The Saudi-Iranian War

by Ted Halstead

Books by Ted Halstead:

The Second Korean War (2018)
The Saudi-Iranian War (2019)

To my wife Saadia, for her love and support over more than thirty years.

To my son Adam, for his love and the highest compliment an author can receive -"You wrote this?"

To my daughter Mariam, for her continued love and encouragement.

To my father Frank, for his love and for repeatedly prodding me to finally finish my first book.

To my mother Shirley, for her love and support.

CHAPTER ONE

Near Sa'dah, Yemen

Prince Ali bin Sultan grit his teeth in frustration at the familiar sight. His tank company was too late again, and the missile had already been fired at Riyadh. Though the missile attacks were a response to Saudi Arabia's intervention in Yemen's civil war, now they were a principle reason for the growing number of Saudi troops in Yemen. The possibility that if the Saudis left Yemen the attacks might stop genuinely never occurred to Ali, or for that matter to any other member of the Saudi royal family.

Ali surveyed the ballistic missile launch site from the cupola of his M1A2 tank, identical to all of the other eleven tanks in the company deployed for this mission. He spotted smoke that was still rising from some of the debris ignited by the back blast from the missile's launch, and smiled grimly. They were getting closer.

Technicians were already scrambling across the site collecting samples of debris and fuel. Part of Ali knew that it was important to determine whether the missile had been a Burkan-2H, a Qiam 1, a Shahab-2, or a missile the Houthi rebels had never used before. From the size of the blast crater the missile left when it was fired Ali suspected it was a missile larger than the ones the Houthis had used so far.

A much bigger part ached to be able to attack the country supplying the Houthis - Iran.

Iran had always denied supplying the Houthis with missiles. Of course, it had never been able to explain the missile debris with Farsi characters stenciled into the metal found in both Yemeni launch sites and targets in Saudi Arabia. Farsi, a language spoken almost exclusively in Iran. Or suggested an alternative source of missiles for the Houthis, who certainly weren't capable of manufacturing the missiles themselves.

Ali had made the case to his superiors that they either needed to send more troops and armor to Yemen, or radically change their tactics. He had argued repeatedly that tanks should be sent out in platoon strength, not company. Ali knew that one reason for sending out tanks a dozen at a time was fear of having a prince killed or - even worse - captured. He had offered to give up his command if it meant a smaller, quicker force would be deployed to reported launch sites.

The answer had still been no, because there was no appetite for the political consequences of Saudi casualties in any significant number. Especially since the missile attacks had been largely ineffective thanks to American-supplied Patriot missile interceptors and the poor accuracy of the missiles. So far.

Ali had also argued for greater focus on the missiles by the Royal Saudi Air Force (RSAF). Unfortunately, those assets were controlled by another prince, with his own ambitions. RSAF Commander Prince Khaled bin Fahd believed the Houthis needed to be attacked wherever they were to be found, and that if they could just kill them all there would be no one left to fire the missiles. So, while he would sometimes act on missile site reports, if he had alternative targets to attack with more reported Houthis, that's where his planes would go.

As often as not, either the intelligence reports Khaled acted on were faulty or dated, or his pilots missed their target. The civilian death toll that resulted was becoming a real problem. Not because Ali, Khaled or anyone else in the Saudi royal family was concerned about Yemeni civilian deaths.

Instead, it was because though the Americans had sold the Saudis all the weapons and ammo they'd asked for and supplied them with satellite imagery and other intelligence for free, they were unpredictable. Today they were willing to tolerate the criticism from those worried about Yemeni civilian casualties. One election could radically change that, though, and Ali thought only a fool would count on American support indefinitely.

Ali sighed, and climbed down into the tank to use its radio. Time to find out what damage this missile had caused, and whether someone would be willing to change a strategy that had been failing for years.

Assembly of Experts Secretariat, Qom, Iran

Grand Ayatollah Reza Fagheh nodded dismissal to the servant who had brought tea for him and his guest, Farhad Mokri. Reza showed every one of his seventy years in his lined face, white hair and beard and stooped shoulders, but a sharp intelligence still glittered in his dark eyes. By contrast, Farhad with his slim frame, thick black hair and erect posture looked like the university student he had been until recently, and was only twenty-six.

They were meeting in the Assembly of Experts Secretariat building in the holy city of Qom, about a two-hour drive south of Tehran. Reza was Deputy Chairman of the Assembly of Experts, which both chose Iran's Supreme Leader and advised him once chosen.

Reza was a candidate for Supreme Leader, and was now acting in that position due to the current Supreme Leader's terminal illness. All the doctors could say was that there was no cure, he could die any day, and was unlikely to emerge from his coma before he did. Until he actually died, Reza had the acting Supreme Leader title.

Reza knew, though, that he had to tread carefully. The Assembly expected him to act solely as a caretaker until a new Supreme Leader was chosen, and any new initiatives could hurt his chances in the upcoming selection by his fellow clerics if they became known prematurely.

Reza knew those chances were slim, and that he would probably be passed over for a man he despised, who despite his denials Reza was certain would lead Iran down a new and dangerous path of reconciliation with the West. It was a path that could even lead to the end of control by Iran's religious leaders.

That could never be allowed.

Reza had decided on a risky gamble that would either see him selected as Supreme Leader, or executed for treason. With Iran's future at stake, and at his age only a handful of years left in any case, courage was not hard to find.

"So, Farhad, tell me about the progress you have made since we last met," Reza said, in a tone that made it plain he expected a positive answer.

He was not disappointed.

"I have made contact with one of the surviving Saudi resistance organizations. I was fortunate in being able to reach a Saudi I knew from my student days in the United States. His father was an outspoken critic of the government who simply disappeared while my friend was still a child. I know him well enough to be sure he is not a Saudi government plant, even without that history. The best part is that since we know each other well, I believe it will be relatively easy to obtain his organization's participation in our plan - while making him believe it was his idea."

Reza nodded. "Excellent. So, he knows of your uncle's leading role in our nuclear weapons program?"

Farhad smiled. "Indeed he does."

Reza pursued his lips. "I see you used some of the funds I provided to set up an online presence for the organization that will be the initial facade for our attack. Why did you decide on Al-Nahda for its name?"

Farhad shrugged. "Well, it was obvious that the name should be Arabic rather than Farsi, which would have pointed straight at us."

Reza gestured impatiently, which Farhad knew meant to move on from the obvious.

"I thought 'Renaissance' sounded plausible, and though it has been used by a few political parties in North Africa, I could find no organizations resisting governmental authority using the name."

Reza's face twisted with distaste. "You spent too much time at that American university. 'Organizations resisting governmental authority'? I think you mean 'terrorist'."

Farhad smiled. "Well, I know you agree with me that those of us in the organization's leadership are certainly not terrorists."

As he saw Reza's face begin to turn crimson Farhad thought maybe he had gone too far. After a few seconds, though, he saw Reza visibly regain control.

"You have a point. Did you know that Al-Nahda, besides the general meaning of Renaissance, also refers to a specific cultural movement that began in Egypt about one hundred thirty years ago, and then spread to Ottoman territories?"

Farhad nodded. "Yes, but I don't believe that movement is well known to many besides scholars such as yourself. Anyway, I don't think it stops us from reusing the term."

Reza nodded absently. "I agree. So, what are your next steps?"

Farhad shrugged. "I will be busy. I plan to meet my Saudi friend in Brussels, where we are unlikely to be tracked by Saudi intelligence. While I am here in Iran I will meet with my uncle. Finally, I will meet with the Qatari prince who had expressed interest in striking back against the reimposed Saudi blockade."

Reza smiled. "Yes, you will indeed be busy. Now, what do you need from me?"

Farhad hesitated. "I know this is a delicate subject. But since we last talked, have you given further thought to arming the ballistic missiles we have been providing to the Yemeni rebels with VX warheads? Unless we strike the Saudi's air bases with them, any armored advance we organize towards Riyadh can be easily destroyed from the air."

Reza grimaced. "I'm sorry I told you we had them. When I saw we had the technical capability I ordered the production of VX as a way to retaliate against an Israeli nuclear attack, and we only have enough for two warheads. The truth is Ayatollah Khomeini himself told me he wanted Iran to avoid such weapons at all costs. He saw what they could do when Iraq used them against us in the 1980s, and considered them truly evil."

Farhad spread his hands and nodded his understanding. "But he was thinking about their use against hundreds of thousands on the battlefield, as happened against us. The number of casualties from strikes on Saudi air bases will be far less. And we must be practical. Most of the Saudi's planes will be in hangers hardened against anything short of a direct missile hit if we use a warhead armed with only conventional explosives. A VX strike will kill most of their trained pilots and contaminate the planes, making them useless."

Reza sighed. "Very well. I will give the necessary orders. Some experts in the West must suspect we have a chemical weapons program anyway."

Farhad frowned. "How is that? I have seen nothing in the press, and our enemies are normally very free with their accusations."

Reza nodded. "It was a small slip, and by itself proves nothing. Our chemists synthesized five Novichok nerve agents for analysis and added descriptions of their spectral properties to the database of the Organization for the Prohibition of Chemical Weapons."

Farhad stared. "When did they do this?"

Reza arched one eyebrow. "2016."

Farhad shook his head. "Two years before the Russians used Novichok to attack the spy in England who had betrayed them and his daughter."

Reza shrugged. "Yes. Fortunately, the OPCW's reaction was to congratulate us for adding information to their database that had not previously been available in open scientific literature."

Farhad smiled. "Amazing. Now, I know our missile program suffered a heavy blow when General Moghaddam was killed in 2011, and that development of improved ballistic weapons was set back for years. Has it finally been possible to make Khorramshahr 2 missiles available to the Yemenis?"

Reza nodded. "Yes. Their two thousand kilometer range and improved accuracy will make a meaningful hit on Riyadh far more likely."

Farhad smile broadened. "Excellent. We will need to convince the Saudis the threat from Yemen is real if we are going to draw a substantial amount of their army south."

Farhad then frowned. "Of course, there's no way to be sure that this plan will work. The Saudis could simply leave Yemen and end their blockade against Qatar, and it would be over."

Reza nodded gravely. "As always, we must put our faith in God. If we are carrying out his will, obstacles will fall before us. If not, then it was not meant to be."

Reza paused. "Of course, he still expects our best effort."

Farhad smiled. "Naturally. Now, once I find out from my uncle what we have to work with, can I call upon you for help with transport?"

Reza gestured dismissively. "Of course. I know for a fact that the program developed at least one nuclear weapon and that it still exists, but could find out no more without arousing suspicion. That is one secret that is truly...secret. As it should be. It would be unfortunate if our enemies in the West were to learn of it. Even worse if the first to find out were the cursed Zionists."

Farhad nodded vigorously, but said nothing. Everyone knew the Zionists had nuclear weapons, and if they learned of their existence in Iran might use one or more to make sure Iran had them no longer.

Reza continued, "I have men loyal to the Revolution with access to trucks, ships and planes. Simply tell me what you need."

Farhad rose, understanding both the reference to the 1979 Iranian Revolution that had installed the current theocracy, and that their meeting was over. "I hope soon to report on further progress towards our goal."

Reza nodded irritably as Farhad beat a hasty retreat. At his age, Reza had no time for pleasantries. His fondest hope was that instead he still had the time needed to keep Iran true to the Revolution and its sacred goals.

Brussels, Belgium

"I know how to bring down the House of Saud," Abdul Rasool declared with a confidence his Iranian friend Farhad Mokri found amusing. He was, though, successful in keeping the smile from his lips.

"Well, if anyone would know how, I'd expect it to be a Saudi," Farhad said gravely. "Let us keep our voices down, though. Even here, you can never be sure who is listening," he said, looking around the square as he spoke, and taking a sip of the excellent Belgian coffee.

It was a chilly and windy March morning, and Brussels' Grand Place had very few tourists in it besides Abdul and Farhad. The waitress had looked at them dubiously when they told her they wanted a table outside, but had shrugged when Farhad had explained they wanted to "take in the view." And it was spectacular, with impressive structures on all sides enclosing a vast space, dwarfing their small table.

After delivering their coffees the shivering waitress had beat a hasty retreat and given Abdul and Farhad, bundled in warm jackets, the privacy that was the real point of their selection.

"We do it by taking away the source of their income. Ultimately, the Saudi monarchy depends on the money coming in from the sale of petroleum, both refined and crude. Take that away, and the whole structure collapses," Abdul said confidently.

Farhad nodded. "In general, I agree with you. We must remember that the House of Saud has used its oil money to buy vast assets overseas, such as the refinery at Port Arthur, Texas which is the largest in the US. But many of those assets, like that refinery, could not quickly be turned into cash to pay bills at home."

Abdul smiled. "Exactly. And even if the monarchy had enough money to keep the lights on for a while without a continuous flow of oil money, the shock of an immediate future with no source of national income would be enough to provoke the revolution we need to rid ourselves of the House of Saud."

Farhad shrugged. "Very well, that leaves the obvious question - How do you propose to cut off the petroleum income that keeps the Saudi monarchy in power?"

Abdul grinned and punched Farhad in the shoulder. "Remember when we watched an old Bond film where the conclusion was set in the Middle East while we were in college?"

Farhad rubbed his shoulder, sighed and nodded. "Yes, I remember you saying the plan to use nuclear weapons could never have worked in Saudi Arabia. You said that the fools running the country had depleted the underground aquifers like those shown in the film to grow wheat. I also remember you saying they did it when some in the West threatened a food boycott to match the OPEC oil boycott, and the Saudi monarchy decided self-sufficiency in wheat was critical. But they grew the best wheat for desert conditions, which turned out to make bread no Saudi would eat. So they exported the wheat at world market prices, about five percent of the cost of production. And so much of the groundwater is gone, and most drinking water is now from desalination plants, produced at enormous expense and piped hundreds of miles inland."

Abdul nodded. "I have always known your memory was impressive. But did you ever consider the use of a nuclear weapon to contaminate the Saudi oil reserves and make petroleum from them impossible to sell abroad?"

Farhad shrugged. "Two problems immediately come to mind. First, how would we get a nuclear weapon? Second, how could we deliver it to the target?"

Abdul smiled. "When i saw you a few months ago, you mentioned you had an uncle who had gone back to teaching after the deal the Americans reached with the Iranian government shut down its nuclear program. Are you still in touch with him now that the deal is off?"

Ministry of Defense, Riyadh, Saudi Arabia

Prince Ali bin Sultan looked around him at the others at the conference room table at the Ministry of Defense. At the head of the table was the Crown Prince, the Defense Minister. Everyone else at the table was either a field commander in Yemen like him, or one of their counterparts in the Ministry.

Ali and the Crown Prince were the only ones at the table who were both princes, and had trained at the United States Armor School. The Crown Prince had gone in 2010 just after the Armor School moved to Fort Benning, while Ali had gone almost a decade later. It still gave them a connection that Ali knew everyone else at the table envied, particularly Prince Khaled bin Fahd.

Khaled had gone to No. 1 Flying Training School in the UK, which claimed to be the oldest continuously operating military pilot school in the world, and was there for its 100th-anniversary celebration in 2019. He had gone to become a Eurofighter Typhoon pilot, which Ali had thought an odd choice considering that the RSAF also flew the F-15. Until Ali read an article quoting US Air Force Chief of Staff General John Jumper, the only pilot who had flown both the Typhoon and the F-22 Raptor, praising the Typhoon as "absolutely top notch."

Ali had learned several American idioms while he was at Fort Benning. The one that applied here, he thought, was "Even a stopped clock is right twice a day."

The Crown Prince put down the folder he had been reading from and looked around the table, which everyone knew was the signal that the meeting was going to start. He spoke into the sudden silence.

"You have all seen the casualty reports from the missile that detonated here yesterday."

They all nodded. Over a hundred had died and many more had been wounded after the hit collapsed an apartment building, though exact numbers would take days to establish. Rescue crews were still finding survivors, though they were finding far more bodies. Nearly all of its residents were Saudis, which had led to surprise in the Western press, where they seemed to think all Saudis lived in palaces.

That had never been true, even in the 1970s when Saudi per capita income at about 40,000 US dollars had been one of the world's highest. Now that number had been cut in half, thanks to a population that had tripled over the past thirty years. So now, Saudi per capita income of about 20,000 dollars a year was a third of the 60,000 dollar a year level in the US.

Plenty of Saudis lived in apartments.

"His Majesty has instructed me that no more missiles may strike the Kingdom. We are here to decide how best to accomplish this. Ali, you have spoken before about changes to our strategy in Yemen."

All heads swiveled towards Ali, who nodded.

"Yes, Minister. I've proposed before that we move more of our M1A2 Abrams tanks to Yemen. I think we should increase the number deployed there to four hundred. I also recommend that we distribute our forces at the platoon level, which will let us respond to any reported missile launch site far more quickly."

Ali paused. "I will defer to my colleague from the Air Force regarding air deployments."

The Crown Prince smiled. "Not so fast, Ali. I called this meeting for options. Let's hear yours, all of it. Khaled will get his say."

Ali nodded dutifully. "Very well. I believe missile launch sites should have an absolute air targeting priority. We will, of course, still move Abrams platoons on any reported site. However, in many cases, an air strike could get there first."

The Crown Prince smiled. "I would recommend close communication, to ensure you don't arrive at the same time."

Everyone laughed at the image, though internally Ali winced. So far he hadn't been impressed by the aim of Khaled's pilots, and wouldn't be surprised by a battlefield accident - even a little.

The Crown Prince turned his head. "Khaled, what do you think?"

Khaled's expression was impassive, though Ali knew that internally he had to be seething at a tanker making deployment suggestions for his precious planes. This time, though, he was surprised.

"I agree with Ali. After the casualties caused by this attack, missile launch sites must take targeting priority over troop concentrations."

Khaled then turned towards Ali, who was still absorbing this first-ever agreement from his rival.

"I am not a tanker, but if four hundred M1A2s are deployed to Yemen, how many will be left to defend the Kingdom?", Khaled asked.

And there it is, Ali thought bitterly, even as he answered. "We will still have two hundred Abrams in the Kingdom, as well as several hundred M60s."

The Crown Prince's eyebrows rose, and he said dryly, "Let's not forget the AMX-30s."

Ali winced internally again, though he was still successful in keeping his expression impassive. They had bought the AMX-30s from France decades ago, and though they were carried on the books as "reserve" tanks, Ali knew as well as the Crown Prince did they'd never be taken out of storage again.

"As you know, the M60s are still in active service and are a match for the armor fielded by the enemies on or near our borders, except for the Israelis. I have seen nothing from our colleagues in the GIP suggesting that either the Israelis or anyone else is planning to attack us. Besides, we'll have nearly the entire force in Saada province, just over the border from the Kingdom. That's not going to change, because their missiles barely have the range to make it to Riyadh. If we need to, we can get back in a hurry using the rail line we just built to Jaizan."

What Ali had just said had been...mostly true. The General Intelligence Presidency (GIP), the Saudi equivalent of the American CIA, had not warned of anyone besides the Houthis even potentially planning to attack. The M60s were a match for the T-72s that constituted the bulk of the Syrian Army's armor, and one of the few realistic scenarios of a land attack against Saudi Arabia was one or more of the T-72s captured by Syrian rebels being used in a raid. And that scenario required them to pass through Iraq, since no part of Syria bordered the Kingdom.

What was left of the Syrian rebel forces now, though, would never use its few remaining tanks on such a pointless suicide mission.

Most of the countries that bordered the Kingdom were either allies like the United Arab Emirates, Kuwait and Oman, or dependent on Saudi financial and military aid like Jordan and Bahrain.

They were addressing Yemen. That left Iraq. Since the Americans ended Saddam Hussein's regime Iraq had been far too occupied with its own survival to threaten anyone, up until very recently. Even now, there were regular bombings in Baghdad markets, and though ISIS no longer had a Caliphate it still had followers. The last election there had put in a government that seemed friendlier to Iran, but it still seemed quite a stretch to call it an Iranian ally. Anyway, the GIP didn't see Iraq as a threat.

Of course, the GIP had also failed to predict Iraq's annexation of Kuwait.

Ali pushed that thought firmly out of his head.

The Crown Prince nodded, and then asked in a neutral tone, "You have seen the reports that the last deliveries of Leopard 2A7s have been made to Qatar, replacing their AMX-30s. Do you think our M60s are a match for the Leopards?"

Ali shrugged. “Tank for tank, no. But even after the latest delivery, they only have a total of two hundred Leopards. They have to know that if they attacked us we could end their tiny country and make it a Saudi province. Since Qatar kicked out the Americans last year, they no longer have a protector, unless you count Iran on the other side of the Gulf. I just don’t see them as a threat."

The Crown Prince nodded again. "GIP agrees with you. I'm still not happy to see the Qataris arming themselves with a tank that has a better main gun than our M1A2s."

Ali shrugged agreement, but said nothing. It was true that Rheinmetall, the German company that had manufactured the main gun used on both the original Leopards and every M1 model, had developed the improved 120mm smoothbore cannon fitted in the Leopard 2A6 and later models. The key improvement was that the L/55 cannon added fifteen hundred meters to the range of the original L/44 cannon mounted on his M1A2s. As a bonus, the L/55 increased the velocity of armor piercing ammo to 1,800 m/s.

This would be bad news for any of his M1A2s facing a Leopard 2A7. It would be worse news for any of his M60s.

The Crown Prince continued, "Qatar said they asked the Americans to vacate their Central Command headquarters in their country because they had sided with us when we reimposed the blockade. That made sense, and I never questioned the GIP's reports on the matter. I wonder now, though, whether they did it to have the freedom to break out of our blockade."

Before Ali could even think of a way to politely reply that the idea was ridiculous, the Crown Prince beat him to it.

"No, Ali, you're right. The Qataris don't have the nerve to risk their independence by attacking us, and the Iraqis are busy with their own problems. We will proceed with your proposed deployment to Yemen."

The Crown Prince paused. "But I want to inspect those M60s personally. They need to be in fighting shape and ready for deployment to our northern and eastern borders before your extra Abrams move to Yemen. And all the M1A2s that aren't already blockading Qatar or going to Yemen will stay right here in the capital region."

Ali simply nodded and said, "Yes, Minister." It was easy to agree since his fellow tanker, as he privately thought of the Crown Prince, was telling him to do what he had planned to do already.

"And Ali," the Crown Prince continued, "make sure you stay put in Saada province, and don't push further south. If there is any trouble, I want to be sure your M1A2s can get back in a hurry."

Ali nodded, privately thinking to himself that the Crown Prince was starting to show his age. He was worrying like an old woman.

It would not be long before Ali looked back at this moment, and remembered that with age also came wisdom.

CHAPTER TWO

Ash Sha'fah, Syria

Colonel Hamid Mazdaki sat on his pack in the shade of his Zulfiqar-3 tank, ate his meal, and looked at the Euphrates flow by. Smoke was still rising from some of the buildings the tanks of his regiment had just leveled, and he knew that one of those thrice-cursed rebel snipers could be taking aim at him as he chewed.

He was too tired to care.

This was supposed to be their last mission before they passed out of Syria and crossed through Iraq on their way to home in Iran. Most soldiers were especially cautious when reaching the end of a deployment, and normally Hamid would have been no exception.

The difference this time was that their most important mission was still ahead. And it was one Hamid did not expect to survive. He was willing to undertake it because he would finally achieve his lifelong dream of avenging his father's death at the hands of Saudi soldiers during the 1987 "Mecca Incident" which killed over four hundred people, most of them Iranian pilgrims like his father. Hamid had been just an infant at the time.

Hamid's mother had been crushed by his father's death, and sought to go on the pilgrimage herself to honor his memory. After being told she would be able to go the year after his death, her Saudi permit was revoked when the number of pilgrims allowed from Iran was reduced from 150,000 to 45,000. Iran boycotted the pilgrimage for the next three years, during which his mother wasted away, and finally died. Hamid was raised by an aunt and uncle who treated him...harshly.

After Hamid enlisted, he repeatedly tried to go on the pilgrimage himself, but every year either duty intervened or he was not lucky enough to get one of the limited spaces the Saudis doled out by nationality. Then after the 2015 stampede in Mecca where 2,400 pilgrims died, over 400 of them Iranians, pilgrims from Iran were again no longer welcome. Of course, both the Saudis and Iranians blamed each other.

Then, many Iranians started calling for a boycott of the pilgrimage, because the Saudis were using profits from it to fund their war against the Shi'a in Yemen.

As far as Hamid was concerned it was clear who was responsible for everything he, his family and his countrymen had suffered when trying to perform the pilgrimage to Mecca. The Saudis.

The mission that would give Hamid the vengeance he had craved for so many years was also one that almost nobody in Iran knew about. Not so long ago, that would have been impossible.

In 2008 a drastic reorganization of the Islamic Revolutionary Guard Corps (IRGC), or Pasdaran, had created thirty-one autonomous provincial corps. This new decentralized structure gave corps commanders substantial leeway, from the equipment they requisitioned to selection of regimental commanders, and even the missions they requested.

In the case of Hamid's provincial corps the equipment was tank-heavy, the regimental commanders were loyal solely to the general in command of the corps, and they volunteered for duty in Syria at every opportunity. The tanks were a mix of Zulfiqar-3 and recently purchased Russian T-90s, and a single very new Russian T-14 Armata.

The Zulfiqar-3 was the latest in a series of tanks designed and built in Iran, a necessity forced upon it by years of international sanctions. However, it was a challenge many Iranians welcomed, since sanctions or no it was important not to depend on foreigners for the defense of the revolution. It was primarily based on the American M60 and Russian T-72 tanks, but Hamid thought its fully stabilized 125mm smoothbore cannon, composite armor, autoloader and improved fire control system gave it an edge over both tanks. Hamid would admit, though, that he didn't particularly look forward to facing a Saudi Abrams tank in his Zulfiqar-3.

Hamid had talked to an Iraqi tank commander who told him that though they had bought T-90s as a reaction to American annoyance at several M1A2 tanks ending up in the hands of Shiite militia forces, the T-90s actually had some pluses. First, at 2.5 million US dollars the T-90 cost less than half as much as an Abrams tank. It had better gas mileage, and was a target about thirty percent smaller than the M1A2. Its internal filters required cleaning much less often. Also, unlike the M1A2 version sold to the Iraqis the T-90 came equipped with reactive armor, giving it a much better chance of survival against rocket-propelled grenades and anti-tank rockets, even the TOW-2.

Iran had produced dozens of the new Karrar tank, which was intended to match the T-90's performance. However, problems with both the Karrar's engine and its reactive armor made Hamid pleased his corps had decided to buy T-90s instead.

The single T-14 Armata was supposed to be an opportunity for Iran to decide whether it wanted to buy more of them, rather than the far cheaper T-90s. Hamid knew there was no chance Iran would spend the money required, and didn't even believe they were really necessary.

Hamid also strongly suspected the Russians' real purpose for making the Armata available to Iranian forces in Syria was to gain information on the tank's combat performance without risking Russian troops, or the tank's reputation. Russia had already sold T-14s to India and Egypt, and clearly saw it as an export cash cow. Anything that went wrong with the T-14's performance in the hands of Iranian soldiers could be blamed on their incompetence, while any successes would be credited to Russian engineering.

Hamid shrugged. The truth was that if they didn't cost more than twice as much as a T-90, he would have wanted the T-14 instead. It had automated defenses against incoming rounds that had proved effective against both rocket-propelled grenades and anti-tank missiles. It wasn't clear how well those defenses would do against tank shells, but fortunately the rebels had very few of those.

The Armata could fire a wide range of ammunition, though here the rebels' lack of tanks had made using many of the rounds pointless. The anti-tank guided missile called the Sprinter had been developed specifically to take advantage of the greater energy of the T-14's 125mm smoothbore main gun, and had an effective range of up to twelve kilometers. The Vacuum-1 armor-piercing fin-stabilized discarding sabot round had a penetrator that could punch through nearly a full meter of rolled homogeneous armor (RHA) equivalent, meaning no tank's armor should be able to defeat it. Using either on anything but a tank, though, was like using a sledgehammer to kill a fly - a very expensive sledgehammer.

Hamid was looking forward to explaining their mission to his troops, because it guaranteed them the chance to finally use the Armata's impressive capabilities, as well as giving all of them a chance at a place in Paradise. He was also realistic enough to think it was likely most of them would be going there directly.

Cairo, Egypt

As a city, both Abdul Rasool and Farhad Mokri agreed the best adjective to describe Cairo was "overflowing." Its cafes, restaurants, streets and public squares were always packed with people. The largest city in the Middle East with a population of over nine million, the Cairo hotel room they were sitting in provided one of the few possibilities for a truly private meeting. Once they had swept the room for listening devices, of course.

Abdul looked thoughtful. "I don't think striking Saudi oil production will be enough to guarantee the overthrow of the regime."

Farhad shrugged. "Well, I wasn't entirely convinced the last time, but didn't want to discourage you. I still think it would be an excellent start."

Abdul nodded. "I have an idea for an additional step, but for maximum impact it will need to happen at exactly the same time as the strike on petroleum production."

Farhad laughed. "Well, we wouldn't want to make this too easy, would we? So, the second step?"

"Strike at Saudi water production," Abdul said confidently.

Farhad frowned. "Is that really practical? I've read that the Saudis are getting most of their water from desalination plants, and that they have over two dozen."

Abdul smiled. “Actually, they have twenty-seven. But that's a misleading number. Twenty-one plants are on the Red Sea coast, and most of their production goes to Jeddah, Mecca and Medina. There are six plants along the Persian Gulf coast, and most of the production from four of them goes to Dhahran and Dammam. Two plants, Jubail II and Ras al Khair, produce nearly two-thirds of all the desalinated water in Saudi Arabia. Nearly all of it is piped straight to Riyadh."

Farhad stared at Abdul in shock. “Almost two-thirds of their entire water production?"

Abdul's smile grew even broader. "About two million cubic meters per day. Jubail II was the largest desalination plant in the world when it opened in 2009, and Ras al Khair took over that title when it opened in 2014. And many of the groundwater wells that provide the only other available water have run dry. It’s true that eventually enough water to keep people drinking would make it to Riyadh, even if they have to truck it in from other plants. But when everyone in Riyadh turns the taps in their kitchens and showers and nothing comes out, I think we can count on panic."

Farhad frowned. “Surely the Saudis realize how vulnerable they are with so much depending on just two plants. Are there no planned backups?"

Abdul nodded vigorously. “Yes, there was a plan for a large solar-powered desalination plant to be built jointly by the Saudi government and a Spanish company, Abengoa."

Farhad's frown deepened. “And?"

Abdul smiled. "In 2015 Abengoa filed for bankruptcy."

Farhad nodded. “Ah. And you think my uncle can help us with this project too."

Abdul smile broadened, and he said, "Well, yes, Farhad. I think he can."

Cairo, Egypt

"Ok, you were right. They are following us," Abdul Rasool said with a grimace. "Do you have any idea how long they've been on our tail?"

Farhad Mokri shrugged, and shook his head. "That's just one of the many questions I plan to ask them."

Abdul snorted with suppressed laughter as they continued to walk down a crowded street in the center of Cairo. “And what makes you think they'll answer? Either one looks like he could take on both of us."

Farhad smiled. “Because we're not alone. Now, be quiet while I use this Bluetooth earpiece to finalize arrangements to receive our uninvited guests.“ Farhad continued to smile as he spoke in a low voice to his unseen friends, while continuing to look at Abdul and gesture as though his words were intended for him. Abdul concentrated on looking engaged in the conversation and occasionally nodding, while a part of his mind couldn't help thinking how odd this all was.

Finally, Farhad gestured for them to turn left into an alley. They had nearly reached its end when the two men appeared behind them. Being careful not to look behind them, Farhad and Abdul turned left out of the alley into another main street.

The two Russian agents were well trained, and knew an obvious spot for an ambush when they saw it. The problem was that they were looking ahead, behind, and on both sides.

They weren't looking up.

Which is where the sniper was waiting. To be fair, this was no ordinary sniper, and his weapon was just as unusual. He had been trained by the Mukhabarat, the Egyptian secret police. When he joined the Muslim Brotherhood after his conversion to what he now thought of as "true Islam" he had taken the rifle and its ammunition supply with him. Since he knew he'd never get more rounds, both he and the leaders he reported to were very particular about his targets.

The rifle used compressed air cartridges that were impossible to find in stores open to Egyptian civilians, but relatively easy to find in Europe. The dozen rounds he had taken with him when he had left the Mukhabarat were irreplaceable because they had been developed in Egypt by government scientists. Using tetrodotoxin extracted from the yellow boxfish, commonly found in the Red Sea waters off the Egyptian coast, they had developed a round that could somewhat reliably immobilize the target, while still leaving him alive for questioning.

In his training, the sniper had been warned about three variables. The first was body mass. A small man, or even worse a child, could die from respiratory arrest or a heart attack provoked by the toxin.

The second was allergic reaction. A small but unknown percentage of subjects would die from even limited exposure to tetrodotoxin.

The sniper wasn't worried about the first variable once he saw the size of the two muscular men who had been following Abdul and Farhad. There was nothing he could do about the second variable. The third factor he could control. Where on their body the round would impact.

The first shot was perfect. It impacted without a sound in the first man's lower back, and he dropped like a stone.

Unfortunately, the second man's reflexes were excellent, and he wheeled around and was looking up towards the third-floor window where the sniper had just fired his second round. As a result, the round impacted about an inch below his heart.

The sniper had no way to know for sure whether the man was dead when he fell. But his guess that he was turned out to be correct.

As planned, the sniper had already turned from the window and begun disassembling his rifle when four men emerged from one of the doors lining the alley to take the two men inside. He hadn't been told why it was necessary to shoot the two men, why it was worth trying to capture them alive, or what would happen to them now.

The sniper shrugged. He would be the first to admit he had no better reason than curiosity for wanting to know.

FSB Headquarters, Moscow, Russia

Anatoly Grishkov and Alexei Vasilyev both looked as though they needed the support of the sturdy red leather sofa to cope with the meal they had just consumed. As well as the vodka toasts that had followed. Their host, FSB Director Smyslov, smiled at them benevolently over a glass of strong black tea.

Grishkov had been told many times that he looked like his father, who had also been a policeman. Like him, he was shorter and more muscular than the average Russian, with thick black hair and black eyes. His wife Arisha said that his face gained more 'character' every year, whatever that meant. Since she patted his face when she said it and gave him a kiss, he didn't mind. His son Sasha was thirteen and his other son Misha was eleven, and though both had black hair otherwise they thankfully looked more like Arisha.

Circumstances had thrown Grishkov together with FSB Colonel Alexei Vasilyev on their last mission. Following that success, Smyslov decided to make Grishkov Alexei's partner. That had meant giving up his job as the lead homicide detective for the entire Vladivostok region, and being put on "indefinite special assignment", though he was now on the books as a Captain in the Moscow Police Department. It looked like Grishkov was about to find out what that meant in practice.

Grishkov thought Vasilyev was at least a decade older than his age of forty-three, but in fact he was even older. Vasilyev was still in excellent physical condition, in part because unlike most Russian men his age he rarely drank alcohol, and because he regularly practiced his hand-to-hand combat skills. At the FSB's gym many younger agents had learned painful lessons about the value of experience over youth. Since these skills had kept Vasilyev alive in the field more than once, he took keeping them up-to-date very seriously.

Vasilyev was about a head taller than Grishkov, but thinner. His true age was disguised in part by a full head of dark brown hair, which showed no signs of thinning. On his last mission he'd told Grishkov that he didn't even have a dog in his apartment, which was a true statement. Vasilyev had seen several agents suffer because the enemy decided to use family against them, and indeed that had happened to Grishkov during their last mission.

"So, I hope you are both sufficiently fortified to let us begin with your mission briefing," Smyslov said, his smile widening.

Vasilyev and Grishkov both nodded, and Vasilyev added, "I thought that the feast you laid on after we finished our last mission couldn't be surpassed, but you proved me wrong."

Smyslov's laugh rumbled from a frame that Grishkov thought for perhaps the tenth time helped explain the foreign stereotype of the Russian bear. "I'm sending my two favorite agents to a region where decent food and drink are hard to come by, so the memory of this meal will have to sustain you for some time. Nobody should have to face cardamom coffee without some reinforcement!"

Vasilyev smiled wryly. "On that point we're in complete agreement. So, the Middle East then?"

Smyslov's smile disappeared. "Yes. I had thought originally to send you both straight to Iran, but it looks like you'll need to go to Saudi Arabia first."

Vasilyev nodded. "Good. My Arabic was always better than my Farsi. This will give me more time to prepare."

Smyslov grinned and pointed at Grishkov. "And how has your Arabic refresher course been going?"

Grishkov scowled, and shook his head. "Refresher is the wrong word. I was one of a handful of soldiers in Chechnya who learned enough Arabic to make out most of what we overheard from foreign fighters using handheld radios. But the vocabulary we learned was limited to what we were likely to hear on the battlefield. So, if anyone is setting up an ambush within earshot, I'll know. Polite dinner conversation, not so much."

Smyslov laughed and shook his head. "My friend, as usual you are too modest. Your instructors tell me you have made remarkable progress, and are the most motivated student they have ever seen."

Grishkov blinked, and then shrugged. "I'd like to make it back to Arisha and the kids."

Smyslov nodded. "Of course you shall. But I'd be lying if I didn't tell you the vocabulary you remember from Chechnya may come in handy."

Vasilyev frowned. "So, our target is aware of our interest?"

Smyslov sighed. "Possibly. The men we had following them both disappeared, and our efforts to locate them have failed. We have to assume they were captured, and were forced to tell the target everything we know. Both fortunately and unfortunately, that's not much."

Grishkov's and Vasilyev's eyebrows both rose, but they said nothing.

Smyslov shrugged. "So, here's what we know, and what we suspect. We know that an unknown organization is gathering men and weapons for the purpose of overthrowing the Saudi monarchy. We know that they have help from elements of the Iranian government. We know that they have been planning their attack for over a year, and that the attack will happen soon."

Smyslov paused. "That's what we know. We suspect that Iraq may also be involved. We suspect that the attack will be on Saudi oil production, and that there may be another target as well. I have been informed by the President himself that preventing these attacks is a top national priority, and that we may request any resources necessary towards this goal."

Grishkov and Vasilyev looked at each other, but said nothing.

Smyslov nodded. "You're wondering why we care so much about an Arab monarchy that has been America's closest Middle Eastern ally for generations. In fact, it was just before the collapse of the Soviet Union that we resumed diplomatic relations after a gap of over fifty years. Why the Saudis are important to us is a complex matter."

Smyslov frowned, and pointed to Grishkov. "What is Russia's most important export?"

Grishkov answered almost immediately, "Oil and gas."

Smyslov nodded. "And Saudi Arabia's?"

Grishkov's answer was even quicker. "Oil and gas."

Smyslov nodded again. "So, what does that give us in common?"

Grishkov looked thoughtful. "Didn't I read that a Russian company was involved in gas exploration in Saudi Arabia?"

Vasilyev's eyebrows flew up as rapidly as Smyslov's.

"Excellent!," Smyslov said. "And quite right too. LukOIL signed a contract good for 40 years in 2004, suspended operations in 2016, and resumed gas exploration last year. But that's not why this matter merits the President's attention."

Vasilyev nodded and said quietly, "Supply coordination."

Smyslov nodded vigorously. "Exactly. The pact we made with the Saudis in 2018 has had its ups and downs, but it's been successful in maintaining an oil price high enough to keep our economy in reasonable shape for years. Two of the largest petroleum exporters limiting production did what OPEC failed to do for decades - keep prices stable at a sustainable level."

Grishkov shook his head. "So, if something happens to Saudi production wouldn't that reduce supply further and drive prices up, giving us a windfall to spend here at home?".

Smyslov clapped his hands and grinned. “Yes, it would - for a while. And then what would happen?"

Vasilyev said quietly, "The West would ramp up production again."

Smyslov nodded. “Just so. The Americans with their fracking. The Canadians with their tar sands. The Brazilians with their new offshore oil deposits. But this is only a secondary concern for the President."

Vasilyev cocked his head. "The German model?"

Smyslov looked grim. "Exactly. By 2012 a quarter of Germany's power came from renewable sources. By 2016 that had increased to nearly a third. It's now over half. Push the price of petroleum high enough, and even the Americans and Japanese will turn to renewables. And once the renewable infrastructure is in place, petroleum will never come back."

Grishkov frowned. “But aren't we supposed to be moving away from petroleum anyway? I read that we supported the Paris climate change agreement, and that there had been a change in the government's thinking about global warming."

Smyslov snorted. "Well, yes and no. The May 2017 storm that killed sixteen in Moscow, the worst storm to hit the capital in over one hundred years, was hard to ignore. The thawing of the permafrost supporting much of our petroleum infrastructure in Siberia, causing it to sink into a new sea of mud, also helped focus attention on the problem. However, we have so far failed to identify a candidate to replace the role petroleum serves in our economy. Right now, our only other export generating significant earnings is weapons systems. We have other possibilities, like civilian nuclear power plants and aircraft, software and other technology. But we need time to make this transition. If the terrorists are successful, events are likely to spin out of control before we have that chance."

Grishkov looked puzzled. "You said that Iraq might be helping elements inside Iran to attack the Saudis. Don't the Americans control Iraq? After all, it's not so long ago that the Americans saved them after ISIS came within an hour's drive of Baghdad."

Smyslov nodded. “Yes, you would think that a trillion dollars and thousands of casualties would have bought the Americans at least a little Iraqi loyalty. In the real world, not so. In 2016 Iraq bought 73 T-90S and SK tanks from us, after the Americans started asking the Iraqis why some of the Abrams tanks they had provided to the Iraqi military had been given to Iranian-backed Shi'ite militia. They took delivery of the first 39 T-90S tanks in 2018, and have now fully converted to Russian armor. There are even reports of Iranian troops stationed inside Iraq, and we know that Iran has had troops stationed next door in Syria for years."

Grishkov shrugged and spread his hands. "Fine. The Iraqis have no loyalty to the Americans. What do they have against the Saudis?"

Vasilyev grunted. "I always thought it was interesting that the Saudis waited until 2016 to reopen the embassy they had closed in 1990 after Iraq invaded Kuwait."

Smyslov nodded. "There is little love lost in either direction. The fundamental issue is, as usual in the Middle East, religion. Iraq and Iran are majority Shi'a, in Iran's case almost exclusively so. For some time Sunnis have been leaving Iraq, a trend that has accelerated over the past few years. That has made possible the election of increasingly radical Shi'a controlled Iraqi governments, starting with one in 2018 dominated by Shi'a cleric Moqtada al-Sadr. He was an enemy of both the Americans and Iran, but after his death other Shi'a leaders have moved closer to Iran. They all share one belief with Iran - Shi'a religious leaders should control Mecca and Medina, not the Sunnis running Saudi Arabia."

Grishkov smiled. "So, at least we know that the attack will take place in either Mecca or Medina, or both."

Smyslov sighed and shook his head. "No, my friend, this is the Middle East. Matters are never so direct. In fact, what our agents have learned so far suggests that the attack - or attacks - will take place in the Eastern Province, on the other side of the country."

Grishkov scowled. "Right, you said one attack focus would be on Saudi oil production, which is mostly in the Eastern Province. But what about the other target? You said it looked like more than one. Couldn't that be either Mecca or Medina?"

Smyslov shook his head again. "We can't be sure of anything, but we don't think so. Iran and Iraq would face universal condemnation in the Muslim world if an attack on either Mecca or Medina were traced back to them. More to the point, it's hard to see how such an attack could endanger the Saudi royal family's grip on power. It's more likely that such an attack would make ordinary Saudis rally to their defense. Besides, our agents reported that the attackers were focused exclusively on the Eastern Province, but it appeared in more than one location."

Vasilyev nodded. "So, where do we start?"

Chapter Three

University of Tehran, Tehran, Iran

Kazem Shirvani knew he really had no reason to complain. When the US had signed the Joint Comprehensive Plan of Action (JCPOA) ending Iran's progress towards its rightful place as a nuclear power in 2015 it had been over Kazem's strident objections. He had been joined by every single scientist working on Iran's nuclear program.

It had made absolutely no difference. All Iran's corrupt politicians cared about was money, and the sanctions levied against Iran were costing it about forty billion dollars per year in lost oil revenue. Kazem, his fellow scientists and even the few honest politicians had argued that Iran was within reach of a nuclear capability, and that just a little more time would let them take Pakistan's path.

In 1998 Pakistan had tested its first nuclear weapon, and was promptly sanctioned by the US. The month after the 9/11 attacks the US abandoned the sanctions after it became clear Pakistani help would be necessary to remove the Taliban regime in Afghanistan. So, the sanctions against the first Muslim country to obtain nuclear weapons lasted...three years.

But the politicians eager for immediate sanctions relief pointed out that the Americans were unlikely to need Iranian help, and Iran would be unlikely to give it. Kazem and others wanting to get nuclear weapons for Iran argued that the greed of American and European countries eager for access to Iran's market could be counted on to weaken their resolve. Besides, how long would Russia and China really go along with sanctions once their only point was to punish rather than prevent?

None of these arguments had worked.

So, Kazem and everyone else who had been forced to look for new jobs after the JCPOA had been approved had rejoiced when the Americans had walked away from the deal in 2018. Especially the ones who hadn't been as lucky as Kazem, and hadn't been able to get work making some use of their skills. And even more so for the ones who hadn't managed to get work at all.

But it hadn't worked out quite the way Kazem imagined. There were still politicians hoping that the Europeans would eventually defy the Americans, in spite of threats against anyone trading with Iran. Russia could offer little but weapons, but the Chinese would buy all the oil Iran had to sell and there was little the Americans could do to stop them. On condition, the Chinese had told the Iranian government privately, that it did not resume a full-scale race to obtain a nuclear weapon.

So, threats to resume weapons-grade uranium enrichment? Certainly. Maybe some enrichment out of view of the International Atomic Energy Agency inspectors? Sure. How about some ballistic missile testing? Absolutely.

What about rehiring Kazem and everyone else who had been fired in 2015 and finally getting Iran enough nuclear weapons to keep it from being pushed around by the Americans, Saudis, or anyone else ever again?

Well, no.

Kazem sighed and looked around his office at the University of Tehran. He knew he'd been lucky to get a job here as a full professor of nuclear physics. Not because he had any doubt about his qualifications. His mother and father had both studied at an American university, and so he had been born in the US. That gave him the US passport he needed to study at Michigan State University, to his surprise the school with the top nuclear physics program in the US, and some would argue in the world.

Of course, MSU didn't teach anyone how to build a nuclear weapon. With the knowledge of the science behind one, though, the challenge was really to make the most effective use of the plutonium or highly enriched uranium needed to create a weapon.

Kazem smiled sourly at the University of Tehran motto, engraved on a sign in his office - "Rest not a moment from learning".

That was really what bothered him about this job. He was certainly helping his students learn, and that was good. But now that he had been separated from the concrete, tangible results of what he knew, he felt as though he would never learn anything more himself.

If only, Kazem mused, he could do something to change that.

Dammaj Valley, Yemen

Captain Jawad Al-Dajani was pushing the tanks of his M1A2 platoon as fast as they could go, which on the dirt road they were using wasn't very fast. Still, he was optimistic. The RSAF Typhoon that had spotted the missile being readied for launch had already dropped its ordnance load on another target, and by headquarters' calculation it would take longer to reload, refuel and return than for his tanks to reach the launch site.

Jawad was determined to make sure that HQ's calculation was correct.

He smiled grimly as he thought about the Typhoon pilot who had tried to take out a missile launch site the previous week with his cannon. After hearing about the incident Jawad had looked up the cannon's specifications out of curiosity, and had been impressed by what he read. The Mauser BK 27 gas-operated cannon fired a 27 mm round at a selectable rate of fire ranging from one thousand to seventeen hundred rounds per minute. Though mounted in many different aircraft, the BK 27 in the Typhoon was a special model that used a linkless feed system to improve reliability.

Jawad had nodded as he read that Mauser had later become Rheinmetall, the same German company that had made the cannon in his M1A2 tank. Well, he thought, who could blame the Typhoon pilot for wanting to try it out once on a live target?

Unfortunately, it ran straight into an ambush. The Houthis had an Iranian-supplied truck-mounted Herz-e-Nohom, a compact radar and electro-optically guided mobile air-defense system based on the Chinese HQ-7, itself a copy of the French Crotale, both of course unlicensed. Hit during its attack run while it was pointed straight at its ground target objective, the Typhoon had no chance to recover before it slammed into the Yemeni earth.

Jawad just hoped its explosion took a few Houthis with it.

As they neared their objective, Jawad spoke over his headset to the rest of his platoon, reminding them to stay vigilant against ambush. Multiple missiles had been launched out of this valley precisely because most of it was difficult to access, and it was still close to the Saudi border. More than one Saudi tank had already met its end here.

Jawad's platoon took a sharp bend in the road that suddenly made their objective visible in the clearing ahead. There was the missile!

Very quickly, Jawad saw that the missile was in fact a decoy made of metal drums and painted cardboard. He thought bitterly that a Houthi with a welding torch and some auto body experience had probably slapped it together in a few hours.

Jawad was wrong. It had taken two Houthis a full day to make it, and the help of three others to put it in place.

Jawad immediately ordered his platoon to search for the anti-tank missile he knew was waiting for them. He knew better than to order a retreat back the way they had come, since outrunning a missile in a tank was...unlikely.

This time, Jawad was right.

The Houti crew of the 9K115-2 Metis-M were in a camouflaged position, that for good measure was also dug-in so only the missile launcher and their heads were exposed. The Metis-M was designed in Russia and produced in Iran under license, so the crew also had the latest missile made for the launcher, the Metis M1. This model increased armor penetration from the original Metis M missile's eight hundred to nine hundred fifty millimeters.

The Metis-M had a well-deserved reputation for lethality from its use in Syria and Lebanon, where its victims included Israeli tanks. Today it would add an Abrams tank to that tally.

The missile only needed seconds to travel from its launch point to the M1A2 tank directly behind Jawad. Like the original Metis M, the

M1 was also wire-guided. It served well to allow its operator to direct the missile precisely to its target.

The Abrams tank took a direct hit, and immediately stopped and burst into flame. Its hatch flew open, and two crew members tumbled out, one of them on fire. The other crew member was able to put out the flames, and both of them stumbled as far away as they could get from the burning tank.

This was an excellent decision. Within seconds either the fuel or the ammo, or perhaps both, inside the Abrams exploded with enough force to turn the tank on its side.

Though the wire was useful in guiding the missile, and was too thin to be easily seen by the enemy, a sharp eye could spot it. Jawad's eyesight was excellent, and so was his gunner's. Moreover, a faint smoke trail led from a point in the bushes in their left flank to the destroyed tank.

The Metis-M crew were in the middle of reloading when they came under fire from both cannon and machine gun fire from the three surviving tanks. Most of the rounds missed. However, only a single hit from Jawad's M256 120 mm smoothbore cannon was more than enough to ensure that no other missiles were fired at his tanks.

Confirmation that Jawad had hit the anti-tank crew came when the three remaining Metis-M missiles exploded simultaneously, creating a fireball that easily eclipsed the gouts of earth thrown up by the impact of the other rounds. It gave him some satisfaction.

But Jawad knew it wasn't going to bring back his two dead crewmen inside the burning Abrams tank.

Next time, Jawad swore to himself, it was going to be different.

University of Tehran, Tehran, Iran

Kazem Shirvani scowled at the knock on his door. He had almost finished preparing his afternoon tea, and did not welcome this break from routine. "My office hours are posted on the door! Come back in half an hour!"

To his astonishment the door opened, but his annoyance changed to a smile when he saw that it was a relative rather than a student.

"Farhad, come in! Sorry not to give you a better welcome, but I had no idea you were coming! The last I heard from your father you were still in Europe." The cocked eyebrow that accompanied his last statement told Farhad that Kazem was actually asking a question.

"Uncle, a pleasure to see you as always. I have just arrived, and in fact am seeing you even before visiting my father," Farhad said with a broad smile.

Kazem smiled back, but it was clear Farhad's statement had come as a real surprise.

"I was just about to have tea. I hope you will join me?," asked Kazem in a tone that made it clear he expected only one answer.

Farhad laughed. "You know I'll say yes. You make it exactly the right way - black, hot, and plenty of sugar. Green tea and aragh - you can keep it!".

Kazem nodded and said nothing, but he was actually pleased. Aragh was a collective name for a wide variety of beverages made from flowers that in other countries would have been called herbal tea. Kazem's reaction to its taste was similar to his hearing Iran's nuclear weapons program had been shut down.

As he poured the tea, he asked, "Well, your father said you were at a conference in Brussels. What did you think of Belgium?"

Farhad smiled. "Quite pleasant. Excellent food, particularly the mussels. Really outstanding coffee. But none of that is why I was there."

Kazem nodded. "Yes. How was the conference?"

Farhad paused, and was immediately annoyed with himself. If he didn't trust his uncle, he should have never made this trip back to Iran. Besides, without his help the plan would be over before it began.

"I actually wasn't at a conference. I was meeting someone who agrees with our view that Iran needs to take its rightful place in the Middle East. And in particular, that we should have custody of the two holy places."

Kazem's eyebrows flew upwards, and he said, "Well, yes, you were right to say 'our view'. But while you were speaking with this mysterious friend, you should have included our views on world peace and the immediate reversal of global warming. An end to world hunger would be nice too," he added tartly.

Farhad just smiled. “Uncle, believe me when I say that I was initially just as skeptical. However, my friend and the organization he represents have the resources to make this plan a reality."

Kazem nodded. “Let me guess. This is where I come in."

Farhad laughed. “I'm not asking you to do anything. First, I'd just like to ask you a few questions."

Kazem shrugged. “Ask your questions. I'll even promise that all my answers will be true. If I don't think you should know something, I'll simply refuse to answer."

Farhad nodded. "Fair enough. You told me the last time we talked that one reason you thought ending our nuclear weapons program was a mistake was that we'd made more progress than anyone knew. Did we succeed in building a nuclear weapon?”

Kazem hesitated, and then nodded.

Farhad nodded back, and said, “Good, good. Did we make more than one?“

Kazem scowled, and this time Farhad thought he wouldn't answer. Finally, though, he nodded sharply.

Now Farhad leaned forward. "Uncle, how many do we have?"

Kazem shook himself like a man coming out of a trance. “Before I say anything else, I want to know what you're planning, and who else is involved. You're not going to attack Mecca and Medina, are you?"

Farhad didn't have to feign his shock. “Certainly not! That would be insane and a sacrilege."

Kazem leaned back in relief. "Good. I would not relish having to tell my brother that his son had taken leave of his senses." Then his eyes narrowed. "So, what exactly do you propose?"

Once Farhad had outlined the plan to attack the Saudi oil reserves and its two largest desalination plants, followed by an attack with armored forces on Riyadh, he could see that Kazem was thinking intently.

"So, your plan would require three nuclear weapons," Kazem said.

Farhad nodded. "Yes. The two desalination plants are both on the Saudis' Persian Gulf coast, but they are about a hundred kilometers apart. I'm not an expert, but I don't think a single weapon could destroy both."

Kazem nodded back. "Correct, these are weapons, not magic. Even a thermonuclear weapon would not destroy them both, and we only have fission devices. As it happens, we have three."

A smile slowly spread across Farhad's face. "Uncle, surely this is a sign from God! To have exactly the tools we need to carry out his will..."

Kazem made a sharp cutting motion with his hand. "God helps those who help themselves." It was one of the very few things he had heard while he was in the US, outside a nuclear physics classroom, that he agreed with completely.

"We have only tested these devices in computer simulations. All of them were rated as over fifty percent likely to work. But none of them made it to the ninety-five percent or better threshold we were aiming for, and all of the simulations assumed there were no mistakes in the manufacture of weapons components or assembly. All three are different designs. Oh, and our simulation software was provided by the North Koreans."

Farhad winced, and Kazem smiled thinly. "Exactly. So, God may indeed be on our side. Or, as we have seen so often, he may be showing us again that he has a sense of humor."

Farhad nodded. "I understand, uncle. I will...restrain my enthusiasm. I know we are only at the beginning of a long road." Now Farhad leaned forward again. "Can you access the weapons?"

Kazem scowled, but slowly nodded. "They require periodic maintenance, and I am one of the few people authorized to go anywhere near them. In fact, I am one of the few people who know they exist."

Farhad smiled. "Excellent! Will it be possible to move them?"

Kazem frowned and looked at his watch. "My office hours are about to begin, and if I'm even going to think about being involved in something like this a break in routine is the last thing I need. My wife will be visiting her sister later this evening. Come to see me at the house at about eight o'clock. And be ready to answer questions about your friend and his organization."

"Yes, uncle. Absolutely!" His eyes shining, Farhad jumped up and left Kazem's office, nearly knocking over a student who had just been reaching his hand forward to knock on the door.

Kazem shook his head as he watched him go. Was this really what all the years of work and study had been for?

Tehran, Iran

Neda Rhahbar had been really proud of her most recent plan. She really hated living as a woman in Iran, but escape had seemed impossible. Her family was solidly middle-class and completely traditional, even though most Iranians living in Tehran were not quite as conservative as those outside the capital. Even if her parents had not been deeply religious, they would have never allowed her to leave Iran.

Her first plan had been to go to university overseas, marry a Westerner and never come back. Her parents had been smart enough not to simply say no to study outside Iran. Instead, they pointed out that the tuition for such study would be more than they could afford, and that she would not be admitted unless she learned a foreign language and radically improved her grades.

They had been shocked when over the next two years Neda had thrown herself into her studies with a fervor they had never seen from her, and she became nearly fluent in English. Her mother had attempted to head off the conflict that was coming by arranging her marriage, but Neda had turned down anyone she suggested flat. Her long black hair, heart-shaped face and attractive figure had produced many suitors. But even though her parents were conservative, they had drawn the line at forcing their daughter to marry someone she didn't want.

Finally, Neda's grades and her English ability had earned her a full scholarship at a British university. But her parents had still refused to let her go. Without her father's signature Neda could not obtain a passport, so no matter how much she screamed and cried and called them unfair, she had still been stuck in Iran.

Neda knew that sitting in the house as an adult would have guaranteed an arranged marriage. So, she had dried her tears and gained admittance to the University of Tehran, where she decided to study physics. Even though she had found herself attracted to several of the male classmates who tried to strike up conversations with her, she always remembered her goal was to leave Iran, which an Iranian husband would make impossible.

Until she'd found what she thought was the answer to her dreams. In Neda's senior year, she had at first been annoyed by a substitute for their regular professor, who was out sick. This professor normally taught only graduate classes, and clearly considered her class a waste of his time. His name was Kazem Shirvani.

But she had really had enough when he began to lecture them on the importance of learning English, since most of the cutting-edge research in physics was being done in the US and "even the work at CERN is written up first in English and then translated into lesser languages." Neda knew all about CERN, the Swiss headquarters for the European Organization for Nuclear Research.

Neda had responded at length and in English, which she had improved to native speaker fluency through study at the British Council in Tehran, both in person and online. She made her points politely but firmly. The first was that CERN's other official language, French, deserved respect as well. The second was that the Americans had made a terrible mistake in abandoning the project to build a massive particle accelerator in Texas, creating the opening the Europeans had seized in building CERN.

Kazem had laughed and agreed, and carried on with the class. Afterward he asked her to stay, and asked her whether she planned to apply to the graduate program in physics. The professor said that though French might deserve respect, a person with her knowledge of physics and English was someone Iran could not afford to waste.

While they had spoken, he had mentioned he obtained his degree from Michigan State University. Neda had been puzzled, and asked how he had managed to study nuclear physics in the US when visas were normally denied to Iranians in such fields.

That's when Kazem had explained that he had an American passport thanks to having been born there, though he had subsequently been raised in Iran.

Neda had done her best to restrain her delight at this discovery, though it wasn't easy. An American passport could be her ticket out! Further conversation had revealed that Kazem had made several trips to the US and Europe after graduating from Michigan State, primarily for academic conferences. This cemented Neda's mental image of Kazem as someone who was free to travel to the West, unlike nearly all Iranians.

This, she decided on the spot, was the man she would marry.

Naturally, turning intention into reality took some time. Neda very quickly realized that Kazem would never see her as a possible candidate for marriage before she graduated, but fortunately that happened a few months later. She was also careful not to pick nuclear physics as her incoming graduate major, even though it interested her the most, because he would be even less likely to consider marrying one of his students. She could always change it later, once she knew one way or the other whether things would work out with Kazem.

Those hurdles passed, Neda approached the most important - her mother. Fortunately, her relief at her daughter's finally having found a man she wanted for a husband overwhelmed what would have been her normal impulse to question Neda's choice. After all, in her mind the initiative should have been hers, not her daughter's.

It helped that Kazem had a completely respectable and solid job, had never been married before, and was substantially older than Neda. There was also no question that they had done anything inappropriate in coming to know each other. Her mother believed Neda when she said that they had only had coffee on campus a few times outside the classroom.

In fact, Neda had found Kazem frustratingly difficult to get to know as anything but a professor. The only reason he was willing to speak to her outside class is that she had been the only student to in any way contradict him. He thought, but didn't add to her, in a way that made me acknowledge to myself I may have been mistaken. Kazem liked Neda, but was completely absorbed in his academic work, and the plans he had not yet abandoned to make Iran a nuclear power. Of course, he would have never discussed Iran's nuclear weapons program with any student.

However, Kazem's parents were just as unhappy as Neda's that they had no grandchildren. Though less conservative than Neda's parents, they had also been patient considerably longer. Once Neda's mother contacted them, Kazem found himself swiftly at a family dinner with Neda and both sets of parents.

After his initial surprise faded, Kazem found himself shrugging internally. He had always planned to marry someday. Neda was beautiful, intelligent, and he respected her. His parents liked her. What more did he want?

Their honeymoon in Paris had fanned the flames of Neda's desire to leave Iran into a roaring blaze. She loved everything about Paris, and would have given anything to live there and never go back to Iran. Neda had been sorely tempted to just walk out of the door of their hotel and never come back.

Only two things had stopped her. The first was that she really did like Kazem, and knew she wouldn't be able to look at herself in the mirror after leaving him on their honeymoon. The second was more practical - she had little money, and no source of income. As a married woman on a French tourist visa, she knew her old plan of marrying a Westerner would no longer work.

So, Neda decided to wait. She would get her graduate degree, get a job and save her money, and then on their next trip out of Iran make her escape.

The first part and second parts of her plan went perfectly. The third failed completely. After graduation her job as an undergraduate lecturer in nuclear physics paid quite well, and she was glad Kazem had turned out to have no objection to her decision to switch majors after their marriage. In fact, Neda thought Kazem believed she had done it out of admiration for him, and been secretly flattered. Neda was happy to let Kazem think what he liked, as long as it got her what she wanted. She had even been able to quietly convert a fair quantity of her earnings from Iranian rials to euros and US dollars.

But Kazem had no interest in traveling outside Iran.

Neda had always been a firm believer in predicting what people would do by what they had done, not what they said. That's why she had never discussed travel outside Iran with Kazem, except for planning their honeymoon. His many trips to America and Europe, including years of study in America and his US passport, all made it a given to Neda that there would be more trips outside Iran.

This was one time, though, that conversation would have served Neda well. She found out after waiting for a year to propose a vacation to Europe that he had no interest in tourist travel outside Iran. As Kazem made clear the first time she brought it up, all his travel outside Iran had been for study or work, with the sole exception of their honeymoon. When Neda suggested a few extra days after an academic conference she wanted to attend in London, the discussion became particularly unpleasant.

It turned out that once Kazem had been identified as the head of Iran's nuclear weapons program, he had become unwelcome at any related academic event. Even after the Americans walked away from the JCPOA, Kazem was still off every invitation list. Neda had never seen Kazem bitter before. It was not a good look.

So, her brilliant plan had backfired completely. Neda was married to a US citizen who could travel to America or Europe anytime he wanted to go.

Which turned out to be never.

What could she do now?

CHAPTER FOUR

Assembly of Experts Secretariat, Qom, Iran

Grand Ayatollah Sayyid Vahid Turani was a patient man. He had learned patience the hard way, waiting over thirty years for his predecessor as Iran's Supreme Leader to finally meet his maker. The day was finally about to come, though, and once the Supreme Leader's coma released him to Paradise then Vahid would finally be able to right the many mistakes made by the last Supreme Leader as well as Iran's elected leadership.

Vahid had recognized long ago that Iran's perpetual isolation, far from being seen as negative by its leaders, was actually desired for several reasons. International sanctions were used to justify government ownership of the bulk of Iranian industry and much of its service sector. Oil and gas production accounted for most of Iran's export earnings, and was entirely government controlled. Iran Electronics Industries was as well, producing everything from semiconductors to satellites. With over a hundred subsidiaries, the government's Industrial Development & Renovation Organization of Iran was involved in everything from auto manufacturing to health care. The Iran Insurance Company used government backing to account for over half of the policies issued in Iran.

As well as guaranteed lifetime government salaries, isolation also justified continued repression, including suppression of legitimate complaints about the miserable living conditions for Iranians not among the lucky few with government jobs. After all, surrounded by enemies how could the authorities tolerate disorder?

Most important of all, Iran's isolation justified its continued control by an unelected theocracy. Obviously, an Iran under continuous threat from the West could hardly afford to experiment with untried forms of government- such as genuine democracy.

Vahid was well aware of the irony of his situation. On the one hand, he would need every bit of the considerable power of the position of Supreme Leader to push through significant change. On the other, the changes he planned would end up weakening his position as Supreme Leader - and maybe even ending the clergy's control of the government.

Vahid shrugged. He had always known he would have to move carefully to have any chance of success. Now he had to hope that the relationships he had carefully built over the previous decades he had served in the Assembly of Experts would supply him with the information he needed to make his plans reality.

The report he was reading on "temporary marriages" made Vahid's upper lip curl, and was a perfect example of the aberrations he planned to remove from Iranian society. Literally translated as 'pleasure marriage' (nikah mut'aa), a temporary marriage typically lasted for three to six months. The woman usually received a sum of money at the start of the marriage, which - incredibly - was recorded as valid by any mullah in Iran following a ceremony at a mosque.

So, Vahid thought, the man could make use of the woman and then discard her without consequence. Of course, no respectable man would ever consider her subsequently for marriage, since she would no longer be a virgin. It did not even occur to Vahid that no Iranian man would ever be held to this standard.

However, Vahid did frown impatiently when the report described the basis for permitting such marriages in Iran, when they were forbidden in most other Muslim countries. Oral tradition. Given credence in Shiite tradition and generally condemned by Sunni clerics, statements attributed to the Prophet Mohammed but nowhere to be found in the Koran were in Vahid's view one of the primary sources of many of Iran's current problems.

Now, if he could just figure out a way to make the case that this and other traditions needed to be ended without being branded as a Sunni sympathizer as soon as he became Supreme Leader.

Tehran, Iran

Neda Rhahbar had never given up on her dream to leave Iran. Her younger sister Azar had married right out of high school, and done it to fulfill her dream of escaping her parents' house. Azar's husband had a government job as an inspector that required him to travel around Iran frequently, which she knew before agreeing to the marriage arranged by her mother.

Azar never went with him on these trips.

Azar was also determined to avoid being tied down by children, and was helped by two factors. The first was that her husband was not particularly interested in having children. The second was that when Azar married, birth control was free and endorsed by both the government and the religious authorities. This was due to a realization that Iran's exploding population was far outstripping the government's ability to provide it with employment and services. So, without telling her husband, Azar had a tubal ligation.

Until Neda married herself, she hesitated about following suit because she thought a potential foreign spouse might balk at a marrying a woman unable to have children. Once she married Kazem, though, those concerns disappeared. Neda had the procedure just in time, before yet another policy change from the government and the religious authorities. They had decided that, even though job prospects for Iranians were still poor, they wanted a rapidly growing population after all.

Neda shook her head in disgust as she remembered a billboard that had appeared all over Iran to mark the policy change. On one side was a family with two parents and two children, looking sad and lonely. On the other was a family bursting with children, who along with the parents were all happy and smiling.

This was one area where Kazem's obsession with his job worked to Neda's advantage. Kazem had never discussed children with her, and Neda guessed correctly that he saw them as a distraction, when he thought of children at all. Though her mother was disappointed, she did no more than make a few comments about Neda having "waited too long" to get married.

This left Neda and Azar free to use each other as alibis when they wanted to leave the house. Neither did anything that would have seemed out of the ordinary for a married woman in any Western country, and sometimes they actually did do things like shopping together. Sometimes Azar invited friends to her home, many of them women from other countries, and Neda came as well to learn about the world outside Iran. But the fact that they had to lie to even go alone to a cafe grated on both of them.

Azar had joined the thousands of Iranian women who had protested the laws requiring head coverings by walking down the street without one, but was one of the lucky few who avoided arrest. After the government crackdown intensified, Azar put her scarf back on, but picked a brightly colored one that served to symbolize her disdain for the practice. Neda sympathized with the protesters, but could not imagine spending even a minute inside an Iranian jail. Besides, she wanted far more than to leave home without a scarf, and one way or another was determined to find the freedom she had been seeking for years.

Whatever it took.

Tehran, Iran

Kazem Shirvani had run into Farhad Mokri less than a block from his apartment.

"Good!", Farhad exclaimed. "I had been worried I would be late."

Kazem shook his head. "No, as usual you are exactly on time, one of the things I've always liked about you. You'll have to give me a minute to make tea. I think I mentioned that your aunt is visiting her sister, so you'll have to put up with my brew again."

Farhad laughed. "Uncle, you know that the chance to drink tea made right is one of the things that always brings me back home."

Kazem thought Farhad was just being polite, but was still pleased.

As they entered the apartment, Kazem snapped on the lights. "It will only take me a few minutes. Please, make yourself at home."

Farhad walked around the living room, looking at the books lining the shelves across from the windows. Unsurprisingly, they were all related to Kazem's work. As he sat on the large sofa and was nearly swallowed by its cushions, Kazem came in from the kitchen holding a large silver tray full of cakes and cookies.

Farhad smiled. "Uncle, this is very nice of you. I'm beginning to believe I really am your favorite nephew!"

Kazem shrugged. "Actually, it is your aunt you have to thank for this. I called and told her you were coming, and not to cancel the visit she had promised her sister. She must have bought these before she left. Obviously, we need to be finished talking about your project before she returns."

Kazem was correct about Neda Rhahbar having visited a nearby bakery after his call, and she had planned to go to a movie while supposedly "visiting her sister." But she had a headache that Neda knew from experience would never let her enjoy the film. So, she had turned off all the lights in the apartment and crawled into bed, hoping the headache would disappear in time to let her spend some time with her nephew, who always had stories about his travels outside Iran.

Neda was still asleep when Kazem and Farhad began their conversation, which began as soon as Kazem had finished pouring their tea.

Kazem took a sip and said, "The first point I must emphasize is that these devices were never intended for use as weapons. Their primary purpose was to give our technicians experience with the challenges involved in nuclear weapons production, and to help us decide which of the three designs we would produce in larger quantities. It is also important to note that while two of the devices were built using Uranium-235, one was built using Plutonium-239."

Farhad shook his head. "I'm sorry, uncle. Why does the radioactive material used in the weapon matter?"

Kazem raised his eyebrows. "Never apologize for asking when you need knowledge. In fact, I will only be upset if you fail to ask questions. I have been immersed in this program for so long that sometimes I forget what is obvious to me is not to most others."

Kazem paused, as he thought about the best way to explain the difference between the two nuclear materials. At the same moment, Neda woke up, and reached for the switch on the lamp next to her bed. What she heard next made her hand freeze.

"If you plan to use these nuclear weapons to attack targets in Saudi Arabia, you must use the plutonium device against the one that is the farthest from a population center. That is especially true if there is a subcritical detonation," Kazem said.

Seeing Farhad's look of confusion, Kazem smiled. “Let me begin at the beginning. There are three possible outcomes when each of these weapons are detonated. First, it may fail altogether. Second, it may detonate as designed. Third, it may explode, but fail to perform as designed. That would be a subcritical detonation, also called a fizzle."

Farhad nodded. “I understand, uncle. But why would such a result be more dangerous to people nearby?"

Kazem shrugged. “It might not be. If the plutonium device performs exactly as designed, it would be bad enough for anyone in the area. However, a fizzle would distribute all of the plutonium in the device over a wide area. The results would be far less spectacular than a successful detonation, but could result in even higher casualties."

Farhad frowned. “Is the fallout really that dangerous?".

Kazem nodded. "Yes. The basic yardstick is that five hundred grams of powdered plutonium has the potential to kill about two million people if inhaled. A fizzle is likely to both pulverize the plutonium contained in the device, and to send it airborne. Of course, prevailing winds and many other factors will play a role in exactly how much plutonium would be distributed from a fizzle."

Farhad cocked his head. "And how much plutonium is contained in your device?"

Kazem waved his hands. "I should point out that as with all such devices, the plutonium is present in an alloy with gallium for stability. However, only about one percent of the alloy is gallium. Our design uses about the same amount of plutonium as the device the Americans detonated at Nagasaki, roughly six kilograms."

Farhad winced as he thought through the figures Kazem had just given. “So, times two million dead..."

Kazem laughed. “No, no! For a start, there aren't that many people living in the entire Saudi Eastern Province! Also, though much of the plutonium may be pulverized in a fizzle, some is likely to be ejected from the blast site in solid chunks. Depending on the winds on the day of the explosion, some powdered plutonium will be blown into uninhabited desert. Still, you see why I say the plutonium device should be used as far from a population center as possible."

Neda, listening in the bedroom upstairs, certainly saw why that was true. What she didn’t understand was why her husband and nephew were talking about attacking Saudi Arabia with nuclear weapons. It was all the more frustrating that she had to strain to hear their conversation, since she didn't dare leave the bedroom.

Farhad frowned. “Uncle, what you say about the danger of plutonium from a fizzle deeply concerns me. Casualties are inevitable. But we must avoid deaths numbering in the millions, or abandon this plan. Is there anything else you can tell me about a plutonium release? Has it happened before?"

Kazem shrugged. “Well, yes. There were plutonium fires in the 1950s and 60s at Rocky Flats, a nuclear weapons plant not far from Denver."

Farhad stared, horrified. "Plutonium fires?"

Kazem nodded. "Yes. Plutonium is pyrophoric, meaning that it can spontaneously combust in ordinary atmosphere, particularly the thin shavings produced during the weapons production process. Safe handing requires working with plutonium in a sealed glove box flushed with argon."

Farhad repeated, "Glove box..."

Kazem smiled. “Yes. I'm sure you've seen them in movies. A clear plastic box with gloves set into them, so that you can reach into the gloves and manipulate whatever is inside the box without allowing the contents to be exposed to the air you are breathing.“

Farhad nodded. "Of course. Didn't they have these at Rocky Flats?"

Kazem shrugged. “They did, in fact some of the largest I've heard of, over sixty feet long. But, something went wrong, twice."

Farhad lifted both hands. "What went wrong, exactly?"

Kazem grinned. “Who knows? Both fires were covered up until the seventies. Even after the Americans admitted they happened, they continued weapons production there through the eighties. Then a joint raid by the FBI and EPA collected enough evidence to shut down the plant. After that it was torn down and turned into a wildlife refuge. The government started to allow in hikers in 2018.”

Farhad shook his head. "What you are saying makes no sense. How could the American government raid itself?"

Kazem raised his eyebrows. "Rocky Flats was run by a private company. Until the government found evidence of wrongdoing, it was bound by its contract."

Farhad grimaced. “Uncle, I am impressed that you were able to stand living there as long as you did."

Kazem laughed. “Well, there's indeed much in America that is difficult to understand. However, they are not to be underestimated. Remember, Americans are the ones who invented nuclear weapons in the first place."

Farhad frowned. “Uncle, this story is interesting, but doesn't really answer my question. What were the casualties from the plutonium fires?"

Kazem smiled. “The government said there were none."

Farhad looked at Kazem incredulously. “None? But what about cancer? I thought you said the plant wasn't far from Denver. Isn't that a big city?"

Kazem nodded. "Yes, it is. But whatever the impact may have been, I think it's good for your plans that the plutonium fires didn't produce casualties or cancer at rates too high for the government to deny responsibility. The problem for our comparison is that the fires consumed much of the plutonium, just as the many successful plutonium-based nuclear weapons tests did. If either the Americans or the Russians ever had a fizzle, they certainly haven't admitted it. Since the very first nuclear weapon the Americans tested was plutonium-based, and successful, it's possible they never had one. So, we can hope that a plutonium fizzle won't be as dangerous as some fear. But the truth is, nobody really knows."

Kazem paused. "That brings us to the next thing you should know."

Farhad said nothing, and waited expectantly for Kazem to continue.

"The Saudis will be able to quickly confirm once the weapons are detonated that they came from Iran. The International Atomic Energy Agency inspectors have samples of the uranium and plutonium we have produced, and they will be able to match fallout particles from a successful explosion within days. Of course, a failed detonation or a fizzle would leave more nuclear material, and make the match even easier. From what you have said of the planned follow up to the detonation that may not matter, but I thought you should know in any case."

In the bedroom Neda's right hand flew to her mouth. Planned follow up? What insanity was this?

Farhad nodded. "You're right, uncle. I don't think it will matter. Still, it's useful to know. Now, how soon are you scheduled to maintain the weapons?"

Kazem shrugged. "There is no schedule, per se. Remember, these weapons are held in secret, and very few people know they exist. There are no formal procedures. The truth is, I decide on my own when to check on them."

Farhad smiled. "Excellent. We have to think about the best way to deliver the weapons to their targets, and decide which weapon to assign to each target. And, now we have to confirm which target is farthest from a population center. I can say offhand that the desalination plant at Jubail cannot be the target for the plutonium weapon, since it is not far from a city of at least eight hundred thousand people."

Farhad paused. "Can you get me basic specifications on each weapon, like dimensions and weight? Also, I presume the men carrying out the attacks will need protective gear to handle the weapons?"

Kazem nodded. "I can give you approximate dimensions and weights from memory right now, with more precise details later once I can consult my notes at the lab. The devices are shielded, though if your men aren't doing the attacks as a suicide mission I'd recommend lead-lined gloves."

Farhad grimaced. "I don't intend these to be suicide missions if I can help it, particularly since I plan to lead one of them myself. Of course, the dimensions and weights will give us a better idea of our options in carrying out the attacks. We have more work to do to determine how tight security is at each of the targets. Our organization is still working to determine which assets will be available to deliver the weapons to their targets. In short, we have a great deal to accomplish in very little time."

Kazem frowned. "What's the rush? Mecca and Medina have been in Saudi hands for centuries. What difference does a few weeks or months really make?"

Farhad sighed, and tiredly rubbed the right side of his face. "Uncle, once a plan like this is in motion, it is only a question of time before our enemies learn of it. There are simply too many people involved to keep it a secret indefinitely. Our only chance of success is to carry out the attacks before the inevitable leaks are pieced together by whoever would like to stop it."

Kazem grunted agreement. "Yes, I see your point."

Farhad looked at his watch. "One last question before I should leave. What is the earliest date we can collect the devices, and will we need to overcome any resistance to their removal?"

Kazem looked at his watch in turn. "I think I will walk with you to your car and answer your question there. Your aunt may return any minute and I don't want to be interrupted, since I know you need this information for your planning. How far away are you parked?"

Farhad shrugged. "Considering the neighborhood, I didn't do too badly." He then named an intersection that brought a smile to Neda's lips. It was about three blocks away, and would let Neda pretend she had returned while Kazem was out.

Kazem nodded. "Good. Let's hurry. I'd really like to get back before your aunt gets home."

Neda waited a full five minutes after Kazem and Farhad had gone before she emerged from the bedroom, her head still swirling from everything she'd heard. There was so much that made no sense. What were the targets? What did the planned attacks have to do with Mecca and Medina? What would be the "follow up"?

One thing was clear, though. The nuclear devices her husband had worked on for so many years, that he had told her were never completed, were real.

And were going to be used.

CHAPTER FIVE

US Embassy, Beijing, China

Mark Bishop looked up as his deputy Tom Patterson entered his office. Since Mark had been promoted to Chief of Station at US Embassy Beijing, he'd lost the ability to do any sort of field work. His interest in field work was why he had joined the CIA, but his new job came with a 24/7 Chinese follow team that represented the best they had.

And that was actually pretty good.

So, instead he got to read and listen to the reports produced by his team, and decide what got passed back to Langley, and with what priority. Though the rest of his staff was followed by the Chinese, even they couldn't do everyone 24/7, and not all of the men they put on the job were truly competent. Or else Tom wouldn't have just produced his latest report.

Bishop looked nothing like James Bond. Middle-aged, slim, medium height, brown hair, wearing silver wireframe glasses and clothes that would have made him at home in any office cubicle in America, there was absolutely nothing remarkable about him.

Tom Patterson looked much the same, except his hair was black, he was seven years younger, and his glasses had a more modern looking bronze metal frame. Nobody passing him on an American or European street would have given him a second look.

"So, Tom, have a seat. Interesting report. I've passed a copy to our DIA friends," Bishop said. One of the perks of his job was that he got to decide who else saw the information they collected, and how quickly. Bishop was a believer in sharing, both because he truly thought every agency at the Embassy was on the same team, and because sharing was normally a two-way street. This time, the Defense Intelligence Agency office at the Embassy had an obvious need to know about Tom's report.

Patterson nodded. "Any reaction?", he asked.

Bishop shook his head. "Not yet. I'm sure their first question will be the same as mine - why in the world would the Chinese sell a pair of Chengdu J-20 stealth fighters to the Iranians? And what are the Iranians planning to do with them?"

Patterson shrugged. "You saw in my report that I asked my Chinese contact at the Ministry of Foreign Affairs both questions, and he said he didn't know. I'll add that I believe him, mostly because I had the strong impression he was annoyed that he didn't know. As I said in the report, I think he was just as motivated by a desire to expose the sale as by the money I handed over."

Bishop grunted. "But he did take the money."

Patterson grinned. "Well, sure."

Bishop shook his head. "The People's Liberation Army Air Force got their first dozen J-20s in 2016, and they weren't made operational until 2018. They're still working out issues with the J-20's engines and flight control systems, and deliveries aren't even half complete. It's the only true fifth-generation stealth fighter to be fielded by anyone but us, and they would have never managed it without the technology they stole from our F-35 program. So, why would they sell even two to Iran?"

Patterson chewed on his lower lip. "OK, now I'm going to go to speculation, which is why it wasn't in the report."

Bishop nodded, and made a "give it to me" motion with both hands.

"My contact made references that I noted in the report about irregularities in the sale. When I pressed him he refused to give me details, and of course that normally means bribes."

Bishop nodded. Patterson continued, "I had the sense, though, that it was more than that. Like the J-20s were going to Iran, but not to the Iranian Air Force."

Bishop stared. "That's quite a leap, Tom. Who else in Iran would know what to do with a J-20?"

Patterson shrugged. "I'm no expert on Iran. But I do remember reading that the Pasdaran is basically a parallel armed force, and there are also government-sanctioned militias, called the Basij if I remember correctly. Or maybe some other organization we don't know about. I warned you this was just speculation."

Patterson paused. "I just think the guy was hoping we'd spill that we knew about this sale, and then it would be called off, and the planes returned."

Bishop cocked his head. "Really? The J-20s have been there now for months, so how likely is it that the Iranians would give them back? Also, isn't he smart enough to worry that if we did that then our learning about the J-20 sale might get traced back to him?"

Patterson nodded. "Even though he's smart enough, I think he really believes the sale is a bad idea that's worth some risk to stop."

Bishop made rapid notes. "OK, Tom. You were right not to put this in the formal report. I'm going to add some detail, though, based on our conversation. Maybe our stations in the region can find out something."

Patterson nodded, but knew as well as Bishop did that their ability to find out what was happening inside Iran was limited at best.

As Patterson left his office, Bishop weighed whether to recommend that US knowledge of the sale be disclosed as widely as possible within the administration. Bishop was old school, from the days when the ideal still existed that the CIA should be solely the collector of intelligence, and leave policy decisions about what to do with that intelligence strictly to the State Department and the White House.

With a firm shake of his head, Bishop made his decision. Whatever the Iranians were doing might not, strictly speaking, be his problem. But whatever the Chinese were doing to stir the pot in the Middle East, he knew it wasn't going to be good news for the US. No, it was time to ring a few alarm bells, even if he had to risk upsetting his superiors to do it.

Tehran, Iran

Neda Rhahbar didn't have any idea what to do about the terrifying plans she had heard her husband and nephew discussing just two days earlier. She was sure, though, that she needed to know more before either confronting her husband or doing...something else.

So, when Neda told Kazem Shirvani she was going to visit her sister Azar, she was pleased to see that his reaction was relief quickly followed by poorly acted disappointment. She guessed that the relief came from knowing the apartment would be free for Kazem to meet with Farhad again.

This time, instead of coming home and falling asleep, she actually prepared a hiding place in the bedroom wardrobe. Filled with full-length garments, it would be impossible to see her hiding in the back unless it was both opened and the clothes swept aside. Neda doubted that either would happen, but was concerned that it would be even harder to hear than when she had listened before at the bedroom door. She finally decided to keep the same perch as last time next to the barely open bedroom door, with the wardrobe door open in case Kazem came upstairs.

Their cat Shiri was normally not interested in either being played with or being shown any sign of affection, and only perked up when food was being placed in her bowl. Naturally, it picked this time to circle around her ankles. Finally, out of exasperation Neda picked Shiri up and tossed her onto their bed. Shaking herself, Shiri curled up in a pillow and looked at Neda reproachfully, but made no further moves.

Finally, Neda's patience was rewarded when she heard her nephew Farhad Mokri's voice, along with her husband's, as they entered the apartment.

"I regret that there will be no snacks to accompany the tea today," Kazem said. "I was concerned that if I told your aunt you were coming she would have canceled her plans with her sister to see you, and we obviously need privacy for our discussion."

Farhad nodded. "Understood. Besides, I'm honestly too nervous to eat. I hope you have good news for me."

Kazem frowned. "As usual in this life, both good and bad. But, first things first. Let me make the tea."

They were shortly sitting together in the living room, sipping from Kazem's usual strong black tea.

"Excellent," Farhad murmured. "Now..."

"Yes, yes," Kazem growled in response. "I well remember how my father used to complain about the impatience of youth. Proof I am growing old myself, I suppose."

A brief glare at Farhad was met by the wisest response - silence.

"Very well. I was able to make a quick trip to the nuclear weapons storage facility. When I left I told the guards I needed additional tools to complete my maintenance work, so they should expect to see me again soon."

Kazem paused. "I confirmed the information in my notes regarding the weapons' dimensions, and consulted the technical documents on site to confirm the weights. The good news is that each weapon can be transported in an ordinary delivery truck, and we have the equipment on site to assemble and load each weapon."

Kazem had also used his cell phone to take careful photos of the technical documents, which he later copied to his personal laptop, but left that out of his account.

Farhad nodded. "And the bad news?"

Kazem shrugged. "Actually both good and bad. Two of the weapons will have to be delivered to their targets by vehicle, or I suppose by boat if you wanted to attack a port. That is, both the plutonium weapon as well as one of the uranium-based devices. The other uranium weapon is designed to be dropped from an airplane. But it won't be easy."

Farhad shook his head. "I'm not a military man, but don't you just drop such a weapon from a bomber?"

Kazem smiled. "I'm no more a soldier or pilot than you. But I have had many discussions with those who are. In order to be dropped from a modern bomber, the weapon would have to be fitted with a mount allowing it to be attached to the bomber's wing, in such a way that the bomb could be jettisoned by the pilot when he was over the target. It would also need to have an aerodynamic shape, in order to prevent problems with aircraft handling."

Farhad grimaced. "I thought bombers could just...open their bay doors, and push a bomb out."

Kazem nodded. "I thought the same thing. I was told, not by anything we have, or by any bomber built in the last thirty years. So, our tentative plan was to drop it from a cargo aircraft designed to do air drops. We do have C-130s, so that's probably what we'd have used. Until, of course, we were told to drop the entire project."

Farhad looked puzzled. "I don't understand, though, why only one of your weapons could be dropped by air. If you're pushing it out of a cargo aircraft, couldn't you do that with any of them?"

Kazem shook his head. "Not at all. We had to spend more time on the design for the air-dropped weapon than the other two combined. There are two approaches to successful detonation of an air-dropped nuclear weapon. The first is to time detonation to occur prior to the bomb's impact. The advantage is that you don't have to worry about the detonation mechanism surviving its encounter with the ground. The disadvantage is that unless your timing is accurate, and both the plane's altitude and your speed high, you may be caught by the detonation. C-130s have many advantages. Their great speed is not one of them."

Farhad nodded. "So you used the approach that allows the weapon to detonate on impact."

Kazem smiled. "Correct. It took a lot more work and ended with a device heavier than the other two, but just like you, I didn't want to send anyone on a suicide mission."

Neda's eyes widened as she realized this was absolutely not some theoretical discussion. They were going to use three nuclear weapons in an attack on Saudi Arabia.

Neda was so distracted that she didn't notice the hairbrush on the nightstand until she knocked it off. It fell on the tile floor with a clatter. Her heart in her throat, Neda walked silently to the wardrobe, burrowed into the spot she had chosen and closed its door after her.

A few minutes later, the door opened and the light snapped on. Neda could hear Kazem's footsteps move closer to the wardrobe, and the spot that had seemed so safe just moments ago now left her feeling naked and exposed. Neda closed her eyes.

A thump was quickly followed by a startled oath from Kazem. Neda guessed, correctly as it happened, that Shiri had come to her rescue. Neda prayed that Shiri would take the blame for the dropped hairbrush. As Kazem's footsteps started to retreat, Neda mentally retracted all of her earlier unkind thoughts about Shiri.

Neda's heart felt as though it had stopped as soon as Kazem's footsteps did. She then heard a sound she recognized as Kazem opening his briefcase, which he always kept locked. This was followed by a faint whirring and beep that told her Kazem had turned on his laptop. A few minutes later, the sound of the bedroom light being snapped off and the door closing told Neda it was safe to emerge from the wardrobe.

At last, a stroke of good luck! Neda could see that though he had pulled the lid partway down, Kazem had not turned off the laptop. She carefully lifted the lid up, and with her background in nuclear physics saw enough to recognize the document on the screen for what it was - information on the operation of a nuclear weapon.

Neda had kept a USB flash drive on her key ring ever since her student days, replacing it whenever a newer model struck her fancy. The latest measured slightly less than an inch long, but could still hold 64GB of data. Thankfully the Chinese had never paid much attention to international sanctions, so such items were freely available in Iran.

In moments Neda had transferred the handful of files in the laptop's documents folder onto the USB drive. She then carefully folded the laptop screen back to exactly where it had been when Kazem left it, and returned to her listening perch at the bedroom door, which she eased open just a crack.

Kazem shook his head and sat back down across from Farhad. "Your aunt's cat. I have no idea why she bought it. All it does is eat and cause trouble."

Farhad laughed. "I could say the same of some people I know."

Kazem smiled tightly. "It does remind me, though, that we need to wrap this up before your aunt gets home." Holding up a USB flash drive, he said, "I had originally planned to give this to you later, but it occurred to me that you should have some time to study its contents. The documents on it detail the operation of the nuclear devices we will be using. Since you will be leading the team detonating one of them, you must become thoroughly versed in its contents."

Farhad accepted the USB drive, but was clearly troubled. "Uncle, when you say 'we will be using' surely you do not mean..."

Kazem interrupted him with an impatient wave of his right hand. "That is exactly what I mean. At least one of these teams needs a real expert on it. I don't know what communication will be possible, if any, between the teams once the attacks have begun. But I know if I stay here on this couch in Iran you will have no hope of reaching me from the Saudi's Eastern Province."

Farhad bent his head, clearly overwhelmed. "Uncle, I and all who follow me will never forget what you are doing to make our mission a success."

Kazem grunted. "Admiration I don't need. Proper planning to give us all a fighting chance to make it back home to Iran I do. Let me walk you back to your car, and we can discuss the transport of the weapons from storage."

A few minutes later, both Kazem and Farhad were gone. This time Neda had taken the precaution of ensuring that a cafe in her neighborhood would be open, so she could spend enough time there to avoid returning right on Kazem's heels. No, she reminded herself again, Kazem was no fool.

Just a monster, willing to kill thousands.

Riyadh, Saudi Arabia

Grishkov swore as the car he had driven from the airport to the traffic light they were now waiting to turn green was struck by the car behind them. The first startled oath became much more descriptive as continued taps on the car's rear bumper slowly moved them into oncoming traffic.

Grishkov was astonished to see that Vasilyev was smiling.

"Truly," Vasilyev said, "I learn more from you on every mission. I would not have thought that anatomically possible."

"Well, I think you'll find this a lot less amusing in a few seconds once the idiot behind us finishes pushing us into traffic," Grishkov responded. To accent his point, the drivers crossing in front of them were beginning to honk and swerve.

Still smiling, Vasilyev said, "You don't understand. It is your fault for having stopped at the red light at this left turn only lane. The driver behind you wishes to go straight, and after this vehicle is struck by an oncoming car will probably have a clear way to do so."

As the force of repeated taps on their car pushed it further into the intersection, Grishkov snarled, "Enough!" After putting the car in park and applying the emergency brake he had just reached for the door handle when the light turned green.

Vasilyev now said soberly, "Remember the mission." A vein in Grishkov's temple was throbbing quite alarmingly, he noted.

His hands blurring and with a new stream of invective Grishkov put the car back into drive, released the brake and executed the left turn nearly fast enough to set the car on two wheels. With the high-end American owned hotel that was their destination now a few blocks in front of them, Grishkov snapped, "Are you going to tell me that was normal?"

Laughing, Vasilyev said, "Consider yourself welcomed to Saudi Arabia."

Ten minutes later, they were checked in to the hotel, and Grishkov was frowning as he sipped his black coffee in a cafe in its ground level. It was mid-afternoon on a weekday, and they were in the back corner of a nearly deserted establishment.

Vasilyev peered over his cappuccino and smiled. "Something is bothering you. Care to share?"

Grishkov shrugged, but if anything his frown deepened. "Well, I'm no expert in these matters. But here we are in an American hotel. They have sold billions in weapons to the Saudis. After Iraq seized Kuwait and its oil, if it hadn't been for the Americans everyone knows the oil just a few hundred kilometers south in this country would have been next. And without their support, the Saudis could never continue their campaign in Yemen."

Grishkov paused, and looked expectantly at Vasilyev.

Vasilyev's smile simply broadened, and he took another sip of his cappuccino.

Now Grishkov's frown became a scowl. "Fine, I'll come right out and ask. Why aren't we working with the Americans on this? They certainly have greater resources and more contacts in this country than we do. Or am I wrong about that?"

Now Vasilyev's smile disappeared, and he put down his cappuccino.

"You are not wrong. Of course, the decision about whether or not to work with the Americans, or for that matter the Saudis, was made far above our level. Probably above Smyslov's, and considering the stakes possibly by the President himself. So, I can only speculate about why we are dealing strictly with unofficial contacts during this trip."

Vasilyev paused and looked at Grishkov, who nodded acknowledgment that he understood what would follow was only Vasilyev's best guess.

"You are correct to think that the direct approach would have many advantages. Your police training has taught you to look for the most effective solution to a problem, and sharing all we know with both the Saudis and the Americans would appear to be just that. But, there are many possible negative consequences as well."

Vasilyev picked up his cappuccino and took a sip while he gathered his thoughts.

"The first problem is our friendly relationship with Iran, at least as far as military sales go. Though we do not believe the attack is sanctioned by the Iranian government, what we have learned so far suggests that the organization planning it includes multiple Iranian government officials. So, if the attack is not stopped, we may be blamed for assisting it."

Grishkov gestured impatiently. "That makes no sense. If we were involved with the attack, why warn its target?"

Vasilyev nodded. "I understand your confusion. However, consider that so far we don't even know the specific targets. The vague warning we could provide now could be dismissed as an attempt to evade responsibility, particularly if the attack is not prevented."

Grishkov paused, and then shrugged acknowledgment. "But I am sensing that even if we learn of the targets, we may not automatically tell the Saudis and the Americans."

Vasilyev smiled broadly, and nodded vigorously. "You are a quick study, my friend. Yes, even then there would be problems. Do you imagine we would be free to intervene in this matter if the Saudis and Americans knew about it? Even if we weren't escorted to the first flight back to Moscow, any supposed joint effort would just be a way to track our every move. How likely would our success be then? And how likely do you think it is that our President would leave the solution to this problem in the hands of the Americans?"

Grishkov grimaced, and shook his head.

Vasilyev laughed. "Yes, exactly. Add to that the possibility that the plotters may have ears within the Saudi government that could tell them about our warning. Though I doubt they do within the American government, remember that their security is truly very poor."

Grishkov nodded, and said simply, "Wikileaks."

Vasilyev smiled. "Just so. Can you believe a low-ranking officer was able to put thousands of highly classified documents on a USB drive, and simply walk out with them? And that the documents had no encryption to slow down their distribution on the Internet even a little?"

Vasilyev paused, and lowered his voice. "We must also acknowledge that after certain recent actions by our government, some Americans may not believe our warning would be...well-intentioned."

Grishkov shrugged. "Everything you have said makes sense. But at some point we may have to call on the Saudis for help, yes?"

Vasilyev nodded. "Yes. We will hardly be able to take on a well-funded and highly capable terrorist organization on our own. We have agents in place throughout the Kingdom, and there are Saudi officials we consider reliable. But we are not to contact them unless we have actionable intelligence, and then only if we cannot deal with the matter ourselves."

Grishkov glanced at his watch, a metal specimen that was obviously far from new. Vasilyev smiled and gestured towards it.

"That looks like a Sturmanskie. Is it original?"

Grishkov shrugged. "I have no idea. The pilot who gave it to me in Chechnya said it was the most valuable thing he had. I tried to refuse, but he insisted."

Vasilyev nodded. "You saved his life, I suppose?"

Grishkov frowned, obviously annoyed. "I told him I was simply doing my duty, but he wouldn't listen. I finally accepted the watch just to be done with the matter."

Vasilyev laughed. "Well, you've obviously taken good care of it since then. Did you know that's the same model watch Yuri Gagarin wore when he became the first man in space? Or that for years they were only available to Soviet Air Force pilots?"

Grishkov's eyes widened, and he simply shook his head.

Vasilyev nodded. "Yes, and the company that made them has an interesting history. The Soviet government bought two American companies in the 1930s. All of their equipment along with about two dozen former employees from Ohio were brought to the USSR to start our first watch factory. After they produced your watch and many others, the company went on in the 1970s to produce Poljot, the most popular watch brand of the Soviet era."

Grishkov smiled. "My father had a Poljot. He loved that watch. We buried him with it."

Vasilyev nodded. "And unlike many young people today, you do not rely on your phone for the time."

Grishkov snorted. "Certainly not. Phones are far less reliable. I have had many fail over the years. This watch has never failed to tell the correct time. And now it is telling me that the meeting with our contact is due."

Vasilyev smiled. "Well, as in many countries, how late he is will tell us much. In particular, how much does he need us, versus how much we need him."

Grishkov shook his head. "While we wait, I have to ask you how you could take that business at the intersection so calmly."

Vasilyev smiled. "Traffic here is far less dangerous now than during my first trip to the Kingdom, which was even before we opened our embassy. Then the rumor was that the death rate from traffic accidents was higher than the birth rate."

Grishkov stared. "Surely an exaggeration!"

Vasilyev shrugged. "Perhaps. But the government was certainly concerned. For example, truly spectacular wrecks would be featured on the evening news. I remember one in particular where the voiceover said, as the camera panned over pieces of wood with Arabic lettering on them, 'Yes, the driver of this Maserati drove right through this sign saying The Bridge Isn't Finished Yet.' The camera then zoomed to the scorch mark on the other side of the gorge as the voiceover continued. 'Yes, the driver almost made it across - but not quite.' Then the camera angle zoomed down about two hundred meters to the bottom of the gorge, where you could see pieces of a white Maserati scattered over a considerable distance."

Grishkov shook his head. "Come now, we have such stories in the news in Russia, and I'm sure in many other countries."

Vasilyev nodded. "True. Very well, imagine this. A TV program which begins with an Indian doctor on the top floor of a Riyadh hospital. He looks into the camera, and without preamble opens one of the windows. He then asks, 'If you were in a big hurry to leave this hospital, would you jump? No? So, why are you driving double the posted speed limit inside the city? You need to stop doing this.' He then walks down the hallway and stops in front of a door. 'Let's talk to some people who did not follow my good advice.' He then opens the door to the quadriplegic ward."

"No," Grishkov said, horrified.

"Oh, yes," Vasilyev nodded. "He then proceeds to ask the patients questions like 'Are you sorry you drove double the posted speed limit inside the city?' This program was rebroadcast multiple times."

Grishkov frowned. "It still doesn't prove much. Whoever was in charge of programming may have had a family member killed in traffic and had that show produced."

Vasilyev nodded. "Also true. I'm glad to see that some of my skepticism is rubbing off on you! So, picture this. After each serious accident, the dead and injured would of course be removed. However, instead of towing away the wrecks they would be moved to the side of the road and left in place for a week or so, as a warning to other drivers. One wreck even featured above it a fender dangling from a second-story balcony, where it had evidently been thrown by the impact. You couldn't drive any significant distance without passing multiple instances of such examples."

Grishkov shrugged. "I saw none on our drive from the airport."

Vasilyev smiled. "Just so. As I said, it is far safer to drive now than on my first tour. And here comes the man we have been waiting so patiently to meet."

Chapter Six

Doha, Qatar

Prince Bilal bin Hamad looked at Farhad Mokri skeptically. For this highly unofficial meeting they were in the offices of one of the many businesses controlled by the Qatari royal family, of which Prince Bilal was a high-ranking member. Bilal was wearing the same traditional white thobe and red-checkered ghutrah as nearly all other Qatari men, making him difficult to pick out from the busy office crowd. Farhad wore the slacks and dress shirt common for foreign businessmen visiting Qatar, and was equally inconspicuous.

"Are you sure it will be possible to detonate three nuclear weapons against Saudi targets simultaneously? You say the loss of Muslim lives will be minimal, but will not tell me which places are targeted. Who will provide these weapons?", Bilal asked, and then paused.

"I have many more questions, but those will do for a start."

Farhad nodded, and said, "I can assure you that we can deliver on the attack we have promised. In fact, we can give you the best guarantee of all. Qatari tanks will not be expected to cross the border into Saudi Arabia until at least one of the nuclear weapons have detonated. The weapons are untested, and one or two may not work. But even a single nuclear explosion will be enough to create the chaos and confusion we need for success."

Farhad saw with satisfaction that he had scored a hit from Bilal's reaction. He knew from it that it was a condition Bilal had planned to demand anyway.

"As for the targets, you understand that for the security of our operations we cannot share them, even if you decide to participate in our plans. The same is true for the source of our weapons. However, I can guarantee that we are not targeting any Saudi city. We know that mass casualties would turn the entire Muslim world against us. War is not simply killing. It is truly about breaking the enemies' will to resist."

Bilal shrugged. "Maybe so. But it will take more tanks than we have to fight through to Riyadh, even after the confusion that will doubtless follow your attack."

Farhad smiled. "And you shall have them. Another armored force will join your push to Riyadh from a different direction."

Bilal's eyebrows flew upwards. "And the source of this mysterious assistance?"

Farhad laughed. "Your Highness, if your father is willing to commit to our plan I promise that much, at least, we can reveal. In fact, it will be critical for your forces to be in touch with the other armored force as you both close on Riyadh. After all, it wouldn't do to have you shoot at each other."

Bilal nodded. "Well, I will discuss your proposal with my father, and see whether he has any interest in pursuing it. Before the Saudis decided to impose their blockade again I know he would have refused. Now, though, I think he will at least consider it."

Farhad nodded in turn. It was what he had expected. The Saudis had led the blockade when it was first imposed in 2017, supported by the United Arab Emirates, Bahrain and Egypt. It had never been completely effective, thanks to help Qatar received from Iran and Turkey, though it had inflicted severe hardship and cost Qatar billions. Within a year the blockade had proved ineffective, and after both sides spent over a billion dollars each on public relations campaigns that even included Western TV ads, the Americans had finally appointed a former head of US Central Command to resolve the crisis.

That special representative quit in 2019, citing "the unwillingness of the regional leaders to agree to a viable mediation effort that we offered to conduct or assist in implementing."

The Saudis then escalated the entire blockade concept by beginning excavation of the "Salwa Canal." First proposed in 2018, the goal of the sixty-kilometer long canal was to turn Qatar from a peninsula into an island. Not stopping there, the Saudis proposed to make one end of the canal a tourist destination, effectively stealing tourists away from a massive Qatari seaside resort under construction just a fifteen-minute drive from the Saudi border.

To grind in the canal's function of cutting off Qatar from the rest of the Arabian peninsula, the Saudi government also announced that its other end would be used as a nuclear waste dump. Never mind that though the Saudis had signed construction deals with both the French and the Koreans, no nuclear reactor had yet been built.

Of course, once Qatar had been turned into an island there would be no need for the Saudis to maintain substantial forces at its border to maintain the blockade.

Qatar appealed to the Americans to help end the blockade, but they just pointed to their earlier failed effort and refused. Fed up, Qatar's ruler kicked them out of the US Central Command's "forward headquarters" at Al Udeid Air Base.

And now there was every reason to hope the Qataris would join Al-Nahda, for the oldest reason of all.

Revenge.

Assembly of Experts Secretariat, Qom, Iran

Grand Ayatollah Reza Fagheh looked up as Guardian Colonel Bijan Turani was escorted into his office by his assistant. With a nod Reza dismissed him, and waved the Colonel to a seat across from his desk. Reza looked him over critically, not for the first time thinking it had been a mistake for Pasdaran soldiers to abandon the custom of wearing beards. However, he could find no other fault, for Bijan's military bearing and obvious physical fitness made him look like he had just stepped out of a recruiting poster. Well, time to see if performance matched appearance.

"Report, Colonel."

Bijan nodded. "I believe we have developed a plan with a high probability of success. I must warn you, however, that the plan is complex, and will require our best men and equipment to implement."

Reza said nothing, and gestured impatiently for Bijan to proceed.

Bijan paused, and then said, "We realized first that we could never fly a nuclear weapon directly from Iran to Riyadh. No matter how many fighters the Saudis divert to the war in Yemen, there will be more than enough left to respond to a flight originating in Iran that proceeds to overfly the Kingdom. In fact, the flight might be intercepted the moment it approaches Saudi airspace, since we know they monitor all air traffic crossing the Gulf, and fly regular patrols along the coast. Instead, we will fly the weapon into Bahrain Airport, where we have agents who can prevent its discovery by Bahraini officials."

Reza nodded. This made sense. After all, Bahrain was just a short drive from the Saudi border.

Bijan continued, "We will have a Boeing CH-47 Chinook already at Bahrain Airport, ready to carry the weapon to its final destination. It will have a flight plan showing its destination as an oil field about twenty minutes flying time south of Riyadh. Since Chinooks are routinely used to deliver oilfield equipment and we have agents in place at Saudi Aramco, we will have no trouble with clearance."

Reza scowled. "It will take the Saudis no more than a few minutes to set their fighters on this helicopter once it fails to land at the oilfield. Unless you want me to believe that the Saudis don't have an air patrol over their capital, and the best radar coverage possible for many kilometers around it."

Bijan nodded. "I agree that the Chinook will be detected and attacked before it reaches Riyadh, but I think it will take more than a few minutes. Flying low will make it difficult to detect, and a senior commander will have to authorize an attack on a previously cleared flight. Also, some attempt to communicate will be made before fighters are cleared to engage, and the pilot will claim navigation failure once contacted. We estimate ten or even fifteen minutes will be needed before the Chinook is actually under attack."

Reza grunted sourly. "So, the helicopter will be shot down with Riyadh on the horizon. I think that will be scant consolation for its crew."

Bijan laughed, and shook his head. "I would have never wasted your time if we had no plan for the Chinook's survival. I'm sure you recall the pair of J-20 fighters I asked you to obtain for us from the Chinese last year."

Now Reza's scowl was back, and deeper than ever. "I was going to ask you about that. The Chinese demanded over a billion dollars worth of oil in barter for those planes, and more on top of that for the trainers and equipment you told me would be necessary to get them flying with our pilots. Plus a bribe for the Chinese officials authorizing the sale. Keeping them a secret has also been difficult and expensive. Yet so far we've made no use of..."

Reza's voice trailed off as realization hit him. "These Chinese planes will protect the helicopter and the weapon it carries! Are we ready? Can these planes really succeed against the Saudis? Surely, they will have their best planes and pilots protecting the capital."

Bijan nodded. "I think the J-20s can succeed. We only have to keep the Saudi fighters off the Chinook for ten minutes or so. The J-20s will be difficult to hit for the same reason I am confident they can make it across Saudi airspace without detection. They are fifth generation fighters that are nearly invisible to radar. Our radar has been unable to detect them until they are practically on top of us. The Saudis' radar may be better, but I don't think it's that much better."

Reza looked doubtful. "Don't the Saudis have American made fighters? Aren't they just as good as these Chinese planes?"

Bijan shook his head. "The Americans have fifth-generation fighters, including the F-22 and F-35. They have sold none to the Saudis. The fighters they do have such as the F-15 are capable, and they could get lucky. I must repeat - there is no way to guarantee success in such an operation. All we can do is prepare as well as we can, in the time we have available. Still, I believe we will succeed."

Reza sat mute for several moments, and Bijan started to think that the operation would be canceled.

Then Reza nodded sharply. "Continue your preparations. I will let you know when whatever nuclear weapons we have are available."

Doha, Qatar

Emir Waleed bin Hamad stood in front of a glass expanse giving him a spectacular view of Doha, a city that had been transformed over the previous generation into a modern metropolis with one and a half million inhabitants. Though affairs of state required him to spend much of his time at the Royal Palace, the penthouse he owned at the ninety-first floor of the newly completed Dubai Towers was where he was happiest.

The Palace required an army of servants to clean and maintain, and also housed many of those responsible for arranging and executing state functions. It had its place, but he found it difficult to think clearly in its constant buzz of activity.

This penthouse, by contrast, was almost eerily quiet. Fewer than a dozen servants and security staff were present at any one time, and were restricted to the suite's outer rooms. No one came without being invited, including family.

Today, though, marked a rare day that Waleed did have an invited guest, his younger brother Prince Bilal bin Hamad who commanded Qatar's army. As Bilal knocked and without asking entered, Waleed looked enviously at his trim figure and the dark locks peeking out from his gutrah, which contrasted sharply with his portly figure and thinning hair. Well, Waleed thought, let's see what he looks like in twenty years.

"Bilal, it's good to see you," Waleed said, while kissing him on both cheeks.

"Come and sit," Waleed said, leading the way to an array of comfortable chairs arranged around a small table full of food and a large thermos of strong coffee.

A few minutes later, Bilal smiled and said, "I see you brought some of the Palace's best cooks with you to this penthouse."

Wailed smiled back. "Well, being the Emir should give me some privileges."

Bilal laughed. "Indeed it should. After all, it certainly carries weighty responsibilities."

Waleed winced. "Ouch. Even as a child you were always painfully direct. Well, I suppose people never really change. So, straight to business?"

Bilal shrugged. "It seems there is little time to waste, particularly if we decide to join Al-Nahda in their planned attack on the Saudis."

Waleed nodded. "Before you describe their plans, tell me what you have been able to find out about this Al-Nahda organization. Who is really behind it?"

Bilal frowned, and said, "The honest answer is I'm not sure. The name Al-Nahda is of course Arab, but that proves nothing. The man I'm talking to is certainly Iranian, but that proves even less. A better indication Iran is behind it is that he says Al-Nahda has access to nuclear weapons, and nobody else in the region who wishes the Saudis ill has been trying to produce them."

Waleed grunted agreement. "Certainly the Pakistanis would never support an attack on the Saudis, their number one source of petroleum and provider of billions in loans and outright cash assistance. But I thought everyone, even the Israelis, believes that Iran does not yet have nuclear weapons?"

Bilal nodded. "All you say is true. I can only say that I believe it is probably the Iranians, because I can't imagine who else it could be."

Waleed rubbed his forehead tiredly, and Bilal could see the privileges that went with the title of Emir came at a price. "Did he say how many weapons they have?"

Bilal nodded again. "Yes. Three. However, he refused to say where they would be targeted."

Seeing Waleed's instantly furious expression Bilal hastily added, "However, he assured me that the weapons would not be used against a population center, and made it clear that we would not be expected to intervene until the successful use of at least one of the weapons."

Waleed's anger was replaced by doubt, but he finally shrugged. "At least then we know the weapons are real, and they're not planning lunacy like a nuclear attack on Riyadh. I will have nothing to do with the mass slaughter of my fellow Muslims, no matter how evil their leaders may be. Now, I know you have been putting your training at the German Armor School in Munster to good use since we got those Leopard tanks from the Germans. Are you happy with them?"

Bilal smiled broadly and said, "Yes, I am. At first I'd thought about getting the M1A2 Abrams tanks, and I would have if the Americans had been willing to sell us the latest model with the best depleted uranium and reactive armor. But, they weren't. Now that I've actually got my hands on the Leopard 2A7+, I don't regret that decision. They're fine tanks, and against the M1A2 version the Saudis have, I like my chances. I'll like them even better after the camouflage netting is delivered for the last shipment of one hundred thirty-eight tanks, but if I have to I'll go into battle without it. Together with the sixty-two Leopards we already have that do have the camo netting installed, that brings us to an even two hundred Leopards."

Waleed frowned and shook his head. "I like your enthusiasm. But does Al-Nahda seriously expect us to pit our small armored force up against the Saudis alone?"

Bilal shook his head. "I would not be wasting your time if they had said so in our last meeting."

Waleed looked up sharply. "Yes, and who will join us?"

Bilal looked distinctly unhappy and replied, "He refused to say." Seeing Waleed's expression, he quickly added, "But he promised to tell us if we commit to attacking once the Saudis are hit by their nuclear weapons. He added we would have to get the details to coordinate the attack."

Waleed grunted. "You mean to be sure we don't shoot each other instead of the Saudis."

Bilal smiled. "That is in fact close to his exact words."

Waleed shook his head. "And do we have any real chance to make it to Riyadh? Even if much of their armor is committed in Yemen, they still have planes armed with Hellfire missiles that could make short work of our tanks."

Bilal nodded. "But we do have thirty-six F-15s, thirty-six Rafales, twenty-four Eurofighter Typhoons, and twelve Mirage 2000s available to fly cover. Anyone attacking our force will pay a heavy price."

Waleed grunted. "I think our F-15s and Typhoons still have the price stickers in the windows, and I think that's also true for a dozen of the Rafales. Just how experienced are our pilots with their planes?"

Bilal shrugged. "You know the answer - not very. Before we told the Americans they were no longer welcome in Qatar, we did participate in some joint strike missions against ISIS. All of the pilots who carried out those missions are now serving as flight instructors, as well as pilots who received advanced air combat training in the US and UK. We also have a few flight trainers for the Typhoons from the Royal Air Force, and some retired French Air Force pilots for the Rafales and the Mirage 2000s."

Bilal paused. "I have faith in our pilots. I believe they will give our enemies a very unpleasant surprise."

Waleed nodded. "Very well. Now, the key question- what does Al-Nahda want to achieve by attacking the Saudis? And why would anyone else join us in attacking them? Obviously, nobody else really cares about our desire to end the blockade of our country. So, what does anyone else have to gain?"

Bilal looked uneasy. "You're right. I've wondered the same thing. The Al-Nahda representative has talked in vague terms about the need to end the royal family's tyranny, and bring democracy to the Saudi people. But I have heard little about plans for internal uprisings, and much more about armor and air attacks from outside the Kingdom."

Bilal paused. "So, should we abandon this path?"

Waleed shrugged. "Before the Saudis launched their first blockade, I would have rejected Al-Nahda's approach out of hand. Even after this second, I am still frankly unsure. On the one hand, will the Saudis attack us once they are done with Yemen? Is this alliance with Al-Nadha our only hope to keep our independence? Or will Al-Nahda prove untrustworthy, and make us squander our limited military assets while leaving the Saudis no choice but to end Qatar's existence?"

Bilal nodded. "There is a middle way. We can tell Al-Nadha we are committed to their plan, and find out more about this mysterious armored force that is to join us in our drive to Riyadh. I can also press for more details about what happens after we succeed, obviously assuming we do. If we don't like what we hear, we can end it then. If we do, we will wait until the promised nuclear attacks. If they fail, or if Al-Nahda lies and does inflict mass casualties, we can still stay put."

Waleed still looked unsure, but finally said, "Agreed. Let me know what you learn. In the meantime, we will continue our military preparations. They will serve equally well as preparation for attacking the Saudis, or defending us from their attack."

Tehran, Iran

Guardian Colonel Bijan Turani yanked open the door to the laboratory where he had been summoned by a senior technician named Arash Gul. One who would soon take up residence in Evin Prison if, as Bijan suspected, he was wasting his time.

"So, what was so important that I had to..." Bijan's voice trailed off as he took in the thick cable stretching the length of the laboratory, and the section propped up midway on a metal table. The cable's black casing had been sliced open, revealing additional smaller multi-colored casings inside. One of these interior casings had been sliced open as well, and the thin glass fibers inside it attached to an electronic device covered with lights and digital readouts. A small cable snaking from the device was attached to a nearby PC, and its screen displayed data that meant nothing to Bijan.

But he imagined he was about to get an explanation.

"You will recall several months ago you asked me for help in avoiding detection by automated border monitoring systems, specifically at the Saudi land borders. I suggested we put a notice on the dark web saying we would pay well for such information, without of course identifying us," Arash said.

Bijan nodded impatiently.

Seemingly undeterred, Arash continued. "I also recommended that we not say we were interested in defeating the sensors at the Saudi land borders specifically, to avoid alerting them. The Saudis don't have the capacity to monitor dark web traffic in detail, but their American allies do."

Finally, Arash appeared to notice Bijan's impatience was moving quickly to anger.

"I am pleased to report that we have finally been contacted by someone who says he has information that can help you. I paid the small sum of about ten thousand US dollars in cryptocurrency for the first part of his information, and you see the results of that here before you. For full details of how to defeat the sensors, he wants one million US dollars. I am not authorized to pay such a large amount, so I thought you should see what we have so far in detail."

Bijan took a deep breath and nodded.

"Very well. You have acted correctly. So, what am I looking at here?" Bijan asked.

Arash pointed at the exposed section of cable. "This is a fiber optic cable, of the precise type the man says is used to carry sensor data from the Saudi land border to their military headquarters in Riyadh. For ten thousand dollars he also gave us instructions on how to tap into the cable, and tamper with the data being transmitted. In short, he recommends recording data being sent through the cable over the time period needed, and then repeating it."

Bijan grunted. "And you have confirmed that the instructions work?"

Arash nodded. "Just as he said. I could easily train any of your military communications technicians to do the work."

Bijan frowned. "So, why am I going to pay another one million dollars?"

Arash shrugged. "For the precise GPS coordinates of the buried cable. He claims to have been one of the contractors who did the installation."

Bijan pursed his lips thoughtfully. "This could be just a clever story, with nothing waiting for us at the GPS coordinates but sand."

Arash nodded. "I said exactly that in our last exchange. He said he is willing to take half now, and the other half after we confirm the GPS coordinates. However, he recommends against that approach."

Bijan smiled. "I'm sure he does. Why?"

Arash shrugged again. "Well, he says that if you dig up the cable once to confirm its location and then again when you really need to, your chances of discovery go way up."

Bijan laughed. "Maybe so, but why not get the coordinates, use them when we need to and then never pay him the rest?"

Now Arash looked uncomfortable. "Because he says for the full million dollars up front he has some helpful tips on avoiding detection when we tap into the cable. He also says there is a wireless backup data transfer system, and he'll include information on it as well. But only if we pay the million up front."

Bijan scowled. "This man seems to have an answer for everything. So, how long does it take him to respond when you contact him?"

Arash smiled. "Very quickly. I think he is looking forward to getting his money."

Bijan nodded. "I'm sure he is. Have our hackers been able to trace his location?"

Arash shook his head. "Not at all. When the first hacker was unable to do so I went to his supervisor, who failed as well. Finally, I had the head of the cybersecurity department try, who was also unsuccessful. He told me that if the man knows as much about communications as he does about maintaining his anonymity, our payment will not be wasted."

Bijan grunted. "Very well. If it is everything promised, it will indeed be money well spent."

Bijan then picked up the nearest phone and punched in the numbers for his assistant, quickly giving him the necessary instructions.

"You should have access to one million dollars in cryptocurrency within ten minutes. Once you do, contact the man and tell him we agree to his terms."

Half an hour later Arash and Bijan had a set of GPS coordinates, and were reading several pages of instructions.

Bijan frowned. "So, he included the transmission frequency for the wireless backup data transfer system, but warns it may have been changed. He recommends blanket jamming of all frequencies for a radius of several miles around the border crossing point."

Arash's eyebrows rose. "An R-330ZH automated jammer?"

Bijan smiled. "Exactly. I had already planned to allocate one to the commander of this mission anyway. We have several, and they are often useful."

Arash nodded. "I see that my initial plan to loop a short recording of ambient noise from the sensor collectors would have been a mistake."

Bijan shrugged. "It was my first thought as well. I have no desire to have our force linger at the border any longer than necessary. However, we can send a team ahead of the main force to carry out the mission. As I understand it, software will alert the Saudis if we loop a short recording. But, if we leave at least a five-minute gap between the recording we collect and the one we switch to, we can get away with using the recording once. That means to give us enough time to get across the border undetected the recording will need to be at least ninety minutes long."

Arash frowned. "I am no military expert. But will it really take that long? I ask because there are technical issues with making and properly replaying such a long recording. Training someone to go with our force will not be as easy as I thought."

Bijan nodded. "I hope it won't take so long to cross. But the first thing you learn in the military is to prepare for the unexpected. There is some good news, though. You won't have to worry about training anyone."

Arash frowned even more deeply. "Why not? This really will not be so simple..."

His voice trailed off as he saw Bijan's smile widening.

Arash's voice rose in near panic as it finally dawned on him why he would not need to train another technician.

"I cannot be spared here! I am overseeing numerous projects of the highest priority!"

Bijan's smile didn't waver. "I know. But your boss agrees with me that this mission is more important than all the others put together."

Bijan could see Arash's thoughts race as he tried to find a way out. Then, to his surprise, Arash turned to a nearby wooden crate and flipped off its lid.

"Well, my beloved boss told me not to show you this, because I think he has his own plans for it. But if I'm going on this adventure, I want us to have every advantage we can get."

Bijan's eyebrows rose. What was inside the crate was...cloth. What was so special about it?

As though reading his thoughts, Arash said "You cannot imagine how difficult this was to obtain. The manufacturer calls it the Ultra-Light Camouflage Netting System. The American military uses acronyms for everything, and calls it ULCANS."

Bijan shrugged. "So, what makes it different than any other camouflage?"

Arash smiled. "The honest answer is that we don't know. That's why the company selling this to the American military was able to get a contract for half a billion dollars. What we do know is that it is effective at blocking detection not just in the visible light spectrum, but in all wavelengths used by current military sensors, including radar and thermal."

Bijan frowned. "So, you mean that radars and thermal imaging won't detect a vehicle covered with this material, even if it is on the move?"

Now Arash's smile widened. "Please watch the video that the manufacturer has helpfully uploaded to the Internet."

When the short video had finished, Bijan rubbed his chin thoughtfully. "They talk about customizing the fabric to different environments. I imagine that was not possible for this shipment."

Arash shook his head. "No. That would require collecting data in the area where the fabric would actually be used. However, as you can see we did make the obvious choice from the manufacturer's generic terrain selection."

Bijan grunted. "Yes, desert. I believe you when you say this was hard to get. How much do we have, and can we get more?"

Arash looked uncertain. "I can give you documentation showing the precise quantities and dimensions. But from what I have been told of your plans I cannot say if it will be enough. The material obviously has to be cut to size. You will have many vehicle types. For application in the field you will want attachment mounts designed to fit the pre-made cuts. There are several different application approaches that we should test to see which can be done most quickly, and give the best coverage."

Arash paused. "The simple answer to your second question is no. We were able to get a man inside the Americans' manufacturing facility in Kentucky in their shipping department. After months of learning their systems, he was able to fake documents routing a shipment to the manufacturer's headquarters."

Bijan frowned. "And where is that?"

Arash grinned. "Israel." When he saw Bijan's reaction, he had to laugh, and after a moment Bijan did too.

Bijan shook his head. "Obviously, we did not steal the shipment from Israel."

Arash nodded. "Correct. Our agent had the shipment routed through Antwerp, and we were able to intercept it there. Unfortunately, he had to flee after this success, just one step ahead of the authorities. So, there is no way of knowing if or when we may be able to get more of this fabric."

Bijan shrugged. "Very well. We will make whatever use of it we can. And Arash, don't worry about your boss. I will speak with him on my way out and remind him - again - that my mission has top priority."

Arash nodded, but Bijan could see that he was still unhappy.

Bijan clapped him on the shoulder and told him with a grin, "Cheer up! Thanks to you we have a fighting chance of success. Look at it this way - how many Iranians will ever get to visit Riyadh?"

Chapter Seven

Artillery Group 22 Garrison, Isfahan Province, Iran

Guardian Colonel Bijan Turani had to suppress a smile at the poorly concealed nervousness of the artillery captain standing at attention in front of him. If their positions had been reversed, Bijan had to admit to himself he might have reacted the same way.

"Captain Dabiri, I know you have had little time to prepare for this exercise. That was precisely the point. I want to see how well your unit can perform under pressure. Do you have any questions about your orders?", Bijan asked.

"No, sir," the captain responded.

Bijan nodded. "Excellent. I have one change to those orders we need to communicate to your troops before we begin."

The captain looked even more nervous as he carefully asked, "Sir?"

Bijan smiled. "The obsolete tanks you have rigged as targets for your artillery can be moved remotely, correct?"

Now the captain appeared close to a stroke. "Yes, sir. But as you know, the Basir artillery round requires a laser designator for an accurate strike. We have men in the exercise area targeting the tanks now. If we begin moving the tanks, we risk hitting the men."

Bijan nodded. "In that case, Captain, I suggest you move the tanks away from your men rather than towards them."

The captain paused and then wisely swallowed his objections, which Bijan knew would have included the finite range of the laser designators, and simply said, "Yes, sir."

A few minutes later, the new orders had been transmitted and the captain said, "Ready, sir."

In spite of himself, Bijan was impressed. It was obvious the unit had practiced using the Basir artillery round on a moving target before. Bijan had been told this was Iran's best artillery regiment, and now felt his hope rising that its reputation might be justified.

Well, let's see if they can actually hit the moving targets before we celebrate, Bijan thought.

Aloud, he said, "Proceed, Captain."

Ten HM-41 155 mm howitzers fired simultaneously at the ten moving tanks. Both the howitzers and the Basir artillery round had been developed and manufactured in Iran. While the HM-41 howitzer had been reverse engineered from the American M114, the Basir was an Iranian product from start to finish, and made Iran one of only five countries in the world with a laser-guided artillery shell.

Bijan and Dabiri were about five kilometers away from the targets, and half a kilometer away from the HM-41 howitzers. They were protected from the noise with earplugs, but they could still feel the vibration of the howitzers' firing in their bones. Both had binoculars trained on the distant forms of the moving tanks, which very quickly stopped moving as each was hit.

Bijan was surprised to see multiple secondary explosions, and then quickly chided himself. The tanks may not have carried ammunition, but to move they had to contain fuel.

Dabiri rapidly swapped his earplugs for a headset, and called for a report. Bijan was not so quick to remove his earplugs, and so missed the first part of an exchange between Dabiri and one of the spotters, but knew better than to interrupt before he was ready. Bijan had been in Dabiri's position before, and had always detested officers who interrupted his efforts to get the information needed to report by demanding answers before he could possibly have them.

After a few minutes Bijan could tell from the newly relaxed slump of Dabiri's shoulders that the news was, if not good, at least not disastrous.

Dabiri drew himself up and saluted. "Ready to report, sir."

Bijan's eyebrows rose. Was the news really that good?

"All targets destroyed. One spotter was lightly injured by shrapnel, but will not require hospitalization."

Bijan smiled. "Excellent, Captain. Shall we have a look?"

Both climbed into the nearby Safir 4x4 transport vehicle. Externally a close visual match to the WWII American Jeep it was Iranian made, except for a 105 horsepower Nissan engine which gave it nearly twice as much power as the original Jeep. It came in multiple configurations, including ones mounting everything from twelve 107 mm rocket tubes to anti-tank missiles. This one was outfitted as a command vehicle, with nothing onboard more lethal than multiple radios.

They pulled up first next to another Safir with a Red Crescent insignia marking it as used for medical transport, where they saw a medic packing up next to a bandaged noncommissioned officer. As soon as the soldier saw them he began to stand, but Dabiri quickly waved him back down.

"Report," Dabiri said calmly.

The NCO looked at Bijan's rank insignia and his eyes widened, but to Bijan's approval made no comment.

Instead, the NCO said, "My laser designator worked with no issues. Even though the target was moving, I had no trouble keeping it illuminated. I admit that I moved a little closer when I realized the target was moving away from me to avoid losing contact."

The NCO paused and looked at his bandages. "I didn't anticipate the force of the secondary explosion. In my only previous exercise with these rounds the targets were stationary, and hadn't been fueled. Not an excuse, sir. Glad I'm alive to have learned the lesson."

Dabiri smiled. "That's the right attitude, soldier. I'm told your injuries aren't serious, and you don't need time in hospital. Do you agree?"

The NCO nodded. "It was just a few stitches and some scrapes. I've done worse as a child falling off a bicycle. If I hadn't been hugging the ground it could have been more serious. I could feel things passing right over my head. If there had been ammo in that tank I don't think I'd be here talking to you."

Bijan glanced at Dabiri, who nodded. It was just a courtesy, but Bijan knew from his own experience it mattered.

Bijan asked, "Do you think you were the only one to move closer when you saw the targets were moving?"

The NCO hesitated. "As far as I saw, yes. I have to be honest, though, and say my attention was focused on the target in front of me."

Bijan nodded and turned towards Dabiri. "Let's take a closer look at what's left of your targets."

At that the NCO looked visibly uncomfortable, and looked up at Dabiri.

"Yes, soldier?" Dabiri asked quietly.

"Well, Captain," the NCO replied, "I would keep a respectful distance as you travel around the exercise area. I think some of these targets are still cooking, and I wouldn't want to be around when they're ready to serve."

Now both Bijan and Dabiri laughed. Bijan said, "Well said. I think we can chalk this up as a lesson well and truly learned."

As they drove around the smoking hulks of the destroyed targets, Bijan silently counted to himself until reaching ten, and nodded with satisfaction. He doubted Dabiri would have tried to claim unearned kills, but he had seen it happen before in exercises.

Both of them started involuntarily as one of the targets erupted in a new explosion, fortunately on the other side of the exercise area.

Bijan grunted. "Your soldier was right. Apparently it takes time for fire to reach the gas tank in some of your targets. Squinting he asked, "Are these all T-54s, or are some T-55s?".

Dabiri smiled. "Good eye, Colonel, particularly considering the damage the targets have taken. Seven T-54s, and three T-55s. It took some work to get these mobile again."

Bijan snorted in amusement. He didn't doubt it considering the age of the tanks, which he guessed at over fifty years old.

"Obviously we're not going to use our best tanks for target practice. Based on the damage you see here, do you think the Basir will kill more modern tanks?"

Dabiri nodded vigorously. "Absolutely, sir. Top armor is the weak point of every tank, new or old. No tank ever built is going to survive a 155 mm round dropped on top of it. The only question is whether we can deliver that round on target. Frankly, I'm not sure how easy it will be to shine a laser designator on a tank without being spotted."

Bijan nodded, but said nothing. There was one place he could imagine that being possible, but Dabiri had no need to know that. Yet.

Dabiri continued, "If the spotters have the chance to dig in I think it would help their survival chances, but unless they're good with camouflage it could make their detection more likely. If we can get laser designators with a longer range I think that would help too."

Bijan smiled. "Excellent points, Captain. Please be sure to include them in your report."

Finally, the Safir pulled back up at Dabiri's mobile command post, and they sat back on either side of the folding table where Dabiri would draft his preliminary report.

"Just one question before I let you get to your report, Captain. How long would it take you and your men to pack the howitzers used in today's exercises for transport?"

Dabiri's eyebrows flew upwards and he hesitated, which surprised Bijan, who had expected a quick answer. The reason quickly became evident, though.

"It depends on whether you want these particular howitzers, sir. We actually have twenty new HM-41s still in their original crates we could move anytime, along with a full supply of Basir rounds to go with them. I'd rather use the howitzers from today's exercise, though, since we've used them multiple times and know they have no issues. We could have them ready to go inside a week, or five days if we drop everything else we're doing."

Bijan smiled. "I think a week will be fine. I suggest you assemble and test another ten HM-41s while I clear your orders, and then crate them back up for movement. I'm glad to hear you have spares in case there are any issues discovered with those ten. Expect your new orders within a week to ten days."

Bijan climbed aboard the Agusta-Bell 212 helicopter that had brought him from his office in Qom to the exercise area for the return trip. He would have the report Grand Ayatollah Reza Fagheh expected. Bijan also planned to add some questions, now that this operation appeared more and more likely to actually be possible.

Assembly of Experts Secretariat, Qom, Iran

Grand Ayatollah Reza Fagheh scowled as he read another report on the damage American sanctions were doing to the Iranian economy. Of course, he mused, a much longer report could be written on the problems caused by corruption, price controls, subsidies and a long list of other government interventions.

Not to mention that about sixty percent of Iran's economy was centrally planned. Reza smiled grimly as he thought about one comment he had heard about on social media that the proportion of Iran's economy controlled by the government was greater than China's. This had set off a lively debate about whether anyone could really know who controlled what in China, and how its control of the economy explained why Iran's clergy was so resistant to change.

Of course, the author of the most perceptive comments quickly found himself in Tehran's Evin Prison. Reza made a mental note to check whether he was still alive, and if he was to put him out of his misery.

Reza smiled again as he thought about the religious foundations called Bonyad, which represented more than thirty percent of Iranian government spending. He effectively controlled one of those Bonyads, though his name appeared on none of its documents. Yes, the poor fellow in Evin Prison had no idea how right he was.

Not that Reza planned to change anything about how Iran's economy was managed. Though he was aware of the role that both the clergy and the government played in Iran's economic problems, fixing them was impossible without the clergy ceding its control of Iran's government. On the contrary, Reza wanted that control tightened.

Reza only cared about the performance of Iran's economy at all because its failure had begun to cause demonstrations that were too large to ignore or easily suppress. He had been part of the demonstrations that had brought down the Shah, and knew first hand that the effectiveness of violent repression had a limit.

The effectiveness of blaming all of Iran's economic problems on American sanctions also had a limit, as the size of the recent demonstrations showed. Reza had ordered the report to see if there was anything new the government could use to point the finger at the Americans again, but now that he'd read it had seen nothing likely to help.

People were fed up. With its oil and gas reserves Iran had the fifth largest total value of natural resources in the world, worth an estimated twenty-seven trillion US dollars. This was not a secret to anyone.

And yet, a study by the International Monetary Fund in 2016 detailing what Iran's citizens could buy in their country ranked it...67th.

Many were starting to ask dangerous questions about the clergy's share of the country's wealth. Others were starting to ask about the money being spent on Iran's interventions in Yemen, Syria, and Lebanon - and whether spending the money at home instead might help stop the seemingly endless sanctions.

Reza was determined to provide a different answer to Iran's economic problems. He smiled as he thought back to an economics lecture he had attended decades earlier, where the professor had said that if you didn't want to share the pie differently, bake a bigger pie.

Reza's smile grew even wider as he thought about his pie's prime ingredient. Then, his pleasant imaginings were interrupted by reality, in the form of a knock announcing Guardian Colonel Bijan Turani's arrival for his scheduled briefing.

"So, Colonel, I understand the exercise was a success," Reza observed, waving Bijan to the seat across from his desk.

Bijan nodded. "Frankly, it succeeded beyond all my expectations. I'm beginning to think this plan may work after all."

Reza smiled thinly. "Yes, I remember your objections. I'm glad to see you coming around. I understand one soldier was injured?"

Bijan frowned. "Yes, but not seriously. I plan to get improved laser designators for the troops in this mission to avoid more casualties like his, caused by his being too close to the target. In fact, I already have orders en route to our purchasing agents in the US."

Reza's eyebrows flew upwards. "America! Are you sure we can get them here in time, and without detection?"

Bijan grinned. "This is hardly the first time we have needed a rush shipment of American military equipment. I placed the orders yesterday, via free two-day air shipping. Once our purchasing agents in the US receive them, they will fly with them as checked baggage through a variety of routings. The Americans and Europeans will scan their baggage for explosives, but nothing else. Even if the bags are opened, security screeners will find only legally purchased civilian laser designators."

Reza frowned. "Civilian? Won't they be weak and useless to our soldiers?"

Now Bijan's grin grew wider. "On the contrary, the American soldiers who thoughtfully reviewed them said they were comparable to the ones they had used in the military."

Reza shook his head. "This makes no sense. Isn't such equipment restricted, and ridiculously expensive? How could you make these purchases without my authorization?"

Bijan shrugged. "The price of well under two thousand dollars each fell well within my spending authority, and in fact they were even on sale! As for restriction, the website did say that they could be sold only to US citizens, and were not for export. So, on the online order form I did have to...check a box."

When he saw Reza's expression in response, Bijan couldn't restrain his laughter. After a few seconds, Bijan was astonished to hear Reza join him. He had honestly never imagined the dour cleric capable of laughter.

After a few moments their laughter wound down and Bijan asked the question that had been troubling him during the entire trip back from the exercise.

"If we get all the pieces in place in time, the first phase of the plan may be successful. But even so, do you really believe the Saudis can be defeated with the limited forces we have available? It may take time for them to move the forces they have in Yemen, and I have some ideas for how we can slow that redeployment down. But make no mistake- most of their troops and armor will be back to fight us far sooner than we'd like. Of course, the aircraft now in Yemen will be back within hours."

Reza nodded. "Yes, I think it is time to tell the others the real plan, not the one I have had "Al-Nadha" selling to everyone. First, while I do intend for two of the nuclear devices to be used on Saudi desalination plants, the third will not be detonated in a major Eastern province oil field. Instead, now that you have confirmed it is possible, I plan to drop it on Riyadh."

If Reza had expected shock from Bijan, he was disappointed. "Well, that makes sense. Nearly all of the central government is there, including almost all high-ranking members of the royal family. Command and control of Saudi armed forces will be severely disrupted, and the substantial military forces guarding the capital will be destroyed. More of the Saudis' oil money has gone to building hospitals, universities and other institutions in Riyadh than any other city."

Bijan paused. "But above all, the city has well over five million residents, about a fifth of the entire Saudi nation. Yes, losing Riyadh would be a mortal blow."

Reza smiled. "I'm so glad you approve."

Bijan ignored Reza's sardonic tone and asked, "Are you concerned about the American reaction to the likely destruction of Eskan Village Air Base, as well as the death of their diplomatic personnel at the US Embassy? I am not sure how many American diplomats are in Riyadh, but I recall about two thousand Americans are stationed at Eskan. It is true that the base is on the outskirts of the city and so some at Eskan may survive, but I think the odds are against it."

Reza shook his head decisively. "No. The Americans will not use their nuclear weapons against us. They would think of it as sinking to our level, since any nuclear attack on Iran would kill far more than two thousand. I think a conventional military strike is certain, probably by air. We will need to move the Assembly of Experts to a prepared location as soon as the weapon detonates in Riyadh."

Bijan cocked his head. "Not sooner?"

Reza shook his head even more vigorously. "Definitely not. What would we tell them? No, the attack must be kept secret until the last possible moment. Besides, the fact that Qom is a holy city may prevent the Americans from attacking it at all. They may limit their strikes to our military bases, since after all an American military base will be what we destroyed."

Bijan decided not to raise the casualties among US Embassy Riyadh personnel again, since Reza clearly saw them as unimportant. "Well, at least there we are prepared. We've spent years anticipating an American or Israeli air attack, so our most important military assets are underground, in mountain excavations, or in hardened bunkers that can withstand all but the largest conventional warheads."

Reza nodded. “Excellent. But I see from your expression that you still have concerns.”

Bijan frowned. He wasn’t aware he was that easy to read, but quickly realized that was a skill to be expected from someone sitting in the chair of Iran’s Supreme Leader. Even if he was a temporary occupant.

Of course, if this plan succeeded Reza might be in that chair a lot longer, he thought. Not for the first time.

Aloud, he asked, “Even if the attack on Riyadh is successful and the Saudis are thrown into chaos, do we really expect to take over the entire Kingdom? Because that’s what we’d have to do to take over Mecca and Medina. I think the resistance we’d face would make what the Americans dealt with in Iraq child’s play by comparison.”

Reza simply nodded. “i am aware of the problems you describe. However, control of Mecca and Medina is not my goal.”

Bijan started, genuinely surprised. “Then, what is?”

Reza smiled. “You know that most Saudi oil is in the Eastern Province, near the Persian Gulf. Where the majority of its residents are Shi’a. Who have been severely repressed by the Saudis. If we destroy Riyadh, and appear in the Eastern Province with a substantial armored force, wouldn’t most there greet us as liberators?”

Bijan was silent for a moment. Having just spoken of Iraq, the Americans’ naive belief that they would be welcomed because they had overthrown Saddam was still fresh in his mind. He quickly realized, though, that this time Reza was right.

After the best known Saudi Shi’a religious leader, Sheik Nimr Baqir al-Nimr, was executed in 2016 the authorities added to the Shi’a community’s sense of outrage by refusing to give his body to his family for burial. The following year the Shi’a town of Al-Awamiyah was razed by government forces claiming it was a terrorist base, forcing those of its twenty-five thousand inhabitants who were not killed outright to flee.

The Eastern Province just might rise in rebellion if given the chance.

Bijan slowly nodded. “Maybe. But what if they don’t? They might not actively resist us, but instead just hide in their homes. After all, many of them probably have relatives living in Riyadh they’ll never see again after our attack.”

Reza frowned, and Bijan sensed he'd raised a problem that hadn't occurred to him before. Of course, he thought grimly, when you're inflicting mass casualties unforeseen problems were to be expected.

"Well, if occupying the Eastern Province turns out not to be feasible, there are two other possibilities," Reza said with a smile.

Bijan wasn't sure he wanted to hear the answer, but knew he had to ask the question. "Which two would those be?"

Reza's smile now reminded Bijan of a cartoon he had once seen of a shark swimming up to a beach, and grinning as it pointed up at the legs of the swimmers with one of its fins.

"Bahrain," Reza said simply.

Bijan frowned. "Yes, I remember hearing a few years back that they had discovered a large new offshore field. About eighty billion barrels of oil and twenty trillion cubic feet of natural gas, if I remember correctly. But we have plenty of oil and gas of our own, surely?"

Reza nodded. "We do. But access to Bahrain's resources could give us far more. And since over seventy percent of Bahrain's citizens are Shi'a, we can expect them to welcome our help in overthrowing the Sunni Al Khalifa dynasty in Manama. Remember that in 2011 the Al Khalifas nearly came to an end as protesters overwhelmed the police. Only the intervention of the Saudi military saved them that time. This time, the Saudis will be far too busy to rescue them."

Bijan shrugged. "Perhaps. But do we have the resources to take on the Saudis as well as launching an invasion of Bahrain?"

Reza smiled, but this time instead of a shark Bijan thought of a sly fox. With some irritation, he thought that Reza might be a bit too impressed with himself.

"You know that about one hundred thousand Bahrainis, or about fifteen percent of the total population, are Ajam?"

Bijan raised his eyebrows and shook his head. "No, I didn't know that the number of Bahrainis of Iranian origin was that high. I do know that they speak both Farsi and Arabic."

Reza nodded approvingly. "Correct. The Ajam are key to our plans. We have been smuggling them weapons for the past two years, and have secretly brought their leaders with military experience here for further training. I have had Pasdaran agents in Bahrain coordinating with them as well as other Shi'a leaders during that time. If our plans succeed in Saudi Arabia we will seize Manama Airport, and fly in whatever additional forces we need. But the bulk of our invasion force...is already there."

Bijan knew better than to ask why he, a high-ranking Pasdaran officer, had not been told about these actions. Up until now, he hadn't needed to know.

"You mentioned two possibilities?"

Reza leaned forward. "Indeed I did. And you should be able to guess the second, after the report you gave me about the exercise."

Now Bijan was truly shocked. "But the Qataris will be attacking the Saudis alongside us!"

Reza showed no emotion at all. "Yes, and they will leave their country defenseless as a result. And we will have weapons capable of great destruction in Qatar, at their invitation. The howitzers are self-propelled, correct?"

Bijan nodded numbly.

"So, after the attack on the Saudi blockaders, we can move the howitzers to the port at Doha under the guise of preparing to return them to Iran. That will put them in perfect position to threaten the Qatari capital. I imagine it would take no more than a few volleys to bring down many of their famous high-rise buildings. Plus, we already have some troops stationed in Qatar," Reza said with satisfaction.

Bijan shook his head. "But Qatar is majority Sunni, and its population has shown no signs of rebellion. Can we really force regime change just by threatening to destroy some of their buildings?"

Reza smiled. "No, you're right that we couldn't bring down Qatar's monarchy so easily, but it will make them willing to listen to our proposal. What we will offer is an alliance guaranteeing that no canal will be built cutting off Qatar from the Arabian Peninsula, and no embargo will be allowed against it. After the damage we will do to Saudi Arabia, I think Qatar will be far down their priority list. Of course, our protection will come at a cost."

Bijan frowned. "Are you sure the Qataris will give in so easily? They could call their tanks and planes back from attacking Saudi Arabia, and make short work of our howitzers. For that matter, they could probably do it with whatever forces they leave behind."

Reza's smile grew wider. "Of course, at the right time you will need to make sure the Qataris understand that at the first sign they are doing any such thing our howitzers will immediately open fire on downtown Doha, and the armor we have not far away to attack the Saudis will switch to targeting them. Besides, think logically. Who else will protect Qatar from an eventual revenge attack by the Saudis?"

Bijan grunted, and at first said nothing. Reza had a point. Having kicked out the Americans, Qatar had few options left. They certainly weren't going to ask the Russians for help. Iran could well be in a position to dictate terms, since the Saudis would eventually attack Qatar for its role in the war that was about to start, even if the Qataris were initially successful.

Finally, though, Bijan couldn't restrain himself. "But is this really all something we can call 'war'? Two small armored forces, a few nuclear weapons that may or may not work - isn't all this a huge gamble in taking on the best-armed country in the region behind only Israel and Egypt?"

To Bijan's surprise Reza didn't appear even a little upset or offended. "I understand your concerns. But think about Russia's success in Crimea. Propaganda, some Special Forces troops, and repeated denials that the Russian government had anything to do with what was happening were all that they deployed. Still, in a matter of months, somehow a territory of twenty-seven thousand square kilometers with a population of over two million was under Russian control. You can say what we're going to do isn't a war. I say it is war - as it's practiced in the modern age."

Bijan had to bite back the comments that came to mind at the incongruity of the lecture in modernity being delivered by the black-robed cleric before him.

Besides, he was right.

Aloud, he said, "I see your point. In the end, all that matters is whether we can apply sufficient pressure at enough points simultaneously to bring an end to the Saudi royal family's rule."

Reza nodded. "Good. Now that you understand our options, all that's left is to get our forces in place. Remember to stop by before you leave when you have plans finalized to deal with securing the Assembly of Experts. Once you are in Qatar I may send you further orders, depending on the success of our nuclear and ground attacks."

Bijan nodded, rose and left.

Reza looked at Bijan's retreating back and sighed. He had known a military man like Bijan would not be happy with what he would see as treachery. Well, high-minded principles had no place in his plans to secure Iran's future in the few years he had left. Reza was fighting for the souls of his countrymen, and sentiment had no place in that battle.

Now that Farhad Mokri had convinced his uncle to hand over the weapons his team had developed, Reza would have to convince him that bombing Riyadh was necessary. Farhad would then need to convince his Saudi friend that this step was unavoidable.

Well, Farhad was the one who'd convinced Reza to authorize the use of VX against the Saudis' air bases. And Farhad's Saudi friend had his father killed by the Saudi government.

Yes, they might not like it. But Reza was betting they would go along.

Assembly of Experts Secretariat, Qom, Iran

Grand Ayatollah Reza Fagheh looked at Guardian Colonel Bijan Turani's expression for a clue about whether he would be pleased by his news, and was happy with what he found. Bijan's normally serious expression wasn't smiling, but did appear...satisfied.

Bijan wasted no time confirming Reza's impression. "I believe we have a plan to keep the Assembly of Experts occupied while the operation is underway."

Reza nodded with relief. One of his great worries had been that once their plan was being executed, one or more of the other Ayatollahs in the Assembly of Experts would discover Reza's role in the war and call for an immediate election to select a new Supreme Leader. For Reza to have a chance to win that election, he had to delay it until the war was at a minimum successful at overthrowing the Saudi royal family's grip on Saudi Arabia. Anything else he managed to accomplish, like helping the Shi'a majority in Bahrain to overthrow its Sunni monarchy, would help even more.

Bijan continued, "Everything depends on the successful detonation of at least one of the three nuclear devices against a Saudi target. My men can then quickly rush into the Secretariat building, and tell the Ayatollahs that they must be moved to a nearby bomb shelter for their safety in case of a retaliatory raid by either the Saudis or the Israelis, who have threatened to attack anyone using nuclear weapons in the Middle East with their own nuclear stockpile. Once they are in whatever we decide to call a 'bomb shelter,' they will be under our control. We will naturally say they cannot contact anyone outside for security reasons."

Reza nodded thoughtfully. Warning the Ayatollahs about a strike by the Israelis would not only be credible, but much more likely to work than trying to scare them with an attack by the Saudis.

"If you agree with this concept, I will have a building near the Assembly of Experts Secretariat secured and prepared. I have already identified one with a large below-ground level that I believe will do nicely."

Now Bijan hesitated.

"If the Ayatollahs prove difficult to control, or vote to select anyone other than you as Supreme Leader, more drastic steps may be required. I suggest we wire the 'bomb shelter' with explosives in such a way that after detonation, the building would appear to have been struck from the air. We can then blame their deaths on either the Saudis or the Israelis, depending on which appears to be more credible at the time. You can then continue as Acting Supreme Leader until a new Assembly of Experts can be selected. By you, of course."

Looking at Reza's expression, for a moment Bijan feared he may have gone too far. Then he relaxed, as Reza's expression became more thoughtful.

Reza shrugged. "I don't want to take such an extreme step unless there is no alternative. Some of the Ayatollahs are good men, who I will be able to count as allies in moving Iran forward on the correct path. But, there are those like Sayyid Vahid Turani who must be stopped at any cost."

It was now Reza's turn to hesitate.

"Very well. Make the preparations you described. But the explosives are not to be detonated without my personal order. That means even if you, or whoever you select to carry out your orders while you are in Qatar, thinks it would be the best option."

Bijan nodded. "Understood. And I agree, it would be best if we could secure your election as Supreme Leader with the current membership of the Assembly of Experts. I remain optimistic that our plan will achieve that goal."

Reza simply nodded, and Bijan strode out of the office, and on to Qatar to begin the first stage of the plan.

Reza sighed, and looked unseeing at the papers on his desk. After so much effort and preparation, now they would finally see whether the plan to remove the Saudi royal family would work.

Chapter Eight

Salwa Beach Resort, Qatar

Guardian Colonel Bijan Turani was out of uniform for the first time in many years. As the supposed construction manager in charge of finishing the Salwa Beach Resort, he was dressed in the khakis and polo shirt he'd been told would be typical for the job. Now, he had to get the Pakistani foreman of the construction crew he'd hired moving without arousing his suspicions. All while praying that the resort's real owners didn't hear about all the new activity at Salwa before it was too late to stop him.

The truth was, he'd been lucky to get Fuad Siddiqi. Competent foremen were in high demand in Doha's busy construction industry, and few were eager to leave the capital for a site without amenities for many kilometers in any direction.

Fortunately Fuad, or more precisely his family in Pakistan, needed the money. His first month's salary had been paid up front, and a generous bonus promised for on-time completion. Fuad had rounded up construction material, hired a crew, and was ready to start when Bijan arrived. He was bald, but sported a mustache and beard that seemed to be trying to make up for it.

As soon as he spotted Fuad, which was easy due to the crowd of workers listening to his shouted orders, Bijan pushed his way forward until he was standing in front of him. Bijan thrust his hand forward and said simply, "Bijan."

His hand was quickly enveloped by one covered with calluses from a lifetime of hard work. The power that went with its grip was not challenging, simply a reflection of the sturdy muscular frame of the man behind it.

"Good to meet the manager. I understand that after this resort has been left to sit in the sun for years you're finally going to finish it," Fuad said with a smile.

Bijan nodded. "Yes. Getting these two warehouses up so we can store the construction materials we'll need is my first priority." Waving his right hand at the pile of prefabricated components laying on the sand, he added, "I see you've already got the warehouse materials unloaded. You've got the blueprints, right?"

Fuad frowned, "Yes, but one point I wanted to check with you. There are no roof components among these materials, or shown on the blueprints. Instead, we've got blue plastic sheeting we're supposed to put in place of a roof. Which will work fine to keep out dust and insects."

Bijan nodded calmly. "Correct."

Fuad's frown deepened, and Bijan thought to himself that the absence of hair on his head made the frown seem to go higher. Probably his imagination.

"OK, I'm sure you know like everywhere on the Peninsula it doesn't rain much. But it does rain sometimes. If it does in any quantity, this plastic sheeting is going to collapse and dump rainwater all over the contents of these warehouses. I know that this sort of storage method has been used before here, and that warehouses this large had to cost quite a bit. But it won't cost much more to add the roof components, and my crew can have the roofs added in just a couple of extra days."

Bijan nodded as though he were seriously considering Fuad's arguments. "I will talk to the owners and pass on your concerns. I'm sure you understand that I'll need their approval to spend the extra money. Frankly, I had the same thought and have already checked the weather report for the next ten days. Fortunately, it shows clear skies ahead. I'm glad to hear you say that the roofs can be added in just a couple of days if that changes."

Fuad looked relieved. "Yes, that's right. I'm glad you're willing to think about my advice. I always want the bosses to be happy, and soaked construction materials are a sure way to slow down the finish time for this project."

Bijan smiled. "And that wouldn't help your chances of getting that on-time completion bonus, would it?"

Fuad smiled back. "No sir, it would not."

Bijan nodded. "So, how long to finish the two warehouse buildings based on the blueprints as they stand?"

Fuad shrugged. "The components are all prefab, so my crew should have no trouble getting them done in the three days you asked for, as long as you don't have any side projects in the meantime."

Bijan laughed. "Spoken like an experienced foreman. No, you'll get no surprises from me. Just get the warehouses up, and then we'll get the materials we need to start on finishing up the resort stored away."

Fuad nodded. "Very good, sir. I'll get the crew started." With that, he walked to where the crew was sitting around two plastic tarps stretched out on the sand and held down with rocks, makeshift tablecloths for an outdoor breakfast. As Fuad explained what they would be doing to the crew, Bijan smiled with satisfaction. Now, if everything else just went this smoothly...

Assembly of Experts Secretariat, Qom, Iran

Grand Ayatollah Sayyid Vahid Turani was one of the very few members of the Iranian clergy to have contacts within the regular Iranian military. There was a reason a large and well-armed parallel military answerable only to the clergy had been set up after the Iranian Revolution. That was the Shah's use of the regular military to successfully suppress dissent for years, until the Iranian people were finally willing to face machine guns in crowds numbering tens of thousands to defy them.

Vahid smiled as Colonel Arif Shahin was escorted into his office by his secretary, who quickly left. Arif was in command of a tank regiment stationed near Tehran, which meant he was considered reliable by both the Iranian military and the Pasdaran, who would have never allowed a military commander they suspected near the capital.

"Arif, it's good to see you! Please, we must have some tea." Vahid said, gesturing towards a low table surrounded by comfortable chairs, where tea and cookies were already waiting.

There was only one possible answer to that invitation, though Vahid could see Arif was anxious to begin speaking immediately about something important. With a sharp nod, Arif sat in the indicated seat, and visibly willed himself to relax as Vahid poured tea.

Arif took the offered glass and sighed as he inhaled the tea's fragrance. "I must remember, we have ancient customs for a reason."

Vahid laughed. "Indeed we do. Now, tell me what brings you here with such urgency."

Arif set his glass down and frowned. "First, I have to say I wish I had more to tell you. Much of what I've learned is incomplete, and I'm not sure what action we can take to stop whatever's happening. But, here's what I know so far."

Arif spent half an hour explaining what he and his men had discovered.

Vahid listened intently, and once Arif had finished shook his head. "Very well," he said. "Let me sum up what you've told me. Reza Fagheh and his allies in the Pasdaran plan to attack Saudi Arabia, and their plot includes at least one nuclear weapon and the Qataris. We don't know exactly how or when this attack will take place, but we believe it will be soon. Reza is doing this because he thinks it will provoke a rebellion against the Saudi royal family's rule, and that if he can claim credit for sidelining our main rival for influence in the Gulf, he will be elected Supreme Leader."

Arif nodded, and then shrugged. "I know it's not much to go on."

Vahid shook his head sharply. "I can't go to any of my fellow clergy with this, let alone try to warn the Saudis. We've all heard rumors that we built one or even several nuclear weapons, but I've never seen a document referencing them, or talked to anyone who claims to have seen them with his own eyes. And who would take the Qataris seriously as a military threat? The Saudis could squash them like a bug."

Arif looked distinctly unhappy, but simply nodded.

Now Vahid smiled. "Cheer up, Arif. I didn't say I don't believe you. We may not have enough information to stop whatever attack Reza is planning against the Saudis. But there is one step not covered in the plan you outlined that Reza will have to take if he's to become Supreme Leader. And that, we can counter. Now, here's what I want you to do..."

Tehran, Iran

Neda Rhahbar called her sister Azar, and was relieved when she answered for a change, rather than letting the call go to voicemail.

"Sister, it is good to hear from you! How have you been?" asked Azar.

"Bored, to be honest. I was hoping you might be having one of your gatherings sometime soon," Neda said, trying to keep her voice casual.

Azar laughed. "I'm glad to hear you say so! As it happens, I'm having one tomorrow. I would have called you, but I thought you weren't so interested anymore."

Neda forced a laugh of her own. "Well, I was a little hasty there, I think. So, where are your guests from?"

Azar paused and thought briefly. "Well, the foreigners are from Pakistan, Azerbaijan, Indonesia and Russia. Were you hoping for someone from any country in particular?"

"No, not at all," Neda said quickly. "Just curious."

Azar replied in a tone that made it clear she wasn't convinced, "Sure. So, I'll expect to see you tomorrow at seven?"

Neda answered immediately. "Look forward to it! See you then!" and hung up.

Neda had really been hoping for someone from France or the UK. She knew that an American was too much to hope for, but this group was not very promising. Maybe the Russian...

Neda grimaced. She had a vague plan of trying to trade the information she had overheard for a ticket out of Iran.

But would Moscow really be an improvement over Tehran?

Neda again thought about going directly to a West European embassy, but after a few moments rejected the idea. All foreign embassies were watched by VEVAK, the Iranian secret police. She also believed that they all had VEVAK agents working in them covertly as ordinary local employees and was correct for all but one. Only the Russian Embassy refused to hire local employees to work inside its mission, which they regarded as an elementary security precaution.

Neda had thought about posing as a visa applicant, and only once she was inside the embassy building revealing her true purpose. However, she was right to think that if she were to be believed and admitted to an office other than the visa lobby for interview, this would be noted and reported to VEVAK.

Life in Moscow with its endless cold, dark winters was the opposite of appealing. On the other hand, she was certain that women there had more freedom than in Iran. After her experience learning English, she was also certain that she could quickly learn Russian.

Neda also thought that her information would be worth money to the Russians, not just a ticket out. When they had gone on their honeymoon in Paris she had told Kazem she needed to buy some "lady products" to give her the time needed to open a French bank account she could access online, so she would be able to demand and receive payment before providing all she knew.

Though it was tempting to wait for a better opportunity, Neda finally decided that she had to act on her information immediately. Kazem and Farhad had never mentioned a specific date for the attack they were planning, but it sounded as though it would be soon. Neda knew that if the attack happened before she could sell her information, it would be worthless.

Besides, she thought to herself, it wasn't as though Tehran never had snow and ice. Neda also realized that on her own in Moscow, there was a good chance she could find someone from a West European country to marry. She still had her looks, and her excellent English.

Leaving Kazem would have made her hesitate before, because she used to have real feelings for him. Not now, though. Hearing him casually discuss the slaughter of thousands of her fellow Muslims had horrified her, and now having him anywhere near her made her skin crawl. That was actually another pressing reason to go with any credible buyer of the information she was selling. Neda didn't know how long she could go on pretending everything was fine before Kazem realized something was wrong between them.

Kazem was many things. Stupid was not one of them.

So then, Neda thought with a decisive nod. That's it. I'm going to Moscow.

Riyadh, Saudi Arabia

Anatoly Grishkov and Alexei Vasilyev both stood to greet their contact, who they had been told was Saudi but little else. He was dressed in the standard thobe and gutra worn by nearly all Saudi males, had dark hair and a neatly trimmed beard and mustache. Both guessed his age, correctly, as in his thirties. After brief handshakes, they all sat and the man gave his coffee order to the waiter who appeared almost immediately.

"I imagine you were told little about me," the man said. "We keep it that way for security reasons. You may call me Mohammed. Please, ask your questions."

It was clear that Mohammed had no interest in learning more about them, so Vasilyev decided to get straight to the point.

"Have you heard anything about a terrorist attack planned anywhere in the Kingdom, particularly in the Eastern Province?"

Mohammed's eyebrows rose but he said nothing, clearly considering his response. During his pause, the waiter appeared with his latte. Nodding his thanks, Mohammed waited until the waiter had gone to reply.

"Nothing specific. However, there have been some rumors about plans for a mass uprising among the Shi'a community there. Of course, there have been such rumors before. The government had to take action some years back against one rebel Shi'a group in Al-Awamiyah. You have probably heard of the incident?"

Vasilyev and Grishkov both nodded, and Vasilyev saw with relief that Grishkov managed to keep his feelings from showing. As part of their briefings in Moscow they had been shown footage that was considerably more graphic than the videos available on the Internet. Vasilyev could see that they had stirred Grishkov's memories of his time with the Russian Army in Chechnya, which he knew would never leave him. While Grishkov had no love for the Chechens fighting for independence from Russia, he had fiercely disagreed with the indiscriminate slaughter of women and children.

"The government keeps close watch on Shi'a terrorists and their sympathizers in the Kingdom. However, we have seen nothing recently to suggest specific targets that might be attacked in a bombing, or a town like Al-Awamiyah that terrorists might try to take over," Mohammed said.

Vasilyev observed Grishkov's lips twitch when Mohammed mentioned Al-Awamiyah, but saw with relief that he was still keeping his temper in check.

"So, it appears we have been listening to the same rumors. Is there anyone you could suggest who might give us any additional insights? We have a report to prepare, and even background information would be useful," said Vasilyev.

Mohammed paused and appeared to be giving the request serious thought. Finally, he shrugged and nodded.

"Ayatollah Sheikh Massoud al-Ahmadi. After Ayatollah Sheikh Hussein al-Radhi was convicted, he eventually became the senior Shi'a cleric in the Eastern Province. Most of what he'll say will naturally be the standard complaints about the government's handling of terrorist activities. However, he may let some detail slip that might prove useful. Naturally, if he does we'd appreciate hearing about it," Mohammed said, arching one eyebrow.

Grishkov finally couldn't restrain himself, but Vasilyev was pleased to see that he did no more than ask a question.

"This Ayatollah al-Radhi. Any chance he'll be released before we make the trip? We wouldn't want to see the wrong person," Grishkov said.

Mohammed at first looked surprised, and then laughed. "He was sentenced to thirteen years. Since he was in his sixties when he was imprisoned, I'd be surprised if he lives long enough to see the outside of a jail cell. No, there's no danger of seeing him instead of al-Ahmadi."

Grishkov simply nodded.

Mohammed then rose, immediately followed by Grishkov and Vasilyev. "I will send you details on how to arrange a meeting with al-Ahmadi once I am back in the office. I wish you good fortune on your trip," Mohammed said, and shook each of their hands before departing.

Once he was gone, Vasilyev and Grishkov sat back down and looked at each other.

"It would be wrong to root for the terrorists," Grishkov said, soberly.

Vasilyev smiled. "It sounds like you're trying to convince yourself, not making a statement."

Grishkov grunted. "Hatred motivated by religious differences I understand, like the Chechen Muslims resenting being ruled by Russian Orthodox Christians. But different sects of Islam? From what I've read, the similarities in their beliefs far outweigh the differences."

Now Vasilyev couldn't restrain his laughter. "My friend, I will find you a good book on the Hundred Years War, where Catholics and Protestants in Europe slaughtered each other with abandon for a century. The total killed was over three and a half million. Sadly, our classes in Russia focus on more recent history, so I can't say I'm surprised you're not familiar with it. I wouldn't know myself if I hadn't started reading about history as a hobby."

Grishkov smiled. "Well, you have never married and have no children. It's good you found something productive to fill up all that free time besides drinking, like most Russian men your age."

Vasilyev smiled in return, and lifted the fresh cappuccino the waiter had just brought him at his signal. "Who says I don't drink? I just prefer caffeine to alcohol."

Then Vasilyev arched one eyebrow, and said, "I was impressed with the Arabic expressions you worked into your...expression of discontent at the intersection. Obviously, you have gone beyond your classroom curriculum."

Grishkov shrugged and replied, "My instructors appeared to have taken an interest in me. How was Arabic training for you?"

Vasilyev smiled. "First, I should mention that it was before my very first assignment in Morocco, with language training being given at the Embassy in the capital city of Rabat. Perhaps the most memorable moment was when we were each made to sing a song in Arabic. The songs were all sad, about either a man or a woman losing their lover, so "lover" was the key word in each song, which in Arabic is..."

Grishkov nodded and said, "Habibi."

"Yes, very good," Vasilyev said, smiling. "The problem was, one of my fellow students sang one of these songs while omitting the first syllable of that key word, "habibi." So instead of singing about how he couldn't live without his lover..."

Grishkov shook his head, horrified. "He was singing about how he couldn't live without his turkey."

Vasilyev nodded, and said, "The instructor was laughing so hard she was gasping for air while I and the other students looked at each other helplessly, wondering when the poor fellow would stop, but he soldiered on until the end of the song."

Grishkov shook his head again, and said, "Surely the most memorable training experience for all concerned."

Vasilyev smiled, and said, "Not so. As a sort of graduation exercise, we were each sent on a separate two-day trip to a much smaller city well outside the capital with an instructor who would not assist, but only evaluate. One student nearly failed before even leaving for the exercise."

Grishkov frowned. "How could he possibly do that? Were his language skills so poor?"

Vasilyev laughed and said, "On the contrary, they were superior to mine. No, the instructors were cross because the student refused to believe where he was being sent was not a joke."

Grishkov's frown deepened. "How can a place be a joke?"

Vasilyev pulled out a pen and wrote a word on their cafe receipt, "Ouarzazate," and then slid it towards Grishkov, who shrugged and said, "Never heard of it."

Vasilyev nodded, and replied, "No reason you should have, though you may have seen it, since it has been the backdrop in several movies set in the Middle East. I wrote it as it was transcribed by the French from the original Arabic. Now, I will write it phonetically, as it would be heard by an English speaker," and then wrote again on the receipt, and returned it to Grishkov.

Grishkov read it slowly, and then smiled. "Where's iz at?"

Vasilyev nodded. "As KGB agents posted overseas, we all spoke fluent English. The agent being sent to 'Ouarzazate' was certain we were all pulling his leg, until I finally dug out a map of Morocco with enough detail to show its location."

"Very good," Grishkov laughed. "So, have you ever been back to Morocco?"

"Yes, though I was not amused by what I found," Vasilyev said with a frown.

"How so?," Grishkov asked.

"Well, first I should explain that one of my favorite memories on my first trip was a conversation with a young Moroccan woman whose professor had assigned her a biographical paper on Lenin. Since the Kingdom of Morocco's libraries had little on the topic, she hit on the idea of visiting the Soviet Cultural Center in Rabat."

Grishkov smiled. "I'll bet it wasn't a busy place."

Vasilyev snorted. "She said she was the only visitor, and that at first the staff appeared puzzled by her arrival. But once she conveyed her purpose, she said they were overjoyed to find someone interested in Lenin, and left staggering under the weight of all the materials they gave her for her paper."

Grishkov laughed and said, "Well, that sounds like a happy ending."

Vasilyev nodded, and said, "Yes. I also told her about my favorite biography of Lenin, written by a British author. His forward described his methods, which included trying to find absolutely everyone still alive who had spent any time with Lenin."

Grishkov frowned, and shook his head. "After Stalin, not an easy task."

Vasilyev's smile was rueful. "Yes, just so. He described going to the British Museum where Lenin had done some research, and asking everyone if they had met him, to no avail. Just as he was about to give up, someone said to try the caretaker, who had been there 'forever.' But he also said no. Then it occurred to the biographer that the caretaker might have known Lenin under his real birth name of Ulyanov. The caretaker brightened and said, 'Yes, indeed, I spoke several times with Mr. Ulyanov. A very nice, well-spoken man. Whatever became of him?' And that's how he began the biography."

Grishkov clapped his hands. "Excellent. You must tell me who wrote the book. But first, what didn't you like when you returned?"

"Well," Vasilyev scowled, "when I came back to Morocco after many years the Soviet Cultural Center was no more, no surprise since the same was true for the USSR. But I was not pleased by what I found in its place."

Grishkov shook his head, and said, "I'm afraid to ask, but will. What was it?"

Vasilyev replied grimly, "A certain American hamburger restaurant."

Grishkov stared and asked, "Not..."

Vasilyev nodded. "Yes, the one with 'golden arches.' I will not say its name."

Grishkov shook his head, and said, "I can see why you were not pleased."

Vasilyev scowled and said, "Yes, we already know who won the Cold War. Whoever at corporate headquarters decided on that particular location didn't need to make the extra effort to underline the point. From time to time, though, I think we can remind the Americans that we are still in the game."

Grishkov nodded, and then asked, "Do you really think this Shi'a cleric will tell us anything useful, or will this just be a waste of time?"

Vasilyev shrugged. "Your guess is as good as mine. My instincts, though, tell me that getting to the Eastern Province with the Saudi government's blessing is the best we can hope for at this point. And besides - maybe we'll be there in time to witness the attack!"

Grishkov choked on his black coffee, while Vasilyev laughed.

"I know, I know - we're supposed to prevent the attack. Well, who knows? We may just get lucky!"

Grishkov wiped his mouth with a napkin and glared at Vasilyev, who he could see was completely unrepentant. Well, he couldn't really argue. What they needed most now was some good luck, and soon.

CHAPTER NINE

Dammam, Saudi Arabia

As they trudged towards the airport exit with bags in hand, Anatoly Grishkov saw a twinkle in Alexei Vasilyev's eye. Sighing, he said, "OK, out with it. Another fascinating bit of trivia to share?"

Vasilyev laughed. "Well, yes, and I think this one will surprise you. Did you know that Dammam's King Fahd Airport is the largest airport in the world?"

Grishkov snorted. "For once I know you're wrong. I'll bet even Sheremetyevo Airport is bigger, and I know that many airports in Europe are bigger than ours in Moscow."

Vasilyev raised one eyebrow. "You'd like to bet? Very well, how much would you like to wager? Oh, and to settle the bet, I propose we rely on the Guinness Book of World Records."

Grishkov sighed and shook his head. "You've forgotten my service in Chechnya. I know an ambush when I see one. So, explain how this could really be the world's biggest airport."

Vasilyev grinned and said, "With pleasure. It is indeed biggest in terms of land area officially deeded to the airport authority. In fact, in terms of sheer acreage it is larger than the country of Bahrain. Only a small fraction, though, is used for actual airport operations."

Grishkov scowled. "So, it hardly counts then. Really, what's the point of learning such trivia?"

Vasilyev's grin now grew wider. "Ah, you still need training to think like an intelligence officer, which like it or not is what you've become. What question should you be asking now?"

After a brief pause, Grishkov asked thoughtfully, "Why did the Saudis deed so much land to the airport authority?"

Vasilyev punched Grishkov in the shoulder and nodded. "Exactly. To answer that question, you need to know that this airport was built in the 1990s to replace a much smaller one. We are here in the heart of the Eastern Province, near Dhahran and Saudi Aramco headquarters, as well as their most important oil production operations. The Shi'a here have always been a security concern. So, now draw on your military and police background. If you had decided to build a new airport, what would you want?"

Grishkov grunted. "As much fenced and alarmed space between the airport and any potential attackers as I could get."

Vasilyev nodded with satisfaction. "Just so. The fact that most of the land is desert with no other real use may have encouraged our Saudi friends to go a bit overboard, but from a security standpoint the result is quite impressive. An attacking force of any size would stand no chance of approaching the airport without detection long before it could do any real damage."

Grishkov nodded. "Helps to give you some idea of how the government thinks about the threat here. They really are worried, aren't they?"

Vasilyev shrugged. "Well, I'd say we can hardly blame them."

Grishkov scowled. "The Shi'a are even worse. I'm surprised you agreed to their terms for this meeting."

Vasilyev nodded. "Yes, you are quite right. Ordinarily I would never agree to allow the subject of the investigation to provide the car and driver that will take us to meet him. Too likely to be a one-way trip. This time, though, there was no choice. We must get information on the coming attack, and quickly."

As sliding glass doors opened in front of them, Grishkov jerked his head wordlessly toward a car idling near the entrance. Its driver was staring straight ahead.

Vasilyev smiled. "And why this car?"

Grishkov's head swiveled back and forth as he observed the surroundings outside the airport terminal.

"Because it contains the only driver who didn't look right at us when we exited. I think we're a bit noticeable."

Nodding, Vasilyev walked up to the open passenger-side window and asked in Arabic, "Who are you supposed to take us to meet?"

Now the driver slowly turned towards Vasilyev. "Ayatollah Sheikh Massoud al-Ahmadi."

Vasilyev opened the rear passenger door and gestured for Grishkov to enter, which he did with the same degree of enthusiasm Vasilyev remembered from his last dental visit.

Vasilyev pushed away the smile the comparison brought to his lips, not wanting to explain it to Grishkov in front of the driver, and entered behind him. As soon as they were both seated, the car moved forward.

Once they left the airport terminal the driver made a right turn, and then settled into a broad, multi-lane road.

Vasilyev turned to Grishkov and said, "This is King Fahd Road. In about thirty kilometers we'll get to Qatif via Route 605, followed by Route 617."

Grishkov simply nodded, since he knew Vasilyev was just demonstrating situational awareness to their driver, who appeared to be paying no attention. Nevertheless, Grishkov would have cheerfully bet a month's pay that the man had listened carefully to every word.

With little in the harshly lit desert landscape to attract his attention and conversation on any matter of importance in earshot of the driver out of the question, Grishkov's thoughts turned to names. King Fahd Airport. King Fahd Road. Now that he thought about it, the massive structure connecting Saudi Arabia with Bahrain was called King Fahd Causeway.

Well, Grishkov thought shaking his head, no Russian could really criticize the Saudis. Leningrad, Stalingrad- they had renamed entire cities for their leaders, even while they were still alive. It was fair enough that the Saudis had named several important landmarks after one of their kings following his death.

Bored with both his thoughts and the passing scenery, Grishkov realized that while they couldn't discuss their mission in front of the driver, he was unlikely to be interested in a foreigner's past experiences in the Kingdom. So, he asked Vasilyev, "What is your most vivid memory of your past trips here?"

"Well, to Dhahran specifically I would say a trip I took from Riyadh by train. The only difference between second class and first class, where I was, that I could see was we had a TV. During the entire trip the only muted program playing was American professional wrestling starring someone named 'Hulk Hogan' which everyone watched in complete silence." Vasilyev shrugged. "Of course, back then there were no cell phones or laptops."

"No," Grishkov said, shaking his head. "I meant in general."

"Well then, prison visits," Vasilyev answered with a smile.

"Ah, one of your duties when you were with the Embassy," Grishkov said.

"Correct," Vasilyev nodded. "Not so much for the Russian citizens I visited. Their cases were fairly straightforward, and the Saudis treated them reasonably well. No, it was talking with the warden that was particularly interesting."

"For example?" Grishkov asked.

"Well, I saw one article in the local paper that puzzled me. A man had been convicted of murder, and now after seventeen years had just been executed. There is no lengthy appeals process here, so I wondered what could have accounted for the delay. I asked the warden on my next prison visit."

Vasilyev paused, and was clearly thinking back to the visit. "When I asked him if he knew of the case, the warden laughed and said 'Of course! He was at this prison. The delay was caused because under the law, the nearest male relative of the victim had to be given a choice of a cash payment from the guilty man's family, or the man's execution. This provision was put in the Koran to prevent endless warfare between tribes, with one revenge killing answered by another, by providing an honorable alternative. Of course these days the relative always asks for execution."

"So I said, OK, but I still don't understand the delay. The warden said with a smile, 'Because in his case the nearest male relative was an infant. They had to wait for him to grow up to make the choice.' I nodded and thanked him for clearing up the mystery. I then commented that such a thing must happen only every fifty years or so. He laughed and said 'Not at all! We have a whole wing devoted to such cases!' I must have appeared doubtful, because he then insisted on giving me a tour, describing the crimes and the sentences of each inmate as we passed their cells. I asked him about the mental state of these prisoners waiting years for certain death, and he laughed again, saying 'Oh, they're all quite insane.' It is indeed a vivid memory."

Grishkov shook his head. "I've heard that executions are public?"

Vasilyev nodded. "Yes. Though I've never attended, I have spoken to Russians who have. Both then and now, execution is carried out through beheading by sword."

Grishkov shrugged. "Surely, an effective deterrent?"

Vasilyev shook his head. "You would think so, but not based on the TV coverage I saw."

Grishkov frowned. "Surely they didn't televise the executions!"

Vasilyev smiled, "No, certainly not. But every week, as part of the news there would be a map of the Kingdom with little dots appearing all over it, and the newscaster saying 'Here is where executions took place this week, and what the criminals did.' That's when I first learned that besides murder, other crimes were punishable by execution."

"Such as?" Grishkov asked.

"Opposition to the government, rape and adultery. Adultery, though, was not punished by beheading," Vasilyev explained.

Grishkov nodded. "I think I have heard of this. An adulteress is killed by stoning, yes? And it would always be a woman, correct?"

Vasilyev gave an answering nod. "Correct. The old method involved a crowd that would chase the woman, pelting her with rocks until she died. The new method involves staking out the woman on the ground, backing up a dump truck full of rocks and dropping its contents on her. It is, at least, faster."

Grishkov frowned, "I've also heard that they chop off hands for theft. That must scare off potential thieves!"

Vasilyev smiled ruefully. "You'd think so, but no. When I was with the Embassy I lived in a housing compound we shared with a local bank. Thieves broke into the homes of my neighbors many times, each time stealing only currency while the residents slept, so that once the thieves were in the street there would be no real evidence against them. After all, almost everyone carried multiple types of foreign currency. I, however, was never robbed."

Grishkov laughed. "And how were you so lucky?"

Vasilyev snorted. "Luck had nothing to do with it. My neighbors, even after being victims of theft, persisted in believing that nobody would risk losing their hand and so were careless about locking their doors and windows. I knew that the thieves would, as long as they believed the risk of capture minimal. So, I locked my doors and windows. However, I did notice one thing that forced me to ask the warden another question on my next prison visit."

Grishkov smiled. "And what was that?"

"Well," Vasilyev said slowly, "I noticed that nobody I saw in the Kingdom in my first year was missing a hand. Not in airports, train stations, shopping malls, open-air markets - nowhere. This made me suspect that the entire business was a fiction designed to scare criminals."

Grishkov nodded. "I would have had the same thought. So, what did the warden say?"

Vasilyev frowned. "Well, first he told me some history that didn't really answer my question. He said there had been a period of about a year when it had proved impossible to carry out the punishment. He said this was because Saudi doctors began coming back to the Kingdom who had been trained in the US and UK, and refused to carry out the punishment. Everyone agreed that a doctor had to do it because simply cutting off a hand untreated would lead to death from shock and blood loss, and the punishment for theft was not intended to be fatal. He said that this impasse was finally resolved by the authorities wrapping the convicted person's hand in cloth, pounding it with a sledgehammer, and then presenting the results to doctors for treatment. Because of the damage, that treatment had to include removal of the hand. Doctors quickly agreed that the intermediate step with the sledgehammer was unnecessary, and so removals were back on track."

Grishkov frowned. "But that doesn't explain why you weren't seeing people who were missing hands."

"Precisely," Vasilyev nodded. "The warden went on to explain that in every case he had seen, the thief had been a foreigner. Though many Saudis are not rich, none are poor enough to have to take the risks involved with theft. The typical foreign thief had either reached the end of a work contract and stayed, or never been given their promised salary. So, after being caught and having their hand cut off they were then imprisoned for some period, and finally deported. So, the warden told me, if you want to see persons subjected to this punishment you need to visit Pakistan, Bangladesh, Yemen and the many other countries sending large numbers of foreign workers to the Kingdom."

Grishkov shrugged. "It's true that I have noticed many foreign workers in the short time we've been here."

Vasilyev nodded. "Yes, but the proportion is far lower than it used to be. Saudis are now in many positions that used to be manned exclusively by foreigners, and this is the result of a deliberate government program. The most expensive foreigners, Americans and Europeans, were the first to be replaced."

Grishkov smiled. "I remember you telling me that you knew quite a few of them when you were here earlier."

Vasilyev laughed. "They were an excellent source of inside information, as well as some amusement. One even drew cartoons!"

Grishkov frowned. "Dangerous, if they ever ended up in the hands of the authorities."

Vasilyev shrugged. "They were not political, but you are correct that they could have easily led to expulsion. One that I thought summed up the viewpoint of many foreign workers quite well used characters from an American comic strip called 'Peanuts' without, I am sure, authorization."

Grishkov smiled. "I know the strip. I'm quite sure you're right."

Vasilyev continued, "In the strip, Charlie Brown has a stick on his shoulders with a bucket at each end. Linus asks him 'What are the buckets for?' Charlie Brown replies, 'One is for all the money I'm going to make. The other is for all the shit I'm going to have to take. When one or the other is full, I'll know it's time to go home.' In the next panel we see the same two characters and the same two buckets. The only difference is that one of the buckets is dripping. Without being asked, a glum Charlie Brown tells Linus, 'I punched a hole in the shit bucket.' Particularly after the 2003 bomb attacks that killed dozens of expatriate workers in their residence compounds, I think most Americans and Europeans have crossed the Kingdom off their overseas employment list without regret."

Their conversation ended as the car pulled up outside an unimpressive two-story building that looked much the same as those on either side of it. All were the same drab off-white color, and Grishkov would have bet they had been built at the same time using the same blueprints.

The driver exited the car and without saying anything to his passengers walked to the door of the building, which opened at his approach.

Vasilyev looked at Grishkov, and they both shrugged and followed the driver.

Qatif, Saudi Arabia

It took a moment for Vasilyev and Grishkov to adjust to the gloominess of the interior, a sharp contrast to the bright light outside. They quickly realized that the only illumination came from a few narrow windows set high in the wall. Grishkov glanced at Vasilyev who simply nodded, and was sure he had the same thought. Whoever had designed these buildings wanted to make it impossible to enter except through the heavy metal front door.

As they emerged from the entry hallway Grishkov and Vasilyev saw an elderly man sitting on a heavy carpet, surrounded by cushions. A large, low wooden table was in front of him, which held a large teapot and a plate piled high with cookies. There were also three glasses full of a dark liquid that Grishkov fervently hoped was black tea. The man was stirring sugar into one of them, at the same time gesturing impatiently for them to come and sit.

"You will have to forgive my failure to rise and greet you properly. I regret that I am not as mobile as I used to be," the man said, pointing to the cushions on the other side of the table.

Grishkov noticed that the man, who did appear elderly, nevertheless seemed quite alert and intelligent. He was dressed in a fashion nearly identical to Sheik Nimr al-Nimr in a picture Grishkov had seen taken not long before his arrest and execution, and was even thinner. The low white turban on his head marked a sharp contrast from the gutra worn by nearly all Sunnis in Saudi Arabia, and instead looked very much like the turbans worn by Iranian clerics.

Grishkov had a sudden moment of understanding. So, the Sunnis in this country saw the Shi'a as foreigners, no matter how many generations they had lived in Saudi Arabia.

This reminded Grishkov of a discussion about Chechnya he had engaged in many times with Vasilyev. Grishkov argued that you were either a rebel or someone who gave them material aid and deserved death, or you were an innocent bystander who deserved protection and the full rights of any Russian citizen. Vasilyev saw guilt or innocence as a continuum, with few people in such a long conflict either completely one or the other. So, shoot back at rebels shooting at you - absolutely. But for the rest, perhaps local autonomy and removing the right to vote in Federal elections made more sense.

Grishkov argued that such measures would only fuel resentment and increase support for the rebels. And so their arguments had gone. He wondered what Vasilyev would make of the situation here, and how it would affect their reports back to Moscow.

As they both sat, Vasilyev said, "First, allow me to compliment you on your excellent English. We have the honor to address Ayatollah Sheikh Massoud al-Ahmadi?"

The man smiled. "You do. And I have the honor to meet Anatoly Grishkov and Alexei Vasilyev?" he asked, pointed at each in turn.

Noting Vasilyev's raised eyebrows, Massoud laughed and said, "I was told the older man would be Vasilyev. No offense."

"None taken," Vasilyev said dryly, noting Grishkov's barely successful effort to suppress a smile. "I have always believed that with age comes wisdom. Or, it can if the person makes an effort in each passing year."

Massoud nodded approvingly. "An important addendum. As for my English, I am sure you know that I went to university in England. It is one reason I was chosen to lead our community at this troubled time. We need to let the world know what is happening here, and the countries that the Saudis will listen to speak English."

Vasilyev shrugged. "What you say is true. But as you have seen recently in Syria, Russia is not without influence in the Middle East."

Massoud smiled and said, "Please, I am neglecting my duties as host. We must drink this tea before it gets cold. I understand that most Russians like their tea strong and black. Happily, so do I."

Grishkov's opinion of their host rose with his first sip.

Massoud pointed at the sugar bowl. "I took the liberty of adding some sugar to each glass, but you are welcome to add more. I find it is better to add it as soon as the hot tea is poured in the glass, or it will not dissolve properly."

Grishkov found himself nodding. It was remarkable how such a small thing could make him look more kindly on a man the Saudis considered one short step removed from a terrorist worthy of arrest and execution.

Next Massoud pointed to the pile of cookies next to the teapot. "You must try these. They were made by my wife. These are called Nan-e Nokhodchi and are made of chickpea flour, so are safe to eat even if you have a problem with gluten," he said with a smile.

Vasilyev and Grishkov were both surprised that a Saudi cleric had even heard of gluten, but both knew they had no choice but to try one of the cookies. Grishkov in particular disliked chickpeas either whole and cooked or puréed into hummus. Both were pleasantly surprised, though, since the cookies tasted nothing like chickpeas. Instead, the flour practically melted inside their mouth, and the flavor left behind was that of pistachios.

Well, that makes sense, Grishkov thought. Iran is world famous for its pistachios, and the Shi'a community here would certainly have access to a supply.

"These are excellent," Vasilyev said sincerely, while Grishkov nodded vigorously and reached for another.

"Very good!" Massoud laughed, "I must remember to tell my wife. Now, I understand that you are looking for information about what is happening here in the Eastern Province."

Vasilyev nodded. "Anything you could tell us, even background information, would be helpful."

Massoud leaned forward. "I am sure you have heard what happened at Al-Awamiyah, and the execution of my predecessor Sheik Nimr al-Nimr. You have probably heard about the execution of several of his relatives, as well as the summary shootings of several others."

Vasilyev simply nodded.

"What you don't know is just how many Shi'a died at Al-Awamiyah, and how many have been killed since. Now, anyone can toss around numbers, and have them dismissed as propaganda. We realize that. So, what I am giving you now is different. It is proof."

Massoud held up a USB flash drive.

"On this device, you will find a complete list of all the Shi'a killed by the Saudis at Al-Awamiyah and later. For each name you will find their date of birth, Saudi national ID card number, and the date we either know they died or simply disappeared."

Massoud paused, clearly working to keep his emotions under control.

"You know that in these times nobody can live without leaving a digital mark. You Russians have quite a reputation for being able to access any network. If any country can confirm that the people on this list are dead, it's yours."

Vasilyev nodded. "We will certainly pass this information on to our superiors."

Massoud now looked particularly grim. "All we ask is that if we are wrong about any of the names on this list and you find evidence they are still alive, you will let us know."

Vasilyev nodded. "Of course. I think that brings us to the obvious question - what does your community plan to do in response?"

Massoud shrugged. "What can we do? A few of us have guns. As you saw at Al-Awamiyah, they are of little use against tanks. The sort of rebellion you saw in Iraq against the Americans is impossible here. There it was led by the men from Saddam Hussein's army, who had hidden many of their weapons and explosives after their surrender. We Shi'a have nobody with military experience, and no vast store of weapons. Nobody from outside the Kingdom is giving us aid. Our demonstrations are crushed, and the world ignores us. Without outside help, we are doomed."

Vasilyev cocked his head to one side. "Are you expecting the Russian government to intervene on your behalf?"

Massoud laughed bitterly. "After how it treated Muslims in Bosnia, Syria and Chechnya? Certainly not. If anything, we expect your government to continue selling military forces around the world the tanks they use to crush Muslim rebellions as long as they have the money to pay."

Vasilyev pursed his lips. "Of course, I have no authority to speak for the Russian government. However, I must ask - if you expect no help, why see us?"

Massoud nodded. "A fair question. The answer is simple. We know the names on that USB drive I gave you may not change any minds at the Kremlin. But I have always believed in the power of truth. Who knows, maybe someday someone in your government will find a reason to care about what is happening here. At worst, we have nothing to lose."

Vasilyev nodded and rose, followed by Grishkov. "I promise to pass what we have learned, including the information on this USB drive, to our superiors. After that, anything is possible."

Massoud's answering smile had no warmth in it. "As you say. The driver outside will take you to your hotel, or back to the airport. Just let him know where you want to go. Safe journeys."

As they walked to the door, Vasilyev's cell phone buzzed. He looked at the screen and frowned. Grishkov looked at him questioningly, but Vasilyev just shook his head and opened the car door. The same driver was at the wheel.

"To the airport, please," said Vasilyev.

Without a word, the driver put the car in gear and less than an hour later they were back outside the Dammam airport terminal. As soon as they left the car clutching their bags, the driver sped off.

The glass doors slid open in front of them, and Grishkov turned towards Vasilyev as they walked.

"So, here we are back at the world's largest airport. I hope the next destination will be less a waste of our time."

Without breaking stride Vasilyev laughed. "Waste? Is that really what we did?"

Grishkov shrugged. "Well, was there some part of our exchange I missed where we learned the targets of the planned attacks? Or when they will happen?"

Vasilyev smiled. "No. But, let me ask you a question. How would you describe our host, in two words?"

Grishkov frowned, and finally shrugged. "Angry. Desperate."

Vasilyev's smile grew broader. "Excellent. Now, if someone asked for his help and the help of his people in attacking the Saudis, what do you think his answer would be?"

Grishkov grunted. "OK, I see your point. We did learn something worth knowing. So, care to tell me where we're going?"

Vasilyev nodded. "Tehran, via Dubai. We should be there by evening."

Grishkov grunted. "Lovely. I know someone has thought about the need for an Iranian visa, which I didn't notice in my passport."

Vasilyev smiled. "Of course. We are good at such details. A man will meet us at Dubai airport with passports containing the correct visas for a short business stay."

Grishkov sighed. "And may I know why we are going to Tehran?"

Vasilyev shrugged. "No idea. Such details are never included in a cell phone message even when the device is encrypted, as is ours. We will be given a summary readout by the agent who passes us our new papers in Dubai, and a full briefing once we arrive in Tehran."

To that Grishkov had no answer, since his time in both the Russian Army and the Vladivostok police had drummed the need for operational security into him at often tiresome length. Well, he mused, having paid attention to security requirements helped explain why he was alive to be walking here beside Vasilyev, in spite of several serious attempts on his life when he was in Russia.

It didn't make him any less curious, though.

Dubai International Airport, United Arab Emirates

Grishkov and Vasilyev were waiting for the next Iran Air flight to Tehran, after an uneventful flight from Dhahran and a smooth handover of new documents from one of their agents in Dubai. Grishkov thought, not for the first time, that it was good to be part of a truly capable organization. Russia had many problems. An incompetent intelligence agency was not one of them.

Now, though, he saw the twinkle he dreaded in Vasilyev's eye. "OK, out with it. What's so special about this airport?"

Vasilyev smiled. "Why, it's the world's biggest, of course!"

Grishkov groaned. "Not again! OK, Dhahran was the biggest by land area. So, this one has the most passengers?"

Vasilyev shook his head. "Close, but not quite. It has the most *international* passengers. Construction is underway to add further capacity, so it's likely to keep that title for some time."

Grishkov frowned. "But, since we are literally passing through, this time it really is trivia with little importance for our mission."

Vasilyev grinned. "Well, alright. You have me this time."

Grishkov nodded. “At last! Let me turn instead to a subject where I hope you can shed some light. The brief report we just read says the defector we are on our way to assist is an Iranian woman. I know that women throughout this region are repressed, but not the details. Perhaps you could contrast the situation of Saudi women with Iranian women, since you have lived in both countries.”

Vasilyev smiled. “An excellent approach. Let me begin with the positive. In both countries some women have always been able to obtain both degrees and employment, primarily in areas such as education, medicine, and administration. Women have obtained employment in other sectors, but only in small numbers. One example I saw personally during a tour of a Saudi jewelry factory was the design and production of high-end gold jewelry. The owners admitted they had been unenthusiastic about employing women when a small quota was forced on them by the government, but quickly changed their minds."

Grishkov frowned. "Why? Did the women impress them immediately with the quality of their work?"

Vasilyev shook his head, and explained, "Their work quality was fine, but that's not the real value they brought to the factory. Once the women told their friends that jewelry they made themselves was available at a particular shop and showed them pictures of what they'd made, it immediately disappeared from the store shelves. In part, this was friends showing solidarity. In many cases, though, the owners believed it was that women were better at designing jewelry because they knew what women like. That's because even the jewelry these women designed that was exported to surrounding countries like the United Arab Emirates and Oman sold better than the rest of their products."

Grishkov frowned and asked, "But isn't segregation still the rule?"

Vasiloyev nodded. "Segregation by gender exists in both countries, and the need for totally separate facilities including entrances if women work at a company is often cited as a cost factor in refusing to hire them. Such segregation is generally more strictly enforced in Saudi Arabia, so that the women in the jewelry factory, for example, have to work in a separate area. Likewise for the requirement that women be accompanied by a male relative outside the home, and need a male relative’s permission to obtain a passport, make a report to the police, or to take most other significant actions. However, thanks to recent liberalization in Saudi Arabia women no longer need a male relative's permission to apply to a school, for a job, or for medical care. Plus, as long as they obtain the permission of their nearest male relative, Saudi women can now drive."

Grishkov nodded. "Yes, I had heard of this. And the negative?"

Vasilyev frowned. "Perhaps the most disturbing development in Saudi Arabia has been forced divorce. This happens when a relative of a married woman, often her brother, decides to contest the legitimacy of the woman's marriage. He would usually do this by going to a religious official, often making a 'contribution', and asking for a ruling that the marriage was invalid. A typical basis would be that the marriage was beneath the status of the woman's family, and as its head he disapproved."

Grishkov shook his head. "Why would he do this?"

Vasilyev grimaced. "Money. The most common motivation is to take control of a woman's share of an inheritance. Though a woman only gets a half share, that is often more than the males in the family want to give, particularly if giving that half share would require selling property or businesses and splitting the proceeds."

Grishkov frowned. "What happens to the woman in such cases?"

Vasilyev spread his hands. "Their marriage is annulled as if it never happened. Any children are given to the father to raise. The woman is required to move in with her closest male relative, usually the man who forced the divorce, and must place all her assets under his control. This means not only her share of an inheritance, but any assets she retained after her marriage, such as a bank account or salary."

Grishkov shook his head again. "How often does this happen?"

Vasilyev shrugged. "There are no statistics. However, at one point there were articles about the issue even in the Saudi English language press, which demonstrated both that the government was aware of the issue and disapproved of the practice. It's important to understand that the Saudi government has only limited control over the actions of the clergy, though that's still better than Iran where in spite of elections the clergy is actually in control of the government."

Grishkov frowned. "I think I have heard enough about women in Saudi Arabia. I hope their situation is better in Iran."

Vasilyev smiled. “It is, to some degree. Women have been allowed to vote and hold office for years, though in the 2009 presidential election many women were arrested for voting for a candidate not favored by the clergy, and their votes were not counted. Women make up only about three percent of the members of Iran’s parliament. In other areas the record is also mixed. Women are allowed to participate in some sports, but not to enter stadiums as spectators to watch football or volleyball matches. Though they can drive, few have the money to buy a car of their own, and strangely women are not allowed to ride bicycles.”

Grishkov nodded. “Not so surprising then, that this particular Iranian woman would like to live elsewhere.”

Vasilyev grinned. “Fortunately for us, since otherwise we’d have no leads worth pursuing.”

CHAPTER TEN

Tehran, Iran

Anatoly Grishkov placed his request for black coffee with the waiter as soon as Alexei Vasilyev had finished ordering his latte. Waving his hand around the back patio where they were seated, he asked "Why is it we seem to always be in coffee shops? And why did you specify this one in particular?"

Vasilyev smiled, and said, "Good. We will continue with your training. Think, and then answer the questions yourself."

Grishkov scowled, and then nodded. "Very well. It is obvious that we should not meet our Russian Embassy contact at the Mission building, since it is sure to be under observation by Iranian intelligence. This cafe is within walking distance of the Embassy, and there is nothing strange about our contact sharing a coffee with two other Russians."

Vasilyev arched one eyebrow. "And?"

Sighing, Grishkov looked around the patio. "Well, I did notice when we arrived that you told them we had a reservation, and we were shown outside to this patio. I suppose not all cafes take reservations, and we wouldn't want to stand in line waiting. I also notice that we have good table separation here, and in this patio with the ambient noise from the city around us overhearing our conversation would be quite difficult."

Vasilyev grinned and clapped his hands. "Outstanding. I'll add that along with excellent reviews Google was nice enough to include customer photos, including one showing this cafe's latte art. Just the basic heart design, but enough to make me hope the latte will be drinkable. Tehran is not really known for its coffee."

With that a tall woman with blond hair showing under her sheer scarf walked into the patio, and made straight for their table. She sat down without any preamble, and placing a black briefcase beside her said in a low voice, "You may call me Alina."

Before either could say anything Alina gestured impatiently and added, "Introductions are unnecessary. I know who both of you are. I am here to give you the details of your mission. First, you will receive an overview from Director Smyslov."

Both Grishkov and Vasilyev started with surprise. Vasilyev asked, "He is here in Tehran?"

Alina smiled dryly. "In a manner of speaking," as she pulled a small laptop from her purse and attached earbuds. "One earbud each, but for this you will not need stereo."

The waiter appeared and Alina ordered coffee, with cream on the side.

As soon as the waiter left, Alina turned on the laptop, placed her fingertip on a sensor and entered a password to open the video file. She then turned the screen towards them, and handed them each an earbud.

Shortly Smyslov's smiling bearded face filled the screen, and his voice boomed through the earbuds. "My friends! We are finally able to send video files to our embassies with proper security. I've always wanted to do this, like the Mission Impossible movies, yes? But there is a serious purpose - I want there to be no doubt in your minds that these orders are coming directly from me.

Your mission will not be impossible, but I will not lie. It will not be easy. The first part will be to help an Iranian woman leave Iran for Iraq overland. She is the wife of the man leading Iran's nuclear weapons program, and has vital information on the attacks coming in Saudi Arabia. An Iranian who has worked with our Embassy before will accompany you as guide until you have reached Iraq."

Smyslov paused. "Now for the difficult part. Once you are in Iraq, a Russian Army helicopter that has already been cleared to enter Iraqi airspace will pick you up and fly you to our military headquarters in Syria. There you will meet with the commander of Russian forces in Syria, General Stepanov. The purpose will be to brief him on the planned attack. The defector has told us that part of it will be by air, and we expect the Iranians to use a pair of J-20 stealth fighters they have recently obtained from China in carrying out the attack. Particularly since the Saudis are heavily engaged in Yemen, we think the attack may succeed unless we intervene.

General Stepanov controls the only pair of SU-57s stationed within range to defend likely targets. He has refused to commit these stealth fighters to that mission, saying they are needed in Syria. The President will not overrule the commander on the ground, which I...reluctantly...understand. However, he has agreed to order General Stepanov to hear details of the planned attack directly from the defector.

Now we come to the most difficult part of your mission. The defector has provided us with many details, but has told us she has withheld many as well until she reaches Moscow. We pointed out that once the attacks begin her information is useless. We also threatened to refuse to help her leave Iran at all, and even to give her to Iranian authorities. She has proved quite stubborn.

You will need to overcome her reluctance to talk to have any chance of convincing General Stepanov to commit his SU-57s.

The Embassy will give you all the other details of your mission. Good luck to you both."

Grishkov shook his head in bewilderment. "Can it really be so hard to persuade this defector to talk? Does whoever at the Embassy debriefed her know what they're doing?"

Alina flushed angrily. "I'd like to think so, since that person is me. As the only woman at this Embassy's intelligence station, I was selected because it was thought the defector would relate better to a woman. That may not have been the best choice, but it cannot be changed because after our initial report Moscow ordered that no one else at the Embassy is to speak with the defector."

Grishkov winced. "I'm sorry. I meant no offense. I'm frustrated because we've been hitting our heads against a wall for days trying to find details on the upcoming attacks, and to be told a person has the answers, came to us but refuses to tell us everything is...maddening."

Alina was still clearly unhappy, but seemed at least somewhat mollified. "Maddening is the right word. But put yourself in her position. By now she has certainly been reported missing. Considering her husband's position, there is sure to be a police alert for her. Without our help, she'll never make it out of Iran. And once she's told us everything, why should we take the risk of helping her?"

Grishkov shook his head. "We would never betray..." His voice died away as he saw the expressions on the faces of both Alina and Vasilyev. It was Vasilyev who spoke first.

"No, we would not betray her in this case, because there will be those in Moscow who wish to speak to her personally. But betrayal is simply another tool for an intelligence officer, however distasteful they may find it personally. I doubt that any of us makes it through a career without using it at least once."

All Grishkov had to do was look at Alina's face to see the truth of Vasilyev's statement. She looked up and said, "She has told us a great deal. You will find the information in your briefing materials. But she has held back the target locations." With that she laid a hand lightly on Vasilyev's, who withdrew it with a smile. She withdrew hers with an answering smile.

Grishkov frowned and asked, "Do we really need this Iranian guide who is supposed to take us across the border to Iraq? I can read a map, and I have plenty of experience getting through wilderness without being seen by the enemy."

Alina sighed and shook her head. "There are many dangers not marked on any map. Minefields left over from the Iran-Iraq War in the eighties. Others said to have been put along smuggling routes more recently. And, of course, Iranian Army patrols. The area of Iraq you will cross into is controlled by the Kurds and there is no love lost between them and the Iranians, so they keep a sharp watch there."

Grishkov grimaced. "So, why are we going that way?"

Alina waved her hand, clearly frustrated. "Not my decision, in fact I argued against it. Director Smyslov ordered it, precisely because the area is controlled by the Kurds. When our forces pick you up by helicopter, he does not wish a detailed report of who was aboard immediately passed to the Iraqi government, and from there almost certainly to Iran. Mind you, that will happen eventually. But it will take longer this way, since the Kurds do not cooperate especially closely with the Iraqi government."

Grishkov shook his head. "Assuming we make it at all."

Alina smiled wryly. "Well, yes. That was the crux of my argument against this route. The Director seems to believe you both have nearly superhuman abilities. He said something about how I would never believe what you have already accomplished, and how I should be feeling sorry for the Iranians," in a tone that made it clear she was not convinced of anything of the sort by the two sitting in front of her.

Grishkov snorted. "I feel very ordinary, and I'm sure bullets would work on me just fine."

Vasilyev sighed. "We shall have to have a long talk with the Director after we return home."

Alina leaned forward. "Another important point to remember is that it would be suspicious for the defector to be traveling without a male family member, particularly because she is fairly young and quite attractive. You should wait to speak to her until you are far from observation by any Iranian."

After first looking around to make sure they were not being watched, Alina passed her black briefcase under the table to Vasilyev.

"Documents for your trip, local currency and US dollars, and train tickets are inside. So are some other necessities, so you should not open the case where you may be observed."

Seeing Vasilyev's raised eyebrows, Alina smiled and said, "No offense. I know you have far more experience than I do, but I have found it is best to take nothing for granted."

This earned her an answering smile from Vasilyev. "So, Mikhail is still training at the Academy?"

Alina nodded. "Yes. The instructor everyone hopes they don't get, but sooner or later everyone did. I thought he was tough but fair, as long as you paid attention."

Vasilyev nodded approvingly. "It's obvious you did. When you said 'it is best to take nothing for granted' I could hear his voice."

Alina glanced at her watch. "I have hired you a cab which should be pulling up front in the next five minutes. It will take you to the train station. The defector and our Iranian escort will be taking the same train. You will be in the same car to provide security overwatch in a neighboring compartment."

Vasilyev frowned. "They have been briefed not to approach us?"

Alina nodded. “Yes. Security checks on train trips that do not leave Iran are usually not a problem, but it will not take much to attract attention. Note that the security guards on Iranian trains are armed.”

Vasilyev smiled. “We promise to be on our best behavior.”

En Route to Mahabad, Iran

“So, you said this was going to take about thirteen hours,” Grishkov said, looking out the train window at the passing scrubland.

Vasilyev nodded. “Yes. Then we take a bus to Naqadeh. Alina has arranged for us to pick up a rental car there stocked with the supplies we will need for the hike to the border. The defector and her Iranian companion will accompany us from there. We can safely drive as far as the outskirts of Nalous, and will hike from there in the direction of Sidakan. The helicopter pickup point is only a kilometer from the border, where a hill will prevent observation from the Iranian side.”

Grishkov frowned. “How far from Nalous will we be hiking?”

Vasilyev rocked his right hand side to side, which Grishkov knew meant he was guessing. "Including detours to avoid minefields and patrols, about fifty kilometers.”

Grishkov grunted. “A walk in the park in Chechnya. I am, though, concerned about our defector. How ready is she for this little stroll?”

Vasilyev shrugged. “We will soon find out.”

Grishkov shivered. He had been relieved to see on the ticket that the train was air conditioned, which had indeed been useful during the day. Now that night had fallen, though, the temperature had plummeted with no answering heat from the vents. He rummaged through his bag, finally finding his jacket.

Vasilyev nodded. “Yes, this hike will definitely feature temperature extremes. I am sure that Alina had appropriate clothing packed for our defector. When we prepare our packs for the hike, though, we will need to make sure that what she needs ends up either on her back or one of ours.”

Grishkov held up the brochure he’d been reading, or more accurately examining the photos, since he didn’t read Farsi.

"This was in our briefing papers. What does it have to do with our mission?"

Vasilyev smiled. "With luck, nothing. It is for the Teppe Hasanlu, ruins dating back to 6,000 BC. It's the reason we would give for going to Naqadeh and renting a car, if anyone asked. Plenty of tourists visit there, and it's about seven kilometers outside Naqadeh. For this train trip, though, we'll just say we're meeting a business contact in Mahabad. It's a decent size city of about one hundred seventy thousand people, so we wouldn't be the only foreign businessmen there."

Grishkov frowned. "One last question. Isn't our being in a car along with two Iranians going to attract attention?"

Vasilyev nodded. "A fair point. First, remember that the old USSR actually bordered Iran, and the mix of people that resulted helps explain why both of us could pass for Iranian, at least through a car window. The local clothes Alina put into the trunk of the cab in Tehran for us to wear on this trip didn't hurt either."

Vasilyev paused. "Of course, as soon as either of us opens our mouth any Iranian will know we are foreigners, since my Farsi is far from accent-free. However, we Russians are far more welcome here than you might guess. Our friends at Rosoboronexport have been selling the Iranians weapons for decades, and we are one of the few countries to have kept up good relations after the Revolution. Two Russian businessmen, their Iranian contact and his wife decide to visit Iran's cultural treasures? Odd, maybe, but not unbelievable."

Grishkov grunted. "But we're staying away from the defector and her Iranian escort until we have to travel together."

Vasilyev grinned. "Well, yes. No need to push our luck. For this train trip, they have papers showing they plan to visit the Mirza Rasul baths in Mahabad, which has nothing to do with us or any documents we carry."

Grishkov nodded, and then asked, "What did you pass to Alina at the cafe? I know you well enough to know you weren't holding hands because you're planning to date her."

Vasilyev laughed and slapped his knee, and replied, "Excellent! I'd been wondering whether you were paying attention. That was the USB drive with the names of dead Shi'a from the Eastern Province. I promised to get it to Moscow, and so was simply keeping my promise."

Grishkov grunted, and shook his head. "Do you think anyone in Moscow really cares?"

Vasilyev shrugged. "Perhaps not. But in this business, you never know what information will be useful, perhaps in trade. It could be that someone else cares, after all."

They could both hear the door to their train car slam open and closed, and a few seconds later the door to their compartment flew open, revealing a scowling train security guard.

"Papers," the guard growled in Farsi, thrusting his right hand forward.

Vasilyev and Grishkov mutely handed over their passports. After glancing at the covers, and then opening them to see that the photos matched the two men in front of him, the guard visibly softened.

Handing back the passports, the guard said in Farsi, "You are welcome in Iran. Enjoy your trip."

Vasilyev and Grishkov both nodded and smiled, but said nothing. The guard next moved on to the defector's compartment next door, leaving their door ajar.

Grishkov raised his eyebrows and whispered, "It appears you were right about Iranians liking Russians."

Vasilyev shrugged. "I didn't say all Iranians. But I'm betting you have Rosoboronexport to thank for that happy exchange."

Grishkov and Vasilyev could both hear the guard requesting papers again, but could not clearly hear the exchange that followed. Within a few moments, it was clear from the guard's angry tone that something was wrong.

Vasilyev moved silently through the door, listening intently to the exchange. Something had provoked the guard's suspicions, and he could see an Iranian woman in the compartment holding her hands over her veiled face and sobbing. The guard reached for the radio clipped to his shoulder.

Vasilyev shot the guard twice with his silenced pistol, and he crumpled forward without a sound. Vasilyev grabbed him before he hit the floor and quietly told the Iranian man he could now see sitting across from the woman, "Help me get him inside."

The man was clearly shocked by what had happened, but quickly moved forward to help. Simultaneously Grishkov appeared in the doorway, and quickly closed it behind him.

Vasilyev turned to Grishkov and whispered, "We have to get rid of the body, but if we just dump it off the train it will probably be discovered before we reach Mahabad. Ideas?"

To his surprise the voice answering Vasilyev was not Grishkov's, but that of the Iranian man now gingerly holding the guard's body sitting upright next to him.

"We are coming up to the Zarrineh River. If we hurry, we can have the body ready to throw off the trestle and with luck into the water below. That should buy us some time. It will take two of us to get him out of the compartment."

Vasilyev nodded, and gestured to Grishkov to help. Then Vasilyev turned to the Iranian man and hissed, "Keep her quiet."

Grishkov glanced at the woman who sat as still as a statue, evidently in shock. He knew Vasilyev was right, though. She could start screaming at any second.

With some difficulty, Vasilyev and Grishkov maneuvered the guard's body through the door of the compartment, and out the door of the car into the small metal platform connecting the two train cars. A nearly full moon cooperated with a bend in the track to show them an oncoming trestle about a kilometer ahead.

Vasilyev sighed and muttered, "About time we had a break." He grabbed the guard's shoulders and Grishkov grabbed his legs, and they began to swing the body back and forth. By the time the train reached the trestle they had built up plenty of momentum, and let the body go. It disappeared over the side of the trestle, but it was impossible to see whether the body had fallen in the water or instead on the riverbank.

As they walked back into the train car, Grishkov whispered, "A good thing there wasn't much blood."

Vasilyev nodded. "A combination of subsonic ammo and knowing where to shoot."

They walked directly to the compartment with the defector and her escort. Both were sitting silent and motionless as Vasilyev and Grishkov entered, closing the door behind them.

Vasilyev pointed at himself and said his name, and then Grishkov did the same. The Iranian man nodded and said, "Esmail." After a pause, the woman pulled back her veil and said shakily, "Neda."

Vasilyev turned to Esmail. "What happened?" he asked quietly.

Esmail shrugged. "The guard asked for our papers, looked at them and handed them back. He asked me why we were going to Mahabad, and I told him. Then, he asked Neda the same thing, and she said nothing."

"I just froze," Neda whispered.

"He kept asking her over and over, getting angrier each time she didn't reply. That's when he reached for his radio. You know the rest," Esmail said.

Vasilyev nodded, turning to Neda. "Are you alright? Will you be able to continue this journey?"

Neda drew a deep breath. "I suppose I have to be. I certainly can't go home." She paused. "Didn't anyone else in this train car hear what happened? Won't they report it?"

Vasilyev shook his head. "The woman who arranged this trip bought tickets to all the seats in this train car. A standard security precaution. Of course, sometimes unoccupied seats attract passengers, whether they have been paid for or not. That is why we picked this train with its relatively unpopular departure time, when it is usually less than half full. I checked after the train left Tehran, and we are the only ones who took seats in this car."

Neda shivered. "Won't anyone come looking for him before we get to Mahabad?"

Vasilyev shrugged. "It's not impossible, but I don't think it's likely. These trains normally have a single conductor whose job is to take tickets, and a single guard. The train has already made the last scheduled stop before Mahabad, so I'll bet the conductor is asleep somewhere. The train's crew is unlikely to leave the locomotive. Given what we saw of the guard's disposition, I can't picture anyone looking for him to engage in conversation or a friendly game of cards."

Neda frowned. "So who was he going to call on his radio?" she asked.

Vasilyev spread his hands. "I'm only guessing, but probably the train crew. Since he was suspicious of you, he would have asked them to stop at the next station even though no stop is scheduled, and to radio ahead to have the police waiting there. Once the guard said even a few words to the crew on his radio it would have been over, since they certainly would have called police to meet us at the next station if his call suddenly cut off."

Neda shuddered. "Once we reach Mahabad, though, won't someone notice he's missing?"

Vasilyev nodded. "It's possible. My guess, though, is that once the train reaches Mahabad his job is done. After a thirteen hour ride I'm sure he gets a chance to sleep before he does another trip. With luck, he won't be missed before we're long gone."

Grishkov bit back the observation that immediately occurred to him - unless they'd missed the water, and his body was in full view on the banks of the Zarrineh River. He doubted it would help calm Neda.

Neda frowned and asked, "So we just carry on, exactly as planned?"

Vasilyev shrugged. "I can't think of anything better. Did the woman you met at our Embassy, Alina, strike you as capable?"

Neda nodded.

Vasilyev smiled. "Well, you don't know us, but have some faith in her. This is her plan, and I think it's a good one. We will soon have you on your way out of Iran."

It was obvious to all of them that Neda was far from convinced, but finally she nodded, and Vasilyev said no more. At least she appeared to have recovered from her initial shock at the killing of the guard.

Now, Vasilyev thought, we just have to hope she won't freeze again at the wrong moment.

Chapter Eleven

Mahabad, Iran

Grishkov and Vasilyev both wore caps, which provided some protection from the sun as well as helping obscure their faces. Especially when the brim was pulled aggressively low, as Grishkov was now doing. "I almost miss the Vladivostok winter," he declared.

When Vasilyev's only answer was a smile, Grishkov shrugged and smiled back. "OK, I've gone too far."

Making their way through the crowd milling outside the Mahabad train station, they both simultaneously tried to keep an eye on Neda and Esmail walking ahead and look for the bus station, which was supposed to be nearby. Esmail had said he knew the way, and it turned out he'd been telling the truth. Within a few minutes they were in a line that though long, moved quickly.

Once they reached the head of the line all Vasilyev has to say was "Naqadeh," and hold up two fingers to be handed two bus tickets in return for the Iranian rials he placed on the counter.

Grishkov had kept track of Neda and Esmail, who were boarding a bus about a dozen meters away. A few minutes later Grishkov and Vasilyev had handed their bags to a porter for storage in the bus' luggage compartment, along with a generous tip that saw they were placed there immediately instead of being "lost." They found seats at the back from where they could observe Neda and Esmail in front of them, and would have time to react if the bus were to be boarded.

However, fortune was with them this time, and the only excitement was provided by an American action movie playing simultaneously on small flat screens mounted in the front and middle of the bus, which had been dubbed into Farsi. It was a low budget rip off of "The Terminator" featuring an evil robot with a human appearance that seemed to spend most of its time breaking into motel rooms to kill moderately attractive women. Grishkov had to work hard to suppress his laughter when the robot decided to deal with dents in his metal body caused by police bullets with an iron that his latest victim had been using on clothes.

He also had to admire Vasilyev's concentration, which though it never left Neda and Esmail avoided being obtrusive in a way that might be noticed by the other passengers.

The driver made good time, and they arrived at the bus station in Naqadeh just before the movie finished. As they exited the bus, Grishkov thought to himself that could help explain why such a poor quality movie had been chosen.

Who would complain about missing the ending?

Naqadeh, Iran

Esmail Mohsen climbed out of the bus just ahead of Neda once it arrived at Naqadeh. The cursed Russians were seconds behind them, as they had been during the entire trip. Esmail had spent nearly every minute since this job had started thinking about how to get rid of them, or to call his cousin with the border guard.

The Russians weren't stupid. The first thing they did when he arrived for a job was to search him for a cell phone, and he'd had no chance to slip away to get one.

Esmail also couldn't wave down a passing policeman. Not only might the Russians shoot him the way they had the train guard, something almost as bad might happen - he might not get paid. He had to negotiate a price and place to hand over the woman and the Russians, and for that he was counting on his cousin's help.

Esmail wasn't going to betray the Russians out of patriotism. The only thing he was loyal to was money, and so far the Russians had paid well. This job would be the most lucrative yet.

Still, Esmail was sure his own government would pay even better. Nobody had told him who the woman was, and he hadn't asked. But the fact that for the first time ever two Russians were going with him on a job told him Neda was someone very special.

Fortunately, he had planned ahead. Soon, Esmail thought, soon I will have my chance.

En Route to Nalous, Iran

Grishkov and Vasilyev sat in the back of the rented sedan, a white Peugeot 405. Alina had chosen it not only because it was large by Iranian standards, but due to its status as one of the most commonly seen cars throughout the country. Manufactured since 1987, it had been retired in France a decade later, but not in Iran where thanks to a lack of options caused by sanctions production continued. Though Chinese manufacturers were now giving Peugeot stiff competition, a Peugeot 405 was still as close to camouflage as you could get on Iranian roads.

Esmail was driving, since he knew where they would be leaving the car. Neda sat silently beside him. Vasilyev in particular was worried about her mental state, but Grishkov was not concerned. Unlike Vasilyev he was married, and his own wife had gone through worse. In his opinion, women were at least as tough as men, if given the chance to prove it.

The next stage of their journey, though, did concern Grishkov.

"Isn't anyone going to complain when we don't bring this car back, and maybe report it to the police?"

Esmail answered, shaking his head. "No. Alina has an arrangement with the rental car manager. She gives him far more than the regular rental price, which goes right into his pocket. I'm sure he suspects that the cars are used for smuggling. But as long as the cars come back undamaged, and so far they have, the money is enough reason to play along."

Grishkov frowned. "But how will the car get back to the dealer?"

Esmail smiled. "Alina did not tell you that part, because I handle it myself. I have an arrangement with three families with farms outside Nalous, all related to each other. I leave the car with them, and they return it to the rental car manager. We aren't going past Nalous because farms closer to the border are watched much more closely by the police."

Grishkov shook his head. "I don't like this. What is to stop them from turning us in to the authorities?"

Esmail laughed. "Many things. First, they will never see you. When I pull the car off this road and onto their driveway, you will not be visible from their house. Land this far from a major city is relatively cheap, and the farm is quite large. We will be walking through one of their orchards for some time before we reach the first of several trails that will take us to the border. Second, they know that if they turn us in they are certain to be imprisoned as well, since any investigation of their finances will show income that cannot be explained. Finally, the same is true for the other families involved. If one is discovered, the police are sure to find out about the others as well. Greed might tempt one person to take a chance. But to risk the entire extended family? Very unlikely."

Grishkov nodded, and looked at Esmail thoughtfully. "My apologies. You appear to have thought this through quite carefully."

Esmail smiled. "It's why I'm still alive, and many of my competitors are not. Don't worry - I'll get you to the border."

Grishkov nodded and looked at Vasilyev, who arched one eyebrow and said nothing.

En Route from Nalous to Iran-Iraq Border

Esmail looked over his shoulder at Vasilyev and Neda, who were following behind him. Grishkov was walking a short distance ahead, looking back every now and then as though daring Esmail to correct him. So far, Esmail had said nothing.

After they finished walking through the farm's apple orchards, Esmail called for a stop.

Pointing at the trees around them, Esmail said, "We will continue walking through forest for some time, though the trees will thin as we approach the border. If you have anything to discuss do it in the next two hours, while we are still far enough from the border not to worry about patrols. After that, do not speak or make noise for the rest of our journey. If you need to stop, wave your hand at me. We will make camp at nightfall."

Turning to Grishkov, he said, "It's obvious this is not your first walk in the woods. You are welcome to take the lead. Once we approach the border, though, you should let me earn my pay. There are old and new minefields along the border, and neither are marked."

Grishkov nodded. "Is there any wildlife we need to be concerned about?"

Esmail shook his head. "Iran has many dangerous creatures, ranging from cobras and crocodiles to cheetah and leopards. We are far from the habitats of cobras and crocodiles, and cheetahs and leopards have been hunted to near extinction. Though we could encounter a viper or a wolf, it's unlikely since they usually avoid people. At least, I've never seen either in these woods. The best reason to keep your eyes open is the uneven ground. It's full of rocks and tree roots. A sprained ankle or worse for any of you will be a problem for all of us."

Though he was careful not to look at Neda as he said it, she answered anyway. "This isn't my first time in the woods either. You'll have nothing to worry about from me."

Esmail nodded. "Very well. We've been making good time so far. Let's get back to it."

Once again, Vasilyev and Neda brought up the rear. Vasilyev asked quietly in English, "Have you thought about what you might do in Moscow?"

Just as quietly, Neda answered in Russian, "I plan to teach physics."

Only Vasilyev's years of experience let him keep his feet steady, and keep his astonishment from reaching his face. "I didn't know you spoke Russian," he said, again in Russian.

Switching to English, Neda shrugged. "I've just started to learn. It's obviously something I will have to know."

Vasilyev nodded. "You are right. Many Russians speak English, but most do not. It is good that you have already started to learn. I compliment you on your accent."

Neda smiled, the first time Vasilyev had seen her do so. "Thank you. I've just done some online instruction, so it's good to have feedback from a native speaker. I was able to learn Urdu pretty quickly when I spent a year as an exchange student at the Pakistan Institute of Engineering and Applied Sciences in Islamabad, so I'm hoping to have the same luck with Russian."

Then her smile faded. "But let's be serious. You're not really interested in my plans in Russia. You want to know whether I'm going to tell your General all that I know."

Vasilyev shrugged. "I am actually interested in your plans. One of America's great strengths is its willingness to welcome outsiders, and I have often thought Russia could learn from their success. As someone with an advanced degree in physics, I have no doubt you will make important contributions."

Now Neda's smile was back, but she shook her head. "Really? It's not as though there aren't plenty of other physicists in Russia."

Vasilyev smiled back. "Perhaps. There were plenty of them in the United States in the early 1940s. Do you know how many of the two dozen scientists on the team that created the first atomic bomb were born in America?"

Neda shook her head.

Vasilyev said, "Two. And one of those two obtained his degree outside the US. I think the lesson is clear. Any nation, no matter how great, can always use some help."

Neda looked at Vasilyev with new respect. "I believe you are sincere. I will tell you frankly that Russia was not my first choice. Hearing from you, though, I'm starting to think it was not a bad one."

Neda paused. "I will tell you this much. When I see your General in Syria, I will tell him absolutely everything I know, instead of waiting until I arrive in Moscow. Until then, I will not say another word. I threw away everything I had to leave Iran, and my last reason for staying disappeared when I found out my husband was a monster willing to kill thousands of innocent people. I want to save those people, and I've told Alina as much as I did already to give you a chance to stop their deaths. But I also want to stay alive myself."

Vasilyev said quietly, "Even if you told me everything right now, I would still do all I could to get you to Moscow alive."

Neda's smile now was real, but bitter. "I believe you and the other Russian would as a matter of honor. But there is honor, and then there is duty. Keeping me alive because I still know something your country needs is about professionalism, and your obligations as a servant of the

Russian state. I think you will try harder and sacrifice more to keep me alive if that is your motivation."

Vasilyev nodded. "I think you will fit in very well in Russia."

Esmail held up his hand, now barely visible in the gathering shadows. Vasilyev, Neda and Grishkov quickly gathered around him and they all began to unpack their food and sleeping bags. Esmail pointed to a fallen log nearby, and sat down. They all followed his example, and began to open their food packets.

The temperature was plummeting, and Vasilyev wondered idly whether chattering teeth would affect his ability to eat. Grishkov, with far more recent outdoor experience, knew the answer was that hunger overcame all obstacles to food reaching a stomach.

With a flourish, Esmail produced something that looked like a bulky lantern. Vasilyev was about to object when Esmail shook his head and whispered, "It produces very little light."

It took him several tries, but Esmail was finally able to light the device, which as promised produced only a faint red glow. He nevertheless surrounded it with a thin sheet of flexible metal, which blocked the dim light in every direction but straight towards them. To everyone's astonishment except Esmail, the small clearing began to warm rapidly.

"It contains a small propane bottle," Esmail whispered. "Not enough fuel to last for long, but we will eat and go to our bags warm. Helps for a better night's sleep."

The rest all nodded, and fell to their food with a will. After they had finished eating, Neda was the first to head for her sleeping bag. Vasilyev nodded at Grishkov, and said, "I will take the first watch." Grishkov shrugged, and unrolled his bag as well. Turning off the heater, Esmail whispered, "Time to answer nature's call," and walked towards the nearby bushes, where he was quickly out of sight.

Grishkov had just slipped into his sleeping bag. Once Esmail left, he slipped out of it and just as quickly moved silently in the same direction.

Vasilyev was becoming concerned about their absence when Grishkov walked back into the small clearing, and tossed him a small black device. Vasilyev caught it with a frown, and looked at it closely.

As Grishkov sat next to him, Vasilyev commented quietly, "It looks like a cell phone, but the name on the front is a company that I thought only made GPS devices. I see you took the precaution of removing the battery."

Grishkov nodded, and responded in an equally low voice. "I am familiar with these because we had a grand total of one for the entire Vladivostok police department. It is a satellite radio handset, but you cannot use it to make calls. It can only send text messages. As you would expect from a company that mostly makes GPS devices, it can also tell you where you are located."

Vasilyev smiled. "Let me guess. This is what our guide went to retrieve. Once he had done so, you retrieved it from him before he had a chance to use it. And he will not be returning to our little camp."

Grishkov shrugged.

Vasilyev nodded. "I know we have no tools to bury a body. Were you able to conceal it well enough to give us time for our escape?"

Grishkov frowned. "From people, yes. From local scavengers and buzzards, I'm not so sure. We must also remember that the train guard's body may be discovered at any time. Any competent policeman will check his last route and see that it pointed straight at the border."

Vasilyev nodded. "We must be ready to move at first light."

Grishkov glanced towards Neda's sleeping bag. "And we will have to pick up the pace. We need to be ready to cross the border soon if we are to have any real chance." He paused and said, "I will stand watch now. You may as well go to your bag, since I won't be able to sleep."

Nodding his understanding, Vasilyev quickly squeezed Grishkov's right shoulder as he moved to his sleeping bag, and then turned.

"Just one thing. Each of us must have gone into the bushes a half dozen times on this hike. Why did you follow him tonight?"

Grishkov shrugged. "This was the first time he announced it."

Neda woke as the first rays of light penetrated through the surrounding trees into the small clearing. Like all of them, she had slept with her clothes on. She lifted herself to a sitting position, still in the sleeping bag, and saw that both Vasilyev and Grishkov were sitting on the fallen log and eating. When they saw she was awake they nodded in her direction, but said nothing. She nodded back, and slowly extricated herself from the sleeping bag.

Neda walked to the log and sat next to Vasilyev, who handed her a food packet, saying in a low voice, “The last one.” She nodded her thanks, and quickly ate it. Once she had finished, she looked around and quietly asked with a frown, “Where is our guide?”

Neither Vasilyev or Grishkov had any readable expression. Vasilyev answered carefully, “He decided he’d gone far enough and turned back. We have a map that will show us the rest of the way.”

Neda shook her head and said something low in Farsi that Vasilyev barely caught, but he knew translated roughly in English to “in a pig’s eye.”

With a different animal, of course.

Neda continued, “You killed him.”

Grishkov nodded.

Neda glared at Vasilyev and said in a fierce whisper, “I’m not a weakling or a child. I never trusted that man. Did he betray us?”

Grishkov shrugged. “He tried to. Even though I hid it, his body still might,” pointing upward at a buzzard circling lazily high above them.

Vasilyev looked upwards and bit back an oath. “How can it possibly know so quickly?”

Grishkov nodded. “Yes, I wondered the same thing in Chechnya. I’m sure the scientists have an explanation. I and the other troops there simply believed they had made an agreement with the devil.”

Neda shivered, only partly from the cold. “Do we still have a chance?”

Grishkov smiled. “Absolutely. There’s no way the border guards here have enough men to follow up on every buzzard sighting. They’ll only bother looking if they’re near here anyway. Plus, we’re still kilometers away from the border. But, it does mean we’ll need to move faster.”

Neda nodded. “I’m ready. How far do we have to go?”

Grishkov frowned. “I think we can be ready to go for our final push by tonight. When night falls we’ll get a few hours of rest, and then cross the border in the hour just before dawn. There is enough light from the moon to see if we move carefully, and the border guards should be at their least alert. Many will be asleep, and the vigilance of the night watch will be fading.”

“What about mines?” Neda whispered.

Grishkov grinned. "You're lucky to be with a soldier who's seen plenty of them, and actually had to plant some. There's ground where they're easy to plant, and other terrain where it's difficult or impossible without special equipment. I have looked closely at a geological chart of the border area, and I know exactly where to cross."

Vasilyev nodded approvingly. "Excellent. Now, I think we should be off."

With that, Vasilyev and Neda quickly followed Grishkov's example, discarding all upper clothing except their cotton shirts, and donning the new Ratnik 3 ballistic vests placed in the bottom of their packs at Grishkov's request. He hadn't been sure Alina would be able to find one small enough to fit Neda, but as she strapped hers on was pleased to see Alina had been successful. Thanks to the use of boron carbide in the vest's armor ceramics, it provided better protection than the vest Grishkov had used in Chechnya, and yet was about thirty percent lighter.

Grishkov had already hidden Esmail's belongings, including the heater. They would have to bear with the cold at night for the rest of their hike. He hurriedly put their now empty packs in the same hiding spot.

Grishkov took the lead for this last stage of their march, with Vasilyev and Neda close behind. As the hours passed the temperature once again rose. By the time they stopped at midday to rest, the thinning of the forest had become more noticeable. The chirping of birds, which had been the only sound other than their own footfalls, nearly ceased.

On the one hand, there were far fewer tree roots to avoid. On the other, the rocks were growing larger and more plentiful.

By late afternoon the trees had dwindled further in both number and size, to be replaced by rock and brush. Fortunately, the brush was high enough to provide good cover.

Finally, night fell just as they reached the area Grishkov had picked to rest at before they made their pre-dawn crossing. So far, they had not seen or heard any hint that there were any other people nearby, let alone border guards. Yes, Grishkov thought to himself, we just might make it after all.

No sooner had Grishkov had the thought than a dull "pop" was followed by the brilliant illumination of an area about a kilometer away.

The light lasted less than a minute, and then suddenly went out. Before it did, a machine gun chattered briefly, and was then silent.

"What was that?" Neda whispered fiercely.

"An 82 mm illumination mortar round, or something very much like it. The color of its light looks exactly like what we used in Chechnya, so I'd bet it's one of ours that we sold to the Iranian Army," Grishkov responded.

At the same time he chastised himself for his earlier optimistic thought. He might as well have issued the illumination round an engraved invitation, he thought morosely.

"So, what now?" came in another angry whisper from Neda.

No, not really angry, thought Grishkov. Frightened. He didn't blame her, since he was a bit worried himself.

Grishkov answered in a low voice. "We wait and rest, just as we planned. They're at least a kilometer away. We've still got a good chance, as long as we keep our heads."

Finally, Neda nodded and sat down on the ground with her back against a large rock. She found that while the air had quickly cooled, the rock's surface still retained some of the day's warmth. Well, she thought to herself, at least God is showing me some mercy. She pressed her back harder against the smooth rock, and tried not to think about the border guards.

The night seemed to stretch on forever, but finally Grishkov made a hand gesture with an unmistakable meaning. Forward.

Hunched over as Grishkov had instructed, they crossed single file over rocky ground leading to a grass-covered hill. Grishkov's reading of his map told him that the base of the hill was the border with Iraq. They had been promised a helicopter pickup on the other side of the hill, where they would be safe from observation by troops on the Iranian side of the border.

Grishkov was elated as rock gave way to grass, and had just thought "We made it!" when he heard a "pop" that was much closer and louder than the last one. It was quickly followed by brilliant light, and an impact in his back that felt as though a giant was pushing him face-first into the grass. Only then did he hear the chatter of the machine gun.

It took several seconds before Grishkov could turn his head far enough to see that Vasilyev and Neda were also flat on their stomachs, but he couldn't tell whether they had also been hit or were just seeking cover. A quick look around confirmed his first impression. Aside from hugging the ground, there was no cover. In the dying light of the illumination round suspended from its parachute, Grishkov could see the Iranian border guards moving forward. The only question left was whether they had been ordered to shoot them on the spot, or bring them back for questioning.

A sudden roar of multiple engines from the other side of the hill, followed by the brilliant glare of spotlights, announced the arrival of the Iraqi Army. Grishkov had to squint to see through the sudden glare, but counted at least five Humvees mounting M-2 .50 caliber machine guns and spotlights, as well as two Bradley Fighting Vehicles. Iraqi flags were flying from all of them.

Grishkov had seen many cannons larger than the 25mm variety mounted on the Bradley. He thought to himself that it had to be perspective. They looked so much larger pointed in his direction.

The man with the loudspeaker mounted to one of the Bradleys quickly made it clear he was not their target.

"Iranian forces at our border. Retreat immediately. The intruders in our territory will be arrested and tried under Iraqi law. Any attempt to interfere will be met by force." This message was given first in English, and then what Grishkov correctly believed was Farsi.

Neda would tell him later, very bad Farsi with a heavy Kurdish accent.

A voice shouted back something in Farsi. The answer was a burst from one of the M-2s that kicked up rock and dust close enough to the Iranian troops to send a clear message, but without killing or injuring them. The professional in Grishkov admired the placement of the rounds, while another more human part calculated their survival chances if the Iranians responded.

Low. Very low.

With much shouting and yelling, the Iranians moved back as two of the Humvees moved forward. Without waiting for an invitation, Grishkov, Vasilyev and Neda climbed aboard the two vehicles, which quickly reversed and sped to the other side of the hill. Minutes later, they could hear what Grishkov recognized as a Kazan Ansat-2RC light helicopter. It was even better to recognize the familiar white, blue and red Russian insignia on its side. They were all quickly aboard, and Vasilyev was yelling in his ear to be heard over the noise of the engine, "How badly were you hit?"

Grishkov shook his head and answered, "The armor took the worst of it. What about you and Neda?"

Vasilyev grinned and said, "We are better at ducking!"

Grishkov smiled back, not because he was amused but to give Vasilyev some reassurance that the round's impact really hadn't been so bad.

The pilot yelled back, "Make sure you stay strapped in. We'll be doing evasive maneuvers as soon as we reach the Syrian border that will continue all the way to base. Anything that flies in a straight line in Syria doesn't fly long."

They had to stop at the Syrian military base south of Al-Hasakah to refuel. Grishkov started to admire how neatly and professionally the facility had been laid out by the Syrians, and then stopped himself as he remembered one of his briefings. The Americans had pulled out of this base, built to fight ISIS, just the previous year.

CHAPTER TWELVE

Khmeimim Air Base, near Latakia, Syria

Grishkov had been impressed as they approached Russia's primary air base in Syria at its size and scope, which exceeded that of many of the bases he had used in Chechnya. Originally built to support one thousand airmen, it now had nearly double that. Russian bombers, fighters, and transports of all sizes came and went with dizzying regularity. Grishkov had identified Su-24, Su-25, Su-34, Su-35, IL-76, AN-124, and Tu-214 model aircraft, and he hadn't really been trying.

All three of them were immediately taken to the base hospital, where Grishkov found himself stripped and flipped onto his stomach with a speed that had doubtless saved many lives in the past. It did remind him, though, of a comedian he'd watched on TV who said "Russian" and "gentle" went together like "German" and "easygoing".

Grishkov had laughed, because he wasn't wrong.

The doctor told him to turn around, and shook his head as he stripped off his plastic gloves. "You should write a letter to the manufacturer of your body armor. Aside from a deep bruise, I see no sign you have suffered any other injury. Even the bruise is not as bad as I expected."

He paused. "I can offer you nothing for the bruise but painkillers."

Grishkov grunted. "I'll take a bottle of aspirin."

The doctor nodded. "Good choice. An effective anti-inflammatory and it avoids turning you into yet another addict. I've seen opioids kill more good soldiers than the terrorists we're here to fight."

Grishkov nodded back. He'd seen drugs do the same in Chechnya.

Grishkov was given clean fatigues to wear, and then escorted to a small conference room where Vasilyev and Neda were already waiting. Vasilyev was wearing the same fatigues as Grishkov, but Neda was wearing a simple yet attractive dark blouse and skirt.

Vasilyev smiled when he saw Grishkov was dressed the same way he was. "It appears we've both been drafted. Neda was luckier thanks to Alina. She radioed ahead to a Syrian contact in Latakia with Neda's sizes, who brought her clothes to the base just this morning. I've been doing this work for a long time, and even I am impressed."

Neda smiled wistfully. "It is a small thing, but for the first time in many years, I feel hope that things may be about to change for the better."

The conference room door swung open, and into the room strode the commander of Russian forces in Syria, General Stepanov. Tall, bald, and with a trim muscular build he had been able to keep up in spite of his age, Grishkov's first thought was, "I'd hate to run into him in a bar fight."

An aide followed behind, who quickly took up position at the far end of the conference table and turned on a small laptop. Vasilyev, Grishkov and Neda all started to rise from their chairs, and were impatiently waved back into them by Stepanov.

Pointing at each of them in turn, he said, "Vasilyev, Grishkov, Rahbar." They each nodded, and then Neda said softly, "Please call me Neda, General."

Stepanov scowled, as all the Russians present knew he would at the interruption. He then visibly reminded himself that he wasn't speaking to one of his soldiers, nodded and said, "Very well. I understand your English is good, so we will speak in that language."

Glancing at the file that had been placed in front of him, but leaving it unopened, Stepanov said, "I understand that you promised to give us further details on the planned attacks in Saudi Arabia once you were out of Iran. I am here to listen."

Neda looked thoughtful. "I must stress first that my husband's part in these attacks is limited to the ones using nuclear weapons. There was to be a follow-up attack using conventional weapons of some kind, but I have no details on that."

Stepanov nodded impatiently.

Neda took a deep breath, and said, "One nuclear weapon will be used against each of the two desalination plants that together supply Riyadh with nearly all of its fresh water. A third nuclear weapon will be used to contaminate Saudi oil reserves with radioactivity."

Stepanov shook his head. "This makes no military sense. Why cut off Riyadh's water supply when you could simply attack Riyadh directly? As for contaminating Saudi oil reserves, I doubt there is a single impact point which could accomplish that mission."

Stepanov paused. "I know you overheard your husband making these plans with a terrorist operative, and I know your husband was the head of Iran's nuclear program. But is there any proof that these weapons really exist?"

Vasilyev's outward demeanor didn't change, but internally he groaned. So their mission ended. Stepanov wanted nothing to do with anything that would take resources from his mission in Syria. He would use the fact that there was no proof Iran had nuclear weapons to justify doing exactly nothing.

Then to the astonishment of everyone, Neda reached inside her blouse and pulled out a USB flash drive, the one measuring less than an inch long.

"Full technical details on each weapon are here, as well as my husband's notes on how each were to be used in the attacks. I am a nuclear physicist myself, and I can tell you that these devices should work."

Stepanov swung towards Vasilyev and quickly asked him in Russian, "Doesn't the FSB search defectors anymore?"

Before Vasilyev could answer, Neda said quietly in Russian, "It's not his fault."

Stepanov shook his head in disgust, and said to Vasilyev in English, "Her speaking Russian is another small detail not in her file."

Neda said quickly, switching to English, "I have just started to learn. Please, do not blame him or Alina. They could never have found the drive."

Neda paused, and blushed deeply. "It was not in my bra before. We women have many hiding places."

Stepanov grunted, and then pursed his lips, obviously thinking. He then gestured for the aide to bring him the laptop, and inserted the drive. A few clicks later, the screen was filled with schematics, and Stepanov's frown had changed from angry to thoughtful.

Stepanov looked up from the screen at Vasilyev. "Very well. Let us assume that everything here is true. What do you propose we do with this information?"

Vasilyev said carefully, "I think we should inform the Saudi government, and leave the response to them."

Stepanov's answering smile had no warmth in it at all. "Very sensible, and what I plan to recommend to Moscow. Why do you think they will refuse?"

Vasilyev shrugged. "There may be concern, if the attack is successful, that the Saudis may believe we were involved and warned them too late only to avoid blame. Our weapons sales to the Iranians might cause them to think this, and maybe even to ignore our warning. They are currently very busy in Yemen."

Vasilyev glanced at Grishkov. "We have already discussed these possibilities."

Stepanov nodded. "I'm sure you have. Other options?"

Vasilyev frowned. "The FSB has assets in the Kingdom that could be activated and used to try to stop these attacks. It would be best if we could be there to lead that effort, but I don't think there's enough time to get us to the Eastern Province."

Stepanov nodded. "Any other options to stop the attacks?"

Vasilyev hesitated. "First, I should say that I believe the attacks on the desalination plants are real. They are primarily targets of opportunity, since they are just on the other side of the Gulf from Iran. Small boats smuggling contraband, primarily alcohol but also drugs, land cargos on the Saudi coast daily - or I should say, nightly. Some are caught, most are not. I think a small boat will land the two weapons to be used on the desalination plants, and local Shi'a enemies of the government will help carry out the attacks."

Stepanov's eyebrows rose. "You call them 'enemies of the government'? Here in Syria we find the term 'terrorists' shorter."

Vasilyev nodded. "Yes, General. They are terrorists planning to kill thousands of innocent people, and must be stopped. But it is important to remember that the attackers will be people with real grievances, who are highly motivated."

Stepanov grunted. "Yes, we have seen this in Syria too. Just when we think the war is finally over, it flares up again. But you said that you believe two of the attacks are as described here," waving at the laptop's screen. "What about the third?"

Vasilyev shook his head. "I agree with you that contaminating all or even most of the Kingdom's oil reserves with a single nuclear weapon is impossible. Whatever the idea's origin, it can only have been proposed to Neda's husband as a way to persuade him to provide the weapons."

He turned to Neda. "Your report to Alina said that he would have refused to hand over the weapons if they were going to be used on cities."

Neda's face twisted, and a bitter laugh emerged. "Yes, that monster is fine with killing thousands. But he draws the line at tens or hundreds of thousands. I think he's just thrilled that all of his years of work are going to be put to use. The devil's use," she said, spitting on the floor next to the conference table with a vehemence that took them all by surprise.

"So," Vasilyev continued, "that leaves the question of the real third target. I think there can be only one answer."

"Riyadh," Stepanov said flatly.

Vasilyev simply nodded.

"And you think it will be delivered by air," Stepanov said, "which is why you wanted my only two Su-57s."

Vasilyev nodded again.

Stepanov sighed in exasperation. "The Su-57 has a range of fifty-five hundred kilometers, and that can be extended with additional internal fuel tanks. But for every fuel tank I add, I have to remove an air-to-air missile. And I will have to add tanks, because Riyadh is about two thousand kilometers away. So even if I send them one at a time with extra fuel tanks, it will be pure luck if we stumble across the attackers. That's assuming we can even identify them. And the Saudis don't penetrate the Su-57s' stealth features."

Vasilyev nodded. "Neda has already told us that all three devices were experimental and designed for testing, not fully finished bombs ready for mounting on an aircraft. So, the delivery aircraft will be either a cargo plane or helicopter. It will almost certainly be coming east to west. It will be much slower than the escort aircraft, which will have to either throttle down, or more likely orbit around it."

Stepanov shook his head. "Such a pattern would surely be noticed by the Saudis."

Vasilyev shrugged. "Assuming they saw it. I am sure you have seen the report that the Iranians have purchased two J-20s."

Stepanov scowled. "I have. If you're right about this, then I'll be putting up one Su-57 with a reduced missile payload against two of the best fighter aircraft the Chinese have got. Not a great deal for our pilot."

Vasilyev nodded. "A challenge, yes. But I see no reasonable alternative."

Stepanov grunted. "I don't either." He glanced at his aide, pushing the laptop towards him. "Prepare the necessary orders." The aide nodded and began rapidly typing.

"You were a bit hasty on one point," Stepanov said, smiling at Vasilyev. Something about the smile made both Vasilyev and Grishkov...uncomfortable.

"You said there wouldn't be enough time to get you back to the Eastern Province in time for this mission. Particularly since there are no direct flights from Syria to Saudi Arabia, that would normally be true. However, you know that the *Admiral Kuznetzov* was ordered to the Gulf?"

Vasilyev nodded.

Stepanov continued, "But you may not have heard of the problems the ship had a few years back, when it lost an MiG-29K because of an arrestor cable problem, and we had to transfer the rest of the carrier's planes to this base. After years in dry dock, and after many had thought repairing and updating it would be impossible, the carrier is now finally refitted and its problems hopefully fixed. But, we still do training for new MiG-29K carrier pilots at this base before they try landing on the *Admiral Kuznetzov.* So, we kept two MiG-29Ks. They are the UBR variant. Would you like to guess what makes them special?"

Vasilyev sighed. "Two seats."

Stepanov roared with laughter. "Exactly! You are about to get to the Eastern Province very quickly indeed. Those orders have already been prepared, and your flight plan cleared by the Syrians and Iraqis. Once you're aboard the carrier, a helicopter will take you to Dhahran Airport. It's good that you both had multiple entry visas."

Vasilyev frowned and looked at Grishkov. "General, has the doctor cleared my friend here for a carrier landing?"

Stepanov nodded. "He has, but I approve of your concern for your comrade. You should know that he may be a bit tougher than you realize. I have read his military record, and more importantly, talked to Colonel Geller."

Grishkov started, clearly taken off guard. "He is here? And a Colonel now!"

Stepanov smiled. "He is assigned to this base. Yes, though he was a Lieutenant when you knew him in Chechnya, he has advanced quite rapidly since then thanks to battlefield promotions both there and here in Syria. I spoke with him just before you arrived. I regret that he is now on a mission, and you will be gone by the time he returns. Still, he asked me to pass on his regards."

Grishkov nodded. "A good man," he said.

Stepanov pointed at Grishkov. "Your decision to reach for a bottle of aspirin instead of something stronger was just as important in my deciding to send you on this mission."

Turning back to Vasilyev, Stepanov said, "Your flight will not be too exciting until its end. Though the MiG-29K is capable of speeds up to twenty-two hundred kph, due to the need to conserve fuel you will be cruising at a mere fourteen hundred kph. The landing will be...exciting. But with luck survivable. Now, I assume you have some calls to make before you go?"

Nodding to the aide who had just finished typing their orders into the laptop, Stepanov said, "Get them whatever they need before their flight." Pointing to Neda, he said to the aide, "Prepare orders for her flight to Moscow, but keep her in comfortable quarters here on base for now. We may have more questions for her before this is over."

Stepanov stood and reached across the table, shaking the hands of both Vasilyev and Grishkov. "Good luck to both of you. God knows you'll need it."

With that, he strode out of the room, and the aide handed Vasilyev a cell phone.

Grishkov looked at Vasilyev and frowned. "How many assets does the FSB really have available in the Eastern Province?"

Vasilyev shrugged as he picked up the phone. "We're about to find out."

Approaching the Admiral Kuznetzov, Persian Gulf

Grishkov looked through the cockpit glass at the tiny postage stamp floating on the water that the pilot had improbably advised him was the *Admiral Kuznetzov.* The pilot had strapped him in so tightly it was good that the mask fed him oxygen directly, since otherwise Grishkov wasn't sure he'd have been able to breathe. The pilot had said it was to minimize the impact of landing, though Grishkov wondered whether it was really to keep him from touching the controls all around him. The truth was, if every lever and switch had been a poisonous serpent, it would have made no difference to Grishkov's interest in touching them.

The sound of the engine changed tone to a low-pitched growl, and a sharp "thunk" announced the MiG-29K's landing gear had been lowered. Simultaneously, the plane's speed dropped until it felt as though it were almost standing still. Evidence that it was not was right in front of him, as the carrier went from "postage stamp" to "how can something this big float?" in less than two minutes.

The jet was on the ship's deck seconds later, and stopped so suddenly Grishkov could feel his teeth clack together. So, he thought, the arrestor cable problem appears to have been fixed.

An hour later, Vasilyev's MiG-29K had also landed without incident and they were aboard a Mil-8 helicopter on the way to Dhahran Airport. They had both been issued headsets, and shown the switches to use to communicate with only each other or also the pilot.

Turning the switch that with the noise of the helicopter's operation ensured privacy, Grishkov asked Vasilyev the question he'd been thinking about the entire flight.

"It's obvious you have no great love for either Saudi Arabia or Iran. Yet here we are, about to risk our life for the Saudis. If there is a war between them, which side should we hope will win?"

Vasilyev grunted. "First, I make a great distinction between the Saudi and Iranian governments, and their people. Saudis and Iranians, like all people around the world, are for the most part just trying to live their lives. Brutal criminal codes and oppression of women are not unique to those two countries, though it is true both are worse than most. It is also clear that most Saudi and Iranian men support both policies."

Vasilyev paused, clearly thinking carefully about his answer. "Both countries have been accused of supporting terrorists. The Saudi government has provided funds and weapons to the terrorists fighting the Syrian government, and our troops supporting it. Years ago, they did the same for terrorists fighting the Afghan government, and our troops supporting them. Since then, wealthy Saudi individuals have funded Al-Qaeda, terrorists fighting the Americans in Iraq, and the Taliban in Afghanistan. Of course, most of the September 11 attackers in New York were Saudis."

Vasilyev shrugged. "The Iranian list is at least as long. Funds and weapons to Hezbollah in Lebanon, the Houthis in Yemen, Hamas in the Gaza Strip and yes, terrorists fighting the Americans in Iraq. Iran's attack on the Israeli Cultural Center in Buenos Aires in 1986 killed one hundred fifty people. But this brings us to one key difference between the two. Some Saudi support for terrorists comes from its government, but most of it comes from the Saudi elite. Every terrorist action traced to Iran was directed by its government."

Grishkov frowned. "Does that make it better or worse?"

Vasilyev smiled. "I would say, more dangerous. Governments have access to greater resources than even the wealthiest individuals, particularly petrostates like Iran. There is evidence the Saudis have begun to rein in some of their wealthy princes, and are consolidating more power in its government."

Grishkov nodded. "Like a few years ago, when some of them were involuntary guests at the Riyadh Ritz Carlton."

Vasilyev laughed. "Just so. But meanwhile, Iran has been developing nuclear weapons and providing Yemeni rebels with ballistic missiles, which have been landing on Saudi cities. No missiles are landing on Tehran. Also, the Iranian government has repeatedly and publicly promised to destroy Israel. We know the Iranians have nuclear weapons, and so do the Israelis. Where would a nuclear war between them end?"

Grishkov nodded. "Very well. Particularly since Iran plans to start a sneak attack with nuclear weapons, I agree it makes sense to support the Saudis. Now, since you've shared so many terrible memories, let's have something funny."

Vasilyev arched one eyebrow. "Funny?" he said, and paused. "Very well, I do recall visiting one Russian in a Saudi prison soon after his arrest who I noticed immediately smelled strongly of alcohol, but did not appear to be intoxicated. When I asked him why he had been arrested, he was quite embarrassed and explained he had gone a bit overboard with a traditional expatriate recipe. It consisted of fruit juice, sugar, and fruit cut into small pieces, which would then be placed into a container and left to ferment to produce alcohol. Illegal, of course, but as long as it was produced and consumed at home unlikely to come to the attention of the authorities."

Grishkov nodded, clearly puzzled.

Vasilyev smiled. "Well, our friend was a bit too ambitious. He bought a plastic one hundred liter trash can and filled it with the recipe I mentioned. Oh, and it had metal clamps on either side of the lid. Which he engaged. The fact that fermentation was complete was announced by an explosion at 2AM which resulted in calls from all his neighbors to police, who genuinely believed there had been a terrorist attack. When they arrived, his guilt was undeniable. Not only did the apartment and our unhappy compatriot reek of alcohol, bits of chopped fruit were splattered on nearly every surface. I think it's unlikely he received a refund of his cleaning deposit."

Grishkov laughed. "What happened to him?"

Vasilyev shrugged. "He got off pretty lightly, mostly because we took an interest in his case. I remember the Ambassador saying no Russian should lose a body part just because he wanted a drink. So, he forfeited his salary, paid a fine on top of that, and after a few months in jail was deported back to Russia."

Grishkov nodded. "OK, not bad. Now, here's a challenge. Tell me something funny about Saudi Arabia in ten words or less."

Vasilyev grinned. "I can do it in three, and I actually have one more funny story after that."

Grishkov made a "come on" gesture with his hands.

Vasilyev, still grinning, said, "They import sand."

Grishkov's answering expression provoked a gale of laughter from Vasilyev that Grishkov was finally forced to join.

Rubbing tears from his eyes, Grishkov said, "OK, that was funny, but now you're going to have to explain how that could possibly be true," pointing down. They had reached the Saudi coast, and indeed there was nothing visible but sand in every direction except the Gulf.

Vasilyev nodded. "On my first trip here I was told this, and refused to believe it. A friend of mine took me to an office building, and we walked outside to its back. Then, he told me to press my fingers against its surface. Nothing happened. He shook his head, and told me to press harder. To my astonishment, my fingers began to sink into the building! It seems that cement requires sand coarser than what is to be found in the Kingdom's deserts. Decades ago contractors could get away with this, but the government had put a stop to the use of substandard construction materials by the time I arrived. After all, inspections to detect the practice were not difficult!"

Grishkov smiled, and shook his head. "And your second story?"

"Well," Vasilyev said, "I had read an official report about Saudi steel production and been surprised at the numbers. You see, world trade in steel is governed by many agreements, and the Saudis only need so much steel for themselves. I wondered, where does it all go? So, I visited a steel factory to talk to its manager. I'd noticed when I drove in that there were piles of rusting steel lying outside the factory, so I started by asking about those.

The manager explained that they were no problem, because once the piles of steel rusted it was easy to run them through the plant again, and cheap to do since the natural gas they were using for fuel would have been flared off if they weren't using it. He was puzzled when I asked whether such 'recycling' was counted as new production. Of course it was, he said."

Grishkov laughed and shook his head. "But we Russians can hardly be too critical of such tales. I have certainly heard many over the years."

Vasilyev smiled and nodded, and said, "I must tell you my favorite. Just after the USSR's collapse, there was a big push to convert military to civilian production. So, a factory that had produced military jet fighters was now to make milking machines. Old equipment was removed, new machinery installed, and in less than a year they were turning out milking machines."

Vasilyev paused and smiled, then continued, "There was just one problem. A government ministry in Moscow still controlled allocation of all metals used in industry, and had not yet changed the ones used by this factory when production began. So, aerodynamics aside, the factory was producing milking machines with metals capable of standing up to the stresses of supersonic flight."

Grishkov frowned, and asked, "How long before the mistake was fixed?"

Vasilyev looked grim and replied, "Not before a German businessman bought the entire first years' production of milking machines, had them exported to Germany and melted them down for the titanium, vanadium and other rare metals they contained. He cleared a profit of triple what he spent to buy and melt down the machines. On the bright side, control of metal allocations was removed from the ministry."

Grishkov shook his head. “So, you are depressing me, and we have wandered too far off topic. Where is the Kingdom headed? Forward, or back?”

Vasilyev shrugged. “Forward, but slowly. Abolishing the religious police a few years ago was a positive step, as was allowing women to drive as long as their nearest male relative gave permission. The government has recognized for some time that the economy needs more female workers if they are to reduce the Kingdom’s reliance on foreign workers who are becoming more difficult to afford. They have begun to develop solar power, an area where the Kingdom should be a world leader, as it is already in desalination. They have investments worth billions in America, Europe and Asia. In short, the Kingdom has much going for it.”

Grishkov nodded. “But...”

Vasilyev smiled. “Yes, but. Saudis are willing to tolerate a certain amount of repression, since many believe the alternative is the chaos we now see in countries like Syria. But for how long? Will tanks prove the right long-term answer to unrest among the Shi’a community in the Eastern Province? The Saudis have subsidized the spread of a radical Wahhabi version of Islam around the world. If the Kingdom does continue in its recent more moderate direction, is that money they will regret spending? So, many questions remain. On the whole, though, I am optimistic about the Kingdom's future."

Grishkov grunted. "Good. I'd hate to think that we're risking our lives for nothing."

Vasilyev laughed, and clapped Grishkov on the shoulder. "Never, my friend! Those desalination plants are sure to have thousands of people in and around them. And, of course, there is always our duty to Mother Russia."

Though he was still smiling, Grishkov knew that Vasilyev was absolutely serious. Grishkov nodded, and they rode the rest of the way to Dhahran airport in silence.

CHAPTER THIRTEEN

Salwa Beach Resort, Qatar

Guardian Colonel Bijan Turani was pleased. Both warehouses were finished on schedule, complete with blue plastic sheeting in place of roofs. His foreman Fuad was supervising the crews using a combination of forklifts and brute force to stack wooden crates in the warehouses according to the instructions he had given. The work had been going well, but now as he expected Fuad was striding towards him with a frown on his face.

"Boss, the work is going well, and everything's on track. Just one question. None of the crates have the contents marked, and some of them are really heavy. Can you give me some idea of what's in them?"

Bijan nodded. "The heaviest are probably the ones containing metal pipe we're going to use to complete the water transport system. Some others have machinery, like pumps. I'm supposed to be getting a list, but like I said earlier my boss says don't open anything until he gets here."

Fuad visibly relaxed. "That explains it then. Well, we'll just carry on until your boss gets here. I guess we've all got one, right?"

Bijan smiled. "I don't see any royalty around here, do you?"

Fuad laughed, and went back to yelling at his crew, who had taken his momentary absence as an opportunity to rest. The truth was, Bijan didn't envy them. It was blazing hot, and he was sure that the crates were indeed heavy.

Bijan had learned long ago that small objects and distant movement were most easily detected with peripheral vision. He used that knowledge now to confirm the presence of the visitor he'd been expecting. A small surveillance drone. It could be American, but probably not. Their drones flew high enough that they were usually impossible to spot. No, this one was almost certainly operated by the Saudis, and he'd bet money that the men watching its feed were with the blockade force just on the other side of the border.

Perfect.

Now, time for a little theatre.

Bijan entered a single word text into his phone. The phone of the driver of a nearby truck, one of the soldiers of Artillery Group 22 Bijan had accompany him from Iran, buzzed a few seconds later. Less than a minute after that, the truck's engine ground into life, and it began moving towards the nearer of the two warehouses.

The truck's right front wheel struck a rock partly covered with sand, causing it to lurch and send several of the wooden cases it carried flying out the back, where they landed on the rocky ground hard enough to burst open.

That's how it would have appeared to the drone, anyway.

In fact, several more of the soldiers of Artillery Group 22 were inside the truck's covered cargo bed, and as it deliberately hit the rock assisted the cases on their journey earthward. They had also removed the screws that secured their lids, so once they hit the ground their contents would scatter for some distance.

These contents were bricks, tile, and cans of red paint. And the cans had their lids loosened before being placed back into their crate.

Bijan had known that the Saudis would have to be curious about the resumption of construction activity at the Salwa Resort after years of inactivity, and would wonder about just what was being stockpiled in the newly built warehouses. As he ran towards the scene of the accident, yelling and waving his arms and trying not to grin at his overacting, he was barely able to resist the temptation to look at the drone's reaction. Was it moving closer?

Half an hour later, Bijan had stalked off after "supervising" Fuad and his crew as they salvaged what they could of the bricks and tiles strewed across the desert floor. Thanks to the red paint, that wasn't much.

Finally, he dared to look for the drone, first with his peripheral vision and then by sweeping his gaze openly in every direction. It was gone!

An outstanding result, Bijan thought to himself with satisfaction, for my first dramatic performance.

2 Kilometers West of the Saudi-Qatari Border

Prince Ali bin Sultan had told Colonel Abdo Barazi that he was placing his trust in him after thinking long and hard about who among his men most deserved it. And at first, Barazi had believed him. After all, the force at his command of forty-eight tanks was by far the largest single armored force under the command of a Saudi colonel. The fact that half of his tanks were M60s detracted only a little from that honor, because they had been carefully maintained and were ready for action.

Barazi had no illusions about how the M60s would fare against the Qataris' Leopard 2A7s. For that matter, he knew that the Leopards even outgunned his M1A2 tanks. And that if the Qataris deployed all two hundred of their Leopards against his force, his command would definitely be overrun.

None of this worried him, for three reasons.

First, the Qataris would never sortie their entire armored force, leaving the country undefended. Bazari guessed half at most, maybe less.

Second, the entire Qatari armored force was stationed just outside Doha, two hours away from Barazi's tanks, even at their top speed. Bazari had the Qataris' tanks under drone surveillance 24/7, with rotating shifts of his best troops watching to see if the Leopards showed any sign of moving out from their base. They didn't.

Well, it was clear that the Leopards were well maintained, and their crews were doing their best to become familiar with the new tanks in the large shipment they had received a few months ago. There was certainly plenty of training activity, and Bazari thought it was likely all the Leopards were now operational, though he'd noticed the most recent Leopards didn't have the same camouflage netting as the older ones. But there was zero indication that the Leopards were going anywhere, let alone planning to attack his force.

The last point, though, was the most important as far as Bazari was concerned. An attack by the Qataris would make as much sense as Danish tanks rolling across the German border. It just wasn't going to happen.

Bazari really did listen when Prince Ali told him to take the Qataris seriously, and to prepare for a possible attack. He had ordered his drones to carry out surveillance of their Leopards, and no matter what wasn't going to slack off on that. If they moved out of Doha he was going to be calling for air support, because Bazari knew he'd need it.

He'd also taken Ali seriously when he told him to keep his tanks moving, because as they'd had drummed into them in training, "a parked tank is a really big sitting duck." Bazari had run exercises with his force, which he thought had really improved its readiness.

Then two things happened. First, the demands of the forces in Yemen slowed the delivery of fuel for his tanks. He still had all he needed in case of combat. But he no longer had a fuel reserve he could burn through in exercises, so he had to order a stop to them.

Next, he and all his troops followed the reports closely about the action Prince Ali's tanks were seeing in Yemen. Barazi and his men cheered when Ali's tanks finally managed to destroy a ballistic missile before it was launched against Riyadh. But it was hard not to wish that they'd been there, too.

It wasn't long before that longing was transformed into a dark suspicion. That maybe this command wasn't such a great honor after all. That instead it was just a joke, a "check the box" exercise that Ali had given Barazi because any idiot could handle it.

When one of his men had called over Barazi to a console because of what he called "suspicious activity" at the Salwa Resort at first he thought the Qataris might be up to something. There had been no official announcement that construction of the resort was going to resume, and his force was only about six kilometers away.

Then this morning he had heard uproarious laughter at one of the consoles carrying the drone video feeds, and quickly joined the crowd clustering around the image. Barazi had joined the laughter as the man ran forward, arms waving, while red paint and construction materials were scattered across the Qatari desert.

Once the laughter died down, though, Bazari had wasted no time ordering the drone to rejoin the others watching the Leopards in Doha. They would still have the drones check on the Salwa construction site when they brought them back for refueling, and when they sent them back to Doha. But unless they saw something unusual, the drones would not linger.

It was obvious that the Salwa Resort was no more a threat than the Leopards parked quietly in Doha two hours away.

Salwa Beach Resort, Qatar

Guardian Colonel Bijan Turani grinned as he saw Captain Dabiri jump down from the truck. "Dabiri, good to see you! How was your trip?"

It was immediately obvious that Dabiri was uncomfortable on multiple fronts. This was his first trip outside Iran. Like many, he had joined the military in part because he sought a stable, orderly life. Bijan smiled to himself as he thought of the English word "regimented," used as a synonym for stability. Called upon now to carry out a covert military mission in a foreign country, Dabiri's life had become much less stable. He had to wonder, with good reason, whether he would make it back to his wife and children in Iran.

Well, Bijan thought to himself, that's the chance you take when you put on the uniform.

And it was clear that Dabiri missed his uniform. In his new role as Bijan's supposed boss. he also wore khakis and a polo shirt, just even nicer ones. There was no avoiding the awkward role reversal, since Dabiri had been needed in Iran to oversee the testing, packing and shipment of the howitzers and their ammunition, while Bijan had to get the warehouses ready for their arrival.

Dabiri nodded, visibly reminding himself that he was supposed to be Bijan's boss.

"Everything is good. I have the last of the construction materials we'll need for the first phase in this truck."

Fuad had walked up as Bijan and Dabiri talked, and now Bijan turned to him.

"Fuad, let me introduce you to my boss, Mr. Dabiri." Bijan then turned to Dabiri and said, "Fuad and his men have done great work so far. I recommend we bring them back as soon as we're ready to start on the next phase of construction."

Fuad's consternation was so clearly shown on his face it was almost comical. "Bring us back? But I thought we were going to be working for weeks..."

Bijan nodded vigorously. "You will, you will. But my boss, here, needs time to review our plans on site and make decisions about priorities with the engineers. He expects to need about three days, but it might be a little longer. I will call you on your cell."

Fuad nodded, clearly unhappy.

Bijan pulled out a large brown envelope stuffed with Qatari currency. "The rials in this envelope should be enough to pay you and your men for the work you have done so far, as well as the next three days. You and your men should head back to Doha, to get some decent meals and rest. There will be plenty of work for all of you to do when you get back."

Now Fuad was grinning from ear to ear. "Thank you, sir! Very generous of you! I will be waiting for your call!"

Half an hour later, Bijan and Dabiri were alone with the rest of the men of Artillery Group 22 selected for this mission, his supposed "engineers." Together, they walked through the closest of the two warehouses.

Dabiri shook his head as he looked from side to side, and then up to the blue plastic sheeting high above. "When I gave you the specifications you asked for to make this attack work, I thought that would end it right there. I'm amazed that you were able to get these up so quickly."

Bijan laughed. "Don't thank me! It's all due to prefab components and construction crews used to working hard and fast. That foreman you just met told me that he pulled his workers out of 2022 World Cup construction projects in Doha in 2018 after the worker death toll topped a thousand. He looked online at other major sporting events and saw that the previous record for the number of construction deaths was held by the Russians for the 2014 Sochi Winter Olympics, who lost sixty. I am proud to say that in putting up these warehouses, we matched the British record for construction deaths for the 2012 Olympics. Zero."

Dabiri smiled. "So, that plus the money I saw you handing over means they should be pretty happy."

Bijan shook his head. "That wasn't the point. I could care less how happy there are. I do care that when they get to Doha, they won't talk to anyone about how good they had it here, or anything else about this project."

Dabiri frowned. "Why not? Isn't it human nature to be proud of success, and to want to share it with others?"

Bijan smiled. "Maybe under normal circumstances. But nothing here is normal. Competition among expatriate workers for the best jobs is fierce, because they're not just worried about themselves. Each worker has an entire extended family depending on them. Nobody will risk a good thing through careless talk. That would guarantee having other contractors turn up offering to do the same work for less."

Dabiri grunted. "And we don't want anyone showing up while we're putting together these howitzers."

Bijan nodded. "Yes. That would be...inconvenient."

Dabiri pointed at a large, six-wheeled truck, which had a trailer behind it. It was parked in the shade provided by the warehouse, and was covered by another large blue plastic tarp on every side except the one facing the warehouse entrance. There were several men inside the truck who appeared to be busy with something, but from the outside there was no sign of their purpose.

"What is that truck doing here? Is there a reason they're so close to us?"

Bijan smiled. "Yes. It is a R-330ZH automated jammer. The Russians used it to great effect against the Ukrainians during the conflict there. Its purpose is to prevent the blockaders from calling for help once we begin our attack. And it is pressed up against the warehouse to keep it from being observed by any nosy drones, though we haven't seen any since our performance a few days ago."

Dabiri nodded. "Yes, I heard about that. But is the equipment on this truck really able to jam all signals from such a distance?"

Bijan shrugged. "Yes. But, in order to increase the effectiveness of its jamming, later this evening it will be driving closer to the border. Once at the spot we have selected, the crew will then deploy antennas from both the truck and the trailer. Finally, they will notify us that they are ready to cut off the Saudis' communications. Of course, our frequencies will be unaffected."

Dabiri smiled. "So, we will have some chance of getting these howitzers moving before the Saudis arrive to return the favor."

Bijan nodded. "Perhaps. But we will have no guarantee of reaching safety, only of making it a bit harder for pursuing aircraft to locate us. The Qataris have no idea we're carrying out this attack, and so will have to decide very quickly whether to defend their airspace."

Dabiri frowned. "Shouldn't we have told the Qataris, so they could have their defenses prepared?"

Bijan shrugged. "I considered it. However, I thought it was nearly certain that they would either refuse to allow the attack to proceed, or that a Saudi spy would reveal our plans. I think there's a good chance that the Qataris will scramble aircraft if they see Saudi fighter jets inbound. After all, for some time they have been the threat that provides the Qatari Air Force with its entire reason for existence."

Dabiri smiled. "Colonel, I sincerely hope you're right."

Bijan grinned. "Me too, Captain."

Salwa Beach Resort, Qatar

Guardian Colonel Bijan Turani clapped Captain Dabiri on the shoulder as he walked up behind him in the warehouse. Dabiri had just laid down a tool he was using to adjust a fitting on one of the howitzers, and smiled tiredly as he saw Bijan.

"We're just about ready. And a full two hours ahead of schedule!" Dabiri laughed, and Bijan laughed along with him. A problem discovered with one of the howitzers only after they had nearly completed assembly had cost them precious time, as they had to disassemble it to make room for their only spare. They weren't laughing with amusement, but with relief. Both of them knew how many soldiers were counting on their success.

"Have you heard from the spotters?" Dabiri asked.

Bijan nodded. "They're all in place. The Saudis reinforced the blockade with additional tanks, just as we expected. The spotters report that the Saudis don't move their tanks much during the day, and hardly ever at night."

Dabiri nodded. "Are they all M1A2 Abrams tanks?"

Bijan scowled. "No. About half are M60s. I don't know how the Saudis expected them to stand up to Leopards. There are also about a hundred armored personnel carriers with supporting infantry, a roughly half and half mix of American-made M-113s and the Saudi-produced Al-Masmaks. And, of course, dozens of supply trucks and fuel tankers."

Dabiri shrugged. "Don't discount the value of the M60s. Any tank can get lucky. Plus, almost any shell at the right angle can knock off a tread. I've talked to a lot of tankers who fought in our war against Iraq back in the eighties, and they all said the same thing. Every tank is a threat - period."

Bijan smiled. "Well said. Are all of your men ready?"

Dabiri nodded. "They are. Every howitzer crew is paired with a spotter, and we have tested our communications with each one. When it's time, we will be ready."

The attack had been scheduled after moonset when the night would be at its darkest, and nearly all the blockaders asleep. To maximize their chances of destroying the entire Saudi blockade force, they had to take advantage of every variable.

Fuad had been puzzled by Bijan's request that ropes be attached to the blue plastic sheeting substituting for a roof, that would allow it to be quickly removed. He had been satisfied, though, when Bijan explained that he hoped the owners would follow Fuad's advice to add a real roof to each warehouse, and that being able to remove the sheeting easily would speed that project.

One of Bijan's first lessons in getting people to do what you wanted was simple. Make people think you were doing what they wanted.

The remaining minutes crawled by slowly, as the howitzer crews checked and rechecked to be sure each was ready to fire.

Finally, the order was given, and in succession each howitzer fired its laser-guided Basir shell.

2 Kilometers West of the Saudi-Qatari Border

The first hint Colonel Abdo Barazi had that his unit was under attack was the explosion of the M1A2 tank next to his, followed by the M60 tank to its right. More tanks exploded in quick succession, but the only clue to the attack's origin was the whistling of shells that seemed to come from straight overhead. Barazi had been asleep, and it took him precious seconds to gather his wits and recognize the attack for what it was. Part of that recognition was what it was not. No jets roared overhead. No shells slammed into the sides of his tanks from enemy armor.

This was an artillery attack.

But as shells continued to rain down, Bazari noticed something else. Every shell seemed to be finding its target. There were no gouts of sand rising into the air, even though some of his remaining tanks had started to move. As he saw again and again, even the moving tanks were being hit dead on.

A sickening realization made Bazari press his eyes against the M1A2's eyepiece of the gunner's sight, where he saw the view displayed by the thermal imaging system. It showed a web of laser range finder images crisscrossing his remaining tanks. Bazari keyed his microphone to give the order to target the spotters at the end of each of those crisscrossing lines.

An artillery round sliced through the turret's top armor and exploded inside Bazari's Abrams tank.

Several of Bazari's officers attempted to radio Army headquarters in Riyadh that they were under attack. However, the R-330ZH automated jammer proved effective, and it was not until much later when one of the surviving APCs had driven outside its jamming range that word of the attack finally reached Riyadh.

All most of Bazari's remaining officers could think to do was to flee as fast as their tanks could go. As one tank after another exploded, some tanks stopped and their crews tried to escape.

None were fast enough. The spotters saw what they were doing, and made their tanks priority targets. Trained tank crewmen were targets nearly as valuable as the tanks they manned. And no matter how fast they ran, the lethal radius of a 155 mm shell's explosion was far too great for their speed to matter. The fuel and ammunition exploding inside each tank hit by a Basir round created even more shrapnel, and ensured that no tank crewmen escaped the attack by running away.

Once every tank was a smoking hulk, the armored personnel carriers were the next priority. Some APCs with alert crew were already out of range of the spotters, but the confusion had been great enough that some M-113s and Al-Masmaks could still be targeted. Without being told, the spotters knew to leave the APCs that were still parked for last. To be fair, some of those APCs weren't moving because they had shrapnel damage from the explosion of nearby tanks, while shrapnel had also killed and injured the drivers and crew of other APCs who had been sleeping in nearby tents.

Though none of the trucks or fuel tankers had been deliberately targeted so far, many had been hit by shrapnel from 155 mm shells and exploding tanks. All of the fuel tankers as well as the ammo trucks produced secondary explosions when they were hit, killing dozens of sleeping soldiers.

The maelstrom of exploding vehicles also took a toll on the spotters, in spite of being dug in and deliberately outside the Bashir round's range. A round from an ammo truck ignited by an exploding fuel truck killed one spotter outright, while shrapnel from a tank hit as it fled wounded another spotter badly enough that he was rendered unconscious. Since there were no medics for the spotters, he never regained it.

Each of the twelve active spotters were assigned to a particular HM-41 howitzer, with three dug in and available as a reserve. Once the two spotters failed to send a "click" over their radios each minute to their howitzer crew, they were immediately replaced by the one-word command "active" sent by radio to a spotter held in reserve.

The main challenge each spotter faced was avoiding the assignment of multiple rounds to a particular target. It wasn't easy, because sometimes a target was lased by another spotter from an angle difficult for the first spotter to see. The problem became more serious as the number of targets shrank.

However, the good news was that few Basir shells were truly wasted. Even when the same target was hit twice, more shrapnel was flung out by the second hit, and there were so many vehicles and men in such a small space that additional damage and casualties were almost inevitable.

Of course, the spotters' good luck couldn't last forever. Omar Abu-Rabia was one of the surviving Saudi soldiers and a veteran of the fighting in Yemen, who had been trained at the US Army Sniper School at Fort Benning. Most of the Saudis fortunate enough to be selected for training outside of the Kingdom were either members of the royal family or closely connected through business or religious ties.

Omar was an exception because he was an outstanding shot. He grew up firing his grandfather's WWI vintage Lee-Enfield rifle, which he said the British officer who had given it to him as a present called "Smelly." His grandfather spoke no English, so had never questioned the name. His grandfather passed it to Omar after his deteriorating eyesight made use of the rifle more of a threat to those around him than whatever he was aiming it at. Omar used Smelly to great effect in defending his grandfather's camel herd from packs of wild dogs and the occasional viper.

Only after he was at Fort Benning did he finally learn from the oldest instructor there that the term Smelly had nothing to do with the rifle's smell, but instead came from the acronym for Short, Magazine, Lee-Enfield. For some reason, that instructor was delighted to find that one of the students at Benning had grown up using a Lee-Enfield rifle, and took a personal interest in Omar's progress from then on.

The vehicle where Omar's M-24 rifle had been stored had been destroyed, but he was finally able to find a rifle that would serve.

The Barrett M-82 was intended primarily as an anti-material rifle for the destruction of targets such as parked aircraft, trucks and fuel silos. However, its .50 caliber round worked even more effectively on human targets, because its large size guaranteed incapacitating or killing the enemy soldier no matter where he was hit.

Finding a night vision scope to mount to the Barrett took more precious minutes. Finally, though, Omar was ready to avenge his fallen comrades.

He caught his breath when he looked through the night vision scope and saw the web of laser designations pointing to the remaining vehicles. Quickly, though, his training came back to him. Focus on the closest target first.

Omar methodically worked his way through the spotters closest to him. A successful shot was easy to confirm, since the laser designator either veered wildly off its previous course or winked out altogether. Of course, it was possible that in the latter case he had only hit the equipment rather than its operator. As far as Omar was concerned it didn't really matter, although the size of the Barrett's round made him think it was likely that both had become casualties.

Four of the spotters quickly fell victim to Omar's accurate fire. However, he forgot one key part of his training. Since the spotters possessed nothing more dangerous than a beam of light, he considered it an unnecessary waste of time to move his position. After all, Omar appeared to be the only one doing something to stop the slaughter of hundreds of Saudi soldiers and the destruction of just as many combat vehicles, and there was clearly no time to waste.

The problem was that Captain Dabiri had anticipated the spotters coming under fire, and was actually surprised it had taken this long. Once the fourth spotter failed to check in, Dabiri had all the information he needed to calculate Omar's likely position. The next six Basir rounds bracketed that spot.

Omar has been lining up his shot on the fifth spotter when the first round impacted and threw off his aim. The second hit while he was trying to reset his aim, and sent a piece of shrapnel into his right leg. Cursing, Omar was tightening a bandage around the wound when the third round made the task unnecessary.

The fourth round guaranteed that Omar's body would never be discovered.

The fifth and sixth rounds impacted on an empty tent that had been filled with sleeping soldiers, and an APC that had already been rendered immobile by shrapnel from earlier shells.

However, the volley's task had been accomplished. Nothing more would disturb the rest of the spotters from directing fire on the blockaders' remaining vehicles.

Only a single M1A2 tank and five APCs survived the Iranian artillery attack, while over three hundred Saudi soldiers had been killed and more than four hundred wounded.

The Iranians lost six spotters.

Colonel Bijan, Captain Dabiri and his men then rushed to prepare the HM-41 self-propelled howitzers for the road to Doha. Whether they would be able to do so without interference would depend on how quickly Saudi Arabia's military leadership realized an artillery attack had been responsible for the destruction of their blockade force.

Chapter Fourteen

Ministry of Defense, Riyadh, Saudi Arabia

Prince Ali bin Sultan rubbed his eyes, willing them to remain open. Sleep on the Bell 412 helicopter that had flown him from his command post of armored forces in Yemen to Riyadh had been impossible, and he had been taken directly from the helipad to this conference room at the Ministry of Defense. Looking at the neatly pressed uniform of Prince Khaled bin Fahd, the Air Force commander, he wondered whether it would have been possible to share the jet that he had used to return to Riyadh several hours earlier.

Given the size of Khaled's ego there probably wouldn't have been enough room, Ali thought acidly.

The Crown Prince walked in and immediately noted the contrast between the immaculately turned out Air Force commander and the armored commander still in the tanker coveralls he'd been wearing when the helicopter picked him up from Yemen. Ali knew the smile the Crown Prince gave them both as he sat down.

It was the same smile Ali gave his children when they'd been fighting over their toys.

Ali willed himself to relax. He had to keep reminding himself that the Crown Prince had gone to the same American armor training school he had. It wasn't that the American military didn't have officers who placed a high priority on "proper appearance." It did. But after more than two decades of constant battlefield operations, those officers were a distinct minority.

"I know you've both been briefed on what we know about the attack on our blockading force at the Qatari border. I've called you both here to get your assessment of what happened, and to make recommendations on what we should do in response. Ali, you go first," the Crown Prince said, nodding in his direction.

"The attack included an electronic warfare capability we haven't seen before in this region. Because of this signal jamming, it took over an hour after the start of the attack for word to reach Riyadh, and another hour after that before the full scope of the disaster became clear. The survivors disagreed about what had happened, including whether it had been an air or ground attack. If it had been a ground attack, there was also disagreement about whether the attackers had used tanks or artillery."

Ali paused and shook his head. "Tanks obviously make more sense, but whose and from where? The Qatari tanks were under constant surveillance, and no other country has a land border anywhere near. American Marines might have hovercraft capable of landing tanks on the nearby beaches, but no other country does."

"Drones have crisscrossed Qatar ever since our blockading force arrived at the border years ago. There's no way massed artillery capable of such a devastating attack could have been missed, no matter what some of the survivors are saying."

Ali nodded in Khaled's direction. "That leaves an air attack, which I recognize is Khaled's field of expertise. I will only say that I think bombing runs by enemy aircraft are easy to rule out, since they would have been detected by what I understand is our highly capable radar network. I think that leaves cruise missiles. I understand Iran has them, but will defer to Khaled on whether they could account for the damage we sustained in this attack.

"We are already doing the obvious - providing aid to survivors of the attack, sifting through the battlefield to discover how the attack was carried out, and to prove what I think is clear, that Iran was the attacker. If so, we need to prepare a military and diplomatic response to Iran's aggression, hopefully with American support. I think reestablishing the blockade will have to wait until we've dealt with the missile threat in Yemen. However, since the blockade force was in charge of deploying and monitoring the drones that had been keeping an eye on Qatar's

Leopard tanks, we need to get replacements up and their feed monitored as soon as we can, though I think our response to the attack should be the top priority."

Ali grimaced. "I know it's not much, but that's my best based on what we know now."

The Crown Prince nodded, and turned to Khaled, who had clearly been displeased when Ali's comments had included reference to a possible air attack.

Khaled clearly struggled to find another way to say it, but in the end he had no choice.

"I agree with Ali. There is only one reasonable conclusion. The force blockading Qatar has been struck by Iranian cruise missiles. First, some history."

Khalid signaled to one of his aides, and a screen dropped at the front of the conference room.

Great, Ali thought. Just what we need in our hour of crisis - PowerPoint slides. When he had gone to the Armor School, two speakers had received by far the most enthusiastic standing ovations. The first had been Colin Powell, former Chairman of the Joint Chiefs of Staff and Secretary of State.

The second had been a speaker who began his presentation with the words, "I'm sorry to tell you that I don't have any PowerPoint slides to go with this talk."

Khaled continued, "Iran first publicly displayed a domestically produced cruise missile in 2015 called the Soumar, based on the Russian Kh-55 cruise missiles Iran purchased from Ukraine over a decade earlier. With a range of between two and three thousand kilometers, it could have easily struck our forces from a base anywhere in Iran. An improved air-launched cruise missile was displayed in Iran's Army Day parade in 2018, which included the capability to be guided to its target by a weapons operator up to one hundred kilometers after launch."

Khaled clicked on slides with photos of each missile to illustrate his points. Ali had to grudgingly admit that as long as Khaled kept the slides to that purpose, they were actually useful. Next a winged drone replaced the Soumar on the screen.

"Another possibility to consider is a drone attack. The Iranians have produced several, but as far as we know only the Shahed 129 model has actually fired a missile that hit a target, Syrian rebel forces in 2016. The next year the Americans shot down Shahed 129s that were attempting to attack coalition forces twice, both times with F-15s."

Khaled clicked again and a similar drone appeared, this time with a bulbous nose.

"This variant has supposedly added satellite control to the drone's capabilities. However, though Iran has launched several small satellites, the Americans advise that none of them could possibly provide the basis for successfully controlling a drone."

Ali nodded. "Too small to contain the necessary communications hardware?"

Khalid smiled. "Precisely. And without satellite control, there's no way the drones could have been guided to attack our forces from Iran."

Ali frowned. "Are we so sure of the Americans' dismissal of Iran's space program? Maybe the Iranians have capabilities they haven't detected."

Khalid laughed, and looked at his notes. "Well, to be fair, they have successfully launched and returned two monkeys, a rodent, a turtle, and several worms from suborbital flights. Sadly, another monkey did not survive its encounter with Iranian space technology."

Seeing from the Crown Prince's expression that he didn't appreciate the humor, Khaled quickly added, "Besides, even fully loaded Iran's entire drone force couldn't have delivered the explosive payload used against our forces."

Khaled clicked his remote again and an image of parked M1A2 tanks inside a hardened hangar filled the screen.

"We should also ask why Iran would have picked our blockade force at the Qatari border as a target. I think the answer is that it was a target of opportunity. We publicly announced we were sending more tanks to reinforce the blockade as a warning to the Qataris not to think about taking advantage of our heavy engagement in Yemen. The only armored force of even greater size is well protected here in Riyadh, as this slide shows. The blockade force was exposed, and easy to target."

A dead silence descended on the conference room, and every head turned to Ali.

"It's true. I've read the reports, and late at night when the attack occurred all of the tanks and APCs were parked in the open. None were on patrol. Colonel Barazi was a good man, and I picked him myself for this command. I had ordered that some of our armor was to be on patrol at all times. I understand that didn't happen because we ran short of tankers to run fuel to the blockade force due to the higher priority we set for the forces in Yemen."

Ali paused. "The irony of this disaster having been made even worse by a lack of fuel in the country leading the world in petroleum exports has not escaped me. I have already offered my resignation to the Defense Minister, who has refused it."

The Crown Prince, who also served as Defense Minister, nodded. "That's right. It's precisely at times of crisis like this that we need our most experienced commanders."

Then the Crown Prince shook his head, obviously unhappy with both the situation and their limited information to address it. "Very well. Until we're able to retrieve and analyze the weapons debris from the attack, we will plan on the basis that this was an Iranian cruise missile attack, launched from Iran. So, your suggested response, Khaled?"

Khaled clicked his remote control again, and another missile filled the screen, this time one with Saudi markings.

"I suggest that we trade Iran missile for missile. The DF-21s we purchased from China have the range to strike any target we choose inside Iran. I have a list of suggested military targets for your review, with a high priority on bases suspected of housing the Soumar missiles that were probably used to attack us. We have a dozen mobile launchers that came with the DF-3 missiles we bought from China earlier, and those would work as a launch platform for the DF-21s."

The Crown Prince grunted, and shook his head. "I thought you might suggest that, and have already discussed the DF-21 option with His Majesty. He is unhappy with it for two reasons. First, we don't have many of them, and if we use them now we won't have a credible ballistic missile deterrent. He knows as well as the rest of you do that the other option, the DF-3s, are old, inaccurate and with their liquid fuel almost as dangerous to us as to the Iranians. Second, we've never test fired either missile. How sure are we that the DF-21s we fire will go where they're aimed?"

Before Khaled had a chance to respond the Crown Prince shook his head decisively. "I know I told you that I called you both here to discuss options. The truth is nothing either of you has said has changed my mind about the course I've already recommended to His Majesty. We will ask the Americans to carry out a cruise missile attack on Iran, once we've confirmed that cruise missiles were the weapon the Iranians used to attack us. The Americans have a submarine stationed nearby that can easily launch such an attack, and if we have proof of Iran's responsibility for the attack on our blockade force I'm sure we can persuade them to do so."

Seeing Khaled's expression the Crown Prince smiled and shook his head. "Your work has not all been wasted. I will give your target list to the Americans. And let's face it- both of you already have more than enough to do in Yemen."

With that the Crown Prince rose, and Ali quickly found himself sitting alone across from an obviously unhappy Khaled.

"So," Ali asked innocently, "can I get a ride with you back to Yemen?"

United States Military Training Mission, Riyadh, Saudi Arabia

Technical Sgt. Josh Pettigrew had never heard of the United States Military Training Mission to Saudi Arabia, or as everyone called it USMTM, pronounced "youse-mi-tim." After his last assignment in Korea Pettigrew had learned from his commanding officer that there had been a lively debate over whether he should be decorated and promoted, or court-martialed.

"Decorated and promoted" because he had helped to stop a North Korean armored attack on the base housing most of the drones used by US forces in Korea. "Court-martialed" because to do it he had violated numerous Air Force regulations, including the unauthorized use of an armed drone that was supposed to have been sent back to the US for decommissioning.

Fortunately for Pettigrew his CO had enough pull to settle the debate by losing his file long enough to send him as far away from Korea as possible. Making his status even murkier was that USMTM was actually funded by the profits from US military sales to Saudi Arabia, which meant he was about as far off the organizational chart as possible while still being in the US military.

When he got the assignment he was immediately hustled on the first military transport headed to Kadena, for the first in a very long series of flights to Riyadh. With plenty of time to read, Pettigrew looked up USMTM's history. He was amazed to learn that it dated back to 1945, when Franklin Roosevelt met with King Abdulaziz on board the *USS Quincy* at Great Bitter Lake, part of the waterway that with the Suez Canal connected the Mediterranean to the Red Sea. The details had changed over the years, but the basic proposition was the same - in order to defend itself the Saudis would supply the money and the troops, while the Americans would provide the weapons and the training.

Looking out at the dozen students in his classroom, all of them Saudis, Pettigrew thought back to a conversation he had with a friend who had tutored a Saudi named Maqbul studying history at an American university. Maqbul had given him a paper to review he had written on the development of trade unions in Egypt during the reign of the leader who overthrew the monarchy after independence from the British, Gamal Abdel Nasser. At one point the paper described a strike at a textile factory, which Nasser ended by using troops to rout the strikers and arrest the strike's leaders.

After reading on a few more pages, the tutor asked Maqbul if he knew what had happened to the strike's leaders.

Maqbul replied, "They were hung."

The tutor, nonplussed, asked, "Don't you think you should have mentioned that in your paper?"

Maqbul shook his head and explained, "That would have gone against the thesis of my paper, which is that overall Nasser was good for trade unions in Egypt."

Pettigrew knew he was going to need more than the PowerPoint slide deck he'd used with new drone warfare trainees Stateside.

The first slide was the standard one, showing a fully armed Reaper.

"In this course, we are going to focus on the drone we have just sold to the Kingdom, the General Atomics MQ-9 Reaper. This marks the first time we have sold the Reaper to a Middle Eastern ally, and one of the few cases where we have sold it outside NATO. Properly operated, it will give the Kingdom military capabilities nobody else in region can match."

Pettigrew paused and pointed at a student in the first row, who had "Fadil" stenciled on his uniform.

"Why do you need this, Fadil?" Pettigrew asked, pointing at the Reaper showing on the slide.

"To defend the Kingdom from its enemies," Fadil said promptly.

Pettigrew nodded. "And can those enemies attack your Reaper?"

Fadil looked confused, and then said slowly, "I read that it can fly very high."

Pettigrew smiled. "Correct. It operates at heights up to fifteen thousand meters. Where do you think the Kingdom plans to deploy Reapers?"

Fadil answered immediately. "Yemen."

Pettigrew nodded and clicked his remote. An online video filled the screen, showing a Reaper falling in flames, while a crowd of Houthi rebels cheered and jubilantly waved automatic weapons in the air. The video ended with Houthis poking at the Reaper's smoking wreckage.

"This happened in western Yemen in 2017. The Reaper was launched and controlled by US forces in Djibouti. We don't know what weapons system the Houthis used to shoot it down."

Pettigrew pointed at another student. "Rahim, why are your forces fighting in Yemen?"

Rahim blinked, and was clearly confused by the question. After a moment he said, "To stop the Houthis from firing missiles at us."

Pettigrew nodded, and clicked the remote again. This time the online video showed a Saudi M1A2 Abrams tank being hit and destroyed by Houthi anti-tank missile fire.

"This happened in Yemen in 2016. A dozen M1A2 tanks looking for Houthi ballistic missiles have been lost to Houthi anti-tank missiles so far."

Pettigrew clicked the remote again, and another online video showed a different burning M1A2 tank.

"This is what happened in a Houthi attack in Jizan in 2018."

Rahim shook his head. "Jizan is in Saudi Arabia."

Pettigrew let the silence that followed stretch for nearly a minute before answering.

"Yes, it is."

The classroom erupted in angry murmurs, which Pettigrew silenced with a chopping motion.

"You're wondering why you haven't already heard about the things I'm showing you. You all know that what you can access online in Saudi Arabia is censored. But as Reaper operators you all need to understand the whole truth."

Pettigrew paused, and looked over the students. Pointing at the burning M1A2 tank on the screen, he said, "The Houthis are bringing the war to you. After I am done teaching all of you how to use the Reaper, they are going to regret that choice."

All the students were now nodding and murmuring agreement.

Pettigrew nodded as well, and pulled up the day's first lesson on Reaper operation.

He had their attention.

Chapter Fifteen

Just North of the Iraq-Saudi Border, Near Highway 50

Colonel Hamid Mazdaki had managed to get his force down to the Saudi border without word reaching the Saudis, a feat that would have been impossible without the help of the Iraqis. Its government wasn't willing to join in a military action against the Saudis, but it was ready to help with any action carried out by its allies that cut them down to size. In this case that had meant shutting down a road for "security reasons" that saw little traffic anyway because, while it led to the border, it didn't lead to a border crossing. In fact, on the Saudi side there was no road at all.

At first, this had confused Hamid. Why have a road to - literally - nowhere? There were two main reasons. First, Saddam Hussein had built roads to Iraq's borders at multiple points to give him options for invasion planning. As he showed with first Iran and then a decade later Kuwait, seizing his neighbors' territory and resources was never far from Saddam's mind. In fact, this highway wasn't far from Kuwait's border with Saudi Arabia, but for the actual invasion Saddam's tanks had used a much more direct route. Perhaps not surprisingly, the Saudis reacted to that invasion by closing its border with Iraq during the years that followed, even after Saddam's overthrow.

Since Saddam's ouster successor Iraqi governments had maintained all of the roads leading to the Saudi border for a second reason - the hope that the border would someday be reopened. Trade was one goal. Another was that overland travel to Mecca and Medina would be far cheaper for Iraqi pilgrims than flying from Baghdad. For many, it would make the difference between being able to fulfill this religious duty and not.

There was a third minor reason. Smuggling. Iraq's well-organized criminal gangs paid many Iraqi officials well to represent their interests, and smuggling drugs and alcohol to Saudi Arabia was profitable indeed. Roads to the border obviously made their work much easier. Of course, it was hard to say that during parliamentary debates, but ironically making the pilgrimage easier provided perfect cover for legislators with a very different agenda.

Finally, in 2019 the Saudis had opened a border crossing at Arar, at first only for pilgrims. The Arar border crossing had then been opened for trade in stages, and now nearly all of the Saudi military and police presence at the Iraqi border was concentrated at Arar.

Which was why Hamid's forces would be crossing over five hundred kilometers away.

First, though, there was the task of refueling all of Hamid's tanks and armored personnel carriers. The tankers, unlike the tracked armor, would not be able to go cross-country. The Iraqis had provided fuel for his tankers, and now Hamid's force would be able to cross into Saudi Arabia with just enough gas to make it to Riyadh. As a safety margin, Hamid had two supplements.

First, Hamid had fuel drums strapped to every vehicle. Next, Iranian agents in Kuwait had leased tankers, filled them with fuel, and prepared shipping documents showing that they contained specially formulated aviation fuel destined for use by the Saudi military. The documents included the contact name and phone number of a real Saudi military officer, part of the Al-Nahda organization. He would soon learn whether they held up to scrutiny, or if he would risk running out of fuel before his forces could reach the Saudi capital.

Depending on whether or not the tankers showed up at the planned highway rendezvous, once his tanks and APCs had burned through the same amount carried in the drums, they would be emptied in the vehicles before they assaulted Riyadh. Obviously, it would not do to go into battle while carrying the fuel drums, or the results could be...unfortunate.

Once the tankers had been emptied and abandoned, another small group of vehicles appeared, one Hamid had been told to expect only at the last minute. These included several large trucks, an R-330ZH automated jammer, and an unhappy looking technician named Arash Gul along with several assistants, who appeared just as unenthusiastic.

Happy or not, Hamid had to give them credit - they were certainly efficient. Working with his troops, in short order they had installed camouflage netting on all his vehicles that they claimed would make it difficult for anyone to see clearly what type of vehicles they were, or for any radar or infrared homing warhead to successfully lock on to any of his tanks or APCs.

Arash also carried orders from his commanding general specifying that he was to avoid highways in order to take full advantage of this camouflage. Hamid shrugged, since he had already decided to do that, and had even mapped out an overland route to Riyadh. The only points where he planned to cross a highway were his rendezvous with the fuel tankers and when he had to cross Highway 85.

Hamid sighed when he reviewed the weather report, and shrugged. There were supposed to be high winds for the next several days, which would be perfect for his mission. The one thing camouflage couldn't do was hide the dust inevitably kicked up by the overland movement of dozens of tanks and APCs. High wind could, though, by kicking up dust everywhere so they could move south unobserved.

So, Hamid should have been pleased by the weather report. He wasn't, though, because experience had taught him that nothing in war ever went perfectly.

The only question was, just what would go wrong?

Saudi - Kuwait Border Crossing Post at Raqa'i, Highway 50

The fuel tankers Hamid was expecting to join him rolled up to the Saudi - Kuwait border crossing post at Raqa'i in the dead of night, and the driver in the lead tanker handed over papers and passports for all the tanker drivers. He could observe the reaction on the face of the very junior lieutenant who had been handed the documents for review, and it was exactly what he'd been hoping to see.

The lieutenant knew that if he questioned the documents he would have to call, and probably wake up, an unknown number of officers until he found one who knew what he was talking about. Of course, if he really had doubts he would be expected to go beyond calling the phone number on the documents.

Or, if he was satisfied the documents were genuine, he could simply allow entry.

The lieutenant had the cabs of several of the tankers searched. He also had two of the tankers discharge a small amount of fuel so he could confirm that was what they were carrying.

Everything was as it should be.

Finally, the lieutenant waved the tankers through, and went back to his office. Shaking his head, he thought to himself that he'd have to be sure to tell his commanding officer about the tankers when he came in that morning.

For some reason, he remembered an expression used by an elderly history teacher when he was a student - "coal to Newcastle." He'd explained to a class even more bored than usual that coal had been mined near the British town of Newcastle in great quantities for years, so it would clearly be ridiculous to bring coal there from elsewhere.

The lieutenant smiled. The expression obviously needed to be updated. "Gasoline to Riyadh" had a nice ring to it.

He was sure his commanding officer would see the humor.

United States Military Training Mission, Riyadh, Saudi Arabia

Technical Sgt. Josh Pettigrew looked over the dozen students in his classroom, and casually asked, "Who's ready to put hands on a Reaper?"

One of the first tasks Pettigrew had set himself was to instill what he thought of as basic classroom discipline in his students. To his mind, that meant first and foremost that students learn to raise their hands, rather than all trying to talk at once.

Pettigrew was pleased to see that his students didn't make a sound. Instead, he faced a forest of raised hands.

Pettigrew nodded. "Very well. Follow me to the hanger next door."

Two guards stood watch over the Reaper, which Pettigrew had armed and prepared for this session.

"Who would like to identify the weapon closest to the right side of the fuselage?" Pettigrew asked.

Once again, every hand went up.

Pettigrew said, "Mousa," and nodded in his direction.

Mousa said carefully, "It is a GBU-12 Paveway II laser-guided bomb."

"Excellent," Pettigrew said, nodding approval. "Who would like to try for the weapon closest to the left side of the fuselage?"

Pettigrew was pleased to see that every student was still confident they could identify the munition.

"Rahim," he said. "Oh, and bonus points if you notice anything unusual about what I've placed on that pylon."

Rahim now looked like he wasn't so sure being picked was such a stroke of luck. "It is a GBU-38 JDAM, which is short for Joint Direct Attack Munition." Rahim paused. "I think it is unusual because you said that normally the same weapon would be placed on each side of the fuselage, to keep the drone balanced in flight."

Pettigrew grinned and clapped his hands. "Outstanding! That is exactly right. Now, someone else tell me why I could get away with doing this if I decided it was really necessary."

Now no hands went up right away. Good, Pettigrew thought. I've got them thinking!

Finally Fadil raised his hand.

'Yes, Fadil?" Pettigrew said, nodding in his direction.

"Well, the GBU-12 and the GBU-38 should be about the same weight, since both are based on the MK-82 bomb. They just have different guidance packages. So long as the operator is careful, it should be possible to fly the drone safely," Fadil said.

Pettigrew whistled, which he could see immediately confused everyone. He laughed and shook his head. "You'll learn that if I whistle, I'm really impressed. You must have picked up that bit about the MK-82 from your own reading, since we didn't go over it in class."

Fadil simply nodded.

"OK, next out towards the wingtip?" Pettigrew asked.

Now every hand went up again.

"Hakim," Pettigrew said.

"This is the AGM-114 Hellfire II missile, which uses a laser guidance system," Hakim said.

"Excellent," Pettigrew said, nodding. "Now, unless you were familiar with all the types of Hellfire missiles it would be difficult to tell which this was just by looking at it. Let's say I told you this is the latest version. What would that make this one?" Pettigrew asked.

Hakim answered immediately. "That would make this an AGM-114R Hellfire II Romeo RX missile, which has an integrated blast fragmentation sleeve warhead. That makes it possible to use the missile against many different target types, which in the past would have required different types of Hellfires."

Pettigrew grinned and nodded. "Absolutely right. So far you're batting a thousand."

Again Pettigrew saw confusion on the students' faces.

Pettigrew laughed and shook his head. "An American expression that would take too long to explain. It means you've answered every question perfectly so far. But I've saved the biggest challenge for last. What's on the outermost pylons?"

Now Rahim raised his hand again. "It is an AIM-9X Sidewinder missile. But I don't understand the point of putting it on the Reaper. After all, the Houthis don't have an air force."

Pettigrew nodded. "Now, I've had officers who thought exactly that way. Students, am I an officer?"

The students all grinned and shook their heads. Pettigrew had already made this point several times before.

"That's why I am not going to prepare you for the dangers you expect. Because while you're doing that, what you don't expect will come up behind you and kill you. If you forget everything else I teach you, remember that."

The students all nodded solemnly.

"Now, is there anyone out there with an air force that just might want to attack you someday?" Pettigrew asked.

Nearly every student said "Iran" at the same time.

"Has anybody here heard of Pearl Harbor?" Pettigrew asked.

The students all nodded thoughtfully.

"How about Iraq's annexation of Kuwait?" Pettigrew asked.

The students all nodded again.

"I think the point is clear. History is full of examples of attacks that nobody saw coming. How do you prevent becoming a part of that history? To the extent you can, prepare for every danger you can foresee."

Mousa raised his hand, and Pettigrew nodded permission to speak.

"Has this drone ever shot down a jet in combat?" Mousa asked.

Pettigrew smiled. "An excellent question. First, let me point out that easier and perhaps more likely targets for the Reaper would include an enemy drone, a helicopter, or a propeller-driven aircraft. The pilot of a combat jet who knew the Reaper was there and had plenty of time to line up an approach could shoot it down every time. But in a crowded threat environment with enemy combat jets and surface to air missiles it would be easy to ignore the Reaper until it was too late."

Pettigrew saw Mousa becoming restive and laughed. "I know, I haven't really answered your question. The answer is that in 2017 an AIM-9X fired by a Reaper shot down a drone that was attempting to evade it. Those are the only details I can give you about that exercise."

Pettigrew paused. "I will add this, though. This is the Block II configuration of the AIM-9X, which gives you the ability to lock on after launch. That's thanks to the Link 16 data link, which will also allow you to supply targeting information to the missile after launch."

Mousa nodded. "So, we could relay targeting data from the much more powerful radars we have access to at this base, and the missile wouldn't be limited to what its own small seeker head can see?"

Pettigrew smiled. "Exactly. Now, it may be a while before you actually get a chance to fire one of these, but don't you think the AIM-9X is a good option to have?"

Much murmuring and nodding followed among the students.

Pettigrew was pleased, but also concerned. How, he thought, am I going to arrange a chance for these students to fire a Sidewinder at a live target?

500 Meters South of the Iraq-Saudi Border, Near Highway 50

Colonel Hamid Mazdaki leaned over Arash Gul's shoulder and asked in a whisper, "Are you sure this is the right cable?"

The technician was shivering in the cold desert night air, and continued attaching a clamp to one of the wires he had stripped from the cable before responding. Fortunately, Arash had spent years in Iran answering questions from non-technicians, and had seen what happened to ones who couldn't keep their tempers when those questions were stupid.

Plus, Arash knew all the men in the trench they had dug out to reveal the cable were also short-tempered, and armed. Never mind that now that the cable had been revealed, he was the only one here actually doing anything.

"Yes. It is exactly where our informant said it would be, and the cable's interior matches the schematic he provided. As for whether the method he provided works to defeat the alert network, we will only know that for sure once your tanks cross the border." With that Arash checked the device in his hand, and grunted with satisfaction.

"I am now ready to begin recording the ambient noise and images collected by the sensors the Saudis have placed at the border. If our informant is correct, a small group such as ours should not have been enough to trigger an alarm. Still, it would be best if we keep speech and movement to a minimum while I am making the recording we will play back while your force crosses the border."

Mazdaki nodded sharply, and whispered orders to the other soldiers who had dug the trench, who all nodded silently.

Arash nodded and said, "Good. In ninety minutes, it should be safe for your force to cross the border."

Arash pressed the record button, and said a silent prayer.

95 Kilometers South of the Iraq-Saudi Border, Near Highway 85

Colonel Hamid Mazdaki scowled at the report from the scout he had sent down Highway 6262. It was exactly what he'd expected. Well, he supposed at some point the Saudis would have to rouse from their slumber.

Highway 85 ran east to west in northern Saudi Arabia, and it was impossible to travel south towards Riyadh without crossing it. He had men with counterfeit Saudi uniforms set up a roadblock on Highway 85, and had the R-330ZH automated jammer turn up its output to full to prevent anyone fuming at the delay from reporting it.

On the one hand, the proximity of King Khalid Military City helped Hamid. This was not the first time that Highway 85 had been shut down to allow the passage of tanks on exercise, and in the dark he was certain nobody stopped a kilometer away at his roadblock would be able to see that they were not Saudi tanks.

However, there was no way to prevent drivers at the tail end of the roadblock from turning around. Able to drive at full speed, it would not be long before those cars were out of jamming range. If someone in one of those cars happened to work at King Khalid Military City....

Well, apparently someone did, and had called KKMC HQ to ask about armor exercises and why nobody had told the caller they were scheduled. Whoever was in command had then probably sent out a drone, which thanks to his jammers would have stopped sending back pictures long before reaching his force.

An incompetent or simply lazy commander could have easily decided to wait until morning to take action. It wasn't unreasonable to hope for such a commander, either, since KKMC had its forces assigned shrunk dramatically after the Gulf War. It was almost sad to hear from his scout that three M1A2 tanks and three M-113 armored personnel carriers were coming. They would hardly pose much of a challenge to his force.

But if any survived to escape jamming range and report, Hamid knew he could find himself dealing with serious Saudi resistance before he was anywhere near Riyadh. And that wouldn't do.

Though he hated to admit it Hamid's Zulfiqar-3 tank wasn't the best choice to take on an M1A2, especially if he wanted to be sure of a quick kill, particularly at night. The Irbis-K thermal sights on their Russian T-90s, the first Russian-produced mercury-cadmium-telluride (MCT) matrix thermal sight, gave them the ability to identify the enemy at a range of slightly over three kilometers. Reluctantly, Mazdaki decided to also commit his lone Russian T-14 Armata to the ambush, since it was even more capable than the T-90s.

Since he knew from the scout that the Saudis were simply barreling down Highway 6262 towards his position, finding a spot where the terrain allowed his tanks to hide most of their bulk while leaving their cannons free to fire was not difficult. Hamid had eleven T-90s and the Armata take position, so that each target could be hit with two rounds.

It turned out that two rounds were definitely overkill for the M-113 APCs. Hamid saw multiple secondary explosions from all three, and correctly guessed that he was witnessing detonations from the onboard ammunition. Two of the M1A2 tanks were also quick kills.

The third M1A2, though, escaped without a scratch. One of his tanks had simply missed. The other had targeted the wrong tank.

The commander of that M1A2 was no fool. He immediately deployed smoke, and left the highway. Even worse than the smoke was the bright light from the burning and exploding armor in front of them, which made their thermal sights useless.

"After him!" Hamid roared into his command radio. All of the tanks in the ambush moved forward, with the faster Armata in the lead.

In fact, the Armata had a rated off-road speed of ninety kilometers per hour, better than double the M1A2 tank's rated speed of forty KPH. Hamid knew that both numbers, though, were misleading. He was sure the M1A2's commander was having his driver press the accelerator to the floor, and that it was going well over its "rated speed." On the other hand, he knew the Armata's commander would not careen across the unlit desert at its top speed, no matter how important the target.

Nevertheless, Hamid was confident they would catch up to the Saudi tank. But would they stop it before the enemy tank had a chance to send its base a warning?

Only one direction made any sense for the M1A2 tank, and that was back to base. For several agonizing minutes, though, there was no sign of it.

Suddenly, Hamid could see the Armata fire once, and then again. The second time Mazdaki saw with satisfaction that the M1A2 was hit, and had stopped moving. The Armata put one more shell into the Abrams to make sure, and this time was rewarded with secondary explosions that lifted its turret into the night sky.

Hamid tried to calculate how far the enemy tank had traveled. The ambush site was already some distance from the R-330ZH jammer, which had to stay near the roadblock.

Finally, Hamid shrugged. There was only one way to find out for sure. Press forward, and see what sort of a welcome the Saudis had prepared.

Chapter Sixteen

Ghale-Morghi Airport, Iran

Kazem Shirvani and Farhad Mokri climbed out of Kazem's car, and walked to the back of a nondescript concrete building next to an airstrip that had weeds peeking out from it in several places.

Farhad shook his head. "I grew up in Tehran and this place is less than an hour's drive from my parent's house. But I had no idea this airfield was here."

Kazem smiled at Farhad's additional unspoken comment, visible in his expression. "Yes, nothing about this closed airport says 'secret nuclear weapons storage facility'. Of course, that's the point."

The building's back door opened readily to Kazem's key, and in less than a minute they were both standing in front of a framed but faded poster celebrating a cultural exhibition that had happened over a decade ago. The only other thing Farhad noticed in the hallway was an elevator door, but it was at the far end of the corridor.

Kazem carefully took the poster off its mounting hook and set it aside. Now a plain white keypad was revealed, with no clue to its purpose.

Kazem leaned over the keypad so that it was concealed from Farhad's view, and quickly punched in a series of numbers.

Nothing happened.

Then Kazem carefully replaced the poster on its mounting hook.

The elevator door at the end of the hallway slid open.

"Step lively," Kazem said, running for the elevator with Farhad right behind him. They reached it just before it shut again, and squeezed inside.

As the elevator began to descend, Kazem grinned and said, "It's good that you're young enough to keep up. If we'd missed it we wouldn't have been able to try again until tomorrow, and I'm going to need some help with this job."

Farhad noticed that there were no floors below ground level indicated on the elevator's control pad. And, he thought, he hadn't seen a "down" button on the outside of the elevator either.

After a ride that lasted only a few minutes, but seemed much longer, the elevator smoothly came to a stop. The door slid open, to reveal a workspace crowded with equipment and storage cabinets. There were also three of the "glove boxes" Kazem had described to him earlier.

As he opened one of the storage cabinets with a key, Kazem began to explain what they were going to do next.

"All three weapons are completely disassembled both for safety reasons, and to facilitate maintenance. The two designed for ground testing we're going to assemble completely with the exception of a single component. The one that will be dropped by air we will assemble completely. You may be wondering why we will do that one differently."

Farhad simply nodded.

Kazem continued, "The reason is that the countdown for the first two weapons begins when they are completely assembled. Remember that our first goal was to successfully achieve detonation of a nuclear device. Only later were we planning to focus on precise control, for example a detonation that could be controlled with a timer."

Farhad mutely pointed at the two digital timers included in the pile of components Kazem had pulled from the storage cabinets.

Kazem laughed. "You're paying attention! Excellent! Yes, we will be using these timers on the ground test devices. However, the timers will not control their detonations. Instead, they will give an approximate countdown to detonation once final assembly is complete."

Farhad raised one eyebrow and asked, "Approximate?"

Kazem grinned. "Yes, approximate. For each design we have in the digital clock's memory the expected time to detonation. But these are experimental devices. I'd love to be able to promise that our predicted detonation time will arrive exact to the second. But not even my ego is so large. I am confident, though, that detonation will not occur for at least two hours after final assembly for both ground test devices."

Farhad nodded. "And I remember you said that the air dropped device will detonate on impact."

Kazem nodded back approvingly. "Exactly. And that's why we can assemble that one completely. If it works as designed, nothing but the impact of being dropped from a significant height should cause detonation."

Farhad frowned, and asked, "How great a height?"

Kazem shrugged, and answered, "It would not need to be very great, but certainly more than simply letting the warhead fall off a table or vehicle. That's why complete assembly of that weapon doesn't pose a safety risk."

Kazem then directed Farhad on which components to place in which glove box, and while Farhad was doing that, entered a combination on a keypad attached to a safe. The safe opened with a click, and Kazem put on a pair of lead-lined gloves.

Kazem carefully withdrew three small metal boxes from the safe, and placed one each in a glove box compartment that Farhad noticed appeared to have an extra lining. Farhad guessed correctly without having to ask that he was looking at the uranium and plutonium components of the weapons.

Kazem then helped Farhad finish placing the remaining components inside the glove boxes, until finally they were done and Kazem nodded towards one of the two chairs on the floor, placed next to the elevator door.

"I don't need any help putting these together, so you can get some rest," Kazem said, which Farhad thought was a remarkably diplomatic way of saying, "I'd like anyone without a degree in nuclear physics as far away from the bomb assembly process as possible."

Kazem then added, "You're not done, though. Once I finish putting these together, you'll need to help me with the crating process."

Farhad nodded, and moved to the chair. He had no idea what the "crating process" was, but he was sure Kazem would explain it.

Farhad did his best to remain silent and motionless during the several hours Kazem needed to assemble the weapons. Finally, with a satisfied nod Kazem straightened and looked toward Farhad.

"Done with assembly," Kazem said, removing his hands from inside the gloves that gave the glove boxes their name.

Kazem had brought a small bag into the room with him, but Farhad had not asked what was in it. Now with a flourish Kazem revealed its contents.

Two bottles of water.

Kazem smiled and said, "I recommend taking only a few sips before we begin crating. We had to move out from Doshan Tappeh Air Base in a hurry when International Atomic Energy Agency inspectors turned up unexpectedly. This replacement facility was built very quickly, so there was no time for luxuries like plumbing. That means no bathroom until we get back upstairs."

Farhad nodded, and took the recommended few sips of water. Next, they worked to assemble three crates from the pre-cut wooden components and metal hinges Kazem pulled from a storage cabinet. Once the crates were done, Kazem opened up the last storage cabinet and pulled out six pieces of styrofoam, each with an interior cut to size. He placed one styrofoam piece inside each crate. Then he placed each crate on a dolly next to a glove box.

Next, Kazem handed Farhad a bulky one-piece rubberized suit, with a clear plastic faceplate.

"At Doshan Tappeh we had suits we could hook up to a dedicated ventilation system, which had the advantage of helping to remove any radioactive particles that somehow entered the suit. Here, though, we're just going to have to be grateful that at least the air conditioning works."

Farhad nodded, and put on his suit. Within minutes they were both sweating inside their anti-radiation suits as Kazem first opened the lid of each glove box, and then together they each lifted one end of the device into the matching styrofoam indentation inside each crate. Two of the crates were longer than the third, to allow room for a separate indentation in the styrofoam for the component that remained for final assembly. They then placed the matching pre-cut styrofoam piece on top of the weapon, followed by the wooden lid.

After screwing in the lids, they rolled each dolly to the elevator, and took the first one up to the ground level. Farhad had wondered why the elevator was larger than usual when they went down. Now he had his answer.

Kazem looked at Farhad as the elevator moved upwards, and looked at his watch. "I see my estimate of how long assembly would take was just about spot on. Do you think the cargo plane we were promised will actually be waiting outside?"

Farhad shrugged. "I have faith in my organization. I suppose we will see soon enough."

The elevator door slid open, and they rolled the dolly with the first weapon to the rear exit door. Sure enough, a large cargo plane with its propellers still slowly turning was sitting on the runway. As they looked, its cargo door opened, and two rather large men emerged.

Farhad said mildly, "I asked our people to send competent help."

Kazem grunted. "Good. We need to make sure these are well secured."

Farhad nodded and said, "I've asked that everyone on the flight, including the pilots, understand that they must follow your instructions exactly."

Kazem smiled tightly. "Well, considering the stakes, I'm glad you made that clear."

The two men spotted them, and quickly trotted up to the door. After Farhad verified they were the men he was expecting, they took over the dolly and he returned with Kazem back downstairs to retrieve the other two weapons. In less than an hour, all three weapons were secured on board the plane, and they had taken their seats in the front.

Kazem frowned as he tugged on his seat belt to make sure it was secure. "I've never been on a seat that folded against the wall of the plane. I'd always thought it was impossible for there to be less comfortable seats than on Iran Air. I see I was wrong."

Farhad laughed. "My travels for our organization have often included even less comfortable aircraft. One flight I remember well was on an Ilyushin cargo conversion, where all of the seats were made of hollow aluminum tubes and cloth, and attached to the floor with wing nuts.

Before the flight left the ground, a bottle of vodka with no label, a shot glass and a rag were all passed to the front of the aircraft. Each passenger was expected to take a shot, wipe the glass with the rag, and then pass everything to the next passenger. The lone stewardess was on hand solely to replace each bottle as it emptied with a full one. When the last bottle reached the end of the cabin, it was still about half full.

The stewardess took that bottle up to the pilots.

About fifteen minutes later, the slightly slurred voice of the Captain came over the intercom to welcome the passengers. He then went on to describe his exploits in the war in Afghanistan with the Soviet Air Force, including how he had developed a 'combat takeoff' to minimize the chance of a hit from Stinger anti-aircraft missiles, which he proceeded to demonstrate. This turned out to involve taking off nearly vertically, with the aluminum-tube seats bending backward until my head was nearly in the lap of the passenger behind me."

Farhad paused. "Of course, the pilot was alcoholic, and clinically insane. But I did wonder whether he was completely wrong about worrying that someone might use such a missile to attack a commercial aircraft."

Kazem shrugged. "I'm no expert, but it certainly seems possible. I don't think that really explains your Captain, though."

Farhad nodded. "No, it doesn't. Anyway, we weaved our way unsteadily towards our destination, finishing with a 'combat landing.' We hit the ground hard enough that all the overhead bins popped open, showering the passengers with luggage and coats. The plane's landing speed was too high, so that the pilots had to stand on the brakes to stop it, and the cabin filled with smoke and the smell of burning rubber. Everyone was crying, screaming, and praying- even, I'm embarrassed to admit, me.

Finally, the plane came to a stop just short of the runway's end."

Kazem smiled. "Well told. I hereby withdraw my complaint about the folding seat!"

Bushehr Air Base, Iran

Kazem Shirvani and Farhad Mokri exited the cargo plane with relief. Both because it had not been a particularly comfortable flight, and because no honest person could say flying in a plane carrying three experimental nuclear devices was a relaxing experience.

"So, we are not far from the port," Kazem said. Though the Gulf wasn't visible from the air base, the feel of being near a coast was unmistakable.

"That's right," Farhad responded. "Once the trucks are loaded, it should take no more than half an hour to drive to the dock. As you heard, I called and confirmed the boat is waiting for us."

Kazem nodded. Jammed against each other as the plane's propellers were still turning after they'd landed, he couldn't have avoided overhearing the conversation if he'd tried.

Farhad pointed at the first pallet being wheeled out of the back of the cargo plane. "I know we've already gone over this, but please check again. I told them to remove the air-dropped device first, because it's going on a flight to Manama on that plane," he said, pointing to a plane with the markings of a well-known cargo airline.

Farhad continued, "We picked this airport because it is a dual-use military and civilian facility. We can maintain security over the shipment, and it will still appear to be a perfectly routine cargo flight. Since Manama is only three hundred kilometers away, the flight won't take long."

Kazem nodded. "Excellent. And did I understand correctly that we will be traveling together with both ground weapons on the same boat?"

"Yes, we will," Farhad smiled. "Smugglers have existed along the Gulf coast for hundreds or indeed thousands of years, and the Saudis have certainly never managed to stop all of them. Of course, our task has become much easier because many of the Saudis' coastal patrol ships have been redeployed to the Yemeni coast, to attempt to intercept our gifts to the Houthi freedom fighters."

Kazem grunted and trotted over to the pallet that had just been pulled from the plane. It took no more than a glance to confirm that it was the air-dropped weapon, since its design was radically different than the two intended for ground deployment. He looked at Farhad and gave him a thumbs-up. Farhad then nodded and told the man wheeling the pallet to proceed with it to the next cargo plane.

Kazem walked back to Farhad, and watched with him as the other two pallets were removed from their cargo planes with a forklift, and onto a large truck with a built-in liftgate. Kazem noticed that the truck's cab had two doors on each side, and so appeared to have room for several passengers.

"Will we be traveling to the port with the devices?" Kazem asked.

"Absolutely," Farhad replied with a nod. "We're not going to take any chances," he added, as two heavily armed men in plainclothes exited the truck and stood silently in front of Farhad, immediately making him think of soldiers reporting for duty.

Kazem frowned and leaned towards Farhad. In a near-whisper, he asked "Aren't these fellows a little conspicuous?"

Farhad grinned and shook his head. "Here at a military base there's obviously no problem. Even at the port, though we won't be at a naval base we've still made arrangements to secure the pier we'll be using. That particular pier is one of several getting no recent use, because they were damaged in a storm last year. Ours has been repaired, but is still marked as off-limits. Port security has been told to keep everyone else well away from the piers as a safety measure until repairs are completed. So, I doubt anyone will get close enough to pay attention to us before we've gone."

Farhad stopped speaking as the last pallet was loaded, and the back of the truck was secured. Then, he nodded towards the truck.

"I will be your driver for this part of our journey. If you'd like to keep me company up front?" Kazem lifted one eyebrow in response, as they all started walking towards the truck.

"I had no idea truck driving was among your many talents. Is there a story?" Kazem asked.

As they entered the front of the truck, immediately followed by the two armed men in the back of the truck's cab, Farhad shrugged and said, "Nothing especially interesting. This work forces you to acquire many skills. Honestly, I'm just hoping that all of them together will be up to this task."

With that, Farhad smoothly put the truck into gear and set off. As promised, less than half an hour later they were at a pier festooned with warning signs, as were the two nearest piers. There was no boat at the pier.

Kazem opened his mouth to speak, but Farhad shook his head. "The British have a term. Wait for it..." Kazem shrugged, and settled back in his seat.

A few minutes later, Kazem saw a ship was on its way, and realized it must have been tied up at another pier nearby. As it drew near, Kazem became aware of a smell that quickly became overwhelming.

Kazem muttered an oath that drew a low chuckle from the two men in back.

Farhad grinned and said, "They grew up here in Bushehr, so they're used to the smell. We're using a fishing boat, and this is a traditional model without refrigeration. Even with stem to stern cleaning, I don't think you'd get rid of the smell. Not, mind you, that I think such a cleaning has ever been attempted."

As the fishing boat was tying up at the pier, a forklift began moving down the dock towards them. It turned out that the fishing boat had a hold sized for cargo pallets, so while Farhad and Kazem watched, within minutes both devices had been loaded on board. One of the armed men had boarded to watch the operation from that side, while the other faced outward, carefully eyeing the minimal activity nearby. As Farhad had said, no one came near.

Once the forklift had gone Farhad and Kazem boarded the boat, along with the second guard. The boat immediately set off, and Kazem resolved to say nothing else about the smell. Obviously, there was nothing to be done about it.

At Farhad's suggestion, they were sitting on one of the benches lining the boat's outer rail. Farhad had pointed out that this had two advantages. First, if he fell victim to sea sickness the railing was nearby so he could avoid making a mess. Second, the sea breeze helped to carry away much of the smell.

Kazem turned to Farhad and asked, "Are we still on schedule?"

Farhad nodded. "Yes. As planned, it will be dark by the time we reach our landing point on the Saudi coast. That will not be far from the desalination plant at Ras al Khair. We will offload both devices there, and move both by truck to their targets. You will stay with the device going nearby to Ras al Khair, while I will go down to Jubail."

Kazem cocked his head. “Just curious. Why go near Ras al Khair rather than Jubail?”

“Because there’s a naval air station at Jubail,” Farhad replied, smiling.

Kazem winced. “Good answer,” he said.

Farhad clapped Kazem on the shoulder. “Don’t worry. The owners of this boat have paid a certain Saudi naval captain a substantial sum to make sure its unofficial landings aren’t disturbed. Normally the landings are to offload cargo such as alcoholic beverages and other high-value contraband. In fact, it’s such a regular visitor that I think its failure to appear is what would be more likely to attract attention.”

Kazem knew Farhad was exaggerating in an attempt to reassure him, but he still appreciated the effort.

“Well,” Kazem said with a smile, “at least I’m going to achieve one goal I had just about given up on.”

Farhad looked puzzled. “What’s that?”

Nodding towards the boat’s hold Kazem said, “Well, I’m going to see whether these devices I spent so many years designing and building actually work.”

30 Kilometers North of Ras al Khair, Saudi Gulf Coast

The fishing boat slowly scraped its bow onto the beach, and its engine came to a stop. Lights switched on a truck nearby, and for an instant Kazem Shirvani thought they had been discovered by the Saudi authorities. But no commands over a loudspeaker followed, and Kazem quickly realized that loading the weapon on a truck would definitely require light.

Farhad Mokri grinned at his discomfort, but said nothing.

The truck slowly backed up until it was next to the boat. Several men emerged who immediately deployed its liftgate, which they brought nearly adjacent to the boat, and then used to walk onto it. One burly bearded man grabbed Farhad and kissed him on both cheeks, saying “Good to see you, my brother.”

“And you,” Farhad replied, turning to Kazem. “Meet Masud, the leader of the men who will be assisting you with your mission.”

Kazem nodded politely, and extended his hand. Masud ignored it with a laugh, and gave him the same treatment he'd just bestowed on Farhad. "A professor!" he said laughing. "I'm sure you can teach us some lessons."

Farhad grinned back at him. "Well, he's the one who designed and built these, so maybe he can."

Masud's men had been busy helping the boat's crew use a rope and pulley attached to the side of the hold to retrieve the pallet holding the first weapon, and at that moment it came into view.

Masud looked at the weapon and said thoughtfully, "Yes, maybe so."

Within minutes the first pallet had been retrieved and placed in the truck, which then drove a short distance up the beach and shut off its engine and lights. Another truck then started up, and repeated the procedure with the second pallet. Less than half an hour after the boat's arrival, the trucks were ready to go.

Farhad turned to Kazem and said, "Well, uncle, this is where I have to say goodbye. We have been doing reconnaissance at both plants for the last several days, and have seen no increase in security. As long as that's still true today, you should have time to make it back to this boat. They will pretend to be fixing the boat's engine until they see the signal, and know you'll soon be returning."

Kazem frowned. "What signal?"

Farhad just grinned.

Kazem shook his head and sighed. "Still a joker, just like you were as a child. The big, mushroom cloud shaped signal, right?"

Farhad nodded, but then stopped smiling. "Seriously, it is up to you whether to proceed or not depending on what you find when you get to the plant. Masud knows that you are going to decide whether or not to attach the final component, and that call is entirely yours."

Masud shrugged, saying, "No point in making a big hole in the desert. If we can't get close enough in time, then we don't do it."

Kazem nodded, and embraced Farhad. "Good luck, nephew."

Farhad fiercely hugged him back, and said thickly, "To us all."

Moments later, both trucks were on their way to the targets.

2 Kilometers North of Ras al Khair, Saudi Gulf Coast

Masud put down his cell phone and frowned. Kazem Shirvani looked out the truck's window and could guess the reason. Other trucks' taillights were ahead in a line that extended as far ahead as he could see in the weak dawn light.

"I have confirmation that the truck with the other weapon has joined the men and vehicles that will accompany it to the target, and that they are now about as close to the plant at Jubail as we are to this one," Masud said.

Kazem nodded. It was important that all three devices detonate as close to simultaneously as possible. Of course, once one exploded, security across the country would be on maximum alert.

"The truck bomb is some distance ahead of us," Masud said.

Good, thought Kazem to himself silently.

Masud continued, "Men to storm the plant once the gate has been destroyed are several vehicles behind the truck, but still well ahead of us. One problem is that it will now be harder to tell you when to attach the last component to the weapon."

Now Masud paused. "The other problem is that if they're carefully searching every truck, they've probably added guards. It may take us some time to get next to the plant."

Kazem nodded his understanding, but said nothing.

Masud frowned and asked, "I know that you've said the weapon needs to be adjacent to the plant, but does it really need to be that close?"

Kazem shrugged, and replied, "If it works exactly as I designed it, no. But it may be only a partial detonation. If so, unless we're close to the plant it will be damaged, but may be possible to repair. There will also be residual radioactive material from a partial explosion, but that can be cleared with the right equipment and technicians. I'm sure the Saudis can afford to import those."

Masud grunted, "Yes, they can afford everything but justice for the Shi'a."

Seeing the look that Kazem gave him, Masud said quietly, "My wife and daughter were killed by the Saudis at Al-Awamiyah."

Kazem said sincerely, "I am sorry to hear that."

Masud shook his head and replied, "You of all people shouldn't say that. You've given us our only chance to strike back against the Saudi royal family that oppresses us. When the entire city of Riyadh turns on the taps later today and nothing comes out, then they will feel a little of the fear we live with every day."

Kazem nodded. "So, we carry on. I will go to the back and attach the final component."

Masud looked him in the eyes. "You are certain? With the security I'm sure is ahead, I see no way to place the weapon and escape in time."

Kazem smiled sadly and replied, "I never really thought escaping was a possibility. What I want to see now is for my life's work to have some meaning. What you've just told me has helped me to make up my mind that this is the time, and the place."

With that he unbuckled his seat belt and wedged his body between the two seats, before lifting the heavy cloth flap that separated the cab from the truck's cargo bed. Not a brilliant design, he thought, but it will do. Climbing over the metal divider while lifting the cloth flap wasn't easy, and as he made it over he dropped the flap on his head, which made him immediately aware it was covered with mold.

Rubbing his sleeve vigorously across his face, his eyes watering, Kazem had to resist an impulse to laugh. It had just occurred to him that the respiratory illness he would have normally feared would not have time to be a problem.

Kazem carefully inserted the final component into the weapon, and was rewarded with a "beep" and the illumination of its countdown clock. The countdown time was based on Kazem's own calculations. He smiled grimly as he thought he'd never imagined being able to see in person if those calculations had been correct, instead of standing in some distant observation bunker.

The vehicles of Masud's attack force ground slowly forward, while the countdown clock appeared to Kazem to have somehow speeded up. Repeated checks of his watch reassured him that there was nothing wrong with the countdown clock, only with his relative perception of time's passage.

Finally, just as Kazem was beginning to think they would never reach their goal, a brilliant flash followed by a thunderous explosion announced that the truck bomb had reached the gate. The surviving and still mobile vehicles that were not part of Masud's attack force very quickly did their best to get out of the way, and Masud had already given orders to let them go. They were not the target.

From his position inside the truck bed next to the weapon Kazem could see little, but could hear the rapid fire of machine guns and the intermittent sound of pistol fire that seemed to go on for hours, though his watch insisted only minutes had passed. Then the gunfire began to slacken, and their truck moved past what Kazem could see were the smoking remains of the front gate. The desalination plant filled the front window, but Kazem still wanted to get closer in case of a fizzle.

Kazem was just about to tell Masud that they had to hurry because they were nearly out of time, when their truck was rocked by a burst of heavy machine fire coming from...behind them. He just had time to look out the back and see military vehicles flying the Saudi flag when he felt a heavy weight fling him to the truck bed, and the truck grind to a halt.

Kazem could hear the gunfire picking up again, but not for long. Every time he closed his eyes and opened them again the countdown clock display seemed to have jumped backwards. He realized this must be due to drifting in and out of consciousness.

He looked down and could see he'd been shot, but was surprised not to feel any pain. Shock, he supposed.

The gunfire stopped altogether, and the cloth flap on the back of the truck bed flew up. Kazem heard shouted commands, but was unable to move, in fact it was becoming harder to breathe. He could hear rather than see one of the soldiers jump onto the truck bed and then he came into view as he ran towards the countdown clock, just as it reached zero.

Nothing happened.

After several seconds, Kazem could hear the soldier laughing with relief.

Then he heard a "click" from inside the weapon's casing, and smiled.

Through lips just barely capable of making a sound, Kazem whispered, "Boom."

CHAPTER SEVENTEEN

Jubail II Desalination Plant, Saudi Arabia

Anatoly Grishkov scowled as he looked over the defenses at the desalination plant's entrance gate, a scowl that deepened as he saw Alexei Vasilyev smile in reaction.

"If you had any military experience you wouldn't be smiling! Their preparations are totally inadequate, and these idiots won't even let us use our own weapons! These are ordinary security guards who probably have no training to speak of, and if they have any guns heavier than pistols I have yet to see them. What part of 'attack with a nuclear weapon' did these people fail to understand?"

Now Vasilyev couldn't hold back his laughter though, as he knew it would, it made Grishkov even angrier.

"First, my friend, it is true that we handed over our pistols as soon as we arrived."

Now Vasilyev continued in a lower voice. "However, did it not occur to you that I might have withheld a few items in our cars?"

Grishkov frowned. "But they searched both of our cars..." His voice trailed off as he saw Vasilyev's smile broaden.

"But they're just ordinary security guards."

Vasilyev nodded. "Exactly. And it cannot be such a surprise that ordinary security guards fail to take the threat more seriously. Only the commander is Saudi, and he does not believe the danger is real. The guard force is made up of poorly educated expatriates, mostly from Pakistan and the Philippines. Once a determined attack begins, it is likely that many will throw down their guns and flee. I doubt they are being paid enough to feel obliged to risk their lives. Besides, if they've been treated the way most expatriates are here, I doubt they feel any loyalty to their employers."

Grishkov shook his head. "And where are the Saudi military forces we were promised?"

Vasilyev shrugged. "I am sure they will appear at some point, but we must plan on their arrival being too late to matter. Remember, the nearest large military base here on the coast is naval, and they have little in the way of troops and equipment to assist us against a ground attack. Army bases in the region have had their resources diverted to the war in Yemen, particularly after the recent increase in missile attacks against Riyadh. So, we need to prepare as best we can with what we have."

Grishkov nodded glumly. "Very well. And what is that, exactly?"

Vasilyev smiled. "We were directed to park our cars behind the main building 'to keep them out of the way.' Fortunately, with nearly all of the security forces clustered around the front gate, it also means the cars are out of view. While we walk back to them, please give me your tactical assessment."

Grishkov shook his head grimly as they began to walk from the gate to their cars. "Since most of the guard force is at the front gate, the most likely course of attack will kill almost all of them. That is a truck bomb that will detonate as soon as it reaches the gate."

Vasilyev frowned. "On my previous visits I saw that all of the government ministries in Riyadh had serpentine entrances preventing a vehicle from building up speed on approach. They also had pneumatic bollards raised and lowered from the guard post that physically prevented the approach of an unauthorized vehicle. I saw no such measures here."

Grishkov shrugged. "I'm not surprised. Of course the government spares no expense at taking care of itself, and to be fair I've read that government ministries in Riyadh have already been attacked. I'm sure this was considered a much less likely target. Our biggest problem is that trucks are coming and going constantly."

Vasilyev nodded. "Yes, I heard you suggesting to the guard commander that they close the gate to all traffic, and his refusal. "

Grishkov scowled. "The idiot says that the plant needs the supplies being brought by the trucks to operate. I wonder how well he thinks it will operate as a glowing pile of radioactive ash?"

Vasilyev grinned. "I agree that the plant's efficiency will doubtless be impaired. So, how do we distinguish the truck bomb from an ordinary truck?"

Grishkov shrugged. "If a truck comes barreling up to the gate at high speed, that's probably the truck bomb. However, they did have the sense to fence off both sides of the road leading to the gate. So, because there have been so many trucks coming to this plant since our arrival, unless there's a lull in traffic I don't see how one could make a high-speed approach."

Vasilyev nodded. "So, we probably won't know until the explosion."

Grishkov simply shrugged again.

"Very well. What happens after the explosion?"

Grishkov frowned. "An experienced commander would have another truck filled with attackers following a respectful distance behind. He would also make sure that the truck bomb was carrying a shaped charge directing the force of the explosion forward. If he was smart, he would also have several cars following the attack truck with more fighters. Never good to put all your eggs in one basket. The truck with the nuclear weapon would follow those cars, since you obviously want it as far from the truck bomb as possible."

As Grishkov said this, they reached the spot in the back parking lot where their full-size SUVs were parked.

Vasilyev pulled out his keys, unlocked the trunk of the first SUV and pushed down the rear seat. He then pressed a button on his remote twice, and to Grishkov's amazement the entire rear two-thirds of the SUV lifted to the ceiling, revealing a cavernous storage compartment tightly packed with military equipment.

"I anticipated that we would need to stop something the size of a truck. Do you think this will do the job?" Vasilyev asked, pointing to the largest object in a compartment.

Grishkov stared slack-jawed as his gaze followed Vasilyev's finger. "That's a Kornet! How did they manage to fit it in...oh I see, they've divided the launch tube..."

He looked up at Vasilyev and said solemnly, "Old man, if you were just a little prettier I think I'd kiss you. If the other car's contents are anything like this, I may get back to Arisha and the kids after all. And you may live to collect that pension!" he said, punching Vasilyev in the shoulder.

Rubbing his shoulder, Vasilyev grinned and said, "I'm glad you're pleased. I asked Smyslov to have your service file checked for the heaviest weapons you had trained with in Chechnya that could fit in one of these SUVs. He said this variant is only for special operations use, and there are only a dozen or so in existence. What makes it so special?"

Grishkov shook his head. "Where do I start? OK, this is the 9M133 Kornet anti-tank weapon. When you fire it, you can immediately guess why they call it 'Comet'. The launch tube is a bit over a meter long, and this one has been cut in half to fit. You can see they've added a metal bracket to fit the two halves together. I wonder how well the design will stand up to reuse."

Vasilyev shrugged. "That I can answer. I was told this can only be used once. That's why we have just one missile. It's thermobaric, if that means anything to you."

If Vasilyev had thought Grishkov was happy before, now he seemed ready to dance. "Outstanding! I take back every unkind word I said about the Army when I was in Chechnya. This is exactly what we need here."

Seeing Vasilyev's confusion, Grishkov continued, "You see, this is a weapon designed against main battle tanks. Its normal warhead would indeed stop any truck, but being designed to punch through armor it would just keep going after it hit. I've used this several times against enemy trucks in Chechnya, and each time there were survivors. I told any officer I could find that we needed thermobaric rounds, but all they'd say is that we were lucky to have Kornets at all."

Grishkov paused. "I was in a bar a few years ago talking to a friend who was still in the Army, and was surprised when he told me those officers were right. Most units are still using the old wire-guided Konkurs anti-tank missile because the Kornet is just too expensive, especially this latest model with its fire-and-forget capability. So, a model with a thermobaric round that can fit in an SUV? Nothing short of a miracle!"

Vasilyev nodded. "Excellent. Now, I was told that operating this missile is a two-man job?"

Grishkov shrugged. "I wouldn't mind a hand getting it moved to where we're going to set up for launch. We're just steps from a point where we'll be able to view the front gate. We'd obviously be too conspicuous if we set the whole thing up immediately, but we can move the tripod over to the launch point now, and I can assemble the launch tube and secure the bracket. Once the attack begins the rest of the setup will take just a minute."

Vasilyev's eyebrows flew upwards. "Are you sure you can do it so quickly?"

Grishkov laughed. "We drilled with these all the time in Chechnya, and as you saw in my file I used it several times for real. Any time over a minute was a failure, and my record was forty-five seconds. Targeting couldn't be easier - just shine the laser light on whatever you want to go boom!"

Vasilyev nodded. "That sounds simple enough. Now, have a look at what we've got in the other SUV."

Vasilyev then unlocked the trunk of the second SUV and again pushed down the rear seat, and pressed a button on the second remote twice. This time Grishkov was not surprised to see another storage compartment with military equipment, but Vasilyev was pleased to see he was just as happy with its contents.

"A PKM medium machine gun with a tripod mount, and two hundred fifty round ammunition cans! You know, this is such a reliable, deadly beast that I read American special operations forces are asking their manufacturers to make copies. And here's an RPG-7, which I'm guessing is for you?" Grishkov said.

Vasilyev grinned. "These were around when I did my military service, and they couldn't be simpler to use. The best part is, I don't have to be an expert shot. I'm likely to do some damage if I can just point it in the right direction."

Grishkov nodded. "Well put. And I see we have submachine guns and grenades as well. Yes, with these we can give a warm welcome to whoever survives the Kornet."

Grishkov paused. "One thing does concern me, though. We'll be directing all this firepower towards an enemy holding a nuclear weapon. Isn't there a chance we will hit it and cause it to detonate?"

Vasilyev shrugged. "A fair point. However, the technical documents provided by the defector say that though these devices are experimental, they are quite robust. I would advise against a direct hit by the Kornet. Short of that, though, I think we are safe. The bottom line is that if we don't stop the attackers, we know they will detonate the weapon."

Grishkov grunted. "Your logic is unassailable. So, answer this one. If we are able to take out the bulk of the enemy force with the Kornet, what's to stop them from simply detonating the device where they are, even if they're still outside the gate? After all, it's a nuclear weapon. Surely the blast radius would still be sufficient to destroy this facility."

Vasilyev nodded. "True, but only if the device works exactly as designed. Since it is experimental, the documents also say there may be a 'fizzle' which would release far less energy. That could leave the facility repairable, especially if the detonation is at a distance. So, I think the attackers will try to get the device adjacent to the plant if at all possible."

Vasilyev paused. "I hesitate to refer to the documents, since the weapon may have been modified since they were written. But they do specify that once the ground devices were assembled and armed, a countdown began that could not be altered. We focused on our main concern - that meant we couldn't stop it. But I believe it also means they can't do anything to speed up detonation."

Grishkov nodded, pulled out both halves of the Kornet launch tube and began to assemble them. As he fastened the metal bracket securing the two halves together, he asked, "Since the documents say the weapon cannot be disarmed once it is assembled and armed, what do we do if we capture the device intact? We are certain to have only minutes before it explodes."

Vasilyev grinned. "An excellent question, my friend. I see only one real option. See that pier leading out of the end of the parking lot?"

Grishkov squinted and nodded. It was a fair distance away and partly obscured by intervening vehicles, so he doubted he would have noticed the pier without Vasilyev pointing it out.

"It is intended to provide vehicle access to the main water intake pipe for the plant, so equipment can be easily transported whenever maintenance is required. We will use it to transport the weapon as far out into the Gulf as possible in what I'm sure will be a limited amount of time," Vasilyev said.

Grishkov frowned. "Will the water be deep enough to absorb the force of the explosion? Do we risk causing a tsunami, or contaminating all the fish in the Gulf?"

Vasilyev shrugged. "Also excellent questions. This time, though, I can only say I have no idea. But I see no practical alternative."

Grishkov grunted and continued the Kornet's assembly with a snap of its metal retaining bracket. He then put it back as far as it would go in the SUV and pulled out the launch tube's tripod. A few minutes later, the tripod was set up next to a car that Vasilyev noted Grishkov had picked only after careful examination.

"So, what makes this car the perfect place to send this welcome gift to our visitors?" Vasilyev asked with a smile.

"All will become clear in a moment," Grishkov said with an answering smile, as he used a small metal tool to open the locked right front car door, and then turn on the car's electrical power, but not its engine. He then pressed buttons that lowered all of the car's windows.

Next, Grishkov adjusted the tripod's height so that its launch tube mount was level with the bottom of the car window.

"I see," Vasilyev said with a nod. "You will place the launch tube so that each end rests on one of the car doors. But why go to this trouble?"

Grishkov smiled again, but this time there was no warmth in it. "This is a trick we learned the hard way from the Chechens. The use of the car has two advantages. First, the mount is more stable than with the tripod alone, providing better accuracy. Even more important, I have picked the oldest car here, made mostly from steel rather than aluminum and plastic. When our surviving guests respond to our gift, you will be happy to have over a ton of good German steel between you and them."

Vasilyev clapped Grishkov on the shoulder. "I'm glad we decided to stick together, rather than each going to a different desalination plant. Now all we can do is wait."

They didn't have to wait long. Less than ten minutes later, most of the front gate disappeared in a blinding flash of light and roar of sound. After a few moments of silence punctuated by the screams of the few gate guards who had been wounded rather than killed, automatic weapons fire and the grinding gears of heavy vehicles announced the advance of the main attack force.

Just as Grishkov had predicted, a large truck led the way, grinding over the debris that had been the front gate. With the launch tube now attached to the tripod, Grishkov took careful aim, and pulled the trigger.

A loud "whoosh" marked the thermobaric round's firing, and Grishkov was pleased to see that the backblast was not nearly as pronounced as with the rounds he had fired in Chechnya. He glanced backward and was also pleased to see that Vasilyev had followed instructions and stayed away from the launch tube's exhaust. Even better, he had just finished placing the PKM machine gun on its mount, and had attached its belt-fed ammunition.

The Kornet's round lived up to its "Comet" meaning, producing an explosion that was already impressive even before the truck's gas tank ignited. Grishkov could not imagine anyone inside surviving the impact.

Unfortunately, it was not the only vehicle. It was difficult to see through the smoke and dust thrown up by both the truck bomb and the Kornet's round, but Grishkov counted at least three smaller vehicles behind the burning hulk of the passenger truck, and the dim shape of another truck behind them.

Grishkov grabbed the PKM machine gun and began sending rounds towards the attackers, just as he heard Vasilyev's RPG-7 buck beside him. One of the three cars most clearly visible at the gate exploded, and several armed men near it were knocked down by the blast. They didn't get up again.

Rounds began to impact against the car sheltering Vasilyev and Grishkov. However, they could see that some of the guard force were firing at the attackers through the plant's windows, so the attackers were unable to concentrate all their fire on the two Russians.

Vasilyev's second RPG round barely missed another one of the attackers' vehicles, but hit the ground close enough to the men moving forward that its shrapnel badly injured two of them. Grishkov's PKM machine gun was steadily pumping out rounds, not only killing and injuring several attackers but also discouraging an immediate mass run at their position.

"Last round," Vasilyev said, as he aimed the RPG-7 at a car that was still moving forward.

The professional soldier in Grishkov made him shake his head. Once you knew an RPG was aimed at you, the smart move was to bail out of the vehicle and flank the grenade launcher. Driving straight ahead to give the RPG a better target was probably the worst approach.

Grishkov's assessment was proved correct by another explosion. "Not bad, old man," he said, without stopping his methodical sweep of rounds sent by the PKM towards the attackers trying to advance on their position.

Vasilyev said nothing, but was surprised to feel happier than he had in a long time. He was too busy to think about it, but if he had it would have been easy to explain. There was no doubt that, soldier or not, Vasilyev was making a difference in this battle.

Now Vasilyev threw an RGN grenade towards the closest attackers he could see. Designed to take advantage of lessons learned in Afghanistan, it had both a sensitive impact fuse and a time delay fuse. This meant that it would explode when it hit any surface, even water, and after a brief delay would explode even if the impact fuse failed.

The point was to prevent the enemy from picking up an unexploded grenade and throwing it back, which had happened numerous times in Afghanistan.

The RGN grenade also had a limited lethal radius, which at first Vasilyev had thought was a disadvantage. The armorer on the *Admiral Kuznetsov* had then explained that you could keep throwing it at attackers as they came closer without endangering yourself.

From the screams and curses Vasilyev could hear from their perch behind the German sedan, it worked exactly as he'd been told.

The attackers showed they were still in the fight, though, as the car's front windshield exploded in a shower of glass. Several fragments cut into Grishkov's face and arms, which began to bleed freely.

Vasilyev had a medical kit beside him, and tossed Grishkov some gauze. Grishkov used it to wipe the blood from his eyes, and then stuck part of it to his forehead to stop the bleeding that had threatened to interfere with his vision. That done, he continued to fire his PKM machine gun at the attackers.

Only one of the attackers' cars was still intact and moving, and now it accelerated from its position just in front of the truck that both Vasilyev and Grishkov believed must be carrying the nuclear weapon.

Straight at them.

One man in the front passenger seat and another on the rear driver's side leaned their automatic weapons outside their windows and, without even a pretense of aiming, emptied the magazines in their direction.

Grishkov automatically noted that both men appeared to be using an AK-74, or one of its many variants. Any possibility that the prospect of being killed by a Russian weapon might seem ironic was eliminated by Grishkov's service in Chechnya. Nearly all of the weapons carried by the rebels there had been Russian, either purchased or captured.

Though the car was still too far away for Grishkov to see the driver, he concentrated his fire on where he knew he had to be. Seconds later, the car began to swerve just as they could hear some of the AK-74 rounds beginning to impact the front of their car.

Vasilyev tossed another RGN grenade towards the car, though he doubted he would be able to hit the rapidly moving target. He had never heard the American expression that "close only counts with horseshoes and hand grenades," but he would have appreciated its humor, and its accuracy.

Vasilyev's grenade exploded well short of the speeding car, but one of its shrapnel fragments sliced into the car's right front tire, causing it to deflate immediately. Combined with the swerve caused by the mortally wounded driver's slide into unconsciousness, the result was to flip the vehicle.

No one emerged from its interior.

However, Vasilyev learned the truth of a saying attributed to Stalin and used widely ever since, "Quantity has a quality all its own."

One of the hundreds of rounds fired by the attackers had found its mark.

It had lost most of its energy as it punched through both sides of the sedan that had protected them so far. That was the good news.

The bad news was that it had struck Vasilyev in the shoulder, in a spot unprotected by the ballistic armor he and Grishkov were both wearing. It had passed through rather than remaining lodged in his shoulder, but the shock of the impact knocked Vasilyev to the ground, and made him briefly lose consciousness.

When he came to, Vasilyev saw Grishkov's concerned face hovering over him, and felt the bandage that Grishkov had placed over his wound. He was surprised to feel little pain.

Grishkov smiled with relief. "So, you're still with us! Don't they teach you to duck in the KGB?"

Vasilyev licked his lips and said with a tired smile, "Don't you remember? We're the FSB, and we've reformed!"

Grishkov shook his head and his smile faded. "Don't be fooled by how you're feeling now. I've injected you with a combination of painkillers and stimulants that the doctor on the *Admiral Kuznetsov* was very unhappy to give me. We came up with it in the field in Chechnya, for situations where long-term effects took a back seat to surviving the next half hour. I think this is one of those. Now, try sitting up, but do it slowly."

Vasilyev felt a little dizzy once he was sitting upright, but the feeling passed after a few seconds.

"I think I can go on. It sounds like the gunfire is tapering off."

Grishkov nodded. "Yes, the only movement I see is around the truck. Did I see flashbang grenades in that case?"

Vasilyev smiled weakly. "I insisted on packing some. At some point I was hoping we could capture the vehicle with the weapon, and I think throwing regular grenades at it would be a bad idea. Simply strolling up to the men guarding the weapon would probably be just as bad."

Grishkov grunted. "Yes, especially for us. These look odd to me, so please pull out the ones you know are flashbangs from the case."

Vasilyev picked up two grenades. The first had a metal rod with the arming pin, attached to a plastic ball containing the charge covered on top with short spikes. The second had a shorter metal rod with the arming pin, attached to a smooth oblong plastic body. He held the first one up before slipping it into his pocket.

"The first one is the Zarya-3, and the second the RGK-60SZ. Both should be effective at incapacitating the remaining gunmen until we can reach the truck. I suggest we work our way through the parking lot using the cars for cover until we are close enough to be sure of an effective throw. Fortunately, I was not hit in my throwing shoulder," Vasilyev said.

Grishkov sighed and shook his head as he picked up one of the grenades, and pulled the strap of a submachine gun across his neck. Putting his arm around Vasilyev for support, he asked "Why bother telling me the grenade models? Doesn't every second count?"

Vasilyev shrugged as he bent and picked up a submachine gun as well. "Well, yes. I just wanted to reassure you that these really are flashbangs. I understand mistakes can happen in combat."

With a sharp nod Grishkov said, "Fair enough. Let's work our way to the corner of the building, where we'll have some cover when we throw."

Vasilyev hunched low as he shuffled forward with Grishkov, moving carefully forward from car to car. Fortunately, the men around the truck had their attention focused on the guards firing at them from inside the plant's second and third story windows. Since the attackers' car had made its mad dash towards them and hit Vasilyev, he and Grishkov had ceased firing in the direction of the gate, so the attackers assumed they were dead.

In just a few minutes they had reached the corner of the main desalination plant building, and Grishkov took a quick look around it.

"There are still at least three men around the truck, maybe four. We'll have to move fast once we throw these grenades. Are you ready?"

Vasilyev nodded.

"Good. On three. One, two..."

As Grishkov said "three" both of them threw their grenades, and then ducked back behind the building's corner. Even from there, and with their eyes closed and hands over their ears, they had no doubt that the grenades had detonated successfully.

They ran towards the truck as fast as they could, knowing that the attackers would start to recover from the effect of the grenades in less than a minute. When they got there, they found that all of the four remaining gunmen were still stunned, disoriented and unable to defend themselves.

Grishkov and Vasilyev shot them all without mercy. With a nuclear weapon still to deal with, there was no time to waste and no useful information to be gained by taking prisoners.

One of the men had been Farhad Mokri, who became the first of the Iranians who had plotted the attack on Saudi Arabia to die that day.

Grishkov and Vasilyev had been worried that the guards firing from the plant's windows wouldn't take the time to distinguish them from the attackers, but apparently the grenades had helped to establish that they were on the guards' side. Still, they were just as happy that their current position next to the truck's cargo bed happened to shield them from view.

Grishkov shook his head as he saw the size of the device. "It would have been tough to move that thing even if you were uninjured. But with that wound in your shoulder, I don't see how we're going to get it out of the truck and into the water. Think we should take a closer look at it to see how much time we've got left?"

Vasilyev shrugged. "Why waste time, when we know the answer is 'not much'? As to getting the weapon out of the truck and into the water, I'd say let's get it to the pier before the guards decide to join the party and make us waste even more time."

Grishkov was starting to nod agreement when both of them turned involuntarily towards a brilliant dot that had appeared on the northern horizon. In the following seconds it was crowned by a small mushroom cloud.

"The other plant..." Grishkov said, as he felt an arm close around his throat.

"Sorry, my friend," were the last words Grishkov heard as he lost consciousness. He didn't clearly hear Vasilyev's next words, "I made a promise to Arisha."

Vasilyev checked Grishkov's pulse and breathing and nodded with satisfaction. He would be out for a matter of minutes, but it would be long enough for what he needed to do.

Vasilyev pulled Grishkov into the shade of a nearby car, and propped his head up. There was a chance he would still be unconscious when the guards finally emerged from the plant, but Vasilyev was optimistic, especially since he was sure the guards had seen the other desalination plant disappear in a nuclear fireball.

No, Vasilyev thought they would probably consider it a good day to stay indoors, at least for a while.

Wincing, Vasilyev pulled himself up into the truck's driver's seat. Thankfully, the keys were in the ignition.

At first, he had to drive with care around bodies, debris and wrecked cars. Then Vasilyev had to weave the large truck through the parking lot, until he finally reached the exit to the narrow service road leading to the maintenance pier. The road was obviously intended for a smaller vehicle, but he drove carefully and soon was at the entrance to the pier.

Here the problem was the same. The truck would fit on the pier, but just barely. Unfortunately, the solution had to be different.

Vasilyev wasn't going to go slowly and carefully. He was going to launch the truck into the Gulf as far out as he could.

Vasilyev grit his teeth and pressed his foot on the gas pedal, slowly building up speed as the first half of the pier disappeared behind him. He could feel the steering wheel fight him as he wrestled it straight, ignoring the pain in his shoulder pushing its way through whatever drugs Grishkov had used to keep him going this far.

The end of the pier was just ahead. Now, Vasilyev pressed the gas pedal all the way to the floor, and in seconds the truck was airborne, flying out into the Gulf.

Over his long career in Russian intelligence, Vasilyev had risked his life many times, and had been certain in several missions that he would not survive. In each case, he had been pleasantly surprised to find he had been wrong to be so pessimistic.

This would not be one of those times.

The truck hit the water with the full impact concentrated on the front of the vehicle, which crumpled backward into the truck's cabin. There were no airbags inside the cabin, but it wouldn't have mattered in the face of hundreds of pounds of steel occupying the space where the seats had been a second previously.

Vasilyev's body had no time to feel pain before he was not only dead, but covered in water and on the way to the bottom of the Gulf.

Vasilyev had thought about trying to jump out of the speeding truck just before it reached the end of the pier, but had rated his survival chances as low, particularly because he saw no chance of successfully swimming to shore with an injured shoulder.

It would have pleased Vasilyev to know that his choice was correct because not only would he have drowned, but he would have done something much worse. He would have failed in his mission.

The few extra meters out into the Gulf gained by staying with the truck to the end were not so important in shielding the plant and its personnel from the weapon's explosion. They were critical, though, to whether the device exploded at all.

First, the force of the vehicle's impact broke the weapon free of its attachment to the truck bed.

Next, the weapon struck the truck's metal gate before being ejected from the truck, cracking its metal case.

Finally, it settled on the bottom of the Gulf, about three meters deeper than it would have if Vasilyev had tried to jump. Those three meters made all the difference.

The extra pressure provided by that additional three meters meant that sea water was able to force its way through the cracks in the case with enough force to reach the weapons' electronic components before its countdown was complete.

This would not have mattered for an operational, production nuclear weapon, since waterproofing its interior would have been a routine precaution. However, waterproofing had been considered an unnecessary waste of time for test devices that would be detonated on land.

Kazem had also designed this weapon personally, and would probably have been pleased to know that it would have detonated perfectly if Vasilyev and Grishkov had not intervened.

However, since Kazem had now been separated into his component atoms, he never would.

Chapter Eighteen

National Reconnaissance Office, Chantilly, Virginia

Steve Foster had only been working as a government contractor for the National Reconnaissance Office (NRO) for a few months, but he was already looking for other job options. Looking at satellite images had turned out to be a lot less interesting than it seemed in the movies.

Walking into the NRO's headquarters building in Chantilly, Virginia at first seemed to confirm the movie image. The NRO had used its "black" budget status to hoard three hundred million dollars it used to build its headquarters building without any specific Congressional authorization. Unlike most Federal buildings, the computer systems and network architecture in the NRO headquarters were everything Steve could want. Plus, the offices were much better furnished and equipped than anything Steve had seen in his previous jobs, even in the cubicles where Steve knew he could expect to start.

That's where the good news ended. First, Steve had been surprised to find that American satellites did not image every square inch of the planet every second of the day. Far from it. In fact, every image captured was in response to a specific tasking, and there was a highly classified waiting list of image capture requests that did not have a high enough priority - yet - to get a satellite to capture the requested image. The list shrunk whenever another NRO satellite was launched, but new requests seemed to appear almost immediately to take the waitlist to where it had been before.

So, every image Steve was given to review had someone at a US intelligence agency who was waiting for his assessment. Usually, it meant a series of images with a specific question to answer. This latest assignment had seemed pretty straightforward, but it had just turned into something Steve dreaded. One where he had to ask his boss for guidance.

Steve had a vague idea when he started working for his company as a contractor that he would be supervised by a government employee. In fact, almost no Federal employees worked at the NRO. That meant his boss was simply another contractor with more experience than Steve had, which he realized probably described everyone else in the building.

Mark Rhodes had seen plenty of employees like Steve come and go over his ten years with the company. Not many were cut out for the endless search for a needle in a haystack, but until you put a person in the job it was hard to predict whether they would be a good match. Steve had given the job his best, but Mark was expecting him to leave when he found work that was a better fit.

Steve had pulled up a series of images on his monitor to show Mark the problem.

"Someone at the CIA sent me a tasker to review these images to report on the movements of an Iranian armored force that had been deployed in Syria, but was now on its way home to Iran via Iraq. The tasking said that the Iranians had done this many times before, and I was to report back to the requester when the Iranians were back in Iran."

Mark nodded. "Seems straightforward. What's the problem?"

Steve pointed at the third, fourth and fifth images on the monitor. "They disappeared."

Mark frowned. "How big is this Iranian armored force?"

"Couple hundred tanks and plenty of APCs and support vehicles," Steve replied.

Mark shook his head. "This doesn't make any sense. How broad was the image track you received to support this tasking?"

The "image track" was the area covered by satellite images generated to support a tasking. It could cover a few kilometers around a target, or a radius of hundreds of kilometers if multiple satellites provided coverage.

Steve shrugged. "Pretty narrow. Also, I couldn't find any nearby images to review to support the ones for my specific tasking. And they just show the force exactly where they were expected to be - until they weren't."

Mark scowled. "Since all US troops were pulled out of Iraq again last year it's a fairly low priority for image collection. I'm sure the tasking office expected the Iranians to drive straight down the highway in Iraq to the connecting highway in Iran, like they've done many times before. They just wanted to know when they got there."

Steve cocked his head and spread his hands. "What's to stop the tanks from leaving the highway? Don't they have tracks?"

Mark smiled. "Good question. Yes, they do. But their support vehicles don't. Without gas and ammo resupply, tanks aren't very effective. And from where they were last seen, there's not much but Iraqi desert for a long way in every direction."

Steve nodded. "OK, so what should I do now?"

Mark frowned. "You've done everything you can for now. I'll go back to the office that put out the original tasker and ask them how badly they want to find this task force. It'll be up to them to decide the priority on this, and where to look."

National Reconnaissance Office, Chantilly, Virginia

Mark Rhode stuck his head in Steve Foster's cubicle, and chuckled when he saw his surprise.

"That was pretty fast, huh? It turns out the CIA requestor and several levels above him were very interested to hear that Iranian armored force went missing. We've got a dedicated MA-4C Triton mission out of NAS Sigonella to help us find it, with the feed being sent both to us and directly to the requestor."

Mark had never seen Steve at a loss for words, but he was actually pleased to see that Steve understood just how unusual this response was for an intelligence tasking. Tritons could stay aloft for over thirty hours at an altitude of fifty-five thousand feet, outside the range of many but not all anti-aircraft systems. They cost over two hundred million dollars each, and as Navy drones were usually tasked for maritime or coastal missions. Their most impressive capability was combining what ships, planes, and land-based combat vehicles were seeing and broadcasting to create a common battlefield picture, which they could then rebroadcast.

"Your reaction is a lot like mine. I had trouble believing it too. The Triton should be on station soon, so I'm going to run through how this will work. The CIA thinks the Iranians were probably sent north to Iraqi Kurdistan, maybe around Kirkuk, to pressure the Kurds to share their oil revenue with the central government in Baghdad more fairly. The Iraqi central government did that before in 2017 using its own troops. If now they're using an Iranian armored force, it says a lot of bad things about just how much influence Iran has over the Iraqis. So, the CIA will check out images from northern Iraq that would support that theory."

Steve nodded. "OK, so what are we doing?"

Mark shrugged. "Their next idea is that the Iranians doubled back, and are either on their way to the Syrian border or already back in Syria. The CIA has asked us to check out that possibility."

Steve stared at Mark incredulously. "That's ridiculous, and they know it. The Iranians were already in Syria longer than they've ever been, and their replacement force has just crossed the Iraqi border. They'll be in Syria within a day or so. Yes, it's a little smaller. But there's nothing going on in the Syrian conflict that would support the Iranians needing to send their first armored group back to Syria after crossing more than half of Iraq."

Mark nodded. "I agree. But think about the alternatives. The Iranians headed south to Saudi Arabia. Yes, the Saudis have a lot of their forces tied up in Yemen. But I think they'd have noticed dozens of Iranian tanks crossing their border."

Steve said nothing, and just shrugged agreement.

Mark hesitated, then added, "There's only one other direction left. Back across the border to Iran, where they were supposed to go in the first place."

Steve had never lost his temper in the office before, but Mark could see it was about to happen, so he quickly added, "Look, when the CIA told me they were going to task a Triton I reviewed the images you saw myself and didn't see anything either. So, if the Iranians did go home and we just missed them, I'll have my butt in a sling right beside yours."

Steve visibly reined in his temper, and even managed to smile. “Dozens of tanks should be pretty hard to miss.”

Mark was relieved, and grinned back at Steve. “Right. We should start getting images from the Triton any minute. Let’s find those tanks.”

National Reconnaissance Office, Chantilly, Virginia

Mark Rhode and Steve Foster were sitting side by side in the cubicle, and had each been looking at the images provided by the Triton on separate monitors for hours. Mark’s secure cell phone rang, and after a quick look at the caller ID he answered.

All Steve heard was a terse series of “Yes” and “No” until Mark put down the phone with a visible look of disgust.

Steve said nothing, but was obviously curious.

Mark sighed. “The CIA. They’ve found nothing, and wanted to know if we’ve found anything. I told them no.”

Steve nodded. “I was about to suggest that we look south. We’ve looked east and west and the CIA has looked north, so whether it makes sense or not, that’s what’s left. I also suggest we skip the area between the Iraqi highway where they were last seen and the Saudi border. By now, if that’s the way they went they’re either at the border or have already crossed it. Besides, there’s nothing between that highway and the border but desert, so what would they be doing there?”

Mark looked thoughtful for a moment, and finally nodded. “Agreed. You take the sector near the Saudi-Kuwaiti border, and I’ll look at the Saudi border further west.”

Ten minutes later, Steve tapped his monitor. “Take a look at this.”

Mark leaned over and immediately said, “Fuel tankers and supply trucks.”

Steve nodded. "A lot of them. The Triton‘s pass shows no people, and no vehicle movement.”

Mark frowned. “So they abandoned them? Why?”

Steve tapped another key, and brought up an Iraqi highway map with the tankers and trucks appearing as a dot at the border.

Steve could hear Mark's intake of breath. "The highway ends at the border. Only the tracked vehicles could continue. The tanks and armored personnel carriers."

Steve nodded. "That's how it looks to me."

Mark picked up his phone. "Look for them, starting due south. I have to make some calls."

Steve reviewed images for another fifteen minutes, while his boss made phone calls. All Steve had to do was glance at Mark to get a hopeful, "Something?"

Steve shrugged and said, "Maybe. But I'm not sure what I'm looking at. It's dark there now, so the Triton has switched to thermal imaging. There's not enough of a return here to be the Iranian armored force, or even a substantial part of it. It's all I can find, though, and it's definitely moving. It's also moving faster than anything like livestock. Any ideas?"

Mark looked intently at the series of images, and finally shrugged. "Beats me. None of this makes any sense. I'm going to ask for the Triton to take a more detailed look at that specific area. Maybe then we can figure out what's going on."

National Reconnaissance Office, Chantilly, Virginia

Mark Rhode threw down the crust of the pizza slice that was the last of the only food he and Steve Foster had eaten over the previous ten hours. "So," he said, "dawn in ten minutes."

Steve nodded. "And from what we've been told, the Triton should be getting us the more focused look we asked for any minute at whatever's moving down there."

Right on cue, both their monitors lit up with a "feed active" message. Soon a series of high-resolution images appeared, becoming clearer as the rising sun provided more illumination of the landscape.

For a long twenty minutes, all they saw was Saudi desert that looked exactly like the Iraqi desert they had already looked at for hours.

Suddenly Steve pointed at his monitor. "See that, on the horizon?"

It was a formless cloud of dust. The Triton was headed right for it.

Five minutes later, the Triton's cameras were pointed straight at the billowing dust cloud rising several meters from the desert surface.

Steve shook his head. “Why can’t we see anything but dust? I mean, I see shapes and shadows, but I can’t pick out a single tank or APC. Am I going blind?”

Mark frowned. “If you are, I am too. Something’s producing all that dust, and Iranian armor is the obvious candidate. But I don’t see how they could hide from cameras of the quality mounted on the Triton. Anyway, I’m calling it. Until someone comes up with a better explanation for a dust cloud headed south from the Iraqi border, it looks to me like an Iranian armored force is on its way to Riyadh."

Just as Mark reached for his phone, it rang. Again all Steve heard was a series of “Yes” and “No” responses, but this time followed by a "Is that confirmed?", followed by silence.

“OK, we’re not crazy. They’ve been looking at the same images at the CIA, and have reached the same conclusion we did. It makes just as much sense to them as it does to us.”

Steve raised his eyebrows. “You mean none.”

Mark nodded. “Exactly.”

Steve asked, "What were you asking about confirmation for?"

Mark hesitated, and then shrugged. "It will be on the news soon enough. A nuclear bomb took out a desalination plant on Saudi Arabia's Gulf coast. Nobody has yet claimed responsibility."

Steve frowned. "Couldn't this have something to do with the Iranians moving armor south into Saudi Arabia, if that's what's happening?"

Mark shrugged, and replied, "Maybe. But if it was the Iranians, why not just use the bomb to attack Riyadh? I think there's still a lot here we don't understand."

Steve nodded, and said nothing. On that point, they were in complete agreement.

300 Kilometers North of Riyadh

Prince Khaled bin Fahd was furious, and he knew he had to get his temper in check. First, the Crown Prince had tried to forbid him from flying this mission, even after the Americans had sent their alert and after the armored patrol from King Khalid Military City had failed to report in. Only after he had threatened to resign as Commander of the Air Force would the Crown Prince relent, but then only after making Khaled promise that he would do nothing but observe and report.

Khaled had no intention of keeping that promise.

The Houthis had crossed into Saudi territory many times, but there was little near the Yemeni border but desert. Still, they were doing everything possible to punish the Houthis for their arrogance. Khaled was not one of the spineless who cried over dead Yemeni women and children. Children grew up quickly to take the place of their dead fathers. Women gave birth to more fighters.

As long as the Houthis aimed missiles at his capital and invaded his country, as far as Khaled was concerned they all deserved death.

But none of that compared to the Iranians daring to launch an armored assault at the heart of the Kingdom. How could even the Iranians do something so outrageous, and so suicidal?

Khaled took a deep breath, drawing in the fragrance of the rich leather covering the seat of his Eurofighter Typhoon. Of course, the other Typhoons in the RSAF were not so equipped. Khaled had the seat on this particular Typhoon, on which he had trained in the UK, covered with the same leather used on the seats of a top-end Rolls Royce. To their credit, the British hadn't even blinked when he made the request.

This was one of the many things he liked about the British. They knew how things were supposed to be done in a monarchy.

Khaled had been forced to leave Yemen alone in order to avoid disrupting already planned operations. This meant that the three other planes flying with him today did not have men from his squadron, and were flying F-15s rather than Typhoons. Here too, Khaled had been forced to bow to the Crown Prince, since he would have preferred to fly this mission alone.

Still, there was nothing on his radar return, and his threat warnings were all completely silent. Wait, on the horizon, was that the dust cloud the Americans were talking about?

Suddenly, his cockpit was filled with warning lights and alarms, including ones telling him that the enemy below had not only locked on to his aircraft, but had fired missiles at all four planes in their patrol. The other three fighters did exactly what their American training told them to do. Don't wait for orders - evade, deploy countermeasures, and then if successful in avoiding damage either reform and attack or retreat depending on orders.

Well, the truth was that's what Khaled's British training said he should do, too.

Khaled was damned if he was going to let a foreign invader attack him without an immediate response. Where before there had been nothing on his radar, he now had a faint return that was just barely good enough for his Brimstone 2 missile to get a lock. Exultantly, Khaled pressed his finger on the trigger, sending the missile on its way.

The Brimstone 2 was one of the most successful independently developed items of military technology developed by the British in years. Its range had been tripled to sixty kilometers from the Brimstone 1, and it was rated as three times more likely than an AGM-65G Maverick missile to destroy a modern tank.

Outside Europe, Saudi Arabia was the Brimstone 2's only buyer.

In part this was because not many countries outside Europe flew the Typhoon, and even the British had just finished fitting their Typhoons for the Brimstone 2, followed by the Saudis with the help of British contractors in a project that was still underway. The other part was that though the American military was interested in buying the Brimstone 2, its defense lobby had fought hard against importing such a widely used munition.

Khaled had plenty of experience evading surface to air missiles in Yemen, including the SA-75s the Houthis had modified into surface to surface missiles when they weren't firing them at RSAF planes. Many of those missiles had been fired far closer to his Typhoon, and he was still here to tell the tale.

Khaled knew he could do it again. Though he was surprised to see that the invaders had what his instruments said was an S-300, he knew what missiles it could fire, and he knew he had time.

He yanked his joystick to begin evasive maneuvers, but his Typhoon had run out of time much more quickly than Khaled had thought. The Russian-made missile hit the Typhoon with enough force that ejection would probably have been impossible. Hitting the wing that held the other Brimstone 2 and detonating it meant that Khaled literally didn't know what hit him.

Khaled's death was not in vain, though. The Brimstone 2 was a true "fire-and-forget" missile, and it used its 94 GHz millimeters wave active radar homing capability to avenge the pilot who had launched it. Effective against tanks, it made short work of the S-300, which took a nearby armored personnel carrier with it when it exploded.

In a way Khaled was not to blame for his failure to survive the mission. Two of the three F-15s did not survive either. None of the Saudi pilots knew that they were up against a variant of the Kh-47M2 Kinzhal hypersonic missile recently adapted for surface to air launch. Instead of the SA-75's top speed of Mach 3.5, the Kinzhal's speed was...Mach 10.

The only surviving F-15 pilot had escaped by pointing his plane's nose straight down and pulling up at the last possible second. The Kinzhal's speed had worked against it and the missile had slammed into the ground, close enough to the F-15 for the shrapnel from its explosion to damage it severely. Not badly enough, though, that the pilot couldn't nurse it back to base in Riyadh to give his report on the very real threat advancing on the capital.

Chapter Nineteen

150 Kilometers South of the Iraq-Saudi Border

Colonel Hamid Mazdaki frowned and shook his head at the report from the S-300 radar operator. Well, there was their answer. That cursed M1A2 tank had obviously managed to get off a report, because now they had company. The only good news was that they didn't yet know just how large the force was, or they would have sent more than a four-plane patrol.

Hamid wasn't concerned that the four planes inbound could do any real damage to his force. Instead, it was that they would definitely establish it as a real threat as soon as they were shot down. He had been told that the S-300's missiles outranged anything the Saudis had, and so expected no casualties from this engagement.

That expectation lasted less than five minutes, when a tremendous explosion on his force's far-right flank made him and everyone else in his tank instinctively duck.

A dark circle on his command console that had been lit told Hamid what he had already feared from the size of the explosion - one of his two S-300s had been destroyed. Willing himself to calm, Hamid picked up his handset and keyed the commander of the surviving S-300. Since the S-300s had been added to his force just before they crossed the Saudi border, he did not know either batteries' commander.

"Report," Hamid ordered.

"Yes, sir. Commander Khalilli here. Three enemy contacts confirmed destroyed. The fourth appears to be damaged, and is returning to base at low speed." The commander paused. "The other S-300 has been destroyed by an enemy air-to-ground missile. A nearby armored personnel carrier was also destroyed."

Hamid grit his teeth. Better and better. Now there would be an eye witness account of his force's advance. The weather forecast had been for strong winds to whip up enough desert sand to obscure his force's location. Instead, there was nothing but a mild breeze, so thanks to the dust cloud they created as they moved his force's camouflage didn't conceal their approximate size and position.

Or apparently prevent lock-on to an S-300.

"Commander, explain how the enemy was able to destroy one of the S-300s," Hamid ordered.

"Yes, sir. We have to remove the camouflage netting to fire. It was less than a minute from removal to firing, but it seems that was long enough for one enemy plane to get a lock," the commander explained.

"I was told your missiles outrange anything the enemy planes carry. Explain how an enemy plane was able to successfully fire even a single missile," Hamid ordered, trying to rein in his growing impatience.

"Sir, I have two answers to that. The first is that enemy plane was the only Typhoon, and the others were F-15s. The Typhoon had a Brimstone 2 missile, with double the range of any ground attack missile we thought the Saudis had. So, we waited too long to fire."

There was a deadly silence. "Waited, Commander?" Hamid asked quietly.

"Yes, sir. The commander of the other S-300 was my superior. He ordered us to wait to fire until the enemy was well within our engagement envelope, to conceal our true capabilities. I believed that was a mistake, but was overruled."

Hamid considered this. Of course, he could be talking to the commander who made that mistake, and was now trying to shift the blame to someone no longer alive to defend himself.

But, he didn't think so. Like all senior officers, Hamid had plenty of experience listening to excuses, and he could hear real resentment at being overruled in the commander's voice.

"Very well, Commander. How do we keep this from happening again?" Hamid asked.

"Sir, we will obviously engage any enemy aircraft as soon as they are within range. We will also give launch priority to any attacking Typhoon. Now, there is another matter I need to address."

"Yes?", Hamid said, making a conscious effort to control his impatience.

"A drone flying at high altitude has been observing us for some time. My superior decided not to report it to you because he did not wish to reveal our true capabilities by shooting it down. He also told me he considered it a waste of our limited stock of missiles to use one to destroy a drone that is unarmed."

Hamid shook his head. "And how, Commander, could he possibly know that the drone is unarmed?"

"Sir, I agreed with him on that point. Its flight profile, both speed and altitude, match the American drone called Triton. So does the size of its radar return. Also, if it were an attack drone, they would have logically used it against us before sending in manned aircraft. Where I disagreed was with the decision not to shoot it down."

Hamid nodded to himself. Maybe this man wasn't a total idiot. "Explain, Commander."

"Well, sir, thanks to the current low winds we're leaving a dust cloud behind us as we move that gives away our position to the drone, even through the best camouflage. I'm sure you don't want that. I must point out, however, that the drone has moved well away from us since we downed the enemy aircraft. Though we could still successfully engage it, doing so would reveal nearly our entire potential firing range."

Hamid grunted. So, shooting down this drone now would have a cost.

"Commander, can it still see us from its current position?" Hamid asked.

"Oh, yes. From its current altitude of fifty-five thousand feet it can see about two thousand square miles."

Hamid shook his head. "Presumably the Americans can send another if we shoot this one down."

"Yes, sir," the Commander said. "However, from what we know these drones are based in Italy, and so it would take some time to get here."

Hamid made his decision. "Very well, continue to track the drone, but leave it alone for now. The forecast is still for winds to pick up soon, and if they do I'm hoping the drone will lose us. I'm sure the Saudis will try another air attack soon, and this time I don't want any survivors."

"Yes, sir. And there is some good news," the Commander said.

"Yes, Commander? I would certainly welcome some."

"We keep the replacement missile trailers well separated from the launchers, so the total number of missiles we will be able to launch will not be badly affected, particularly since four of the ones the destroyed S-300 had with it were successfully launched. Our rate of fire will be reduced, but if we prioritize the Typhoons I believe we can still protect this force from enemy air attack," the commander said confidently.

"Excellent, Commander. Keep me informed," Hamid said, signing off.

As he stuck his head outside his rapidly moving tank, Hamid could see the oily smoke rising behind them from the destroyed S-300.

Well, he mused, at least there was no reason to doubt the surviving S-300 commander's motivation.

Bahrain International Airport, Muharraq, Bahrain

Abdul Rasool looked at the massive bulk of the Chinook cargo helicopter, and was impressed that they had been able to fit it in the hangar. When he saw the size of the air-launched nuclear weapon being loaded into its cargo bay, he understood why it had to be the Chinook.

Abdul shook his head. The conversation in the Brussels cafe where he'd talked so casually about overthrowing the Saudi monarchy with Farhad Mokri seemed to have happened years ago. Now in a matter of minutes, it would become a reality.

When Farhad had explained to Abdul that the strike they had originally planned against Saudi oil production simply wouldn't work, and that instead they had to attack Riyadh, at first he had resisted the idea. Then, as they had discussed it further, Abdul finally agreed it was the only way to be absolutely sure of ending the royal family's control. The price would be terrible but it had to be paid, especially since there was no guarantee that all three experimental devices would work, or for that matter that any would.

Abdul also agreed that everything depended on a coordinated strike. Once one of the devices detonated, security all over the Kingdom would ramp up automatically. In particular, Saudi air space would certainly be closed to all but military traffic.

Farhad had explained that the bombs' designer had told him the approximate time to detonation for each device. When he'd pressed the designer for a more precise answer, Farhad had told Abdul with a grin that the man growled, "What part of 'experimental nuclear weapons' isn't clear to you?"

Abdul walked up to the pilot, who he only knew as "Mohammed" and who he also knew had been selected personally by Farhad. Farhad had tried to convince Abdul that the pilot's motives for wanting an end to the Saudi regime were even better than his, but Abdul was determined to see this through to the end, though he knew it was almost certainly a one-way trip.

Abdul had spent several frantic days making sure that the assault teams were in place to get both of the other two nuclear weapons to their targets. If this one worked, though, it would extinguish the Saudi royal family in a single blow.

Abdul had seen brave men lose their nerve in the face of certain death, and had tucked a pistol in his jacket in case Mohammed had a sudden change of heart. Of course, there was a brief delay built into the device's detonation mechanism to give a plane time to escape the blast radius.

But they weren't flying a plane, not even a turboprop. No, they were in an old, slow cargo helicopter. That would certainly have every missile and plane the Saudis had pointed at them once the weapon went off, even if the blast didn't catch them. Assuming they waited that long to open fire.

So, Abdul wasn't expecting to survive this mission, and if he had any sense neither did the pilot.

One thing Abdul did know from experience, though. People always instinctively struggled to survive. If Mohammed had a choice between a bullet from the man sitting in the seat next to him and outrunning both a nuclear blast and the entire Saudi military, Abdul was sure he'd pick the latter.

Walking up to the pilot, Abdul asked, "How long before we can take off?"

Mohammed looked up from his clipboard. "The cargo is loaded and is now being secured. I've already received our flight clearance, so we should be ready to go in ten minutes, which will put us right on schedule. So, you can go ahead and take a seat," he said, pointing at a rolling staircase propped next to the open door on the helicopter's copilot side.

Abdul nodded and headed for the stairs. Sure enough, only a few minutes after he'd figured out how to strap himself into the seat's flight harness while being sure he could still reach the gun in his jacket, Mohammed's head appeared on the opposite side. He said nothing, but just sat down and started to flip switches and levers, while the hangar doors opened and a motorized cart began pulling them forward.

Then Mohammed startled Abdul by leaning towards him and yanking on his flight harness at multiple points, until he was apparently satisfied and began putting on his own harness. Seeing that Abdul was puzzled, Mohammed laughed and said, "I'm pretty sure I'm going to be doing maneuvers this old girl was never designed to perform. Having your body fly into my lap would probably interfere with that."

The Chinook was now out of the hangar, and a few minutes later they were on a cargo runway. The cart detached, and once it was well away Mohammed started up the Chinook's engines. Mohammed was pleased to see that the engine started immediately, and within seconds they were airborne and soaring upwards on a course that would quickly take them away from the busy airport.

Now Mohammed had to speak quite a bit louder due to the engine's loud roar.

"I had a chance years ago to speak to a pilot who flew one of these Chinooks in Vietnam. He told me that the first ones to arrive were slow to start, and slow to build up power to takeoff speed. Pilots pointed out this was a problem in a combat zone, but nobody in authority cared. Until a lot of Chinooks started developing mysterious 'maintenance problems' that prevented their use. Finally, a senior officer got the company that made the Chinooks to send technicians to Vietnam, who quickly became guests on combat supply missions. Turned out one replacement part and a few adjustments did the trick."

Abdul smiled and nodded. "Glad to see we're in a proven aircraft. How will we launch the weapon?"

Mohammed pointed at a large switch in the center of the controls in front of them. "This switch lowers the cargo ramp. The weapon is secured in such a way that it won't move in flight, but once I lower the ramp and angle the helicopter it will roll out."

Abdul frowned. "You said we're on schedule. Are you sure we have enough time to reach the target?"

Mohammed nodded. "Absolutely. We don't have many Chinooks left, but this is the best one. It's got parts from five other scrapped Chinooks in it, and I made sure personally that they were the best ones. It's never failed me, and I know it's not going to start today," he said, patting the dashboard.

Abdul smiled and shook his head. He'd heard of pilots and sailors becoming attached to their craft, but hadn't witnessed it before.

Abdul settled back and looked at the desert landscape passing by, and told himself to be patient. Success was only a short flight away.

Jaizan, Saudi Arabia

Akmal Al-Ghars looked like exactly what he was - one of the thousands of dark-haired, whip-thin Yemeni laborers here in the region of Saudi Arabia bordering Yemen. Even with the war, there were still many jobs no Saudi would do, so Akmal was still here.

For years, Akmal had been working as a janitor at Jeddah's railroad station, which was one of the busiest in the country. Then had come the announcement that experienced volunteers were desired who were willing to work at a new railroad station in Jaizan, which would be at the end of a new line near the Yemeni border. Further south from Jaizan the terrain came in two varieties- "hilly" and "mountainous." Neither Saudi Arabia nor Yemen had seen it as worthwhile to spend the money necessary to overcome those obstacles with bridges and tunnels, so from Jaizan the only way south was still by road. Of course, those with money flew to Sana'a from one of the Kingdom's many airports.

Nobody else was interested in making the move to Jaizan, not even the two other Yemenis working at the station in Jeddah. Both of them were single, and had no interest in visiting parents in a country torn by civil war topped with regular Saudi aerial bombardments. To be fair, Akmal thought, they probably thought their parents would prefer the money they sent to seeing their sons. Travel to Yemen wasn't cheap.

Just like those other Yemeni workers, every spare bit of his salary went straight to his family in Yemen. Especially since the start of the war and the collapse of the already shaky economy, remittances were one of the few reliable sources of income available in Yemen.

With his job at the railroad station, Akmal was more fortunate than most Yemenis. He didn't have to worry that his employer might refuse to pay him, beat him, and have him deported if he complained. He had worked hard and been reliable, so that he had been given more and more responsibility. Now he supervised the janitorial staff at Jaizan station, and had recently been trained to perform minor mechanical maintenance tasks at the station.

Akmal appreciated the higher salary and the benefits that came with the promotion. He appreciated even more no longer having to clean the station's toilets.

Though Akmal was Shi'a, for many years he had not had any love for the Houthis fighting the Saudis. Like many Yemenis, Akmal had seen the Houthis as bearing much of the responsibility for the current disastrous state of his country.

Until a Saudi air strike had killed his brother and his entire family. Akmal knew that none of them had been involved in the war, and that their deaths were impossible for the Saudis to justify.

After he attended the funerals, Akmal had contacted the Houthi leader in his brother's village and asked how he could help. He had been surprised when the man said to keep his true feelings about what the Saudis had done to his family to himself, and to redouble his efforts to convince the Saudis that he was a model employee.

When Akmal asked how this was supposed to help him avenge his brother's family, the man had said simply, "The time will come."

Apparently, after months of waiting that time was finally here.

A Yemeni man Akmal had never seen before had come to his tiny apartment, and given him a large package and instructions. The package had turned out to contain bombs made from a plastic explosive, and the instructions were on where to place them in the station to cause maximum damage. The instructions also said he would be told soon which time to set for detonation, along with the helpful suggestion that he be well on his way to Yemen by the time the bombs were set to explode.

At least that part, Akmal thought bitterly, I had already figured out for myself.

Chapter Twenty

United States Military Training Mission, Riyadh, Saudi Arabia

Technical Sgt. Josh Pettigrew hated the idea of a "teacher's pet," and made it a point to give all of his students equal time on the drones. In fact, if anything he would have been tempted to give some of the weaker students more time. Fortunately, the selection process had come through for a change, and even the weakest of this group would be able to graduate with the amount of flight time Pettigrew had planned.

Mousa was neither the best nor the worst of Pettigrew's students, but instead solidly in the middle. Today he was at the Reaper's controls as it did a practice patrol south of Riyadh, armed with two Hellfire missiles and two AIM-9X Sidewinders. His task was to locate the practice targets Pettigrew had placed earlier for the Hellfires, and successfully destroy them.

Pettigrew had still failed to come up with a way for his students to practice with the Sidewinders. Central Command was unwilling to provide enough target drones to give all his students the experience, which Pettigrew grudgingly understood. Target drones weren't cheap. Anyway, he still loaded every Reaper mission with AIM-9X missiles, if only to get his students used to the idea.

"Target acquired," Mousa announced, placing the display's targeting cursor on the tank mockup Pettigrew had his enlisted team set up for this exercise. Pettigrew was impressed, because he'd had his men alter the tank's outline with sand, the same way that blowing sand in the desert often did naturally. It hadn't slowed Mousa down at all.

Murmuring behind him from the students observing the exercise told Pettigrew they were impressed too.

OK, so maybe Mousa didn't belong in the middle anymore. Pettigrew was too modest to even think his students were improving so rapidly because they had an excellent teacher.

"Air contact within our patrol range," Mousa announced next. For this exercise, they had a real-time data link to the powerful American-installed radars covering the Riyadh Air Defense Region. The display next to the ground attack monitor now showed a contact labeled as a Chinook helicopter.

Pettigrew said nothing, and waited to see what Mousa would do.

After a moment's hesitation, Mousa typed rapidly on the keyboard connected to the air defense display. Instantly a line appeared showing the contact's position and projected flight path, as well as its approved flight plan and clearance.

"Air contact is Chinook helicopter en route to deliver equipment for oil field maintenance. Flight plan is approved and contact is on course. Returning to ground target attack," Mousa said calmly.

Pettigrew nodded neutrally, but was actually suppressing a wide grin at Mousa's performance, both to keep from distracting him and to accurately reproduce a real battlefield environment. He doubted he could have done better himself.

"Hellfire target lock," Mousa said. Now the cursor on the display locked to the mock tank turned bright red and a rasping tone sounded. Mousa looked up at Pettigrew.

Pettigrew nodded, but Mousa did nothing. Again Pettigrew had to suppress a grin. This was his version of "Simon says." He had drummed into his students that a nod was never enough to authorize missile fire from a drone, and obviously Mousa had listened.

"Permission to fire granted," Pettigrew said.

After a final check to ensure that the Hellfire remained locked on target, Mousa pressed the trigger that would send the missile on its way. Less than a minute later, the mock tank was a smoking hole in the desert.

Pettigrew watched carefully, and saw with pleasure that Mousa had no difficulty correcting for the sudden imbalance between the weight carried on the drone's left and right wings after the drone's firing.

"Well done," Pettigrew said, and this time didn't bother hiding his smile. "Now, let's see if you can find the second target so easily," raising one eyebrow in a broad hint that this time his men had done more than blow some sand on the target.

Mousa nodded, and swung the drone into the search pattern he had already planned prior to the exercise. The pattern's quality and effectiveness would go into the grade Mousa would receive for this exercise.

Suddenly, a red light flashed on the communications console, and a buzz that made the drone target lock tone seem soothing sounded.

Pettigrew's frown turned to astonishment as he read the announcement on the console.

"OK, everyone, we've been ordered to the closest bunker. Exercise is over. Mousa, there's no time to return the drone. I'll take care of destroying it, and join you as soon as that's done."

Flying the drone into the ground should take less than a minute, and he was sure Mousa could have done it easily. There was no way, though, that Pettigrew was going to let him do it. Not after the news that a nuclear weapon had vaporized one of the Kingdom's desalination plants, with who knew what to follow.

Mousa frowned and pointed at the display showing the track of the Chinook, which had just changed radically. "That helicopter had almost reached the destination on its flight plan. Now, though, it's heading due north. That's a course straight towards Riyadh."

Mousa looked up. "Towards us. Is the Kingdom under attack?"

Pettigrew hadn't wanted to explain what was happening until he had the students more or less safe in the nearest bunker. Now, though, it looked like he'd need to stay longer than he thought.

Pettigrew nodded. "Yes. A nuclear weapon has destroyed a desalination plant on the Gulf. You need to turn over control of the Reaper to me and head with the other students to the bunker. We don't have much time."

Pettigrew's heart sank as he saw the expressions on the faces of Mousa and all the other students.

Fadil spoke first. "We may be your students, but we are also soldiers sworn to defend our country. We cannot hide while we are under attack."

Mousa pointed at a notice on the communications display saying that Saudi airspace had been closed to all but military traffic. "Obviously this helicopter is ignoring orders to land immediately. As a Saudi soldier I have no problem firing on a target refusing to obey this order. As an American teacher, do you have that authority?"

Well, Mousa had a good point there. The kind of "independent thinking and initiative" that had led him here from Korea had helped him to decide automatically to attack the Chinook. But Mousa was right that he had no authority to do so.

"OK, fine," Pettigrew said, shaking his head. "Select one of your AIM-9X missiles as your primary armament. Then search for the Chinook based on the latest radar return. While you're doing that, I'm going to slave the data link from the defense network to the Sidewinder. We're going to launch as soon as we're in any kind of range, and our chances of a good lock will go way up if we're using ground-based radar."

Mousa nodded, already turning the drone towards the Chinook's latest course. Pettigrew was pleased to see that Mousa had increased the drone's speed without any instruction from him.

After only a few minutes Mousa announced, "Target acquired." Quickly and confidently Mousa designated and locked the target, and Pettigrew immediately said, "Permission to fire granted."

The Chinook detected the Sidewinder's attack less than a minute after launch. By that time the drone had flown close enough that it was visible on Mousa's targeting display. The Chinook dropped altitude and began weaving, and to Pettigrew's surprise flares began emerging from the helicopter.

This was good news, in a way. It took care of any small doubt Pettigrew might have had that this could be an innocent helicopter that had just lost its way. Ordinary cargo helicopters didn't carry flare dispensers.

The flares didn't work. Neither did the Chinook's maneuvers. The Sidewinder had been designed to chase down jet fighters, and a cargo helicopter built in the 1960s was simply not a challenge.

The Sidewinder hit the Chinook in its engine exhaust, exactly where the designers would have expected its heat-seeking sensor to lead it. Because of its low altitude, the AIM-9x's explosion was followed very quickly by the Chinook's impact with the ground.

The cheers of Mousa and all the other students died in their throats as the image of the crashing Chinook relayed by the Reaper was replaced by an instant of brilliant light, and then total blackness.

Pettigrew yelled, "Hit the deck," even as he was doing so himself. The other students followed immediately.

Their building bucked under them like a ship at sea hit by a rogue wave, but remained intact. All the lights went out, but after a few seconds returned to life.

Pettigrew slowly stood up, asking as he did so, "Is anyone hurt?"

His students stood up, obviously shaken, but all shaking their heads.

"Based on our distance from the explosion, I'm nearly certain that had to be a nuclear weapon. The power went out for a few seconds because of the weapon's electromagnetic pulse, or EMP. We've only got power back because we're on a military base where all electronics are shielded against an EMP, and we have generators that kick in automatically when civilian power is cut."

Pettigrew paused. "I don't know for sure, but I'm betting that the EMP took out power to the entire Riyadh capital region. I also think that whoever launched this attack is going to do a follow up on the ground. We've got three control displays here. I need three volunteers to help me load and fuel three Reapers to start hunting whatever's coming our way."

Every student's hand shot up.

Pettigrew nodded. "OK, but I also have to tell you I have no idea what kind of fallout is waiting for us outside that door. Size and type of weapon, wind direction- there are a ton of variables that could make the difference between fatal exposure and treatable radiation sickness. All I can promise you is that you definitely will get sick."

Mousa, grinning, raised his other hand. When they saw this, the other students all did the same.

Shaking his head, Pettigrew said, "Very well. Mousa, Fadil, and Rahim. The rest of you get on the communications console and try to check in with headquarters. Find out what you can. We'll be back soon."

Fadil looked uncomfortable, but said nothing.

Pettigrew cocked his head and asked gently, "Something on your mind, Fadil?"

Fadil slowly nodded. "Yes, sir. What should the men say if they reach headquarters, and they ask for you?"

Pettigrew nodded. "Good catch. Wait to contact HQ until I get back. Just find out what you can."

Fadil still looked uncomfortable.

Now Pettigrew smiled. "You're wondering why I'm not contacting HQ first. Well, I'm certain they'd tell us to wait for things like anti-radiation suits to get the Reapers airborne. I'm pretty sure we don't have that kind of time."

This was met with vigorous nods and murmurs of agreement from Fadil and all the other students.

"Good," Pettigrew nodded. "Let's move out."

75 Kilometers Northeast of Riyadh

Captain Victor Chernin probably had more combat air time than any other Russian pilot, which explained why he had been assigned to one of the few S-57 stealth fighters in service. He had flown combat missions in Chechnya, Georgia, Ukraine (though he knew never to admit those last missions) and now Syria. But none of that experience did him one bit of good today.

Because today he was trying to identify, track and destroy enemy air targets. Every mission he'd flown so far had been ground attack, and he had never even seen an enemy fighter.

That wasn't because Chernin didn't want an air-to-air mission. Far from it. But circumstances had not allowed him to use his extensive - and, he was repeatedly reminded, expensive - combat air training. Chechen rebels had no air force. Georgia and Ukraine did, but had with few exceptions decided to keep them on the ground in the face of overwhelming Russian air superiority.

Syria had seen a few dogfights with Turkish aircraft chasing Russian planes that had strayed into their airspace, but those had ended long before Chernin's arrival in Syria. And just like the Chechens, the Syrian rebels didn't have an air force either.

Chernin was expected to pit this total lack of air-to-air combat experience against not one but two J-20 aircraft. He had no wingman, because keeping even semi-continuous coverage of the airspace between the Gulf and Riyadh meant switching off with the only other S-57 stationed in Syria.

The bad news didn't stop there. The Saudis had excellent American-made radars, and were also trained by the Americans both in the US and in-country, where Chernin learned the Americans had been training the Saudis for decades. He had to not only patrol and avoid detection, but periodically turn on his plane's search radar to try to find two J-20s, which were supposed to be the best stealth fighters the Chinese had produced.

However, there was some good news. At the moment the Saudis' radar coverage was overwhelmingly directed towards intercepting incoming ballistic missiles from Yemen, so as long as he remained in his current search pattern east of Riyadh, he was more or less safe from discovery.

Also, while his air-to-air combat experience might be nil, Chernin doubted that the Iranians who were flying the Chinese-made J-20s had much combat experience, period. There was no way that any veterans of the Iran-Iraq war in the eighties were still flying. He'd heard that Iran might have done some bombing runs against ISIS in Iraq, but even that was unsure. Aside from that, Chernin was hoping these J-20 pilots would be completely green.

Chernin was also very happy with the Saturn izdeliye 117 (AL-41F1) engine that had finally been installed in the S-57, replacing the Saturn AL-31. Lighter yet delivering more power, installed in the S-57 it was like trading in a sedan for a sports car.

Finally, Chernin had to grudgingly admit that this time the GRU, Russian military intelligence, appeared to have delivered. He and the other SU-57 pilot had been given a narrow radar frequency range to search that they had been assured would be most likely to reveal the J-20s. Of course, that presumed the Chinese had not subsequently found and fixed whatever flaw the GRU had discovered.

Still, it helped even the odds. And considering that the odds started at two to one, Chernin would take any help he could get.

100 Kilometers East of Riyadh

Colonel Astan Izad was far too senior to be flying a J-20, both in terms of age and rank. High-speed maneuvering in a modern fighter made demands on the human body that were much easier for younger men to meet. Instead, he should have spent his time on planning and monitoring this important mission, including preparation for contingencies in case the mission went wrong.

Astan didn't care. He had joined the Iranian Air Force as soon as he was old enough, but the fighting in the Iran-Iraq War had ended the previous year. Since then, routine patrols and no wars had left Izad with few opportunities to shine. He had no family connections in the Air Force or government, and no sponsor in the clergy.

With forcible retirement staring him in the face, Astan had called in every favor he had left to get assigned to this mission. He had also made sure that his wingman was a first lieutenant who, while an outstanding natural pilot, was far too junior to receive any of the credit from the success of this mission.

So far the mission was totally on track. The two J-20s had crossed into Saudi airspace without detection, and had no trouble locating and shadowing the Chinook helicopter they were assigned to protect. The only real challenge had been following a flight pattern that let them stay in range to protect the Chinook without stalling. It really was remarkable how slow an old cargo helicopter could be, but Astan and his wingman had practiced the necessary flight pattern over the past few days, and had kept up coverage without incident.

Stealth or no, Astan would have been much less confident in their chances if the Saudis' radar coverage hadn't been so firmly focused westward. Well, he thought with satisfaction, it appears the ballistic missiles we gave the Houthis have the Saudis' attention.

Right now Astan's attention was on two F-15s flying combat air patrol over Riyadh. They gave no sign that they had spotted the J-20s, and could be expected to ignore the Chinook since it had an approved flight plan.

The radios on both J-20s were set to monitor 121.5 MHz, the frequency for International Air Distress. As expected, an urgent message was now being transmitted. Astan just wished it could have been about ten minutes later. Well, he'd been warned that with experimental nuclear devices perfect coordination would be impossible. It could have been worse - at least they were within striking distance.

"All aircraft, all aircraft, land immediately at the nearest available airfield. Any aircraft failing to follow this instruction will be fired upon."

As the broadcast repeated Astan switched it off. No mention of why all aircraft were to land, but Astan was willing to bet that one or both of the nuclear weapons that he'd been told were due to detonate on the Gulf coast had destroyed their target. Good.

Now it was Riyadh's turn.

There had only been a few other aircraft on Astan's scope, and they very quickly disappeared from view as each landed. Only the Chinook and the F-15s were now visible, as well as the fact that the Chinook was no longer on its authorized flight path.

Instead, it had turned towards Riyadh.

The F-15s had not only noticed, it was also obvious they had been cleared to engage. Astan murmured to himself "They must be on afterburner," as the range shrank between the F-15s and the lumbering Chinook.

Time to see if these PL-15 missiles with their active electronically-scanned array radar are as great as the Chinese say, Astan thought to himself. Part of maintaining stealth was avoiding radio contact with his wingman, but launching the PL-15s would make it clear to the Saudis that they had visitors anyway.

"Fire one and two, Target One," Astan said over the encrypted frequency he shared with his wingman, as he launched two PL-15s.

"Fire one and two, Target Two," his wingman promptly replied, as he launched two PL-15s at his target.

The range the PL-15s had to cross at Mach 4 was nowhere near its maximum of one hundred fifty kilometers, but it was still far greater than the range of the AIM-120Cs the F-15s were armed with, according to Iranian military intelligence. If that was true, it meant the F-15s would have no chance to fire back, assuming they could even get a lock on the J-20s.

Yes, Astan thought with a smile, this is my kind of dogfight.

55 Kilometers Northeast of Riyadh

Captain Victor Chernin had received extensive briefings on the SU-57's new capabilities, but had until now never used one of them. That was the active electronically scanned array (AESA) X-band side-facing radars mounted below the cockpit on the aircraft's 'cheeks.' These were to supplement the primarily nose-mounted X-band N036 Byelka (Squirrel) AESA radar.

Chernin was about to use these supplemental radars to strike the J-20s using a technique called "beaming," when a fighter turns ninety degrees away from an enemy's pulse doppler radar array. Because such radars use doppler shift to gauge a target's relative velocity, and filter out low relative velocity objects like ground clutter, the beaming fighter can enter the enemy radar's 'doppler notch.'

This blind spot is where the radar's velocity filter sees a target at low enough relative motion from its perspective that it discounts it. So even though the enemy fighter may be moving at high speed, the right angle to the radar means it sees only small amounts of closure, and doesn't display it as a threat.

This tactic was especially helpful when a fighter pilot was trying to lock up his target in a look-down-shoot-down scenario. Ever since he had detected the J-20s several minutes earlier, Chernin had been slowly increasing altitude to reach an optimal firing position, and was nearly there.

Every other fighter Chernin knew of, including the most advanced American ones, would lose the radar picture of the enemy while "beaming." Even worse is that his radar-guided missiles wouldn't have received mid-course updates. With his side-facing radars, though, none of that was true.

The Americans overcame the disadvantage of lacking side-facing radars with AWACS radar feeds sent to all fighters deployed to a combat zone. Chernin smiled grimly as he estimated the likelihood that the Iranians had any such capability deployed for this mission.

Zero.

Just before Chernin was ready to fire, he heard the order over the International Air Distress channel for all aircraft to land, and saw the

Saudi F-15s turn towards the sole helicopter that had ignored the order. Then he saw the J-20s moving to attack the Saudis.

Chernin had only seconds to decide which target to attack. His preference would have been to hit his primary objective, the helicopter now flying straight to Riyadh which Chernin was certain contained a nuclear weapon. But, it was still out of range.

He could have fired a hasty shot at each of the J-20s, which would be likely to miss but would probably distract them enough to save the Saudi F-15s. Chernin never even considered this option.

There were several reasons, first because saving Saudi pilots was nowhere on his orders. Next was that while the J-20s were focused on the F-15s, they were far less likely to notice his SU-57. Then there was the fact that if he saved the F-15s from the J-20s, rather than thank him they would immediately try to shoot him down as an unauthorized intruder.

Most important though was that unofficial Saudi money was one of the main forces fueling the Syrian rebellion, which had cost the lives of several good friends. Chernin would not lose a minute's sleep over the death of two Saudi pilots.

So, wait for the J-20s to launch on the F-15s. Then, fire on the J-20s. By then, I should be able to take out the helicopter, which was using extreme low altitude and terrain masking to make a lock impossible at his current range.

At that instant he saw the J-20s fire on the F-15s.

Excellent, Chernin thought to himself, as he locked in both J-20s and fired his Kh-47M3 Kinzhal missiles. Slightly smaller than the Kh-47M2 Kinzhal missile carried by the MiG-31 fighter to let it fit in the SU-57's internal bay, it sacrificed some range but none of its sibling's Mach 10 speed.

Chernin had an immediate mental image of a big fish eating a small fish, only to be immediately devoured by an even bigger fish.

It made him smile.

70 Kilometers East of Riyadh

Colonel Astan Izad jerked upright as every warning light and alarm in the J-20's cockpit went off at once, informing him simultaneously of the detection of an enemy fighter, and that it had launched missiles at both him and his wingman.

Astan went from gloating over the two F-15s' imminent destruction to attempting to survive in an instant. He saw to his horror that the enemy missile was closing on him impossibly fast - according to the J-20's instruments, nearly Mach 10! How could he escape?

Ejecting before impact passed briefly through Astan's thoughts, but was instantly rejected. Astan knew that even if he survived ejection and landing, he would certainly be captured. Then, the only question would be whether the Saudis would take the trouble to torture him prior to execution.

As the distance between Astan and the two missiles remorselessly closed, he could think of only one chance.

His wingman was doing what his training told him to - separate from Astan, make radical changes in course and altitude to confuse the missiles' instruments, and deploy flares and chaff when the missiles neared.

Astan flew directly to his wingman. Very quickly Astan heard over his headset, "What the hell are you doing?"

Once his wingman's plane had begun to fill his windscreen, Astan pulled up and released a string of flares and chaff that lit a path to the other J-20, and then veered off as sharply as he could.

Astan heard a snarled, "You son of a" which was cut off by the thunderous explosion of his wingman's plane as it was hit by both Kinzhal missiles.

Astan's J-20 had automatically tracked the source of the two missiles that had just killed his wingman, and he now had a lock. Izad quickly punched out his last two PL-15s. Let's see you escape two of the best missiles the Chinese make, he thought savagely.

With that, he turned his J-20 back east to home base in Iran, and started to increase speed. The two Saudi F-15s had disappeared from his scope, and had almost certainly been destroyed. With no missiles left, he could do nothing more to help the helicopter carry out its mission.

Except, Astan thought grimly, to serve as a distraction for whoever had killed his wingman.

20 Kilometers South of Riyadh

Captain Victor Chernin had watched the drama unfold on his scope as he closed the distance to the helicopter, and shook his head in disgust as one of the Iranian pilots deliberately sacrificed the other to escape his second missile. The two Saudi F-15s had dropped off his scope, presumably destroyed.

Chernin was starting to ready another Kinzhal missile for the surviving J-20, when all of his threat warnings sounded. The J-20 had fired two missiles at him, which according to his instruments were the very capable P-15s. And then immediately turned east towards Iran, and home.

This left Chernin with a choice. Spend the seconds necessary to launch on the J-20, which was probably no longer a threat, and more than likely was leaving the battle because he was out of missiles. Or, conserve the missile for use against his primary target in case his other remaining missile missed.

One argument for attacking the J-20 was that it could carry up to six P-15s, if it used its external hard points in addition to its internal bay, and so might turn back to attack him. If it had those extra missiles, though, it would probably have been easier for Chernin to detect.

None of this made Chernin decide to send another Kinzhal missile after the J-20. He simply couldn't abide the thought of a pilot continuing to draw breath who had so brutally betrayed his wingman.

That done, Chernin had to put his faith in the SU-57's digital radio frequency memory (DRFM) jammers to blind the PL-15's radar seeker heads. He had been told they were the most advanced DFRM version available. He could only hope they would be good enough.

Chernin now turned his attention to the helicopter, which he was annoyed to see had made more progress towards Riyadh than he had expected. He then saw the Reaper drone on his scope, and its launch of an AIM-9X missile at the helicopter.

Well, at least now Chernin was sure he could get a lock if the American missile missed, and if he had time before the PL-15s' arrival. He was close enough now that extreme low elevation and terrain masking would no longer save the helicopter.

Chernin only had time to wonder what was causing a bright light to envelope his aircraft, before thought and existence both ceased.

He would never know that the last Kinzhal missile he had fired had done its job, or that his DRFM jammers might have stopped one PL-15, but never two.

Chapter Twenty One

Doha, Qatar

Emir Waleed bin Hamad frowned as he read the news reports coming out of Saudi Arabia in his favorite penthouse apartment. Something was happening, but nobody seemed sure exactly what.

Prince Bilal bin Hamad strode into the room without knocking. If anything, Waleed saw, he was frowning more intently than him.

"So, do you know anything more than what's on the news?" Waleed asked, gesturing at the several TV screens with news programs he'd set to close captioned.

Bilal nodded. "Al-Nahda's man contacted me. He says that three targets were attacked with nuclear weapons. As we heard on the news, two were desalination plants on the Gulf coast. One of those attacks was successful, but the other was not. He didn't know whether the weapon failed, or there was some other problem. The third exploded in the desert south of Riyadh."

Waleed scowled. "So, they were lying about avoiding mass casualties."

Bilal shrugged. "Maybe. But my contact says the explosion was deliberately well outside Riyadh, and that its purpose was to knock out power to the capital through an electromagnetic pulse."

Waleed grunted. "An EMP. I've heard of them. So, do you believe Al-Nahda meant it when they said they would avoid mass casualties? Can we trust them, or are they lunatics we need to avoid?"

Bilal looked as uncertain as he felt. "The desalination plant that was destroyed was not near a city of any size, and it looks like the only people killed were working at the plant. The other plant was not far from a city of nearly a million, but we don't know how powerful that weapon was, because it didn't go off. I understand some are quite small."

Waleed nodded grimly. "And Riyadh?"

Bilal shrugged. "It looks like some workers in an oil field south of Riyadh were killed. The prevailing winds blew most of the fallout into the desert. The EMP has cut power to the entire Riyadh region, and the loss of one desalination plant has led to an order to use water solely for drinking and cooking. Not that I think gardening and filling swimming pools are probably high on anyone's list at the moment."

Waleed spread his hands. "Yes, but you're not answering the main question. Did Al-Nahda intend to attack Riyadh and fail, or was the EMP the purpose as they claim?"

Bilal nodded. "You're right, that is the real question. The answer is I don't know. The EMP explanation is plausible, but it could be that Al-Nahda intended to destroy Riyadh and hoped we'd still go along with their attack."

Waleed sighed. "Yes, and in spite of everything I've said, it would have been tempting."

Seeing Bilal's horrified expression, Waleed quickly added, "I didn't say I'd give in to that temptation. I may have trouble resisting sweets and some of my cooks' less healthy dinner creations. Mass murder of our fellow Muslims, even if it gives Qatar a strategic advantage, is another matter. So, do you or don't you believe Al-Nahda?"

Waleed could see Bilal's relief at his answer. "I don't know, but when in doubt, I say look to the facts. The facts are that Al-Nahda has used all three of its nuclear weapons, and the result is that the Saudis are weakened, with casualties that are at worst in the hundreds."

Waleed nodded doubtfully. "And what about the mysterious force that is supposed to join our tanks in attacking Riyadh?"

Bilal shrugged. "That's a little more clear. My contact says it's an Iranian armored force that until recently was deployed in Syria, and turned south on its way home. He claims that they have already destroyed a Saudi armored patrol from King Khalid Military City, and shot down several Saudi planes attempting to attack it."

Waleed frowned. “Shot them down? With what?”

Bilal smiled. “Now there is more than their word to go on. They used two S-300s armed with hypersonic missiles.”

Waleed just stared at Bilal. “And why should we believe them?”

Bilal’s smile grew wider. “Because two S-300s, hypersonic missiles and their crews have arrived on a ship in our harbor. I saw them myself just before I came here. I ordered them unloaded, because whatever you decide I think we’ll need them.”

Waleed nodded. “Agreed. So, the armored force is Iranian. The S-300s weren’t put on a ship by terrorists. Is this, then, an Iranian invasion?”

Bilal shook his head. “I don’t think so. If this was an all-out attack by Iran, they have ballistic missiles and aircraft that we could expect to see join the attack. I think Al-Nadha has the support of a faction of the Iranian government. Or ‘Al-Nadha’ is a cover name for that faction. Either way, the question is the same. Join them, or watch and wait?”

Waleed said nothing, and looked out at the lights of Doha spread out below. Finally, he turned towards Bilal.

“Well, they certainly kept their promise to break the blockade. They’ve used three nuclear weapons, but avoided mass casualties. And now they’ve given us the means to protect our armor from air attack.”

Waleed paused. “I don’t think we’re going to get a better chance to end the blockade for good. Order our tanks to execute the planned attack on Riyadh, in coordination with the Iranian force.”

Bilal nodded. “How many tanks do you want to send?”

Waleed shrugged. “All two hundred, brother. If we fail, keeping a few back will do us no good. And commit all our air assets to protect them. The S-300s can’t do the job alone.”

Bilal smiled. “Agreed. I hope this will finally end the Saudis’ attempts to strangle us.”

Waleed nodded. “One way or another, I’m certain it will.”

Jubail II Desalination Plant, Saudi Arabia

Anatoly Grishkov returned to consciousness with his eyes still closed, and his head pounding. He next realized that he was sitting against something, which hard metal against his back told him was probably a vehicle.

Someone was standing in front of him.

With his eyes still closed, Grishkov slowly moved his right hand towards his holstered gun.

Grishkov would not have been surprised by either a blow or a bullet in response. Instead, he was more than a little surprised to hear a laugh.

Grishkov opened his eyes to see the smiling face of the Saudi guard force commander. Vasilyev had dealt with him, and Grishkov didn't even know his name. When the man had refused to take them seriously, Grishkov had decided there was no point in learning it.

Then he saw the man was holding his gun. With relief, as his eyes regained their focus he saw the commander was in fact holding the gun towards him.

"I didn't want you to shoot me out of reflex as soon as you came to," the commander said.

Grishkov nodded as he holstered his pistol and slowly stood. A sensible precaution.

"Where is my colleague?" Grishkov asked.

Now the smile disappeared from the commander's face. "One of my men saw him drive a truck off the end of that service pier," he said, pointing towards the water.

The commander paused. "Did it contain the nuclear weapon your friend was telling me about?" he asked.

Grishkov nodded grimly. "Is there any sign of him or the truck?" he asked.

"No," the commander said, shaking his head. "I have just had a report back from two men I sent to the end of the pier. They said that if he hadn't been seen driving the truck into the water, we'd have no way to know he did it."

Grishkov scowled. "You will have men with the appropriate gear check more thoroughly?" he asked.

The commander nodded. “Yes. There is a naval base not far from here, and divers are already on their way. But I think you’ll be gone by then.”

As he looked around, Grishkov could see Saudi troops and armored personnel carriers securing the scene. Well, better late than never, he thought acidly.

”What do you mean, ‘gone by then’?” Grishkov asked with an even deeper scowl.

“I’m sorry, of course you don’t know. A helicopter is coming to take you to a Russian carrier off our coast. In fact, I think that’s it now,” the commander said, pointing at a rapidly growing dot in the sky.

Now Grishkov simply looked stubborn. “I’m not leaving without my friend.”

The commander nodded. “They said you’d probably say that. I am to relay to you that your superiors wish to keep the involvement of your country from becoming generally known. They also said to tell you that your friend would have approved of this.”

Grishkov could feel tears stinging his eyes, and savagely brushed them away. Damn Smyslov, he knew the only thing to say that would make me agree to leave without at least bringing back Vasilyev’s body.

The Saudi troops had cleared an area for the helicopter to land, which Grishkov could now see would happen within seconds.

The commander hesitated and then said, “I along with everyone else here have been ordered to never say more about today than we succeeded in repelling a terrorist attack.” Then he pointed at the horizon, where a mushroom cloud was still rising. “I and those of my men who survived the attack know that we will be going home to our families only because of your friend’s bravery. We know he was not of our faith. But we will always keep him in our prayers.”

Grishkov nodded, and shook the commander’s outstretched hand.

As Grishkov boarded the helicopter, he wondered whether these nuclear attacks were now finished, or if this was just the beginning.

Jaizan, Saudi Arabia

Akmal Al-Ghars was nervous. It had been two days since he'd been handed the bombs, but he still hadn't been told to plant them. There was little danger that the Saudi police would search his tiny apartment, but having the bombs a few meters from his bed had made it difficult for him to sleep.

A soft knock at the door made him jump. He had been about to leave for work, and as he went to the door, he hoped it would be word that the time had come to plant the bombs.

Akmal cracked the door open, and the man who had given him the bombs quickly slipped inside. He had never given Akmal his name, not that Akmal particularly wanted to know it.

"You must plant them today," the man hissed in a low whisper. "Remember the instructions. You must set them where we told you, the timers must be set to go off after an hour, and you must plant them in the order we told you. Tell me the color order," the man said impatiently.

Akmal sighed. He might be a janitor, but he could read, and each bomb had a small but unmistakable piece of colored plastic next to the countdown clock. "Red, blue, and then green. I will not fail you."

"Good," the man said. "You will be met after you cross the border, and both you and your family will be rewarded."

Akmal hoped that was true, but certainly wasn't counting on it. First things first, he thought. I have to try to make it across the border within an hour, which isn't impossible, but will take some luck.

Aloud he said, "I have to get ready to leave now if I'm not to arrive late for my shift. Today of all days, I don't want to do anything that might attract suspicion."

The man nodded approvingly. "Go with God," he said, and slipped out the door as noiselessly as he'd entered.

Akmal had a large bag he'd carried for years in Jeddah, and now here in Jaizan. In it he had his lunch, a bottle of water, and a complete change of clothes. Before he'd become a supervisor he'd nearly always needed to change at the end of his shift to get access to any bus or taxi to return home, since after a day of scrubbing toilets paying the fare wasn't enough. Even as a supervisor, sometimes his new maintenance duties left him covered in enough oil and grease that he faced the same problem.

Today the bag was quickly emptied, and its contents replaced with the three bombs, covered with a single shirt. Since becoming a supervisor Akmal had never been searched, though he was still required to go through the metal detector. Though ordinary employees were required to hand over their bags for inspection, as a supervisor Akmal had been told to just hold the bag with him while he walked through the metal detector.

The man had told him that the bombs contained very little metal, and certainly not enough to set off the detector.

Akmal hoped that was true, and at the same moment realized that particular hope was becoming a habit.

He willed himself to calm as the taxi dropped him off at the train station. Most days he took one of the minivans that in Jaizan passed for the buses Akmal had been used to in Jeddah, but today he really wanted no chance of being late.

It was anticlimactic when the bored guard simply waved him through the metal detector, which as the man had promised remained gratifyingly silent.

Akmal went to his "office," which was really just an old desk set against the wall at the end of the maintenance corridor. Though Akmal had plenty of paperwork such as time cards, salary worksheets and work orders to deal with, nobody in charge of designing this new station had thought the maintenance supervisor would need an office.

Well, after today he wouldn't, Akmal thought grimly.

Checking to make sure nobody else was in sight, Akmal swiftly placed nearly all the contents of his large toolbox on his desk, and placed the bombs inside it.

Not for the first time, Akmal thought to himself that the planners behind this bombing knew their business. Each bomb location, like the main transformer junction box routing city power to the station, was designed to not only make the station impossible to operate but time-consuming to repair.

Akmal was certainly glad he wouldn't be around to deal with the repair work.

As he planted each bomb and carefully set the timer, Akmal wondered idly why the man had insisted on their being placed in color order. The only thing that made sense was that the bombs were different strengths and needed to be matched to a particular target, but to Akmal it looked as though each contained the same explosive charge.

Well, I guess understanding isn't so important, Akmal sighed as he placed the last charge and set the timer. His last thought as everything around him was filled with white light and a tremendous noise was that he had made a mistake.

In fact, Akmal's only mistake had been in trusting the men who had designed and provided him with the bombs.

Seconds after the last bomb Akmal had placed detonated, the first two also exploded, as they had been instructed to do by the radio signal sent from the last bomb Akmal had planted. This was why the color order was so important. The clocks were only present to reassure Akmal that he would be able to escape after setting the bombs.

The bombs' designers saw nothing evil or treacherous in what they had done. The man planting the bombs would never be of further use to their cause, and had information about their organization that he would certainly reveal under torture. So, he had to be silenced.

Hundreds of Yemenis were dying of hunger caused indirectly by the Saudi blockade or directly by Saudi bombs and bullets every day. One more Yemeni death was a tiny price to pay to ensure the victory that their Iranian friends promised would come soon, and finally force the Saudis to leave Yemen forever.

Ministry of Defense, Riyadh, Saudi Arabia

Army Commander Prince Ali bin Sultan was starting to feel like a ping-pong ball. Within hours of his return to Yemen, he'd been handed a summons from the Crown Prince to return to Riyadh for another urgent conference. Adding to his annoyance was that Khaled bin Fahd, the Air Force Commander, had forced him to take the same Bell helicopter back to Yemen that had brought him to Riyadh. He'd said he "had a few errands to run" and that "no aircraft were immediately available" for a flight to the combat area in northern Yemen.

Well, they'd certainly found one for the return flight to Riyadh. Ali had been put in the back seat of an F-15E, piloted by a grim fellow who hadn't said a word the entire flight. Ali assumed that was because he was in shock, as they all were, at the attacks on the Kingdom by two nuclear weapons.

Ali looked around the conference table and frowned. Where was Khaled?

The Crown Prince strode in, looking even grimmer than the pilot who had brought Ali to Riyadh. Ali once again assumed it was because of the nuclear attacks, but quickly found out there was even more bad news.

Just behind the Crown Prince walked a pilot in a flight suit that looked new. The pilot failed to match his suit, sporting bandages on his neck and right hand, and was clearly exhausted.

As soon as they were both seated, the Crown Prince looked around the table at the assembled high-ranking military officers, and soberly said, "I am sorry to tell you all of the death in action of Air Force Commander Prince Khaled bin Fahd."

A stunned silence fell over the room.

"I'm sure you're all thinking that the commander was shot down in Yemen. He wasn't. His plane was destroyed north of here. Sitting beside me is the only survivor of the three planes that accompanied the commander, Captain Hadi Al-Joud. I will let him tell you what happened, and then you may ask him questions. In view of his condition, I have asked him to remain seated for this briefing."

Hadi made a visible effort to collect himself, and then quietly and clearly described what had happened when they encountered the SAMs. Once he concluded, Ali asked the first question on all their minds - "Can you tell us anything more about the force you encountered?"

Hadi shook his head, clearly frustrated. "I could see a dust cloud that was caused by the movement of a large force. My guess would be armor, but none of my instruments registered tanks or anything else. I don't know how the commander got a lock, but like I said I saw him fire on one of the SAM launchers. I didn't say this before, but I'm pretty sure he hit one."

A growl of approval went around the room. At least the commander had been able to hurt the enemy before his death.

Ali nodded and asked gently, "What makes you think so?"

Hadi gave an exhausted shrug. "I was trying to regain control of my plane after it was hit by shrapnel from a missile explosion. While I was doing that I'm pretty sure I saw an explosion somewhere in that dust cloud."

Ali frowned. "I'm no pilot, but couldn't that have been the missile hitting the ground, or some smaller target?"

Hadi shook his head decisively. "No, sir. For me to see it from my distance it had to be a large explosion, and the only thing I think could account for it would be a SAM launcher and some of its missiles."

Ali nodded. "Do you think there was more than one launcher?"

Hadi looked at him angrily and said, "Give me another plane, sir, because I'd sure like to find out!"

The Crown Prince put a hand on his arm. "I saw what was left of your last plane, Captain. You did well to make it back to report on this new threat. Now, rest while we decide how best to attack these invaders. I will see to it personally that you get a chance to avenge the commander's death."

An approving murmur passed around the table, and Hadi rose unsteadily. Everyone knew, though, that he would not welcome assistance. The Crown Prince leaned towards the aide seated next to him and whispered, "Make sure he reaches his bunk," as Hadi made his way to the conference room door.

Once the pilot was gone, the Crown Prince looked around the room. "Now I will tell you what little I know. I sent out those planes in response to a report from the commander at King Khalid Military City, who said he had sent out a patrol with three M1A2 tanks and three APCs last night to investigate a report of armored maneuvers he hadn't authorized. He got a report back from one tank of an enemy armored force that was cut off before any detail was provided, and has heard nothing since. He wanted authorization to send out his remaining forces in pursuit, but I ordered him to stay put until we can assess the threat."

The Crown Prince paused. "Make no mistake, we will respond. But we will do so in a way that guarantees victory." Heads nodded around the table. Only a fool rushed pell-mell into an enemy's arms.

"The Americans have passed us images collected by one of their drones that show a large force is headed south towards Riyadh. They don't tell us much more than Captain Al-Joud was able to see with his plane's instruments. Whoever they are, the enemy has found some way to conceal themselves from both optical and electronic sensors. We have asked the Americans if they have any idea how this could be done, but have not yet heard back from them," he concluded.

Ali shook his head. "After this and the nuclear attacks, we must return all the armored forces we just sent to Yemen immediately."

The Crown Prince nodded. "Yes. I have assumed command of the Air Force, and ordered most of our planes to return to Riyadh from Yemen, excepting only those already pursuing the most promising reports of ballistic missile sightings. I presume you will move our armored forces back by rail from Jaizan?"

Ali shrugged. "Correct. As you know, our C-130s can't move our M1A2s, and only a single M-113 APC. I wish the Americans would agree to sell us some of their C-5s. Those could take two tanks on each flight."

Now it was the Crown Prince's turn to shrug. "Well, yes. But as I've told you, so far they haven't even sold C-5s to their NATO allies. For now, we will just have to make do with transport by train."

Ali nodded. "I'll get my men on it immediately." Then he hesitated. "You said that the Americans have used one of their drones to provide us with images of the invaders. Could they use some of their armed drones to attack them?"

The Crown Prince spread his hands and said, "I have asked. To sum up a long discussion, the Americans are willing in principle to help, but want to know first just who they are attacking. There is also a practical problem. Their drones use weapons with either infrared or radar guidance. Somehow these invaders can avoid both. Until either we or the Americans can solve this puzzle, I don't think we can count on much help from them."

Ali grunted. "Very well. I'm going from here directly to our armor headquarters to prepare an attack on the invaders. Once we put shells into their tanks and capture some prisoners, we should be able to get answers to some of our questions."

The Crown Prince smiled, but looked worried. "I agree, but keep your eyes open. None of this makes any sense, and we need to understand what the enemy hopes to achieve. Yes, the images from the Americans show a sizable invasion force, but certainly not large enough to make a serious attempt at occupation. We are missing something, and need to understand what that is."

Ali nodded. "Understood. As soon as we engage the invaders, I'll report back on what we find personally."

The Crown Prince nodded. "I would expect nothing less." Then he paused and added, "Good hunting, Ali."

A low and approving growl sounded around the table that would have made Colonel Hamid Mazdaki very uncomfortable had he heard it.

CHAPTER TWENTY TWO

Route 615, South of Al-Hofuf, Saudi Arabia

Lieutenant Salah Beydoun was in charge of two other highway policemen at the roadblock preventing travel south on Route 615. It wasn't the first time the route had been closed, because its main purpose was to connect eastern Saudi Arabia with Qatar through the Salwa border crossing.

So drivers had been annoyed, but not particularly surprised, when they were politely told to travel south via Highway 75 instead. If they were driving as far as the United Arab Emirates, that meant having to cut across east on Highway 10. Anyone with a map could see that Route 615 was much shorter.

But Highway 75 and Highway 10 were far superior, both in original construction and subsequent maintenance, and could be safely driven at about double the speed possible on Route 615. Since Route 615's main purpose had always been to allow travel to and from Qatar, the blockade had meant that the only reason to even keep it open was to make it easier for Saudi tanks and APCs to travel to Salwa to enforce it.

Of course, tank treads weren't especially good for highways.

So, most drivers had figured out that though longer, Highway 75 and Highway 10 were the best way to get from eastern Saudi Arabia to the UAE.

Thankfully, anyone with enough money to have a car in Saudi Arabia also had a smartphone. That meant word traveled fast to other drivers via several apps that provided updates on traffic conditions. After the roadblock had been up for about an hour, traffic to it had nearly ceased.

However, Salah could see that a car was now coming, and his heart sank as he saw it was a highway patrol car. Since it was a late model car and in excellent condition, Salah also knew it contained a senior officer.

Fortunately, he appeared to be alone.

"Fortunate" because though Salah was indeed a real highway patrol officer, the two men with him were not. Instead, they were fellow Saudi members of Al-Nadha that Salah had provided with the appropriate uniforms, which had not been difficult for an officer to obtain.

Just beyond the stretch of highway visible from the roadblock, within half an hour two hundred Leopard tanks were going to start refueling from tankers for their final push to Riyadh, after having already traveled one hundred fifty kilometers. And they were going to do it without being detected, as long as Salah could keep this roadblock in place.

"Captain Harbi! Good to see you, sir," Salah said, with all the enthusiasm he could muster. It wasn't easy, because Harbi was the last person Salah wanted to see. A stickler for regulations, if he sensed something was up this operation could go wrong very quickly.

"Lieutenant, who ordered you to set up this roadblock? And why don't I know these men?" Harbi asked, his eyes squinting with obvious suspicion.

"Why, Captain Badawi, sir. Didn't he tell you? And the men were just transferred to us from Dhahran last week," Salah said, trying to act - but not overact - puzzled. Captain Badawi was Salah's direct superior, and Salah knew he had the day off. He was also well known for not taking kindly to being called on days off for anything but genuine emergencies.

"No, he didn't. He didn't note the order in the duty log, either," Harbi said flatly.

Salah shrugged. "I'm not surprised, sir. He got a call from Riyadh just before he went off shift last night. Something about an incident in Salwa, and that we needed to keep traffic away from there. So far, it hasn't been a problem, sir," Salah said, waving his arm at the empty road in front of them.

"Humph," Harbi said, obviously unsatisfied, but seeming at least a bit less suspicious. "So, where is your motorcycle? One should be here, according to regulations."

Harbi was referring to the motorcycle that was supposed to be available to let a patrolman pursue any vehicle that doubled back upon spotting a roadblock ahead. Such a vehicle was presumed to be carrying contraband of some sort.

"Well, sir, since we're turning everyone back at this roadblock, it seemed like a waste of resources to have a motorcycle here. I can have a patrolman go back to the station to get one, sir," Salah said, as politely and respectfully as he could.

Harbi was silent for a moment, and Salah was beginning to worry that he'd laid it on a bit too thick. Then he startled Salah by clapping him on the shoulder and exclaiming, "Good thinking, Lieutenant! I wish more young officers thought about avoiding waste."

After another look around at the roadblock, the three highway patrolmen and the empty road, Harbi was evidently satisfied. To Salah's immense relief, Harbi turned and began to walk back to his patrol car.

As he did, Harbi pulled out his cell phone and said over his shoulder, "In fact, Lieutenant, I'm going to call Captain Badawi and tell him what a good job you're doing. Officers shouldn't only hear about their men when they've made a mistake."

Salah leaned down over Captain Harbi and checked to make sure he was really dead. Satisfied, he holstered his pistol. Salah wasn't sorry to have been forced to kill him, but was concerned that at some point soon Harbi's absence would be noted.

With the help of one of the other men, Salah got Harbi's body and his car out of sight of the road, which remained blissfully empty.

Minutes later, Saleh could see an armored personnel carrier moving north towards them. By the time it arrived, Salah and his men had moved the roadblock aside. Two other APCs pulled up right behind it, as well as a Leopard tank.

The top hatch on the Leopard opened, and an officer looked at the three men in highway patrol uniforms, finally focusing on Salah. "Your name?" he asked flatly, and with an accent that said "Qatari" to Salah. Of course, so did the insignia on all of the vehicles.

"Salah Beydoun," he answered. The officer nodded and asked, "You are all Saudis?"

Confused, Salah simply nodded.

"Good. You all have vehicles?" the officer asked.

Until Captain Harbi's arrival, the answer would have been, "No." Now, though, Salah could say, "Yes."

The officer nodded. "Good. The vehicles all have outside speakers?"

Now Salah could see where this was headed. Did the other men from Al-Nadha? A quick glance told him the answer was yes.

Aloud Salah also said, "Yes."

The officer said calmly, "You need to drive well ahead of us, and tell anyone you find on the highway that they need to exit immediately for their safety. This will clear the way for the force which will be arriving shortly." The officer's eyes narrowed. "What you will tell them also has the virtue of being absolutely true."

Looking at the officer and his Leopard tank, Salah had no doubt of that.

Armored Force Headquarters, Riyadh, Saudi Arabia

Army Commander Prince Ali bin Sultan was surprised to see the Crown Prince at the Armored Force Headquarters. He had just climbed out of the M1A2 tank he'd been inspecting, and had planned to be underway within half an hour. Ali was about to tell him so, when the Crown Prince shook his head.

"We need to talk," the Crown Prince said. Ali shrugged and pointed to the nearest door. In a few moments, they were seated in an empty briefing room, surrounded by maps of the area where the invaders had last been sighted.

"The train station at Jaizan has just been bombed. It cannot be used to bring back our tanks by rail," the Crown Prince said.

Ali slapped his knee in frustration. "We just finished building that line! There's no other station with the equipment needed to load M1A2 tanks between there and Jeddah. We're going to have to drive those tanks all the way back here!"

The Crown Prince nodded. "Yes. I have already ordered police to close the highways between Jaizan and Riyadh to civilian traffic and clear all vehicles already on those roads. This will take time, but will still be faster than having the tanks come back cross-country."

Ali shrugged. "Yes. Not to mention that they'll get here in better shape. But we'll need every fuel tanker we can get our hands on, and some of those tanks are going to need work before we can put them into combat. The trip is over eleven hundred kilometers long."

The Crown Prince nodded. "True. That brings me to even more serious news. We have reports that the Qataris have crossed our border with their Leopard tanks, as well as support forces. They appear to be headed north to Riyadh."

Now Ali simply stared at the Crown Prince in astonishment. "Leopards? How many?"

The Crown Prince shrugged. "It looks like all they have. About two hundred."

Ali shook his head. "And where are they now?"

The Crown Prince frowned. "The latest report puts them on Route 522, which means they're already past Al-Hofuf. The invaders to the north are going cross-country, probably because using a highway would make them easier to locate and target."

The Crown Prince paused. "The only good news is that whatever the northern invaders are using to mask themselves, the Qataris don't have it. That's probably why the Qataris decided to go straight down our highways. It means they are the more immediate threat."

Ali frowned. "Why are you here delivering this news in person? Why are our intelligence people not briefing me and my officers instead?"

The Crown Prince nodded. "I understand your confusion. You are an officer, and so think first of military necessity. I must think of political necessities as well. If news of two invading forces becomes known throughout the Kingdom before we have a victory to report, we face panic and uncontrolled mass evacuation at best. Those cars will slow your tanks' return to Riyadh, and interfere with the movement of the tanks you have in Riyadh to the battlefield."

Ali looked at the Crown Prince bleakly. "And at worst we could face rebellion."

The Crown Prince shrugged. "I don't think it would happen right away. But yes, if the invaders make it to Riyadh, our legitimacy as a ruling family would be questioned. And frankly, I can't say I'd blame anyone who did."

Then the Crown Prince looked at Ali directly. "But we're not going to let that happen, are we?"

Ali gave him a grim smile in response. “No, we’re not.” Then he paused. “If the Qataris don’t have the ability to mask themselves, can we get the Americans to attack them?”

The Crown Prince shrugged. “Maybe. I’ve asked their President, and he’s talking with his generals now. Since they lost their bases in Qatar and Bahrain, anything the Americans send will be coming from some distance. I’ll let you know if the Americans are able to attack before you reach the Qatari force.”

Ali nodded. “Well, at least now we know this is a real attempt to overthrow us. I still don’t think we know who’s really behind it, though. Certainly not the Qataris.”

The Crown Prince shook his head. “No, they’re just a tool. Whoever sent the northern invasion force is running this show. The obvious candidate is Iran, but if it's them why not use their ballistic missiles and air force?”

Ali stood up. “If I’m going to stop the Qataris in time to find out who that is for sure, I have to get moving.”

The Crown Prince stood up as well, and together they hurried out of the headquarters building.

Qom, Iran

Colonel Arif Shahin had been skeptical when Grand Ayatollah Sayyid Vahid Turani had told him he believed Acting Supreme Leader Reza Fagheh would imprison him and the rest of the Assembly of Experts as part of his plan to take permanent control of Iran’s government. After all, he’d thought, how could such a drastic step be justified?

Well, it turned out, by the threat of retaliation for a nuclear explosion on the Saudi Gulf coast. The Assembly of Experts Secretariat building was indeed a logical target, and from what he’d learned there had been no real resistance to the Ayatollahs' movement to a “bomb shelter.”

Which is where Arif was headed now, at the head of a platoon of Rakhsh APCs, each holding two crewmen and eight heavily armed soldiers. Two of the APCs had a 12.7 mm machine gun mounted on a rotating turret, while the other two had a 30 mm autocannon.

It was 3 AM, and Arif was confident that most of the men theoretically "guarding" the Ayatollahs who made up the Assembly of Experts would be fast asleep. As a regular Army officer, he had a low opinion of the professionalism of the Pasdaran. They might have exactly the same APCs and hand weapons, but because of what he saw as their poor training and discipline he would sincerely prefer one of his platoons to four Pasdaran units.

Arif could have used heavier tracked Boragh APCs for this mission, but had picked these wheeled Rakhsh APCs instead precisely because they were used primarily by the Pasdaran. He had sped through two checkpoints on his way to the building where the Ayatollahs were being held without challenge, simply by keeping himself and all of his other men with their regular Army uniforms inside the vehicles and out of sight.

Once his Rakhsh had turned the corner to the final street, Arif gunned its engine and was upon the Pasdaran guard unit in seconds.

Arif was sure he'd achieved surprise when he saw a cigarette drop nervelessly from the mouth of the Pasdaran officer now standing next to his APC. As Arif had been told, it was one of only two Pasdaran APCs stationed outside the building holding the Ayatollahs. Arif had just popped the hatch and lifted himself out high enough that the officer could see his regular Army uniform.

Arif demanded, "What is your name and rank?"

The man automatically replied, "Guard Captain Izad Pishdar."

Arif nodded. "Good. You are in command of this unit?" he asked.

Izad's head bobbed up and down, as he looked at the four APCs, from which several dozen heavily armed soldiers were now rapidly emerging.

Arif nodded again. "Excellent! You stand relieved. You and your men are to return to base. We will take over guard duty for the Assembly of Experts. Here is your copy of the orders."

Arif held out a copy of the orders that had been prepared for the operation, including the genuine signature of an Army general and the expertly forged signature of the Pasdaran Tehran region commander, a region which included Qom.

Izad frowned and shook his head. "I will have to confirm these orders with my headquarters."

Arif's expression hardened. "You can read for yourself that the orders place me in command from the moment I arrive, and that you are to return to your base immediately. You are welcome to check with your headquarters while you are en route. Considering the hour, I think it will take you some time to reach the Pasdaran commander who signed these orders."

Now Izad looked even more stubborn. "I don't care what this paper says; we're not moving until I get confirmation from headquarters."

Arif had expected it to come to this, and all his men were ready. At his hand signal, the machine guns and cannons on all four APCs wheeled towards the two Pasdaran APCs and the few men outside them, including Izad. At the same moment, the thirty-two soldiers simultaneously pulled back the slides on their submachine guns. The loud "clack" echoed in the cool night air.

Arif's smile had no warmth in it all. "Captain, I have my orders and I intend to obey them. I strongly suggest you and your men get inside your APCs and head back to base, where you can confirm that you have done the same."

Izad looked like he was about to say something, but thought better of it, and instead started to climb into his APC.

Just as Izad was about to climb inside, Arif called across to him. "Oh, and Captain, please make sure that your APCs' weapons stay pointed away from my vehicles. We wouldn't want any...accidents."

With one last scowl, Izad's head disappeared inside his APC, quickly followed by the other Pasdaran men outside. The two Pasdaran APCs' engines rumbled to life, and a minute later they had turned the corner and were out of sight.

Buses had been driven to a public parking garage the previous day, and the drivers were now back in them, waiting for Arif's command. He now lifted his radio handset and gave it, and then climbed down from his APC to begin the hardest part of this mission.

"What's grumpier than a sleepy Ayatollah?" sounded like the beginning of a really bad joke. He had to get the Ayatollahs on the buses that would take them to a nearby regular Army base and safety before the Pasdaran came back in force.

Arif hoped he could convince the Ayatollahs to go with him in time.

Chapter Twenty Three

The White House, Washington, DC

President Hernandez walked into the Situation Room at the White House thinking yet again, "I really wish I could spend less time here."

As a former businessman, he had run for office with an agenda focused almost entirely on domestic affairs. Hernandez had been alarmed by the shortage of workers with even basic literacy produced by what had been one of the world's best educational systems. Collapsing bridges, potholed roads, trains that either derailed or if carrying oil actually exploded, and airports like JFK that guaranteed a visitor's first impression of the US would be negative were just a few of the problems Hernandez was determined to fix.

But it seemed like the rest of the world didn't care how he wanted to focus his time, or America's resources.

"So, somebody set off a nuke that wiped out a Saudi desalination plant, another exploded within sight of Riyadh, and two separate armor forces are on their way to the capital. The Saudis are asking us to help. That leaves me with two questions - Who's behind all this, and what can we do to help the Saudis?"

General Robinson, the Air Force Chief of Staff replied while signaling to a Colonel to stand up. "Sir, we've prepared two briefings that will do our best to answer both questions, one at a time. I'll say up front that there's still plenty of questions left to answer, but we think we know enough to prepare an effective response."

Half an hour later, the President leaned back and shook his head. "When you said there were still unanswered questions, you weren't kidding. It seems pretty clear that somebody suckered the Saudis into putting a lot of their armor into Yemen, and then blew up a train station to make it harder to get back. Somebody blew up the Saudi armored force blockading Qatar. Somebody set off two nukes in Saudi Arabia, and tried to make it three but were stopped."

Hernandez paused and shook his head again. "Both we and the Saudis think Iran is behind all this, but we have no real proof, and Iran's politicians are denying involvement at the top of their lungs. One of the armor groups headed to Riyadh has a camouflage capability we think they somehow stole from us, but we don't know how. And since both armor groups put together don't have the men or tanks needed to occupy Riyadh, even if they get there it's hard to see what they could hope to accomplish."

Secretary of State Fred Popel stirred, and Hernandez nodded in his direction. "Do you think you know, Fred?"

Popel shrugged and said, "This is only a guess, sir, but I think they plan to cause enough damage in Riyadh to spark a rebellion. If, for example, they succeed in destroying one or more royal palaces and maybe kill one or more princes it would probably be a mortal blow to the Saudi family's claim to be the Kingdom's legitimate rulers."

Hernandez nodded. "So, there are probably Saudis in on this, who plan to use this invasion to take over?"

Popel nodded. "I think that's a good guess, sir. But who knows who would end up on top. Probably nobody we want to see there."

Hernandez winced. "Yes, that's how it always seems to work out whenever there's a revolution somewhere. And we certainly don't want a government in charge of a large chunk of the world's oil reserves that owes a debt to Iran. Or even worse, answers to it."

Hernandez paused. "OK, so what are we going to do about it?"

General Robinson nodded to the same Colonel, who gave another half-hour presentation.

Hernandez nodded at its end. "Well, if these Kinzhal missiles are the threat you say they are, I agree we don't want our planes anywhere near them. Now, you said the drones we're planning to use are experimental. How likely do we think they are to work?"

General Robinson frowned. "The honest answer, sir, is that we don't know. But our testing so far has had excellent results, or we wouldn't be recommending deployment. I have to stress, though, that they will only be effective against the Leopards coming from Qatar. They won't work against the fully camouflaged force, so the Saudis are going to have to stop it on their own. Also, we're certainly not going to bag all two hundred Leopards, because it looks like some of them are equipped with a camouflage netting supplied by a European company. But we're sure we'll thin them out some."

Hernandez shrugged. "Well, at least we're not risking any of our pilots. Mission approved."

Hernandez paused. "One question about the Reaper that the Saudis used to bring down that nuke before it reached Riyadh. I thought we just sold those to the Saudis. How were they able to deploy them so fast?"

General Robinson coughed. "That's...a long story, sir. I learned the details on my way here, and I'd like to have some more time to look into it."

Hernandez settled back and fixed Robinson with a baleful stare. Everyone else in the room was very happy not to be its subject.

"Oh, I think we have time, General. Why don't you tell us what you know so far?"

When Robinson finished, Hernandez shook his head in disgust. "So, this US Air Force NCO and his Saudi students shot down the helicopter carrying the nuke just before it reached Riyadh, and the American General commanding USMTM ordered them to return their Reapers to base, and relieved the NCO from duty?"

"Sir, the NCO says one of his Saudi students fired the missile that brought down the helicopter. Other than that, yes, sir," Robinson said, glumly.

"And do you think relieving the NCO and grounding the Reapers was the right response, General?" Hernandez asked quietly.

Robinson shook his head. "No, sir. Regulations may have technically justified those steps, but when millions of lives are at stake we have to use judgment, not just blindly follow what's on paper. At least, that's what I expect from any officer, let alone a general."

"Well put, General Robinson. I will let you deal with that situation, and look forward to your report." Though he took his responsibilities as commander-in-chief very seriously, Hernandez made it a point never to interfere with the chain of command.

But nobody in that room expected a certain General to keep his rank or his command much longer.

"In the meantime, General, don't you think it makes sense to let their NCO instructor and his Saudi students have the Reapers back? Personally, I think shooting down a live nuke should be enough to qualify for graduation, though I'll admit I'm no expert in that area."

Robinson nodded. "Actually, sir, I'd just been thinking that this really falls under 'battlefield commission'. I intend to order that all of the students receive immediate certification as Reaper operators, with any further training needed to follow as soon as their instructor decides they are no longer needed for Reaper operations. I also intend to order that their US Air Force instructor provide his students with any support needed as they operate the Reapers we have sold to the Saudis."

"Excellent, General," Hernandez said.

Next Hernandez turned back to Secretary of State Fred Popel.

"Fred, one way or another this war is going to be over quickly. Either the invading tanks will run out of gas without getting to Riyadh, be destroyed, or will level enough of Riyadh to start a revolution. I'm betting that with our help the Saudis will be able to stop them in time. Then we need to act fast to make sure the aftermath goes the way we want. I suggest we use the Turks as a cutout, and I want at a minimum to get back our bases in Qatar and Bahrain. Here's what I think the settlement should look like, and I'll let you and your team work out the details..."

250 Miles Southeast of the Omani Coast, Indian Ocean

For this mission, the *USS Oregon* had been slated to launch an experimental version of the venerable Tomahawk missile, which had first entered service in 1983. By contrast, *Oregon* was the first Block IV *Virginia* class attack submarine to be completed and represented the newest and best the US Navy had to offer. All Captain Jim Cartwright knew was that they had suddenly been ordered from their quiet corner of the Indian Ocean, far from shipping lanes and all known satellite coverage, to as close to the Omani coast as they could get in the time they had before launch.

Cartwright ran his hand through his closely cut, prematurely graying hair. If his wife had been there, she would have known that meant he was about to start asking questions. Though this was Lieutenant Fischer's second tour with Cartwright, he hadn't yet learned that. Short and thin with sandy hair, Cartwright thought for maybe the hundredth time that Fischer looked like a much better fit for submarines than an officer like him who stood 6'2" without shoes.

"OK, Fischer, I'm going to admit I wasn't that excited when we first received this mission. Tomahawks have been around the Navy longer than I have, and I've seen many versions come and go. What makes this one so special, and why are we going at our top speed before we deploy it? I've seen the targeting coordinates, and we've been within Tomahawk range since before we started this race."

"Yes, sir," Fischer said, his head bobbing up and down. "But for this Tomahawk version to hit with maximum effect, we want it to have as much fuel on board as possible. What makes this version special is that just before impact the remaining JP-10 fuel will be mixed with air to create a thermobaric explosion, which should have at least as much destructive effect as the combined warhead. So, more fuel left equals a bigger blast."

"Combined warhead. So these Tomahawks are carrying cluster bomb warheads," Cartwright said.

"Yes, sir," Fischer said. "Specifically, the BLU-97/B Combined Effects Bomb. According to our new mission orders we're going after tanks, and since they have a combined shaped charge, fragmentation and incendiary effect, I think we'll get good results."

Cartwright nodded. "I'm no tanker, but I remember reading that the top armor is where nearly all tanks are most vulnerable."

"That's right, sir," Fischer said with a smile.

"OK, I just read the mission summary. Why don't you explain to me why when we do our two salvos, we're required to program a small speed reduction for the first salvo. What difference would it make if the Tomahawks' arrival wasn't precisely simultaneous?"

As he asked this, Cartwright reflected to himself that civilians would probably be confused by this dialogue, expecting a captain to know every detail of all aspects of the sub and its operations. One of the things any officer learned as he advanced in rank was that a sub had a crew for a reason. Nobody could run it by himself. Besides, part of his job as captain was training his officers. This Q&A session, which required Fischer to both know every detail of the mission and explain it on his feet, was part of that training.

"Well, sir, to answer that I need to get into the drones that are going to be providing targeting once the Tomahawks reach the attack area. They'll be deployed by the DDV-X, which stands for Drone Delivery Vehicle, Experimental. It's a heavily modified RQ-170 Sentinel with its normal radar, infrared sensors and communications intercept equipment removed. In their place there's a single cargo bay, holding several dozen micro-drones, as well as a single optical sensor to record their performance.

Cartwright nodded. "I've heard of the Sentinel. That's the drone that took and broadcast real-time video footage of the Navy raid that killed Bin Laden."

"Yes, sir. This one, though, just carries these DT-X micro-drones, or Drones, Targeting, Experimental. With a main body a little bigger than a golf ball, each contains a tiny battery and a low-power infrared laser emitter. The drone's circuits are printed into its skin, and its wings are designed to let it take advantage of the power generated by its fall from the DDV-X to loop in slowly to its objective. Once it identifies its target, it remains on station using a tiny plasma jet powered by its onboard battery."

Cartwright frowned. "So, no weapons and no communications capability."

"Correct, sir. They're designed solely to designate a target with its IR emitter using preprogrammed parameters, and avoid designating a target already being illuminated. Once the DT-X's battery begins to run low, it's programmed to use its last remaining charge to send an electronic pulse through its circuits rendering its remains useless to anyone who might find it."

Cartwright shook his head. "I'll bet 'limited' is the right word for its endurance."

"Yes, sir. That's why we'll have to coordinate closely with the Air Force DDV-X operators deploying the micro-drones, to make sure our ordinance package strikes the target while the DT-Xs are on station. You can also see why the Tomahawks have to arrive simultaneously. The blast wave from the explosives deployed by the first Tomahawks to arrive separately would either destroy or brush aside every DT-X in the area."

Cartwright nodded. "Yes, I can see that. Now, we'll be firing two salvos of twelve Tomahawks, and each will deploy about one hundred seventy-five bomblets. Doing the math in my head, that's a bit over four thousand bomblets, right?"

Fischer always had his tablet handy, and he looked at it now.

"Yes, sir. About four thousand two hundred."

Cartwright shook his head. "And these Tomahawks are themselves fuel-air bombs. Well, there's just one thing I'm sure about, Fischer."

"Yes, sir?" Fischer asked.

Cartwright said soberly, "I'm sure glad I'm not in one of those tanks."

Ministry of Defense, Riyadh, Saudi Arabia

The Crown Prince scowled across the table in the command center at Suliman al-Johani, deputy commander of the Royal Saudi Air Force. In most countries, Suliman would have automatically taken command of the RSAF when Prince Khaled bin Fahd had been killed by that cursed missile launcher, at least on an acting basis.

Saudi Arabia was not most countries.

The Crown Prince had decided that the RSAF had to be kept in royal hands, and the truth is Suliman had no trouble with that decision. After all, "Royal" was literally part of the RSAF's name.

No, the problem wasn't the Crown Prince assuming the title of RSAF Commander. It's that he'd started to make decisions as though he knew what the RSAF Commander should do, and Suliman was pretty sure that was about to get some good pilots killed.

"I believe this plan has an excellent chance of success," the Crown Prince repeated stubbornly, as Suliman searched in vain for the words to convince him it was actually suicidal.

"We're going to have six Typhoons go at that missile launcher from every point on the compass simultaneously, and launch the instant they're within Brimstone 2 range. Once we've destroyed the launcher, we can use our air assets to obliterate the invaders long before they make it to Riyadh," the Crown Prince said, again pointing at the graphic he'd had the staff prepare to illustrate his plan.

It was an impressive graphic. It showed six planes converging on a single point from every direction, and then the point representing the missile launcher obligingly exploding.

Suliman doubted very much that the launcher's commander would be waiting quietly while six fighters approached.

The problem was that the Crown Prince was not in fact a fool. But he was trained as a tanker, not a pilot. What made him so dangerous was that, even more than other royals, nobody had ever dared tell him he was wrong.

Suliman tried one more time. "Your Highness, we don't know what model that launcher is, or what missiles it's firing. The only pilot to survive its last attack said the missile that came at him was faster than anything he'd seen in Yemen. I fear it could be capable of shooting down all six planes before they're able to launch."

The Crown Prince shook his head stubbornly, and Suliman knew he didn't believe what he was hearing. "The Typhoons can go faster than sound even without afterburner, correct?"

All Suliman could do was nod. It was true that Typhoons were in the very small group of fighters that could "supercruise" at faster than Mach 1.

"So, the launcher may have time to attack one Typhoon, or even two. I see no way that any launcher would have time to attack all six, let alone shoot every Typhoon down before they can launch their Brimstone 2 missiles. And Prince Khaled did prove that these launchers aren't invulnerable, correct?," the Crown Prince concluded triumphantly.

"Yes, sir," Suliman said stoically.

"Very well, then," the Crown Prince continued, "let me know when the attack is underway. I don't have to tell you that speed is of the essence."

Suliman mutely saluted, and left the conference room. He knew many of his fellow pilots were about to die.

He just hoped that one of them would manage to make the sacrifice worthwhile.

Less than an hour later, they were all back in the command center. This time they were looking at a large LCD display that showed the position of each of the six Typhoons, as well as a graphic representing the Triton's view of the invaders' current position. As planned, the Typhoons were converging simultaneously on that position, and Suliman felt a rush of hope as he saw that their coordination was close to perfection.

Data next to each Typhoon showed their speed and distance to the target, as well as their estimated time before launch. Then, just as planned, each Typhoon cut in its afterburners and went to its maximum speed of Mach 2 for the last one hundred kilometers before reaching the launcher. Suliman nodded and began to think they might just pull this off. It really was hard to see how all six Typhoons could be stopped before reaching the Brimstone 2's launch range of sixty kilometers.

No sooner had Suliman finished the thought than six new graphics appeared on the display, representing missiles fired by the invaders' missile launcher. The number next to each graphic kept rising, until finally settling at a figure that stopped Suliman's heart.

Mach 10.

Suliman heard the Crown Prince shout "No!" and pound his fist on the table, but his eyes remained riveted to the screen. He had already done the math in his head, and the Typhoons' only chance was decoying the missiles.

That chance was low, but not zero. Suliman had seen to it that the Typhoons on this mission were equipped with some of the first self-contained expendable Digital Radio Frequency Memory (DRFM) jammers they had received. He had been with Prince Khaled for an impressive demonstration in the UK where a drone had deployed one and successfully decoyed an AMRAAM. Prince Khaled had ordered a dozen, and then had them installed in his personal Typhoon squadron for testing.

Since these DFRM jammers were ejected from the same 55 mm port used to deploy flares, only a minor software upgrade was necessary to use them. They were supposed to operate for ten seconds, so ejection timing was crucial.

It turned out Suliman's hopes were in vain. In quick succession, the missile and Typhoon icons winked out all over the display, until the only one still showing was the dull red icon representing the invaders.

For the next several minutes everyone sat in stunned silence. Suliman was sure that he was not alone in saying a silent prayer for the brave pilots who had just given their lives for their country.

"How can this be?" the Crown Prince finally asked. "We think these invaders are probably Iranian. How could they have missiles that can fly at Mach 10?"

Suliman nodded and replied, "You're right that we never dreamed any of our enemies could have such a missile. The only one I've even heard of is a Russian missile called Kinzhal, but I've only read about it being deployed on one Russian bomber, the Tupolev 22, and one fighter, the MiG-31K. I've never heard that it has been adapted for use in a missile launcher, or that the Russians have sold it to anyone, least of all the Iranians."

The Crown Prince nodded absently, and then appeared to make a decision.

"General Suliman, I want you to take over planning for the air attack on the Qatari ground force, and the intervention we expect from the Qatari's air force. Be sure to continue coordination with the Americans on their Tomahawk strike against the Qataris. I will plan an armor attack against the northern invaders," the Crown Prince concluded.

"Yes, sir," Suliman said with a salute, as he rose to carry out his orders.

Well, he thought, if the deaths of the Typhoon pilots at least got the Crown Prince out of planning air operations they weren't entirely in vain.

Now, he thought as he punched the elevator button, I have to show that I can do better. Then he thought about the results of the last attack and shrugged.

I can hardly do worse.

Chapter Twenty Four

Shahid Rajaei Research & Training Hospital, Tehran, Iran

Colonel Arif Shahin had believed Grand Ayatollah Sayyid Vahid Turani when he told him he thought Acting Supreme Leader Reza Fagheh might attempt to have the current Supreme Leader assassinated. The Supreme Leader was in a coma following a stroke, and once his guards were ordered away would be an easy target. The first step would be to move him out of the hospital where doctors were just marking time before his death.

The next would be to kill him, probably by doing little more than removing the respirator that had helped the Supreme Leader breathe ever since his stroke. Then it would be easy to claim that he'd been moved "for his security," and simply hadn't survived the move.

So, the first step was to see just how secure the Supreme Leader was. For example, could an armed man wearing an Iranian Army uniform with the rank badges of a Colonel come within firing range?

It was late evening, so Arif wasn't surprised that only a single nurse was on duty in the hospital lobby. He was annoyed, though, when in response to his request for the Supreme Leader's room number she simply gave it to him.

True, Iranian Army uniforms with Colonel insignia weren't on sale in stores. That didn't mean one would be that hard to get.

Arif took the elevator to the Supreme Leader's floor, and exited to find...no guard. So, the only guards would be at his actual room.

"Hey, who are you? You're not supposed to be here at this hour!" Arif turned his head right and saw the source of the sharp voice, a short but attractive middle-aged nurse whose expression at the moment was anything but pleasant.

Finally, Arif thought, someone competent. Aloud, he said "My name is Colonel Arif Shahin, and these are my credentials," holding up his Ministry of Defense ID. "I have been ordered to check on the Supreme Leader's security precautions. May I ask your name?"

The nurse looked at him suspiciously and said nothing, simply holding out her hand towards his ID. Arif suppressed a smile, as well as the thought that he was really starting to like this woman, and handed his ID over for her inspection.

Only after a careful review of the ID, including holding it up to compare the photo on it with Arif, did she finally hand it back.

"You are regular Army. Why are you checking on the Supreme Leader's security, which is handled by the Pasdaran?" the nurse asked.

Arif looked down the hall, and saw that there was nobody in sight, or hopefully within hearing. Looking at the nurse, and the spark of intelligence he could see in her eyes, he quickly decided that nothing but the truth would do.

"We think there could be a threat to the Supreme Leader from within the Pasdaran. Obviously I'm not speaking about whoever is guarding him at the moment, but a person or persons unknown who may gain access to the Supreme Leader, we believe soon."

The nurse looked him in the eye for several moments, and then made her decision. She held out her hand and said, "My name is Roya Maziar, and I am the head nurse on this floor. At this hour, the only nurse on this floor. I am glad to see someone still remembers the Supreme Leader is here."

Arif briefly and firmly shook Roya's hand. He might find her attractive, but right now he had to focus completely on his mission. "Do you know how many guards are with him right now?"

Roya nodded, and said "Yes, one. They started with three, one by the elevator and two with the Supreme Leader. But, as the months passed and every treatment failed, that became first two men and a few weeks ago just one. Or I should say two, who each guard the Supreme Leader for twelve hours. The man there now has been on duty since noon, and his replacement will arrive at midnight."

Arif asked, "Have you ever spoken to the guards?"

Her eyes flashing, Roya said, "No, but they have tried to talk to me. Each did so only once."

Once again Arif found himself suppressing a smile. "Can you tell me anything else about their performance?"

Roya snorted with disdain. "They may be called guards by the Pasdaran, but in reality are no more than common thugs. As to this one's performance, at this hour I think it's likely he'll be asleep."

As a professional soldier, Arif was genuinely shocked by Roya's casual statement. "You have seen this?" he asked.

"Seen it?," Roya replied. "Walk down to the end of the hall, and you will almost certainly hear it. The Supreme Leader is on a respirator and literally cannot snore. When he was first moved here all the other patients were cleared from this floor, so if you hear snoring, it's the guard."

Shaking his head, Arif did exactly as Roya suggested. He had walked no more than halfway down the hallway when he started to hear snoring. When he reached the open doorway, there was the scene he'd expected - the comatose Supreme Leader, and the snoring guard. The only additional details were that the Supreme Leader appeared far older than he remembered, and the guard's head had actually rolled backward in his chair. Arif doubted that anything short of a gunshot would wake him.

Or, he thought grimly, help him sleep permanently.

Roya's arms were crossed and she looked at him defiantly when Arif returned to her station. "So, was I right?" she asked.

This time Arif couldn't help it, and did smile. "Yes, you were," he said. "I appreciate your help with my questions." There was a notepad on the station's counter, and he quickly wrote down his name and phone number. "If anything suspicious happens at any time, day or night, please call or text me at this number. Please also share my name and number, and my interest in the Supreme Leader's security, with nurses who are in charge here at other shifts."

Roya nodded. "You are not speaking with the hospital administrators?" she asked.

"No," Arif replied, shaking his head. "Since we believe the threat is coming from within the Pasdaran, we don't want to alert them to our interest. I feel sure you will not do so, but doubt the same can be said about your administrators."

Roya nodded, and then hesitated. "If men come here to kill or abduct the Supreme Leader, they're not going to want witnesses. How worried should I be?" she asked.

Arif looked at her soberly, and replied, "Remember, contact me at any time, day or night."

United States Military Training Mission, Riyadh, Saudi Arabia

Technical Sgt. Josh Pettigrew was still trying to get used to being back behind a drone control console. Military police sent by the General in command of USMTM had arrested him, and escorted all his students to their quarters before they'd been able to do anything with the Reaper drones. He'd been locked into one of the MP interview rooms for hours, but nobody had ever shown up to question him.

Then, with no explanation he'd been taken back to his classroom where all his students were waiting for him, and told to await further orders. Finally they'd come, and left Pettigrew even more confused. They said he was to provide "all aid and assistance possible" to the Royal Saudi Air Force, and that he would supervise his students as they operated the Reapers they had just sold the Kingdom "as they carried out a mission of national self-defense." For good measure, they said his students had now graduated, and were now to be considered fully qualified Reaper operators.

All US military orders specified the command authority that had issued them. These came from the National Command Authority. Pettigrew had heard of NCA orders, but never seen them. It meant they'd come straight from the White House.

Once Pettigrew gave the orders some thought, he realized his next step should be to find out what the RSAF wanted him to do. While he was trying to figure out the right way to contact the RSAF, the problem was solved for him by the ringing of the secure phone on his drone command console.

Pettigrew picked up the phone and answered it. The voice on the other end said, "Sargent Pettigrew. My congratulations and thanks to you and your students on your success in stopping the attack on Riyadh. I am Suliman al-Johani, deputy commander of the Royal Saudi Air Force. Have you received your orders?"

"Yes, sir," Pettigrew replied. "We stand ready to provide whatever assistance we can, sir."

"Excellent," Suliman said. "I understand you have four Reapers available, correct?"

"Correct, sir," Pettigrew replied. "They're fueled, armed and ready to go."

"Very good," Suliman said. "How are they armed?"

Pettigrew paused, and said, "Just a moment, sir."

Pettigrew motioned to Mousa, who was the closest student. "Did you see whether anyone changed the loadout we did on the Reapers earlier today?" Mousa shook his head, but Fadil replied, "I did, sir. No change, four Hellfires on each."

Pettigrew pressed the hold button again, and said, "Sorry, sir. Just making sure I'm giving you the right answer. Each one has four Hellfires."

Suliman asked, "Am I right to think you could add two Paveways IIs to each Reaper, on top of the Hellfires? Or replace the Hellfires with Paveway IIs?"

"That's correct, sir. We'd need to use GBU-12 Paveway IIs which we've got here on base and are the 500-pound model, to stay under the Reaper's maximum load, but that would give you the totals you want," Pettigrew replied.

"Good," Suliman said. "I want one Reaper to have two Paveways added to the four Hellfires, and the other three Reapers to have six Paveways and no Hellfires. Here's where and when I want to have them deployed..."

Shahid Rajaei Research & Training Hospital, Tehran, Iran

Roya Maziar frowned as she heard the faint ringing of a cell phone. Since the Supreme Leader's guard was the only other person on this floor to have one besides her, she knew that's who had to be receiving a call.

As far as Roya knew, no guard had ever received a call while on duty. She didn't think that was because anyone was concerned about distracting the guards from their important work. On the contrary, she thought it was because nobody cared about the men sent to guard someone who had been in a coma for months, even if he was the Supreme Leader.

So why now?

The answer came a few minutes later when the guard emerged from the Supreme Leader's room, stalked down the hallway, and without so much as a glance at Roya pressed the button for the elevator. It had not been called since Roya arrived for her shift, and so opened immediately. Just like that, the guard was gone.

For the first time since Roya had started working at the hospital, she was completely alone. The other rooms on her floor had been cleared when the Supreme Leader arrived, and a man in a coma obviously didn't count as company.

Roya immediately remembered the officer who had said to contact him anytime if she saw anything suspicious. Well, she thought, this certainly qualifies. Roya sent a brief text explaining what had happened, and was pleased when the officer replied almost immediately that he was on his way.

After a bit more thought, Roya decided to call her friend Farzeen, who she knew was at the desk in the hospital lobby.

"Farzeen, how are you?" Roya asked first, as custom demanded.

"I am well," Farzeen replied. Then, getting immediately to the point, she asked, "Wasn't that the Supreme Leader's guard who just walked past me? And isn't it going to be more than an hour until his replacement shows up? And aren't you all alone up there? Aren't you worried?"

Finally, Farzeen paused for breath. "But I guess maybe that's why you were calling me? Would you like some company? I can have the hospital security guard call if a patient shows up, and be back downstairs in a minute."

Roya smiled. Farzeen really was a good friend, even if talking to her sometimes felt like trying to stop a runaway train. "Yes, Farzeen, that would be great. I'll make us some tea. See you in a few minutes."

As she made the tea, Roya reflected on how lucky they were to work at a hospital that was not only one of the best in the country, but also one that specialized in cardiac and circulatory disorders. It spared them from the endless parade of ambulances with emergency cases at most other hospitals, and also let them work with some of the country's best doctors.

Who, unfortunately, had egos to match.

The elevator announced its arrival with a chime and Farzeen burst out from it, waving her hands and saying in a singsong voice, "I'm here!"

Roya smiled and said, "Yes, indeed you are. Please, have a seat and let me get you some tea."

As she sat next to Roya, Farzeen smiled back. "And you have cookies! I would have come faster if I knew you had cookies!"

Roya poured her tea and just kept smiling. She knew that wasn't true, but she also knew Farzeen loved cookies, or for that matter any other sweet. Roya refused to think of her friend as fat, and instead searched for another word...portly? Ample?

Well, it didn't stop her from being a good friend.

"So, what will you do until the other guard shows up? That is, if he does show up!" Farzeen said, as her hand went to her mouth both to emphasize the horror of the thought and to try to keep crumbs from spilling out. She was mostly successful at both.

Farzeen added, "You know I want to stay with you until you go home, but I don't think I should leave the lobby desk unattended that long."

Roya nodded. She knew that Farzeen was taking a real chance as it was that the hospital security guard would report the time she was already spending with Roya.

"I've actually texted that Army officer who was here earlier this evening, and he's on his way," Roya said.

"Ah, the handsome Army officer! He reminds me of my husband when he was younger. A lot younger. Oh well, I don't look like I did when we got married either. Didn't stop us from having four children. So, do you like him?" Farzeen asked.

"Farzeen!" Roya exclaimed, blushing. "He's coming here to ensure the Supreme Leader's security, not on a date!"

"Humph," Farzeen said around the cookie she was chewing. "Why can't it be both? Tall, handsome and all business sounds like just your type. I'll bet he's the only man you've seen since you started working here who hasn't made a pass at you."

Now Roya was getting a little annoyed, because in fact Farzeen was right. Roya's mother had lost her father in the Iran-Iraq War, and perhaps as a result had never pressured her to marry. Like nearly all unmarried Iranian women, Roya still lived with her mother, and now that her sisters had all married she was the only one left. If Roya married, her mother probably thought it meant she'd be left alone.

Actually, Roya had already decided that if she did marry she would insist her mother continue to live with her. Meanwhile, Farzeen seemed determined to fill in for her mother in the "you should really get married" department.

"Well, maybe you're right about that. One thing I can say for sure is that the young single doctors and the older married doctors have only one thing on their minds when they talk to me, and it's not marriage," Roya said tartly.

Farzeen laughed and patted Roya on the arm. "Oh dear, I think I've upset you. You're right of course. You should get your mother to do a proper arranged marriage for you. Just look at how well it's worked for me!"

Roya suppressed her urge to repeat all the complaints Farzeen had made about her husband over the past few years, and just smiled.

Farzeen looked over the few crumbs remaining on the tray and sighed. "That was good tea! We should do it again this weekend at my house. You can tell me all about how it goes tonight with the handsome officer!"

Roya couldn't help laughing. "You're incorrigible! But, yes, of course I'll come. Just let me know when, and what I can bring."

Farzeen stood up. "I will. And now I have to head back. First, let me help you clean this up."

Together they made short work of cleanup, and then as Roya was putting the tea glasses away she noticed the storage closet was ajar. Sighing at the mess she could see in the cabinets inside, she asked, "Why can't the other shifts ever clean up after themselves?"

Farzeen laughed and said, "Because they're lazy and good for nothing! Not like us hard workers! And speaking of work, I really do need to go back."

Roya gave her a quick hug. "I know. Thanks for coming up."

Farzeen smiled. "See you this weekend!"

With a sigh, Roya turned back to the storage cabinets, and began putting things back in their proper place. What could they have even been looking for?

Roya heard the elevator's chime, and at first thought it was just coming for Farzeen. Then she heard Farzeen's voice saying, "Oh, you must be the replacement guards."

Guards plural, Roya thought with a frown. Why more now, in the middle of the night?

"What's all that you have with you?" Roya heard Farzeen ask, followed almost immediately by a sound Roya couldn't identify, and a distinct thud.

Her heart beating wildly, Roya crept towards the partly open storage closet door and peered around its edge. What she saw nearly made her cry out. It was Farzeen's only partly visible body, with blood beginning to pool next to it.

Roya carefully drew the supply closet door shut, until it was only open a bare crack.

"Idiot!" she heard one of the men say. "Why don't you try talking to people first, before just killing them."

A different, and sullen, voice responded. "We didn't have any good answers to her questions. She would have talked to that security guard downstairs if we'd let her go. And what if then he'd called the police? He already looked suspicious when we went past him in the lobby."

Now the first voice again, this time sounding exasperated. "Well, it's done. Get her body out of sight and clean up this blood. If that guard sticks his head out of the elevator later, I don't want him to know instantly that something's wrong. I'm going to check on the Supreme Leader."

Roya pulled out her cell phone, not even aware that tears for her friend were flowing down her face. The messaging app was still open. She texted, "They killed my friend. Hiding. Hurry."

This time there was no answer. Her heart sank, and then Roya realized it might be because the officer knew texting her back could cause her phone to make a sound that would reveal her presence.

Please, God, let him be that smart, she thought.

For the next several minutes all Roya could hear were sounds that she correctly guessed were Farzeen's body being moved and cleaning up her blood.

Now the sullen voice spoke again. "OK, done with the body. Should I check to make sure there's nobody else on this floor?"

Roya thought her heart would stop, and knew she'd stopped breathing.

The first voice answered immediately. "We don't have time to waste on that. There's only one nurse on this floor, and the Supreme Leader is the only patient. Now get over here and help me move him."

Now Roya did know she was crying, though she managed to do so silently. Without Farzeen having been here, it would have been her lying dead on the floor.

A shadow passed by the storage closet door, and Roya next heard both men cursing at the end of the hall. She opened the door a bit wider, and could now see one of two large men wheeling the Supreme Leader and his gurney out of his room. The other man was wheeling a cart holding his respirator.

Roya shook her head. It was obvious neither man knew what he was doing. She wondered whether the Supreme Leader was even still alive.

She got her answer immediately. "Is that thing still working?" the man in charge asked. The one that she now realized had killed Farzeen answered as sullenly as before. "Yes. It has a backup battery, which should last long enough if we hurry."

Roya had hoped that the security guard downstairs would stop the men, or at least call the police, if he saw them leaving with the Supreme Leader. Her heart now sank, as she saw them moving toward the service elevator. Of course! That way they wouldn't encounter anyone at this late hour.

Just before they reached it, though, Roya exultantly saw Arif Shahin bent low next to another soldier, who both had rifles out and pointed at the Pasdaran men. They were moving silently forward, and Roya wondered why she hadn't heard the elevator chime.

Because they took the stairs, she told herself. Ok, he is smart.

Later, Roya didn't even remember deciding to do it. But at this moment, she lifted the cell phone that was still in her hand and began recording the scene in the hallway.

Now the Pasdaran men finally saw the soldiers and quickly moved the Supreme Leader's body between them, while pulling out their guns.

"Drop your weapons," Arif ordered.

"Drop yours," both of the Pasdaran men said, almost simultaneously.

"You have no authority to move the Supreme Leader," Arif said. "Surrender, or we will open fire."

"And risk killing the Supreme Leader? I think not," one of the Pasdaran men sneered.

"I have more soldiers on their way, and they'll be here any minute," Arif replied calmly. "We'll have to act, because that respirator isn't going to last long on battery. So, your only choice is to surrender."

Roya could see one of the men moving up his rifle to fire. Just as she was going to call out a warning, she saw Arif smoothly move his rifle towards the man and fire a single shot. The sound was deafening.

The Pasdaran man was thrown backward and his rifle flew from his hands. He twitched once, and then stopped moving.

The other Pasdaran man then lifted his rifle and yelled, "Yes, I do have another choice!" before firing several rounds from his crouch behind the Supreme Leader into the comatose man's body.

Both Arif and the other soldier ran forward, and as soon as they had a clear shot both fired at the assassin. From her angle Roya couldn't see, but she was sure the assassin was dead.

Moments later Arif walked to the storage closet and slowly opened the door, to find Roya on the floor sobbing, with her phone lying on the floor beside her.

"They killed her, and now they killed him!" she cried.

"I know, and I'm sorry," Arif said gently. "Are you hurt?" he asked.

Roya shook her head, and unsteadily got to her feet. She felt Arif's hand on her arm helping her rise. His face was full of concern as he asked again, "Are you sure you're OK?"

From anyone else the repeated question would have annoyed her. From Arif, for some reason, it did not.

Roya nodded, and then asked, "Do you really have more soldiers coming?"

Arif replied, "Yes, and I think I hear them on the stairs now." Now Roya could hear them too. Unlike Arif and the other soldier, these were making no effort to conceal their approach.

Arif looked down at Roya's phone, which she had left lying on the floor. Arif bent down and picked it up, and then handed it to her. Then he asked, "I saw us on the screen. Did you record what happened?"

Roya looked at the phone, her expression dazed. "I guess so, though I don't remember deciding to do it."

Arif said gently, "I understand. Is it OK if I borrow your phone, just until we can copy that recording?"

Roya nodded. "Yes. Anything that will help you catch whoever sent those men. Kidnapping the Supreme Leader wasn't their idea."

Arif cocked his head. "What makes you think so?"

Roya's face contorted with hatred, and then she collected herself and said evenly, "I'm surprised those two had the wits between them to lace their boots. Men like that take orders, they don't give them."

Arif looked thoughtful for a moment, and then said, "I think you're right." He paused and said, "My most trusted soldier is going to take you home. You have my word that we're going to make sure your friend's body is treated with dignity. I will see you tomorrow to return your phone, and if you're up to it probably ask you more questions. In the meantime, please stay home and say nothing to anyone. Can you do that for me?"

Roya nodded mutely. It all seemed like a terrible nightmare, but as she looked at the Supreme Leader's body at the end of the hall, she knew it was one that soon the entire nation would share.

Chapter Twenty Five

Near Intersection of Highway 522 & Aramco Road,
228 Kilometers East of Riyadh

Prince Bilal looked around him at the barren desert landscape as the Qatari armored force approached a major highway intersection. This, like the other spots where he thought the Saudis might have rushed an armored force to stop him, was eerily empty.

Bilal had ordered the Al-Nadha men dressed as Saudi Highway Patrolmen he had been told to expect near Al-Hofuf to go ahead of their armored force, to clear the way of civilian vehicles. Over the last half-hour that had proved unnecessary so he had ordered them to depart down a side road, as in battle their patrol cruisers would be useless.

Maybe the word was out that his force was on its way. Or maybe the Saudi military had set up roadblocks. Either way, Bilal was glad the road to Riyadh was clear. Though his Leopards were capable of going up to sixty-eight kilometers per hour on the highway many of his support vehicles were less speedy, so he was going at a relatively sedate fifty kilometers per hour.

Bilal glanced behind him, where most of his two hundred tanks and all the assorted support vehicles and APCs followed, including the two S-300s he was counting on to keep them safe from air attack. He had them spaced out as he'd been taught at the German Armor School where one of the first lessons had been, "Don't let one shell take out two tanks." When a tank suffered a penetrating hit it quite often set off some or even most of the rounds it carried as well as its fuel, which could result in an explosion capable of damaging a nearby tank. That damage would usually not be total but could easily involve knocking off or, even worse, damaging the tank's treads.

Spaced out, there were far more vehicles behind him than Bilal could see, though the view from his perch in the tank's open cupola was excellent. The sky could not have been clearer, and there wasn't a cloud in sight.

A Leopard tank platoon was in front of him for security, and two scout Fenneks were ahead of the entire force. Jointly produced by the Dutch and Germans, Bilal would have never looked at the Fenneks if it hadn't been for the decision to buy Leopards from the Germans.

The Fennek was a light armored vehicle that had proved its worth in Afghanistan, where one had taken a penetrating hit from an RPG that blew off one of the doors, but thanks to its interior spall lining its occupants suffered only minor injuries. Built for reconnaissance, it featured an extendable mast with a camera, thermal imager and laser rangefinder, and was Bilal's best chance of seeing the Saudis before they spotted him.

Bilal noticed the flock of birds, and at first it reminded him of the time he'd spent in Germany. The sheer variety of plants, birds and animals living in the area where he had done his training on the Leopard had astonished him, and his sinuses in particular had gone through a painful but ultimately successful adjustment period.

Then Bilal's blood froze as he realized *there are no bird flocks in the desert.*

Bilal dropped inside the turret, slammed the hatch shut behind him, and grabbed the radio handset.

"Disperse! Smoke! Air attack!," he yelled into his radio, which was keyed to transmit force-wide, and was gratified to see that his crew and all the vehicles in sight were quick to follow orders. They immediately veered off the highway, deployed smoke and began evasive driving.

Seconds later, BLU-97/B Combined Effects Bombs guided by the DT-X microdrones began to fall on the Qatari force. Many Leopards held up well under the bomblet assault. The addition of modular armor to their 2A7 variant proved its worth, and even after hits cleared that away the spaced multilayer armor underneath also proved to be tough to crack.

But turret hits were fatal. So were multiple hits at or around the same spot on the Leopards' top armor. Bomblet explosions directly to the sides of the Leopards did nothing to the crews inside, but damaged or destroyed their tracks and even more critically their wheels. Without functioning wheels to attach them to, replacement tracks were worthless.

Bilal's orders were, on balance, responsible for saving many of his tanks. Not all the DT-X microdrones were able to make the rapid course adjustment necessary to follow their Leopard, and others lost the laser lock on their tank due to dust and smoke.

However, Bilal's orders were a blessing for the DT-Xs in one other regard. Even at the Leopards' fifty kilometers per hour the microdrones had been falling behind, because the tiny plasma jets that powered them were quite weak. The DT-Xs' laser illumination range was impressive, but not infinite. If they had continued on the highway, at least a few locks would have probably been lost.

The DDV-X footage of the attack would later serve as the justification for increasing its battery size to increase the DT-Xs' top speed. But it was agreed by all analysts that if the Leopards had remained on the highway, fewer would have survived.

One of the Tomahawks had malfunctioned in flight and been destroyed remotely by *Oregon,* bringing the number of bomblets deployed slightly below four thousand. Two other Tomahawks successfully deployed their bomblets, but lost their DT-X provided lock, and exploded harmlessly into the desert sand.

Two of the Tomahawks and a dozen DT-Xs had been assigned to the S-300s.

The remaining nineteen Tomahawks found their Leopards, and successfully injected air into their remaining fuel just before impact to produce a thermobaric explosion. The scientists at Los Alamos who had worked on the project had projections for the explosive force that would be released, and later assessed that based on the DDV-X footage of the attack if anything, their projections had been too conservative.

This observation was bolstered by the fact that several of the Leopards were flung into the air by the Tomahawk's explosion, and one actually somersaulted.

The entire attack took less than three minutes.

After five minutes, Bilal ordered his surviving forces to report.

Twenty-seven Leopards had either been completely destroyed or were not repairable in the field. Another fifteen had damage to their tracks that could be fixed. Over half of the remaining tanks had lost all or part of their modular armor, leaving them more vulnerable to a subsequent attack.

Both S-300s had been destroyed, in explosions so violent that five MOWAG Piranha MK-II 8x8 APCs had also been destroyed. Originally designed and built by the Swiss company MOWAG, there was licensed production in many NATO countries including the US, where the Marines used a variant called the LAV-25 with a propeller attached allowing it to ford shallow waters. Qatar's version mounted a Cockerill 90 mm gun, one 7.62 mm coaxial machine gun, and another 7.62 machine gun on the turret. Each had a crew of three and carried five infantry soldiers.

The question now was whether Bilal would continue to Riyadh after this setback with his remaining one hundred fifty-eight Leopards and twenty-nine Piranha APCs, and no S-300s.

Bilal never even considered turning back. Qatar had implemented mandatory military conscription in 2015 with an average of 2,000 graduates per year in response to growing Saudi pressure to change its foreign policy, and the blockade starting in 2017 had just increased the resolve of its leadership.

One way or another, the blockade was going to end.

Bilal reached for his handset to call his headquarters in Doha. With the loss of both his S-300s, it wouldn't be long before he had company in the skies above his force. If he and his men were to have any hope of survival, the Qatari Emeri Air Force would have to prove that its recent purchases were money well spent.

250 Miles Southeast of the Omani Coast, Indian Ocean

Captain Jim Cartwright looked at the feed displayed on one of the *USS Oregon's* screens relayed by the DDV-X thoughtfully as it showed both the DT-Xs' capabilities and limitations.

"So, Lieutenant, it looks like any tank those little drones could lock onto had a bad day ahead. But, it's also clear that some of the tanks were difficult for them to get a lock on," Cartwright said.

"Yes, sir," Lieutenant Fischer replied, his head nodding up and down emphatically. "Some tanks appear to have been equipped with camouflage that was effective against an IR lock. However, as you say if the DT-X could get a lock, it meant one or more hits followed. Any tank hit directly by a Tomahawk was a definite kill, and it looks like the thermobaric warhead performed perfectly. As expected, not every bomblet scored a kill, but we can see many tanks suffering multiple hits that received catastrophic damage."

Cartwright cocked his head. "Define catastrophic, Lieutenant."

Fischer shrugged. "The tank has either flipped, or is missing its turret."

Cartwright laughed and said, "Well, no one will be able to accuse you of inflating the numbers. Do we have a final tally yet?"

Fischer shook his head. "No, sir. First task is already done, designating targets that suffered catastrophic damage. Next is underway, distinguishing mobile from immobile targets. Then we'll see which immobile targets have repair attempts made, as opposed to just checking for injured crewmen. We have software to help automate that task, for example by tracking the time crewman are visible near a target. I'll be able to give you some rough numbers within the next half hour."

Fischer hesitated and then said, "Those tanks took a real hit, sir. But I don't think we stopped them."

Cartwright nodded, and patted Fischer on the shoulder. "That's fine, Lieutenant. I don't think anyone expected us to. I'll bet, though, that we just made life a lot easier for our Saudi friends."

Fischer looked up from his screen and smiled. "Yes, sir. I think our Tomahawks just got a lot more valuable."

Cartwright smiled back. That was exactly the sort of assessment an attack sub captain wanted to hear. He'd read that a *Virginia* class submarine cost a bit more than two and a half billion dollars to build, and about fifty million dollars a year to operate. He thought back to the video footage he'd just seen.

Not for the first time, he nodded to himself and smiled.

Worth every penny.

Dammaj Valley, Yemen

Captain Jawad Al-Dajani was just as frustrated as his commander, Prince Ali bin Sultan. First, he'd lost an M1A2 tank to an ambush with that cursed decoy. He'd just had another M1A2 tank replaced that had been lost to a Tosun anti-tank guided missile, an Iranian-built variant of the old Soviet 9M113 Konkurs. Two of the crew of that tank were also killed, though he took some satisfaction in the success of his own M1A2 tank in chasing down the Tosun fire crew, despite their having fired from over three kilometers away. Those three Houthis wouldn't bother any other Saudi tanks, ever.

But it was a trade-off he knew the Saudi military simply couldn't afford. The Iranians could give the Houthis dozens of Tosuns for the cost of a single M1A2 tank. And there were certainly more Houthis in Yemen than there would ever be Saudis sent to fight them. He and all the other tank commanders were doing the most effective thing they could to avoid repetition of that incident, by sitting in their cupolas and looking for Tosuns or other threats, while the gunner relied on the view provided by the M1A2's thermal and optical sensors.

Even worse was that so far, his platoon hadn't been able to stop the firing of a single ballistic missile aimed at the Kingdom. Every potential launch site they'd been sent to investigate had been either nothing of the kind, or the launch had already happened, leaving nothing behind but smoking debris.

Today, though, would be different. Jawad could feel it in his bones.

None of the roads in Yemen were up to Saudi standards. Some of the highways in the Kingdom had been designed and built by companies like Bechtel, the largest American construction company, which had built some of its Interstate highways. The roads in this valley were worse than average even for Yemen, because only one led anywhere outside it. The others dead-ended somewhere within the valley.

In spite of this, Jawad's tanks were still keeping up a respectable sixty kilometers per hour. Jawad grinned as he thought back to his days at the Armor School at Fort Benning, where Prince Ali and most of his platoon leaders had learned to become tank commanders. One of the instructors had declared, "The M1A2 doesn't promise you the smooth ride of a family sedan. But it can keep up with just about anything else on the battlefield."

That first part was certainly true, Jawad thought. He had to be careful about keeping his teeth shut, because otherwise sharp bumps tended to clack them together. But he was hoping that the second part would be true as well, and they would finally bag a Houthi missile.

There! It was exactly where the reconnaissance drone had said it would be! Only the tip of the missile was visible, and that already told Jawad something. This missile was something new, something bigger than any of the other ones he'd heard about like the Burkan-2H and Qiam 1.

Jawad already had his handset ready, with an extension cable attached allowing him to use it in the cupola. He used it now to order every tank in the platoon to increase speed. He'd deal with bruises and chipped teeth later, once they stopped this missile.

As they turned a corner and the missile came into full view, he could hear his tank's M240 7.62 mm coaxial machine gun chatter, and the reason was immediately obvious - a Tosun was pointed straight at them. He'd told his gunners not to wait for his orders before opening fire on anything that looked like an anti-tank missile, and he was glad they'd listened. Their aim was confirmed by a secondary explosion, as one or more of the Tosun's rounds exploded, taking its fire crew with it.

Jawad had missed the Tosun because the missile in front of him was the Khorramshahr 2, a thirteen-meter tall missile with a range of up to two thousand kilometers, and capable of carrying a warhead of up to eighteen hundred kilograms. Its use in Yemen had been suspected, but unlike the Burkan-2H it had never been captured intact or even clearly photographed in Yemen.

Just like the Burkan-2H, the Khorramshahr 2 was liquid-fueled. It was too dangerous to move while fueled, which meant it had to have propellant added after it was set up at its launch site. Of course, since the Khorramshahr 2 had more than double the Burkan's eight hundred fifty kilometer range, it took longer to fuel.

No sooner had Jawad formed this thought than everyone could see another Khorramshahr 2 missile lift off about two kilometers away. The Houthis who had scattered from the launch site at the appearance of his tanks cheered.

Without the Houthis' cheers ringing in his ears, Jawad might have given his next move more thought. As it was, though, Jawad roared, "Main gun fire!"

There was no need to specify the target. Even the dimmest gunner could hardly mistake his commander's intention, with a thirteen-meter tall ballistic missile standing right in front of them.

Jawad had just enough time to think that he should have moved back into the tank's body and closed the hatch when the tank's M256 120 mm cannon fired an M908 High Explosive Obstacle Reduction round into the Khorramshahr 2 missile. The M908 was designed primarily to reduce concrete obstacles to rubble and was a commonly used round in Yemen, since it was effective against nearly any soft target.

Its results upon impact with the Khorramshahr 2 missile were nothing short of spectacular. Immediately following its detonation, the attached liquid-fuel tanker detonated as well.

Jawad barely had time to register the wall of flame headed his way before it killed him, but his tank and the other two behind it were not just incinerated. The shock wave from the blast tumbled all three like toys, and the sheer kinetic force of the explosion was more than any amount of armor could have withstood.

The fourth tank in the platoon, though, was saved from fire and blast by its position in the rear. It had been the only tank unable to turn the corner from behind the hill to exit the narrow road to the small clearing holding the Khorramshahr 2 missile. When he heard the "Main gun, fire!" command he had also reacted instinctively by ducking into the tank and slamming the hatch shut behind him.

That action saved the crew of the sole remaining M1A2 tank in Jawad's platoon from the fate of the few Houthi survivors of the Khorramshahr 2's explosion. Though there were several who had fled as soon as the tanks' engines could be heard, and so were not killed by blast or fire, they did not escape the Khorramshahr 2's payload.

VX nerve gas.

The force of the blast had ejected the warhead straight up which prevented its complete incineration by the burning rocket fuel, though some of the VX was consumed.

While the surviving M1A2 had a robust and well tested NBC (nuclear, biological and chemical) protection package, the Houthis didn't even have gas masks. Not that masks would have mattered, since any exposed skin surface would allow VX to kill its victim. Only a ten-milliliter dose would have been fatal.

Every Houthi who had been fleeing the launch site received far more.

The sole M1A2 tank to survive radioed to base that they had destroyed one Khorramshahr 2 missile, but had seen another launch successfully. Unfortunately, they did not see any of the Houthis they had left behind at the launch site gasping for air as they died, or they might have been able to give Prince Sultan Air Base some warning.

Because that was the target of the other Khorramshahr 2 missile, which carried the same VX warhead.

Prince Sultan Air Base, Saudi Arabia

Like every country with a significant air force, the Royal Saudi Air Force dispersed its assets in widely scattered air bases. This was both to ensure the widest possible defensive coverage of Saudi air space, as well as to prevent an enemy from inflicting a crippling blow by hitting a single base.

Prince Sultan Air Base had been selected for one of Iran's two VX warheads for many reasons. It was one of the bases closest to the Qatari armored force's march to Riyadh, and was a Sector Operating Center. It had been substantially improved by the US Air Force when it served as a base supporting Operations Enduring Freedom and Iraqi Freedom prior to the September 11 attacks. F-15s from No. 55 Squadron had been recently transferred there, and it contained two of the Kingdom's key strategic assets - its Boeing E-3 Sentry fleet, as well as its Boeing KE-3A refueling tankers. Since it was only about eighty kilometers south of Riyadh, attacking it would remove one of the capital's principal defenders.

But that would not be the only result of the attack. Acting Supreme Leader Reza Fagheh had reconsidered his earlier concerns, and decided to pick a target with multiple impacts.

Prince Sultan Air Base was directly adjacent to the city of Al Kharj, where some of the remaining underground water sources were still replenished by rainwater drained from the Tuwaiq escarpment to the west. Some of the wells were up to a mile deep so that the water extracted was boiling hot when brought to the surface, and had to be pumped into pools to cool before use.

This water was the basis for much of Saudi agriculture, and helped Al Kharj grow from a town of 20,000 to a city of 250,000. Almost every crop imaginable was grown in Al Kharj, and it was also home to nearly its entire dairy industry, with about twenty-four thousand head of cattle.

The amount of VX in the Khorramshahr 2 missile's warhead was enough to ensure it would not only kill most of the bases' military personnel and the quarter-million residents of Al Kharj, it would also contaminate much of the Saudi food supply, and literally kill its dairy industry.

Even worse, VX was specially designed as a persistent nerve agent. That meant that days or even weeks after it was dispersed, it could still kill. As an area denial weapon, that meant not only would the pilots at Prince Sultan Air Base be dead, their planes could not be flown prior to decontamination by suited technicians who would need days to do the work properly.

Decontamination of the soil to allow crops to grow again would take much longer.

So, the stakes were very high for the crew at the Patriot missile battery covering the capital region, even if they had no way of knowing just how high.

The notice provided by the sole surviving tank in Jawad's platoon had been helpful to the Patriot's crew. It gave them the time to establish that the Khorramshahr 2 missile was not merely off-course for Riyadh, but was actually targeted at Prince Sultan Air Base. It also allowed two separate Patriot missile batteries to coordinate their coverage, to ensure that if the missile made a course change to Riyadh it could still be intercepted.

After the Patriot's failure to stop a ballistic missile attack against Riyadh in 2018, the US had approved its upgrade to the MIM-104F (PAC-3) standard. This comprehensive overhaul to the system's computer hardware and software as well as its communications hardware was coupled with a dramatic upgrade to the missiles fired by the Patriot system. Now each launch canister, instead of firing a single PAC-2 missile, could hold four PAC-3 missiles.

The PAC-3 missile was also made more maneuverable, due to tiny pulse solid propellant rocket motors mounted in the front of the missile. An even more significant upgrade was the addition of an active radar seeker, allowing the missile to drop its system uplink and acquire the target itself once it was near, critical when trying to keep up with a fast-moving ballistic missile target.

The accuracy of the PAC-3 missile was improved so it could specifically target the warhead portion of a ballistic missile, giving it the capability to destroy the missile simply by striking it for a "kinetic kill." However, the missile also included a small explosive warhead launching twenty-four low-speed tungsten fragments enveloping the target - just to be sure.

This upgrade had already been underway when the apartment building in Riyadh struck by a Khorramshahr 2 had collapsed. That disaster had dramatically speeded the pace of the conversion to PAC-3 on both the US and Saudi sides of the program, and it was now complete. Today would see its first test.

Since the original Khorramshahr missile had been based on the Hwasong-10, which the North Koreans had sold to Iran, it and the improved version 2 had similar capabilities. These did not include detecting and evading interceptors.

Once the Khorramshahr 2 missile was in range of a Patriot battery in southern Riyadh, it launched two canisters of PAC-3 missiles at the target, for a total of eight interceptors. This left it with another two canisters in reserve while the first two were reloaded, in case of another ballistic missile launch.

The first interceptor malfunctioned and veered off course, eventually impacting harmlessly in the desert.

The second struck one of the missile's tail fins, changing its course from Prince Sultan Air Base to the city of Al Kharj.

The third had been on course to hit the warhead, but could not cope with the last second course change, and also ended up impacting in the desert.

The fourth hit the warhead and the fifth hit the fuselage at almost the same instant. The warhead had been designed to detach and deploy the

VX just before the missile's impact, so that the missile's burning rocket fuel would not consume it.

With a boiling point of 298 degrees Celsius, VX had to reach an even higher temperature for incineration. Fortunately the hypergolic propellant used in the Khorramshahr 2 missile, a mix of unsymmetrical dimethyl-hydrazine and nitrogen tetroxide, served that purpose very effectively.

The remaining interceptors sailed through the expanding cloud of burning fuel and debris. Once the Patriot crew confirmed the Khorramshahr 2 missile's successful interception, they were detonated remotely to ensure they would not impact an unintended target on the ground.

The plan to neutralize Prince Sultan Air Base and cripple Saudi agricultural production had failed.

Chapter Twenty Six

Near Intersection of Highway 522 and Aramco Road,
228 Kilometers East of Riyadh

Though he'd known reorganizing his forces would take time after the beating they'd just suffered, Prince Bilal was dismayed that as the Royal Saudi Air Force (RSAF) planes approached they were still almost exactly where they'd been during the attack. One problem had been getting medical assistance to injured tank crews, which were scattered and in many cases too badly wounded to even reach their radios.

Another problem had been track replacement. Dispersal had reduced the effectiveness of the air attack, but it had made getting replacement tracks to Leopards needing them a time-consuming chore.

Fortunately, the Qatari Emeri Air Force (QEAF) had been on alert from the moment Bilal's force crossed the Saudi border, and had already radioed him that they were en route to provide cover.

Ironically, many of the fighter jets about to meet in the skies above Bilal's force were the same aircraft operated by different countries. Both the RSAF and the QEAF flew the F-15 and the Typhoon, while only the QEAF flew the French Mirage 2000-5 and Rafale.

The QEAF's sole advantage was that its aircraft were newer. With the exception of the Mirage 2000-5, its entire Air Force had been purchased largely as a reaction to Saudi threats, culminating in the blockade and the start of construction on the Salwa Canal.

The RSAF's advantages included more planes and pilots, as well as more experience and training. While QEAF pilots had flown out of Crete to enforce the no-fly zone over Libya in 2011 and had later flown missions against ISIS in both Iraq and Syria, that experience paled in comparison to the combat flying time the RSAF had accumulated in Yemen.

Of course, both the RSAF and the QEAF shared a complete lack of air-to-air combat experience since the Libyans had never sortied aircraft to challenge the Qataris, and neither the Houthis nor ISIS had an Air Force.

The air superiority versions of the F-15 (A/C/I/S) had never been shot down in air-to-air combat, while it had downed over a hundred aircraft in engagements in Europe and the Middle East. The Mirage 2000 had a less inspiring record of one enemy aircraft shot down, and one lost to ground fire. The RSAF had lost both a Panavia Tornado and a Typhoon to ground fire in Yemen. The Rafale had flown in combat before, but had neither shot down an enemy aircraft nor been shot down itself.

All that would change today.

American trainers in Saudi Arabia for the F-15 were employees of its manufacturer, and were based at King Khalid Air Base near Khamis Mushait about one hundred sixty kilometers north of Yemen. British trainers for the Typhoon in Qatar were still considered on active duty in the Royal Air Force. Neither group of trainers would have ever considered flying with their students.

The French instructors for Qatar's new Rafale aircraft, however, were retired French Air Force pilots, and all three volunteered to fly with the QEAF. All of them sympathized with Qatar, disliked the idea that the Saudis could push it around simply because it was bigger, and thought that changing Qatar from a peninsula to an island with the Salwa Canal could reasonably be considered an act of war.

Plus, they had all wanted to fly the Rafale in combat, but had never had the chance.

One of them was Jacques Arcement, who like the other instructors insisted on flying as wingmen, with their Qatari cadets in the lead. One reason for all three was that it was, after all, the Qataris' air force.

For Jacques it was also that he genuinely considered his Qatari cadet to be a better natural pilot. Part of this was a function of age, but by no means all. Mansour Al-Attiyah's situational awareness and lightning-quick reaction time made him one of the best pilots Jacques had seen in any air force. In fact, part of what had motivated Jacques to volunteer was to give Mansour a chance to put those talents to use, since Jacques feared without the experience he and the other instructors could bring to bear the Saudis' superiority in sheer numbers would be likely to overwhelm the QEAF.

Jacques stood on the runway's edge well away from his Rafale as he enjoyed a cigarette from what was likely to be his last pack of Gauloises. As he smoked it to its unfiltered end, he had to smile. Here he was smoking a Gauloise as he prepared to board a Rafale to do battle in a nearly hopeless cause. The only way to make the moment more French would be to find some fitting music played by an accordion.

The Rafales were out in front of the formation because they were one of the few aircraft that thanks to its two Snecma M88 engines could "supercruise," meaning it could travel faster than Mach 1 without using its afterburner, even when fully loaded with four missiles and a drop tank. So could the Typhoons with their two Eurojet EJ200 engines, which followed right behind them, primarily because the QEAF had more Rafales than Typhoons.

When he saw the Saudi attack group on his scope, though, he realized the battle would not be as lopsided as he'd thought. For a start, there were far fewer Typhoons than Jacques had expected. This was partly because all of the RSAF's Typhoons, in Squadrons 3, 10, and 80 were based at King Fahd Air Base near Taif, a full one thousand kilometers from Prince Bilal's force.

Jacques had no way to know the other reason was that only the Typhoon carried the Brimstone 2 air-to-ground missile, the RSAF's only hope to take out the remaining S-300 guarding the northern invasion force. Many of the missing Typhoons were being fitted with Brimstone 2s at the same time as the strike against the Qatari force to do just that.

There were two big questions that Jacques knew would be answered in the next few minutes. The first was whether the Saudis had been arrogant enough to think that they could outfit their strike force with a mix of anti-air and anti-ground missiles to destroy the Qatari armored force and the QEAF in a single engagement, or whether they planned to take out the QEAF first followed by returning and rearming to destroy the now defenseless armor.

The second was whether the Typhoons that were approaching carried the Meteor. The first modern air-launched anti-aircraft missile to be developed by the Europeans, it had a classified range of "well over" a hundred kilometers, while the older AIM-120C that was the best carried on all Saudi fighters as well as the QEAF's F-15s had a maximum range of about a hundred and five kilometers.

A new model AMRAAM, the AIM-120D, increased the missile's range to one hundred sixty kilometers. So far, though, the Americans had only agreed to export it to Australia.

The Meteor's hardware and software had been integrated into Typhoons in European air forces, and French technicians had completed the work for the Rafale in both the French and Qatari air forces, as well as the QEAF's Typhoons. Jacques thought the fact that the first air force outside Europe to receive the Meteor was flying the Rafale might have been because the company making the Meteor had a French CEO.

But Jacques was probably being too cynical.

Qatar didn't have a real military intelligence service, relying on a few paid sources in the militaries of surrounding countries. They said the Meteor was not yet on any Saudi plane.

Today, they would find out for sure.

The Rafale had been upgraded in 2014 to the RBE2 AA active electronically scanned array (AESA) radar with a range of two hundred kilometers, and this upgrade was included in the Rafales delivered to Qatar in 2020. In theory that made it superior to the one hundred sixty kilometer range of the APG-63 in the F-15s flown by both the RSAF and QEAF, and the CAPTOR-D in the Typhoons flown by both the RSAF and QAEF with about the same range. Though only qualified as an instructor pilot in the Rafale, Jacques had also flown both the QEAF's Typhoon and F-15 jets, and thought in practice all three radars' performance was about the same.

Now it let him monitor a sight very rarely seen - the simultaneous launch of five dozen Meteor missiles by thirty-six Rafales and twenty-four Typhoons at the advancing RSAF planes. All Rafale and Typhoon pilots had been briefed before takeoff to launch their Meteors as soon as they all had a lock, even though this would make a hit unlikely.

In training Jacques had told his pilots to wait, if the tactical situation allowed it, to launch from sixty kilometers away from the target. The

Meteor's manufacturer MBDA called this the beginning of the "No Escape Zone." Jacques made a point of telling his students there was no such thing, but it was true that a hit was far more likely at the lower range.

The point of firing the Meteors now anyway was to occupy the RSAF planes with something other than destroying Prince Bilal's tanks. To some extent it worked. All planes with a Meteor locked onto them changed course and began using their electronic countermeasures.

Jacques swore as he heard AGM-114 Hellfire launch warnings, which answered his first question. The Saudis planned to take out both Prince Bilal's force as well as the QEAF.

When no answering swarm of Meteors came, though, Jacques knew he had a happier answer to his second question. It looked like the RSAF didn't have them yet.

Just a few minutes later, the range had been closed to the point that the QEAF's three dozen F-15s could send their AIM-120Cs at the RSAF fighters. An answering and much larger swarm of AIM-120s came from the RSAF jets, though not from all of them. Some of the Meteors had scored hits even from extreme range and many other RSAF fighters were still occupied with evading them, and so were unable to lock onto a QEAF jet.

Now came the most difficult part of the engagement. Jacques and all the other Rafale and Typhoon pilots were going to ignore the AIM-120Cs headed their way, and fire another five dozen Meteors at the RSAF from within the so-called "No Escape Zone." The orders at their briefing had stressed they should still have time after firing a second Meteor to evade the AIM-120C.

Well, Jacques thought grimly, the operative word is "should."

From the point of view of the QEAF Commander, he thought the second Meteor plan made a lot of sense. More RSAF planes would probably be lost to Meteor hits than QEAF planes to AIM-120Cs, and in the meantime nearly all the RSAF planes would be too busy to attack Prince Bilal's tanks.

Jacques' point of view, though, was dominated by an AIM-120C that appeared to be very serious about killing him. Today would see the first real test of the Rafale's self-defense suite, with the French acronym SPECTRA. The capability of greatest interest to Jacques was its supposed ability to do active cancellation. In theory, this worked by sampling and analyzing incoming radar and feeding it back out of phase, which would interfere with the returning radar echo.

As Jacques tried every maneuvering trick he could think of to evade the AIM-120C, all he could think of was that his late father had been right. He had been an NCO in the French Army, and when Jacques had told him he planned to enlist in the Air Force had given him just two words of advice - never volunteer.

Just when Jacques was convinced he would very soon be able to tell his father in person he wished he had taken his advice, the AIM-120C lost its lock and flew off. Had SPECTRA successfully spoofed it? Had it locked onto some other unlucky plane?

Jacques didn't care. While he had been busy trying to stay alive, the RSAF and QEAF jets had continued flying towards each other, and now he was going to experience what an American pilot had told him was called a "furball." He'd said they'd been rare since Vietnam, since missiles had usually settled matters before planes could get close enough for the two key elements to kick in - confusion, and multiple airplanes within cannon range.

The 30 mm GIAT 30M 791 cannon in the Rafale was one Jacques had used several times in exercises, and his score in those had been quite good. He had also insisted that his students take their training with the GIAT seriously, though he had privately agreed with the ones who grumbled that they'd never use them in combat.

Now he was using his GIAT against an F-15 that his instruments told him was an RSAF plane. Jacques hoped it was true, because though he was close enough to target the jet, he certainly couldn't see its insignia. Smoke started to pour from the F-15, and he saw the pilot eject as the jet began to tumble towards the desert below.

As soon as he'd survived his encounter with the AIM-120C Jacques had looked for his wingman but hadn't been able to find him. In the madness of dozens of aircraft firing guns and missiles at each other he hoped Mansour had survived, because at the moment everything was moving too fast for anyone to do more than that.

Just as he had that thought, Jacques watched in horror as two jets slammed into each other and disappeared in a cloud of exploding fuel and ammunition. He joined every other plane nearby in veering off, since the metal debris from the explosion would spell the end for anyone unfortunate enough to suck pieces into their engines.

Each Rafale pilot had been given the option of which missiles to include with their two Meteors, and Jacques had gone with the MICA IR. Capable of lock-on after launch (LOAL), it meant Jacques didn't have to wait to fire, making it perfect for the chaotic conditions around him. Even better was that while at least one was on his plane the MICA IR provided infrared imagery to his attack computer, acting as an extra sensor.

Now Jacques saw that an RSAF Typhoon was within MICA IR range, and without waiting for a lock fired. One reason Jacques had decided to use an IR missile rather than radar-homing was that many fighters lacked the ability to detect they were under IR attack. Only the UK, for example, had equipped its Typhoons with a laser warning receiver.

That's the reason Jacques had picked the Typhoon as a target for his MICA IR.

As it flew closer to the Typhoon Jacques was able to lock the missile on target, and in less than a minute it had detonated near its right engine. Jacques wasn't sure, but he thought it had been a proximity detonation of the missile's twelve-kilogram warhead rather than a direct impact hit, since in spite of smoke and flame the Typhoon's wing appeared intact.

Its pilot, however, apparently concluded that it was best not to wait for further explosions and ejected.

Jacques didn't have time to waste on self-congratulations, though, as the edge of his scope lit up with dozens of new contacts.

So far, the QEAF had faced Typhoons from King Fahd Air Base and F-15s from No. 55 Squadron, which had been recently transferred to Prince Sultan Air Base. Now joining the battle from King Abdulaziz Air Base near Dhahran were Panavia Tornados from the No. 7 Squadron and F-15s from the No. 13 and No. 92 Squadrons.

The RSAF had the distinction of being not only the sole air force in the world to ever fly the Tornado outside the three-country partnership that had produced it (Germany, the United Kingdom and Italy), it was also the only country that still had it in service. The UK, for instance, retired the Tornado F3 air defense model in 2011 and the Tornado GR4 ground attack model in 2019, replacing both with the Typhoon.

The bad news for the QEAF was that these Tornados had been updated to the latest GR4 model by the British and carried the ASRAAM. Developed by the British as a replacement for the AIM-9 Sidewinder, it flew at Mach 3 at a range of up to fifty kilometers. The F-15s were already firing AIM-120Cs at Jacques and the other surviving jets of the QEAF.

With all his attention focused on survival, Jacques had only a dim awareness that so far casualties suffered on both sides had been fairly even, or thanks to the Meteor salvos maybe even slightly in the QEAF's favor. Over half of the aircraft on both sides of the engagement had either been shot down, or in a few cases managed to limp damaged back to base. Prince Bilal's surviving Leopard tanks were back on the highway to Riyadh, and were about to face Prince Ali's M1A2 tanks.

The QEAF had accomplished its mission. It had given its armored forces the chance to reach Riyadh.

But with the appearance of three fresh RSAF squadrons, there was no doubt that today would mark the end of the QEAF as a coherent fighting force, even if a handful of planes were able to make it back to base in Doha.

Jacques managed to score one more victory with his last MICA IR that must have been an impact rather than a proximity hit against the RSAF Tornado, because this one exploded so violently he had to sheer off immediately to avoid damage from its debris.

While he was doing that, another AIM-120C found him. Jacques had no time to even attempt either evasion or ejection.

But, Jacques had fulfilled his dream of flying the Rafale in combat. And his few surviving fellow pilots would agree, he had done so well.

CHAPTER TWENTY SEVEN

Assembly of Experts Secretariat, Qom, Iran

Grand Ayatollah Sayyid Vahid Turani was trying, and failing, to imagine a less receptive audience than the men before him at the Assembly of Experts. They had been forced into cramped and uncomfortable quarters in the name of security, told nothing after that, and then rousted out of bed in the middle of the night - again in the name of security.

Vahid had already decided to get straight to the point. "The Supreme Leader has been murdered by the Pasdaran, on the orders of Acting Supreme Leader Reza Fagheh. He has also launched an attack on Saudi Arabia without any authorization using Pasdaran forces allied with Qatar's military, using both nuclear weapons and chemical agents."

"Where is your proof?" an Ayatollah shouted from the back. Vahid nodded as he recognized one of Reza's allies.

"Play the first video," Vahid said to a nearby technician.

The recording filled the large screen in front of the Assembly hall taken by Roya Maziar of the Supreme Leader being shot by a man in Pasdaran uniform.

Into the shocked silence that followed, Vahid said, "The nurse who made this recording with her cell phone is available to confirm its authenticity. Ask yourself this question- who stood to gain from the Supreme Leader's death, especially with all of you confined for supposed security reasons?"

Another Ayatollah shouted from the back, "Where is the proof Grand Ayatollah Fagheh approved the use of chemical weapons against the Saudis?"

Vahid smiled grimly as he recognized another of Reza's allies.

"Play the second video," Vahid said to the technician.

The next video showed a gruesome closeup of a victim of a missile's premature explosion with a VX warhead in Yemen, due to a Saudi tank shell. The voiceover explained that the Houthis sent to discover what had happened to the missile died themselves not long after taking the footage.

The next view was shot by a drone over the site of the explosion, showing multiple contorted bodies far away from the blast site.

"We all know that the Houthis have only one source for these missiles and the warheads they carry. Us."

Vahid said into an even deeper silence, "This is not the end of Fagheh's crimes. Here is more." He simply nodded to the technician.

A distant view of a mushroom cloud on the Saudi coast was quickly replaced by the view from a drone sent over the blast site. It showed the desalination plant had been utterly destroyed.

Now even the faces of Fagheh's allies showed nothing but shock.

"This is the view from one of our own drones, which I had sent by the Iranian Air Force. This used to be one of the largest desalination plants in the world. We are responsible for the death of everyone in or near this plant. Their only crime was producing fresh drinking water! That is how we decided to use one of our nuclear weapons."

Into the echoing silence Vahid said, "But an even greater crime was planned," and nodded once again to the technician.

Another mushroom cloud appeared, this one closer to the camera and in the desert. The voiceover from the person who had uploaded it to the Internet said that though it had exploded far enough from Riyadh that they believed they were safe from fallout, all power had been cut. The voiceover continued that he had to drive to Jeddah to get online to distribute the video, because all cell phone and Internet service in Riyadh was down as well.

Now it was Vahid's turn to shout. "Can you imagine what would have happened if that bomb had made it to Riyadh? Thousands, even millions may have died. And the deaths would not stop in Saudi Arabia.

Does anyone believe that their American allies would let such an act go unpunished?"

No one had anything to say.

Vahid continued, "But as evil as that crime was, for me using chemical weapons was even worse. A foolish man might claim ignorance of what a nuclear weapon could do. We all know what chemical weapons can do. Some of you in this room have lost sons to the Iraqi criminals who used them against us," he said, looking directly at several Ayatollahs.

They were not the only ones to squirm uncomfortably.

"But even this was not enough for Fagheh. No, he has sent Pasdaran troops without authorization marching to Riyadh. And he has enlisted the Qataris in his schemes, so they have sent their tanks to Riyadh too. Did he get authorization from any of you, or the Consultative Assembly before he did any of this? No, he did not."

Vahid nodded one final time at the technician, who put up a screen grab of the moment that the Supreme Leader was shot by the Pasdaran soldier.

"Ask yourself this question. Do you doubt for one second that the man who gave this assassin his orders was Reza Fagheh? Then ask, who gave the order for you to be moved from this building, and for everything I have shown to be concealed from you? Finally, if you didn't do exactly what Reza Fagheh told you, including electing him as the new Supreme Leader, do you think a man who did everything I have shown you would hesitate for one second to have all of you shot?"

Vahid glared out into the silence. Not one Ayatollah was willing to respond.

"So, how can we stop this madman? And once we do, how can we avoid having our wives and children being made to pay for his crimes? There are many in America who have been waiting for a long time to strike us down, and this criminal has given them the perfect excuse."

Vahid paused and looked out at the Assembly. "If you are all willing to trust me, I can lead us out of this disaster, and to a better future. Here is my plan..."

Doha, Qatar

Guardian Colonel Bijan Turani scowled as once again he was unable to reach the Acting Supreme Leader's office. He had been ordered to wait with his artillery unit in Doha in case pressure needed to be applied to Qatar's Emir, but he had never thought that part of the plan made any sense. Anyone with military experience would know that his howitzers could be easily overrun by infantry within minutes, and at best would manage to fire one or two rounds.

No, Reza Fagheh was far from infallible, even if he was Acting Supreme Leader. And now he also appeared to be unreachable.

Bijan made his decision. He had been worried that the men he'd detailed to deal with the Ayatollahs at the Assembly of Experts, as well as the hospitalized Supreme Leader, would not prove up to the task. While Bijan was leading the attack on the Saudi force blockading Qatar he'd had no choice, since he couldn't be in several places at once. Now, though, all he had to do was disobey orders. Orders he had never agreed with in the first place.

A quick check confirmed that there were three nonstop flights per day from Doha to Tehran, and each one took less than two hours to reach Tehran. That settled it, since even if Reza ordered him back to Doha he'd only have been away for a matter of hours. Plus, whatever the explanation was for his failure to reach Reza, it certainly served as a reasonable rationale for at least a temporary return.

It was nearly ten at night when the flight from Doha arrived in Tehran. As soon as he left the jetway, he saw a squad of Iranian Army soldiers.

None of them were smiling.

Their commander strode forward as soon as he saw Bijan. "Guardian Colonel Bijan Turani," he said, more as a statement than a question. The other soldiers quickly surrounded him, and before he knew what was happening he'd been spun around, and he felt handcuffs being slapped on his wrists.

"What is the meaning of this?," Bijan roared with outrage. "I am a special advisor to Acting Supreme Leader Fagheh, and demand that you contact his office at once!"

In response, the squad's commander slapped him hard on his right cheek. Stunned rather than hurt, Bijan stared at him speechlessly.

The commander said, "The criminal Fagheh is already in custody. You will be tried for your role in the assassination of the Supreme Leader later this evening."

Then the commander nodded to his deputy, and soldiers on each side of Bijan began to march him to the airport exit. Bijan noticed that the few other people visible not only gave all of them a wide berth, no one even looked in their direction.

For maybe the first time in his military career, Bijan sincerely wished he had shown no initiative, and had simply followed orders.

Evin Prison, Tehran, Iran

Grand Ayatollah Sayyid Vahid Turani strode down the prison corridor with the air of a man having a great deal to do. He did; this task was one he did from a sense of duty, not pleasure.

That's not what the man on the other side of the bars thought. "Ah, come here to gloat, have you? I always knew you were a small and petty man." Reza Fagheh had been stripped of his Grand Ayatollah title, but carried himself as though he were still Acting Supreme Leader.

Well, Vahid thought, that will end soon enough.

"No, I am here to inform you of the verdict of the Assembly of Experts, which has tried you for your many crimes. You have been found guilty. The sentence is death."

Reza shrugged. "Once you had regular Army troops drag me from my office and throw me in here, it was pretty obvious what you were up to. Well, you may find that keeping me in this hole won't be as easy as putting me here."

Vahid nodded. "You are speaking of your allies in the Pasdaran, such as Guardian Colonel Bijan Turani. He is in a cell not far from yours. The Pasdaran and Basij have been disbanded. Some will be offered positions in the military. Others will not."

Now Reza looked much less assured. "Yes, and I'm sure they'll all meekly accept that decision," he said, trying to put as much confidence in his voice as he could.

Vahid shrugged and said, “We’ll see. Or more precisely, I will.”

Reza’s eyes narrowed. “What do you mean? What day is my execution scheduled?”

Vahid looked at Reza calmly. “Today. In one hour.”

Now Reza looked at Vahid in shock. “One hour? That’s ridiculous! I have the right of appeal!”

Vahid shook his head. “An ordinary criminal does. But you’re not one of those, you’re a mass murderer. And you’ve already been tried by our highest authority, the Assembly of Experts, and your sentence has been confirmed by the Supreme Leader.”

Reza stared at Vahid wild-eyed. “The Supreme Leader? Who is he?”

Vahid cocked his head, and waited for realization to dawn.

Reza’s breath hissed between his teeth. “You... You can’t do this! Our troops will make it to Riyadh! We can overthrow the Saudis! You’re throwing away a great future for our country!”

Vahid just smiled sadly, and shook his head.

“Your plan was always insane, Reza. It’s time for the rest of us to deal with the consequences of your madness.”

Vahid started to walk away, and then turned. “And it is time for you to meet the final judgment, that sooner or later comes to us all.”

CHAPTER TWENTY EIGHT

Five Kilometers East of Highway 522 and Highway 80 Intersection, 120 Kilometers East of Riyadh

As he sat in the cupola of his M1A2 tank with the rest of the force moving to intercept the Qataris, Prince Ali bin Sultan played back the argument he'd had with the Crown Prince in his head and tried to imagine how he could have convinced him. Ali had argued for another air strike against the Qataris, who had already had their two hundred Leopards thinned out considerably by both the American cluster bomb attack and the RSAF's Hellfires. Another round of Hellfires, in Ali's view, might well have inflicted enough damage to make the Qataris turn back.

The Crown Prince had vetoed that plan, noting first that they needed air assets to be available in case the northern invaders made it past the relatively weaker force commanded by Jamal Al-Qahtani sent to oppose them, especially if during the battle Jamal's forces were successful in destroying their anti-air missile launcher. He also pointed out that some of the Qatari tanks would probably survive, and might make it to Riyadh. That was a risk they simply couldn't take.

Ali thought the bigger risk was splitting his armor so that his deputy commander would have to attack the cloaked force coming from the north with fewer tanks than he probably needed for victory. The Crown Prince countered that Ali could swing north once the Qataris were defeated and finish off any northern invaders still left, plus the tanks on their way back from Yemen would be in Riyadh soon.

Ali pointed out that nothing guaranteed the northern force would stick to its previous slow pace, and that both his force and the tanks from Yemen quite simply might not get back in time. He didn't say that his force could also be defeated by the Qataris, because he never thought for a minute that was possible.

The Crown Prince had then explained that the surviving strike aircraft had to be refueled and rearmed, and that would take as much time as driving his already prepared tanks to meet the enemy. Besides, he'd added tartly, "you won't have to drive far."

What the Crown Prince didn't tell Ali was that he'd been shocked by the losses the QEAF had inflicted on the RSAF, and didn't want to send out its pilots again so soon. It was unfortunate for Ali that Khaled bin Fahd wasn't still alive, since he would have insisted on pressing home the air attack against the Qatari armored force. Khaled would have also known that his pilots weren't asking for rest, and instead wanted nothing more than to strike back against the country that had cut short the lives of so many of their friends.

Ali's tanks were loaded with the 120 mm APFSDS-T M829A2 round. It was two generations behind the rounds used by American M1A2s, having been introduced in 1994. Against Houthi forces this had not been an issue. Against the Qataris' Leopard 2, Ali feared it would be.

It certainly was an improvement over the M829A1. A classified manufacturing process improved the structural quality of the depleted uranium penetrator and there were new composites for the sabot and a new propellant, which all added up to improved penetrator performance. Combined, these features increased the muzzle velocity of the M829A2 by 100 m/sec to 1,675 m/sec.

By contrast, the Qataris' Leopard 2s fired the DM-53 round. It featured a temperature-independent propulsion system (TIPS) which improved accuracy, particularly in the face of the wide temperature ranges often found on the Arabian Peninsula.

Which would be more effective? Since M1A2s had never faced off against Leopard 2s, they were about to find out.

The Saudis weren't blind to the Leopard's advantages. They had tried to buy Leopards since the Leopard 1 was introduced in the 1980s, but been stymied by European concerns over its human rights record.

Initially successful at obtaining German approval for an order of two hundred Leopard 2s, Saudi military intervention in Bahrain in 2011 and renewed concern over human rights led to the order's cancellation.

After the American's drone attack and their own air strikes with Mavericks all Ali knew for sure was that the Qataris no longer had two hundred Leopards. Just how many was anyone's guess, especially because an unknown number were outfitted with that cursed camouflage netting, this time one that had apparently been made by a European company specifically for the Leopard 2 tank. At least, none of the Qataris' other vehicles had it.

Ali had many advantages, though. Even in the unlikely event that the Leopards abandoned the highway and struck out cross-country, he knew their destination. Not only was the capital the obvious target, but the Qataris' route since crossing the border also pointed like an arrow straight at Riyadh.

Bolstering this edge was the unexpected addition of an American Reaper drone, which for now Ali was using strictly for reconnaissance. Camouflage might help conceal some of their numbers, but it didn't stop him from knowing where the bulk of the Qatari force was located, and their heading.

These advantages paled, though, in the face of what Ali could do now that destruction of the two Qatari S-300s had been confirmed. They were finally going to be able to deploy their Apache attack helicopters. Though Ali knew the Qataris must have other anti-air assets, he doubted they could cope with all eight Apaches he had for this battle.

The good news was that these eight Apaches had just been upgraded to the latest AH-64E standard, that the Americans called "Guardian" in place of the earlier "Longbow." It featured multiple improvements including a more powerful engine, new composite rotor blades giving it increased speed, climb rate and payload capacity, and improved radar.

The bad news was that many of their existing Apaches were still being upgraded in Arizona, and the ones they had most recently purchased hadn't yet been manufactured. With some Apaches yet to return from Yemen, he'd only been able to spare five for the force that would attack the northern invaders. Ali thought about the S-300 they would be facing, and said a silent prayer for their pilots.

The news was also mixed for the nearly one hundred Bradley APCs Ali had available for this battle. On the one hand they were plentiful, since none had been sent back to America for refurbishment like the Apaches. On the other, they were still the M2A2 model, two upgrades behind the Americans. Its TOW II anti-tank missile would almost certainly fail to penetrate a Leopard's frontal armor but a flanking hit might damage it, or at least knock off its treads. It was also still a match for the Qataris' APC, the Mowag Piranha.

Knowing where the Qataris were and where they were headed allowed Ali to deploy his Abrams tanks, Bradley APCs and Apache helicopters to maximum effect. Ali planned to hit the Qatari force both directly and on each flank, with the aim of bringing overwhelming firepower to bear. Any vehicle without camouflage would be engaged first, simply because they would be far easier to target. Then, Ali would deal with the camouflaged survivors.

The terrain Ali had picked for this battle was no accident. There was a slight rise in elevation to the front and on both sides which Ali would use to conceal his forces. The Apaches would also be able to use their distinctive top-mounted radomes to obtain a lock on non-camouflaged Leopards before their targets even knew they were there.

To lure the Qataris into the range of his M1A2s' cannons, Ali had ordered that the Qataris' Fennek armored reconnaissance vehicles were to be allowed to move forward untouched. Though Ali knew he risked having his ambush spotted, he thought they had a good chance of keeping the Qataris moving forward until it was too late to escape.

Ali's goal was not simply the defeat of the Qatari force. It was to destroy it, and do so quickly enough that he could hurry north to relieve the weaker force that had been sent against the northern invaders. No matter what the Crown Prince thought, Ali believed they still had a good chance of pushing through to Riyadh.

Once the Reaper operator informed Ali that the Leopards were coming into range, he ordered the operator to engage them with his entire payload of four AGM-114 Hellfire missiles and two 500 lb. GBU-12 Paveway II laser-guided bombs. No sooner had he given that order than he had his eight Apaches each fire a Hellfire against their locked targets.

Within seconds, dozens of 120 mm M829A2 rounds fired by Ali's M1A2 tanks were headed towards the Leopard 2s as well. Many of the

Leopards deployed smoke and attempted to evade the incoming fire, while others immediately fired back at Ali's tanks.

Almost at once Ali began receiving damage reports, and could see with his own eyes Abrams tanks that were destroyed by a single Leopard round. He winced when one M1A2 tank on his left flank exploded with a violence that told him some of its internal store of munitions had been detonated by a Leopard round, but refused to let it distract him from his battle plan.

Ali had put his M2A2 Bradleys on the flanks, and now ordered them to fire their TOW II missiles against any target where they could get a lock. Because their TOW II missiles were wire-guided, Ali knew the Bradleys were going to be some of his most exposed crews against the Qatari force. Unlike the Apaches with their "fire and forget" Hellfire missiles, the Bradleys couldn't quickly pop into and out of the fight. They had to remain in visual contact with their target until the moment of impact.

Of course, visual contact worked both ways.

Many of the Leopards focused their fire on the M1A2 tanks, correctly judging them to be the greatest threat to their survival. As the battle progressed, though, and particularly once some of the Leopards began losing tracks to TOW II fire they started using some of their rounds against the Bradleys.

Some of the M1A2 tanks survived Leopard hits against their frontal armor, though most did not. The Bradleys, on the other hand, had no chance of survival. The impact of a Leopard 2's 120 mm round would not only penetrate its spaced laminate armor, designed for protection against RPGs and 30 mm shells, but often send it tumbling across the desert sand.

The Bradleys also discovered some of the Qatari MOWAG Piranhas were equipped with 30 mm autocannons that quickly managed to punch through their armor, in spite of its supposed resistance to 30 mm shells. The answer was simple. While a single 30 mm hit was indeed unlikely to penetrate, the Piranhas' autocannons were often able to deliver more than one shell to the same area of Bradley armor, particularly if its crew was focused on wire-guiding a TOW II missile to its target.

The Apaches had at first been able to pop up and fire their Hellfires with relative impunity, but after the first two rounds the Qataris were able to deploy man-portable anti-air missiles against them. First one, and then two Apaches were hit. Neither were a total loss, with one able to limp back to base trailing smoke, while the crew of the other was able to escape with only minor injuries after a hard landing. Then a third Apache was hit, and this time exploded with an ear-shattering force that meant its heavy munitions load had detonated.

Snarling curses, Ali ordered his Bradleys to concentrate fire on the locations where anti-air missiles had been fired. Though they were often unable to see the Qatari soldiers and their handheld anti-air missiles, a TOW II missile delivered to the general area where a missile had been fired before usually meant none would be fired again. A few launches spotted at shorter ranges from the Bradleys were dealt with by either its M242 Bushmaster 25 mm chain-driven autocannon, or its M240 7.62 mm coaxial machine gun.

Once the remaining Hellfire missiles carried by the Apaches had been successfully launched, they moved on to the next phase of their orders. Ali had directed four Apaches be given an "anti-armor" load of sixteen Hellfire missiles, and the other four a "covering force" load of eight Hellfire missiles and thirty-eight Hydra 70 2.75-inch fin-stabilized unguided rockets. Two of the downed Apaches had anti-armor loads, so the two remaining returned to base to reload.

The three surviving Apaches with Hydra 70 rockets on board prepared to use them on the remaining Leopards. Few undamaged Leopards left were the ones without camouflage, since fifty-one Hellfire missiles had been fired at them and nearly all had hit. Though not every hit was a kill, most were, and many other hits rendered the Leopard immobile. And any tank, no matter how well armored, that couldn't move on a modern battlefield counted its lifespan in minutes.

The strategy for using the Hydra 70 rockets on the camouflaged Leopards was simple. They might be difficult to target using the infrared sensor in a Hellfire, or in an M1A2 tank turret trying to see through clouds of dust. But, fire enough rockets into the center of that dust cloud, and you'd probably score some hits.

Ali had also stacked the odds in his favor by choosing to arm the Apaches with Hydra 70 rockets containing the M247 high-explosive anti-tank (HEAT) warhead. With a little less than a kilogram of Composition B, a 60/40 RDX/TNT mixture, a single hit was unlikely to kill a Leopard. But the remaining Apaches had enough rockets between them to devote several to each surviving Leopard. It wouldn't be enough to finish them off.

Until that is, they were able to go back to base and reload to the "escort" maximum of no Hellfires - and seventy-six Hydra 70 rockets.

Ali wasn't having it all his way, as the continuing stream of damage reports coming over his headset reminded him. The Leopards' gunnery skills were outstanding, and a hit from one of their cannons was far more likely to kill an M1A2 tank than the reverse. The MOWAG Piranhas were inflicting heavy damage on his Bradleys, as well as any Leopards that were finding them easy targets.

Efforts by the Leopards to push through the ambush, though, were being repeatedly thwarted by the Saudis' superior firepower. Ali was working feverishly to coordinate fire by his armor and air assets on any attempt at a breakout. If he could just keep them pinned down long enough...

One after another, Leopards were hit by missiles, rockets and tank rounds. The first to have their armor fail were ones that had suffered earlier hits from the bomblets deployed by the Tomahawks, but had remained mobile. Often the only damage they'd suffered was having their modular armor cleared away, but that made them far more vulnerable.

One of the principal advantages offered by the 2A7+ Leopard model was modular armor, which improved frontal protection with a dual-kit on the turret and hull front. Without it, the Leopard's integral spaced multilayer armor would eventually fail. Sooner, in the case of a direct Hellfire missile hit. Later, in the case of TOW II missiles, 120 mm M829A2 tank rounds, or Hydra 70 rockets.

One by one, Leopards began dying under the harsh Saudi sun.

By the time the five surviving Apaches returned with their new loads of Hydra 70 rockets, fewer than thirty Leopards remained. One last anti-air missile was fired by a brave Qatari soldier who had burrowed into the desert sand, and it claimed an Apache that blew up with the huge thunderclap to be expected from the simultaneous explosion of seventy-six Hydra 70 rockets.

Ali's remaining Bradleys were quick to direct cannon and machine gun fire to the spot where the soldier had been hidden, and no more anti-air missiles were fired that day.

Three hundred and four Hydra 70 rockets poured into the dust clouds that marked surviving mobile Leopards. Though the number fired at each was not perfectly divided, since the average number of rockets with HEAT warheads available per target was about ten, it hardly mattered.

Quarter was neither asked nor offered. The Qataris were on the Saudi battlefield because they believed the blockade and the construction of the Salwa Canal amounted to a declaration of war. The Saudis saw them as invaders who deserved no mercy.

Once the last Leopard had been destroyed, Ali's armor and air assets began the systematic destruction of the remaining Qatari APCs and support vehicles. Finally, troops dismounted from the Bradleys and searched the battlefield for Qatari survivors.

There weren't many, and they didn't include Prince Bilal, who had died when his Leopard 2 had been hit by a 120 mm tank round and no fewer than nine Hydra 70 rockets. The survivors who were found were put into trucks that transported them to a prison that had been designated by the Interior Ministry. None were ever seen again.

Ali had left the battlefield with his M1A2 tanks and Apaches as soon as the last Qatari APCs had been destroyed, leaving the rest of the battle's aftermath to the Bradleys' commander. He had been in contact with Jamal Al-Qahtani, the commander of the force confronting the northern invaders throughout the battle with the Qataris. The battle with the northern invaders hadn't been going nearly as well.

And then all communication had been abruptly cut off.

The force Ali had left after the battle with the Qataris had been badly mauled. He had lost half of his Apaches, and well over half of his M1A2 tanks had been completely destroyed. An even two dozen tanks were immobile, and though some of those could be fixed, none would be able to rejoin him in time. That left him with just sixty-two M1A2 tanks and four Apaches to bring to the fight against the northern invaders.

As Ali had feared, the latest word from the M1A2 tanks en route from Yemen via highway with multiple refuelings was that they would be in Riyadh soon - about three hours after Ali calculated he would need them north of Riyadh.

Let loose in a city, a tank could do a lot in three hours.

Ali was headed to relieve Jamal at the best speed he could manage - assuming Jamal and the rest of his men were still alive.

CHAPTER TWENTY NINE

40 Kilometers North of Riyadh, Saudi Arabia

Jamal Al-Qahtani was unlike most of the top Saudi military commanders in one key respect. He was not a prince, or in any way related to the royal family. His appearance was unremarkable, except that he was a bit shorter than the average Saudi male.

His father had a long-standing relationship with a prince as his advisor, which had helped him pass some of his colleagues as he moved up the career ladder. But that was not really the main reason he was now a Brigadier General, commanding the force about to engage the northern invaders.

Jamal had been promoted mostly because he was highly intelligent, hard-working, and a natural leader. The fact that he had advanced so rapidly helped explain how Saudi Arabia's government had persisted as one of the very few monarchies left worldwide. Talent, even outside the royal family, was recognized and rewarded.

Being a more recent graduate of the Armor School at Fort Benning than Prince Ali by five years had some advantages as well. Jamal had been exposed to some of the most recent training offered by the US Army, that included hard-won lessons from their experiences in both Iraq and Afghanistan. Many of them applied directly to the Saudis' use of armor in Yemen.

The contacts Jamal had developed had also been useful in securing and expediting a contract to provide the maintenance and spare parts needed for all Saudi armored forces in the far more advanced tempo of multi-year operations in Yemen. Since the only way to keep some

M1A2 tanks on the field had been to take parts from others, getting this contract done had been key to keeping the Saudi Army in the fight.

Now, though, as Jamal looked over the force he commanded on its way to engage the invaders advancing on Riyadh from the north there was one question that he couldn't get out of his head. Was he rolling into battle with a force of fifty M1A2 tanks and fifty-five M60 Patton tanks, plus forty Bradley APCs and five Apaches, because he wasn't a prince?

Yes, Ali was Army Commander. And yes, he understood the argument that since the Qataris were sticking to highways they might get to Riyadh faster, though the Qataris' last reported position made him doubt it. He could read a map.

But the Qataris no longer had S-300s, and their Air Force had effectively ceased to exist. Meanwhile, Jamal wondered how long his Apaches would manage to survive against the S-300 that had already shot down so many of the RSAF's best planes, even one piloted by the Air Force Commander.

Yes, the Leopard 2s Ali faced were formidable opponents. But Jamal had absolutely no idea what he would be up against with these invaders from the north. But he could guess the camouflage that had been so effective against the sensors on drones would probably work just as well against the ones on anti-tank missiles and the M1A2's thermal sights.

That didn't mean Jamal was ready to give up. Far from it. In fact, he planned to surprise everyone and win this battle. Yes, he might have been sent rolling north to buy Prince Ali enough time to claim victory over both sets of invaders before they reached Riyadh. But Jamal wasn't just going to survive. He was going to make the defeat of these invaders the basis for his next promotion.

The first step in Jamal's plan was the elimination of the invaders' anti-air missile launcher. He knew it had some sort of camouflage that protected it from missiles using radar or thermal locks. His attack wouldn't rely on them.

Instead, Jamal was going to use his five Apaches to send unguided Hydra 70 rockets at the launcher, which they would identify by looking for the biggest dust cloud in the invasion force. Between them the Apaches would be carrying three hundred eighty rockets, and Jamal doubted that the launcher could withstand more than a couple of hits before its load of fuel and explosives detonated.

That assumed the Apaches survived to rocket attack range. Jamal had detailed cartography on his tablet covering the invaders' route, which while still off-road was aimed straight at Riyadh. He smiled briefly as he thought about the level of detail, which was extremely high thanks to oil company surveys of nearly every inch of the Kingdom. Nice to know that even in areas like this one north of Riyadh where oil had never been found, the effort had not been entirely wasted.

Jamal had traced out a route for the Apaches that would allow them to approach the invaders by hugging an escarpment that would give them cover from the launcher. He had managed to find a spot where the Apaches could use their top-mounted radomes to peek over the escarpment before engaging the enemy. Jamal knew the invaders' camouflage had been effective so far, but was betting that at a range of under a kilometer the Apaches would be able to get at least a general fix on the bulk of the enemy force.

Everything depended on coordination. The Americans' Triton was still feeding them the invaders' general position and speed. Jamal had to try to confront them with his armor at the same moment the Apaches launched their attack, to give the attack helicopters the best chance of success.

The Crown Prince had promised Jamal personally that if he could knock out the anti-air launcher, he would have RSAF support minutes later. True to his word, the Crown Prince had already ordered that two F-15 squadrons be loaded with Mark 82 unguided bombs, each containing eighty-nine kilograms of Tritonal high explosive. Given the chance, they could deliver enough firepower to the battlefield to end the invasion on the spot.

Jamal's strategy for confronting the invaders' armor depended heavily on his M60s. Though he knew most tankers looked down on them, M60s had performed well in combat in Yemen, and were still a match for most of the tanks actually deployed in the Middle East. Jamal had often pointed out to grumbling crewmen assigned to M60s rather than M1A2s that over five thousand Pattons remained in service in the armies of nineteen countries.

It was true that many of those countries, like Turkey, had invested in upgrade packages that replaced the M60's original cannon. Before retiring the Patton the Israelis had gone further and added armor, as well as replacing its hydraulic system with an electrical one. This cured one of the original M60s' problems- when a shell penetrated its hydraulic system, the fluid would often burst into flames.

Well, Jamal thought, nothing was perfect.

But most of the Pattons the Saudis still had in service were the M60A3 upgrade with an improved engine, turret armor, IR sights, ballistic computer, and a Halon fire suppression system. It also had a crude built-in smoke screen capability achieved by recycling its diesel engine exhaust, called the Vehicle Engine Exhaust Smoke System. All of the Pattons Jamal brought to this battle were the M60A3 upgrade version.

His plan was to put the M60s up front against the invaders' armor to serve several functions. First and most obvious was to do whatever damage they could. Its M68 105 mm cannon would be firing an M152/3 HEAT round capable of penetrating the armor of most tanks, including all but the most modern. It also outgunned any APC. If the invaders were foolish enough to leave their anti-air launcher within its range, a single hit from a round carrying a full kilogram of Composition B explosive traveling at a velocity of over a kilometer per second would probably be enough to destroy it.

The second was to help Jamal solve a puzzle that had vexed him and all the other top Saudi commanders from the start. What were they facing? The Americans had only been able to say that from their analysis of the images captured by the Triton the invaders were not fielding a "uniform force." That meant there was a mix of different types of armor, but that wasn't much help.

Once the M60s actually engaged the enemy, Jamal was confident he would quickly be able to pick out the easier and more difficult targets, camouflaged or not. Then, he would prioritize them between his M60 and M1A2 platoons.

Having seen tank combat in Yemen, where the Houthi rebels actually had their own M60 tanks, Jamal knew that identifying the enemy's advanced tanks was critical. Against a T-55 or its equivalent, he knew the Patton could hold its own. But if the invaders had advanced tanks like the T-90, Jamal would have to push his M1A2s forward quickly before the M60s were slaughtered.

Jamal rode in the cupola of his M1A2 tank as he and the rest of his armor rolled towards the invaders, and chewed his lower lip as he thought about anything else he could do to improve their chances. Finally, he shook his head.

He had done all he could. Very soon, he would find out whether it had been enough.

45 Kilometers North of Riyadh, Saudi Arabia

Colonel Hamid Mazdaki nodded at the scout's report. It was about time the enemy showed himself. He frowned, though, at the estimate that half the tanks he was facing were M60 Pattons, with the other half the M1A2s he'd been expecting as his sole opponents. Since elements of the M60s Iran had bought from the Americans before the Revolution had been used to develop the Zulfiqar-3 he was sitting in, it's not that he dismissed them as a threat.

No. Instead, Hamid's first thought was that the force in front of him was a decoy, intended to distract him while another armor force struck him on the flanks.

Hamid shook his head as he read more reports. Part of his purpose in staying away from highways most of the way had been to avoid a surprise flanking attack, and the terrain he'd picked for his approach to Riyadh had effectively guaranteed against one. There were escarpments on both sides of his force that would halt any flank approach.

By tanks. Hamid froze in his cupola as he thought to himself - What about helicopters?

He dropped into the tank to access its communications console. "Commander Khalilli, can your missile launcher defend us from helicopter attack?"

Khalilli's voice in response sounded genuinely puzzled. "Yes, sir. The S-300's radar will spot helicopters even at low altitude from over a hundred kilometers away."

Hamid gritted his teeth. "I'm not talking about helicopters approaching us on this plateau. What if they flew along the escarpment, and popped up alongside us at the last moment?"

There was a long pause, which Hamid let continue without comment. He wanted the man to think.

"Sir," Khalilli said carefully, "I am glad you brought that possibility to my attention. It is a likely tactic, since I understand the enemy has Apache helicopters. Our crew will be watching for any sudden appearance by unknown contacts, and engage them immediately. Without this conversation, we might have thought such contacts an anomaly. Now, we will understand just how they could have appeared close to us without prior warning."

Hamid grunted. "Good, Commander. Enemy armor is approaching. I think it's likely Apaches are going to join in the attack as soon as their tanks are in range."

"Very well, sir," Khalilli said confidently. "We'll be ready."

Hamid ordered his T-90s and the Armata to the front of his force, and along with the other Zulfiqar-3s fell in behind them. Though ready to die, Hamid wasn't about to take unnecessary risks until they got to Riyadh.

The 2A46 125 mm smoothbore cannon in the T-90 could fire multiple types of ammunition, but for this battle had been loaded with armor-piercing fin-stabilized discarding sabot rounds. These particular rounds were the 3BM44M "Lekalo" with tungsten alloy sabots which would be fired at a muzzle velocity of 1,750 meters per second, and had the ability to penetrate 650 mm of armor at a range of two kilometers.

The T-90 had an autoloader that carried twenty-two ready-to-fire rounds in its carousel, and could reload in less than eight seconds. That meant Hamid's ten T-90 platoons would be able to deliver nearly nine hundred Lekalo rounds with only three minutes needed to reload the shells.

Of course, that didn't include the time needed to aim the T-90's cannon accurately. This had been a major worry for Hamid prior to his unit's last deployment to Syria, their first after receiving the T-90. Their T-90MS tanks included the same "Kalina" automatic target tracker and fire control computer installed in the T-14 Armata. Capable of automatically tracking and continuously locking the T-90's main gun on a target, it had been a godsend for Hamid, since he had not been able to spend as much time as he'd have liked on training many of his tanks' crewmen.

Now Hamid was going to see just how effective the T-90 was against the Saudis. Since the best the Syrian rebels had managed to field against him had been some captured T-55 Syrian Army tanks, all he knew for sure was that this would be a greater challenge.

The Kalina system had locked in the M60s as valid targets from a range of nearly four kilometers, in spite of the Pattons' deployment of a smoke screen. Since Hamid had ordered the T-90s' gunners to wait until the M60s were in the Lekalo rounds' maximum effective range of three kilometers, it gave him plenty of time to ensure they were aiming at separate M-60s.

When the T-90s opened fire on the Pattons, not a single M60 had tried to engage the enemy tanks. Hamid correctly concluded that the M60s' commander didn't believe they had a real chance of hitting his tanks from a three-kilometer range.

The same was certainly not true for his T-90s. Their initial salvo left thirty-eight M60s either immobile or destroyed, with most actually catastrophic hits. Even from three kilometers, Hamid could see multiple tank turrets thrown clear either by the force of a direct sabot hit, or by secondary explosions of fuel and ammunition inside the Pattons.

Now there was finally answering fire, as the enemy's M1A2 tanks rolled forward to replace the Pattons. At the same time, Hamid was notified over his headset that Apache helicopters had launched the attack he'd expected. Two minutes later Commander Khalilli told him four Apaches had been destroyed, and for now there were no other contacts.

So far in spite of the Abrams tanks' best effort only three hits had registered against Hamid's T-90s, and only a single hit had actually managed to kill one. This impressive record was due to the T-90's three-layer defensive approach. The first was the T-90's composite armor, the second its Kontact-5 explosive reactive armor, and the third its Shtora-1 countermeasures suite. Shtora-1 included two active infrared jammers, four laser warning receivers, and two smoke grenade launchers that deployed automatically whenever the T-90 was painted by an enemy targeting system.

By contrast, the Saudi M1A2 tanks lacked the depleted uranium that made the American models difficult to penetrate, had no reactive armor, and manually deployed smoke. Many were killed so quickly they never had the chance, not that it would have mattered. The real surprise was that at a three-kilometer range they were able to damage the T-90s at all.

Just as Hamid thought uneasily that the battle was going too well, Commander Khalilli was yelling over his headset, "Attack drones!" An instant later, a loud explosion behind his tank sent ice through his veins, as he thought to himself the launcher must have been hit.

Several minutes later, Hamid's fears were proved groundless as Commander Khalilli's voice came over his headset again to report that three Reaper attack drones had been shot down, and that once again there were no enemy air contacts visible. He also reported that the R-330ZH automated jammer had been destroyed as well as several of their tanks, though he couldn't say which model. Hamid shook his head with resignation, acknowledging to himself that knowledge of all the different tank models Iran was currently fielding was a bit too much to expect from his missile launch commander.

A quick look answered his principal question- had one of the tanks the Reapers destroyed been the Armata? The answer "no" came in the form of the T-14 firing a 9M119M Refliks anti-tank missile at a Saudi M1A2. With the ability to punch through nearly a meter of armor, any hit was likely to be a kill. So far, the Armata had accounted for the destruction of seven M1A2 tanks on its own, and still stood untouched.

That particular Refliks anti-tank missile ended Jamal Al-Qahtani's dreams of promotion, as it punched through the front armor of his M1A2 tank.

Fortunately, besides the R-330ZH Hamid had brought another tracked electronic warfare vehicle, the smaller 1L262E RTUT-BM. Though its main purpose was to defeat radar-guided warheads, its operator had assured him that it could also jam enemy communications, though over a shorter distance than the R-330ZH.

The commander of the remaining Saudi tanks finally did what Hamid imagined he would have done even earlier. He retreated.

Hamid let the pitiful handful of Saudi tanks and APCs remaining escape, while he collected survivors from the few tanks the Saudis had been able to damage. Even a task as delightful as destroying Saudi tanks had to take second place to his primary objective- leveling as many palaces and government buildings in Riyadh as possible.

There was no doubt that the Saudis had hundreds of M1A2 tanks on their way back from Yemen that could turn up any moment. Hamid knew that even if many of his tanks were better, they couldn't overcome a force twice their size, or even more.

No, there was no substitute for speed. Now that he had brushed this obstacle out of his way, nothing was going to stop Hamid from making it to Riyadh.

CHAPTER THIRTY

The White House, Washington, DC

President Hernandez looked up as Chief of Staff Chuck Soltis came hurrying into the Oval Office. He thought he'd seen every expression possible on Soltis' face, but not this odd combination of excitement, worry, and near panic. At the same moment, he noticed a red light flashing on his phone that told him of an incoming call. Since he had none scheduled, he assumed that's why Soltis was here.

He was right. Soltis stood in front of his desk for a moment, clearly out of breath, and then forced out, "Sir, the new Iranian Supreme Leader is on the phone, and says he wants our help in getting their invasion force to surrender."

Hernandez leaned back in his chair, and gestured for Soltis to sit down, which he did gratefully.

"OK," Hernandez said, "new Iranian Supreme Leader. Do we know that really is whoever's on the other end of the phone?"

"We think so, sir," Soltis replied. "We got a call first from the Iranian Ambassador to the UN in New York, who introduced him and said that he had been elected Supreme Leader by the Assembly of Experts after the old Supreme Leader died. His name is...," and then after a look at the notes in his hand, "Grand Ayatollah Sayyid Vahid Turani." He then handed the notes to Hernandez.

"Interesting. Wasn't the previous Supreme Leader in a coma for months? Quite a coincidence that he happened to die just now, isn't it?"

"Yes, sir," Soltis replied, nodding. "You'll see in my notes that within the past hour the CIA received an unconfirmed report that he was assassinated by the Pasdaran."

Hernandez shook his head. "Pasdaran. Also known as the Revolutionary Guards? Isn't this exactly the sort of thing they were supposed to guard against?"

Soltis shrugged. "Yes, sir, but as you know our understanding of what's happening in Iran has always been limited. No US Embassy in Tehran since 1979, any American who visits risks being arrested on any pretext and effectively becoming a government hostage...getting good information about Iran has been a challenge for a long time."

Hernandez grunted. "And now the new Supreme Leader wants to help get the Iranians just outside Riyadh to surrender. Now, this isn't the same fellow who's been acting as Supreme Leader over the past months, right? I don't remember his name, but I'm pretty sure it wasn't..." Hernandez paused as he looked over Soltis' notes. "Turani," he finished.

"No, sir," Soltis said. "If you look a bit further down the notes, there's another unconfirmed report that the Ayatollah who had been acting Supreme Leader, Reza Fagheh, has been executed."

"Right," Hernandez said slowly, as he read further down the page of notes.

Soltis added, "Fred Popel is on his way here from State and I'm sure he could do a better job of explaining all this, but since this Turani fellow says he can stop the invasion, I thought you'd want to talk to him right away."

Hernandez nodded, and said, "Chuck, remind me about how they handle politics in Iran the next time I complain about having to negotiate with Congress."

"Yes, sir," Chuck said, smiling. General Robinson, the Air Force Chief of Staff, then walked in and Soltis added, "I asked the General to join us in case whatever help Turani wants involves the military, sir. He was already in the building for a meeting."

Hernandez nodded, and waved Robinson to the other chair in front of his desk. "Well, I guess it's time to see what he wants."

Hernandez punched the button that put the call on speaker. "This is President Hernandez. Who am I speaking with?"

The voice that responded spoke in careful, accented, but perfectly understandable English. "I am Grand Ayatollah Sayyid Vahid Turani. I have just been elected Supreme Leader of the Islamic Republic of Iran by the Assembly of Experts. I am speaking to you without an interpreter to try to ensure there is no...miscommunication, but have an interpreter here if one is needed."

Hernandez replied, "I have with me General Robinson, the Air Force Chief of Staff, and the White House Chief of Staff, Chuck Soltis. I understand you would like our help in communicating with your forces outside Riyadh, to persuade them to surrender."

There was a long pause, followed by, "Yes, that is correct. You should soon receive the text of the message I plan to send to them by radio. It is important that they hear my voice, which I am sure they will recognize." Chuck hurried out to see whether any message had been received.

"Are you sure that they will follow your orders?" Hernandez asked. "I understand that you are not the person who sent them on this mission."

The answer this time was quicker. "It's true, I am not the one who sent them to attack a fellow Muslim nation. I am also not the one who attacked that same nation with nuclear weapons, and tried to do so with chemical weapons as well. But I think I can get our soldiers outside Riyadh to listen to me."

Hernandez nodded, and asked, "If you did not do these things, who did?"

Now the answer came instantly, and bitterly. "The criminal who for months had the title of Acting Supreme Leader, Reza Fagheh. He has already been tried, and answered for his crimes."

"I see," Hernandez said, as Soltis returned carrying a fax message in his hand. "Just a moment, please," he said, and pressed the hold button.

"From the Iranian Mission to the UN," Soltis said. "It's the text he proposes to read to his troops. It's pretty chilling stuff, sir."

Hernandez nodded. "Before I get into that, General, do we have the capability to do what he's asking, help him relay a radio message to his forces near Riyadh?"

Robinson shrugged and said, "Yes, sir. The Navy has a Triton on station in the Kingdom, and battlefield communication coordination is one of its primary missions. We just need their forces' command network frequency and any authentication codes they use, and we'll give them the frequency to use to communicate with the Triton and a one-time authentication code. We can easily boost the signal and make sure it's heard by any vehicle in the network that has its radio turned on."

Hernandez said, "Excellent," and then read through the proposed message.

Frowning, he punched the hold button to continue the call. "We have the technical capability to do what you request. Let's discuss what you plan to say..."

The Royal Palace, Riyadh

There were many palaces in Riyadh, but when someone talked about "the" royal palace they could only mean one, where the King had his principal residence. The Crown Prince strode forward through its main entrance to meet his father, for what he knew would be a difficult conversation.

He found the King sitting calmly in one of the Palace's many reception areas, reading a book which he put down at his son's approach. After they had completed the usual greetings and picked up their coffee cups from the service laid out before them, the King looked at him shrewdly.

"So, Talal, there have been developments not necessarily to our advantage," the King said, peering at the Crown Prince over his cup.

It took the Crown Prince all of his self-control not to spit out his coffee at the King's reference to the words Emperor Hirohito had used in explaining Japan's surrender to his subjects after the bombing of Hiroshima and Nagasaki. Well, it wasn't such a bad parallel, considering two nuclear bombs had also been dropped on the Kingdom. Fortunately, their casualties had been much lower than those suffered by the Japanese.

"Yes," he replied carefully. "Though the Qatari invaders approaching from the east have been defeated, we were not able to stop the Iranian force coming from the north."

The King nodded. "You now say definitely that the remaining invaders are Iranian. How did we confirm this?"

"We attacked their force with tanks, helicopters and drones. The drones sent back images from close range that our experts say include Zulfiqar tanks, which Iran builds and no nation but Iran uses. Also, the Americans have just contacted us and said they have confirmed the invaders are Iranian," the Crown Prince concluded.

The King shrugged and said, "Very well. In any case, no other nation ever made sense as an attacker from the north. Did the Americans say anything about assisting us against the Iranians?"

Now it was the Crown Prince's turn to shrug. "They claim they can get the Iranians to stop outside the capital, but said nothing about how. Since the battle took place about thirty kilometers north of the airport, I expect their tanks to reach here soon. I have a helicopter waiting outside to take you to the palace in Jeddah."

The King shook his head, and said, "No, Talal. This is my kingdom, and no invader is going to force me from my home. If it is my time to die, so be it."

The Crown Prince frowned and replied, "Father, you have a duty to your subjects to live, so that you may continue to provide them with the leadership that has helped our country move forward for so many years. Hundreds of our best tanks will be here from Yemen in a matter of hours, and Ali will be here fresh from his victory over the Qataris even sooner. Together they will sweep these invaders away from the capital. Don't make their victory hollow by waiting for an enemy who desires nothing more than your death."

The King shook his head again, and replied, "No, my son. There is no helicopter for my subjects in the capital. If I cannot protect them here, then I deserve to die, and our family should no longer claim leadership of this nation. Now go, and do whatever you can to stop the Iranians. Whether you succeed or fail, I know we will see each other again soon."

The Crown Prince started to speak, and then stopped and simply nodded. After kissing his father on both cheeks, he left in an even greater hurry than he had arrived.

Five Kilometers North of Riyadh, Saudi Arabia

Colonel Hamid Mazdaki grinned, but there was nothing pleasant about his smile. He had just taken a quick look outside his tank's hatch, and in the distance had been able to see the Kingdom Centre, a three hundred meter tall office building in the center of downtown Riyadh. That meant he would reach the royal palaces today, and be able to begin destroying the legitimacy of the Saudi royal family at a minimum.

If the King and his princes had been foolish enough to stay in their palaces, as they had been claiming over the radio, he might be able to deal with the Saudi royal family even more directly.

To his astonishment, he suddenly heard the voice of Grand Ayatollah Sayyid Vahid Turani over the headset that he and every one of his tankers wore. Hamid realized several things in an instant. The first was that Vahid could only have obtained the frequency he was using to speak to his troops from the men who had sent him on this mission, and that could only have happened if Vahid were now the Supreme Leader.

The next was that in order for Vahid to be speaking to his men here, he either had to be in Saudi Arabia, or his signal was being relayed by someone with a more sophisticated communications capability than his force possessed.

Like the Americans with their cursed drones.

The last was that Hamid could do nothing to stop his troops from receiving Vahid's message.

Well, let him try to stop us within sight of victory, Hamid thought savagely. After every obstacle my men have overcome, the prattling of some cleric isn't going to stop us now!

"Brave soldiers of Iran, this is Grand Ayatollah Sayyid Vahid Turani. As provided in our Constitution, I have been elected Supreme Leader by the Assembly of Experts. I am sorry to tell you that you have been betrayed by the men who sent you to attack our Saudi brothers, including the criminal Reza Fagheh, who among others were executed in Tehran this morning."

These words went through Hamid like a lightning bolt. Vahid would not lie about a fact so easily checked. If Reza, who had authorized this entire operation, was dead... There was no way home.

Well, so be it, he thought grimly. I never expected to make it home anyway.

But I'm still going to do what I came here to do. End the House of Saud.

Vahid's voice now came into Hamid's focus again.

"...have fought with courage, but in an illegal and cursed cause. Besides your tanks, the criminals have also used nuclear and chemical weapons against Saudi civilians. Our nation will have to pay a heavy price for these crimes.

But you can end your part in them, and even do more than that. You can atone for the crimes you have committed, and stand blameless in Paradise for the evils you did unknowingly at other's command.

You must turn your weapons on your brothers, and stop the criminals from achieving their illegal and cursed goals.

I am now speaking to you through a drone flying high overhead. That same drone can see all of you, down to the unit numbers on the sides of your tanks. What you do now will be recorded and examined in judgment.

Not of you, because no matter what you do now, you will never live to return to Iran. No, the judgment will be of your family. Because if you are so evil that you do not repent after hearing my words now, surely your family is not fit to live among us.

Now, I will stop speaking. It is time for all of you to earn your place in Paradise."

Hamid frantically mashed on his handset's transmit button. "Men, this is a Saudi trick! Don't let a voice on the radio turn you against your brothers. We all know who the real enemy is, and he's defenseless before us! Let me lead you to victory!"

Nearly thirty seconds passed of complete silence, including within Hamid's own tank, where none of his men said a word.

Shells from three different tanks hit Hamid's Zulfiqar-3 tank at nearly the same moment, killing everyone inside instantly. The fierce battle that followed lasted only minutes, since at the combatants' range missing was almost impossible. The only real question was who decided to fire first. Hesitation meant death, but those quickest to fire often lived only seconds longer as others made their decision.

There was no way to know who fired because of Vahid's words, or simply in self-defense. In the end, it didn't matter.

When Ali's tanks came upon the scene later that day they met no resistance. Every tank and APC in Hamid's force was either destroyed or, as in the case of the Armata, too badly damaged to move. Only a dozen Iranian soldiers were found alive, nearly all wounded, except for one sitting in a daze next to his tank.

Ali did as he had been ordered with all survivors, which was to transfer all of them to the same prison run by the Interior Ministry where the Qataris had been sent. Ali was never told but assumed, correctly, that they were all executed.

In fact, Vahid's threat to the families of the men in Hamid Mazdaki's force had been a bluff on two counts. First, the American President had made it clear he would never agree to provide Vahid with an audio feed for that purpose, or video surveillance to help him carry it out. Vahid had explained, and then promised, that no harm would come to the families of the Iranians fighting in Saudi Arabia before the Americans agreed to broadcast his message.

Probably more important was that Vahid would have never carried out the threat, even if he'd had the opportunity. Indeed making the threat, and particularly doing it with enough menace in his voice to make it convincing, had nauseated him to the point that he was nearly unable to complete the broadcast. Only knowledge of the bloodshed and misery that would have followed an Iranian assault on downtown Riyadh had forced him to swallow his bile and finish the revolting message. That, and the fact that Reza Fagheh would have never hesitated to carry out such a threat, if he had been allowed to live.

CHAPTER THIRTY ONE

Qom, Iran

Grand Ayatollah Sayyid Vahid Turani looked out at the massed television cameras, and thought about the millions of Iranians who would be watching him on every channel. Not to mention the millions more who were likely to be following his every word in other countries. There was nothing like responsibility for the first use of nuclear weapons against a live target since World War II to get people's attention, he thought bitterly. The man behind one of the cameras held up his right hand and silently began folding back first his thumb, and then the rest of his fingers one at a time.

Somehow, Vahid found the primitive countdown in the face of the assembled technology before him comforting. When the man's last finger was folded, small red lights winked on in the front of all the cameras.

Vahid had assumed his sternest expression for the start of his address. "My fellow citizens, I am here tonight to inform you of a terrible crime that has been committed against our brother Muslim nation of Saudi Arabia, and to tell you of many changes happening as we speak to ensure such an outrage never takes place again.

The nuclear and chemical weapons used against the Saudis by the criminals who have now been executed were the only ones we had. We will permanently stop and dismantle our nuclear and chemical programs in all their forms including power production, and invite United Nations inspectors to verify compliance. These inspectors will have full and unrestricted access to all Iranian territory, including military bases, without exception and with no need for prior notice.

Though only the criminals we have executed knew of this cowardly plot, the Iranian government nevertheless takes full responsibility for their actions, and stands ready to provide full compensation to their victims.

The criminals took advantage of a military structure that was too complex to be effectively controlled. Steps are underway to restore the central government's control of all Iranian armed forces."

Indeed, the Pasdaran and Basij leadership was being arrested nationwide, in a move so swift that there was little resistance. Some would be discharged. Some would eventually be integrated into the regular Iranian military, as would all of their equipment.

Some would be executed.

Now Vahid's expression softened and became more thoughtful. "For many years, we have sent our treasure abroad while Iranians at home were going hungry. That stops tonight.

I am announcing the end of our military and financial support for all governments, militias and organizations outside Iran, including but not limited to those in Yemen, Syria, Iraq, and Lebanon.

Iran's military will only conduct operations within Iran and Iranian territorial waters and airspace as defined by international law. In particular, we pledge not to interfere with the free transit of vessels through the Straits of Hormuz."

Now Vahid didn't look merely stern, he looked threatening. "Do not mistake our restraint for weakness. Any weapons launched at us, including under the guise of 'justified retaliation' will be met with twice the firepower used against us. We accept responsibility. We do not accept the death of Iranians who had no role in the criminal attack against a fellow Muslim nation."

Vahid's expression shifted again, now appearing to see into the distance. "Iran was a beacon of civilization thousands of years ago, when most people around the world had not yet discovered the written word. It can be that beacon once again. I pledge to you tonight that the government of Iran has rediscovered the true purpose of the Revolution, which is to make that government serve its people. In the days ahead I will be announcing more changes, all to help unlock the potential of our glorious nation.

For now, though, I will content myself with this. May God bestow his blessings upon all of my fellow citizens, and may he protect the Islamic Republic of Iran."

Vahid nodded to himself as the red lights on the cameras winked out. Next he needed to dismantle the corrupt clergy and government-owned corporate edifice that for so many years had stolen the money that ordinary hard-working Iranians needed to survive.

Once the UN inspectors had done their work and - probably grudgingly - agreed that Iran's nuclear and chemical programs no longer existed, he had to be sure international sanctions were removed without delay.

And to help Iran return to the greatness that Vahid believed was truly its destiny, he had to find a way to integrate women into its society and economy, without allowing them to be turned into the sex objects he so despised in the West.

One step at a time, Vahid sighed to himself. One step at a time.

FSB Headquarters, Moscow, Russia

Dmitry Demchenko was nervous, and with good reason. Anyone at his rank of Assistant Director in the FSB had the right to request an urgent appointment with Director Smyslov. Since he had assumed leadership of the FSB, Smyslov had made it clear his door was open.

Once. If Smyslov decided there was nothing urgent about the request, at best the Assistant Director would find urgent appointment requests refused.

At worst, he would no longer be an Assistant Director. Smyslov was willing to forgive some things, but wasting his time was not one of them.

As Assistant Director for Recruitment most of Dmitry's work was the very definition of routine. Today, though, a file had crossed his desk that made him want to break from that routine radically enough that it would require Smyslov's approval.

As he was ushered into Smyslov's office, Dmitry saw that the file he wished to discuss was already open on his desk. Smyslov waved him to the seat in front of his desk and asked with evident curiosity, "So,

Dmitry, you wanted to speak to me about Neda Rhahbar. What did you have in mind? Recruiting her, I presume?"

Dmitry nodded. "Yes, sir. But I want to do so on an expedited basis, and put her in training immediately."

Smyslov's bushy eyebrows flew upwards. "Most unusual. That would require waiving the usual security screening. She is from a country we don't consider exactly our friend. Do you think that wise?"

Dmitry responded, "I understand your concern, and to some extent I share it. However, the circumstances of her defection suggest she's unlikely to be an Iranian agent. It appears they tried hard to kill her. Anyway, I think a normal security review would add little to what we already know."

Smyslov grunted, and sat quietly for a moment. It was true they were hardly going to learn more from the Iranian authorities, or her deceased husband.

"So, what makes this particular recruitment so urgent?" Smyslov asked in a voice that to Dmitry's dismay was carefully neutral. He thought, incorrectly, that this showed Smyslov thought it was a bad idea.

Nothing to do but soldier on, Dmitry thought. Aloud he replied, "We have nobody with a knowledge of nuclear physics who is a native speaker of Farsi, and who is also fluent in Urdu. You know about my background as an agent in South Asia, and our long-standing focus on Pakistan's nuclear weapons. When I was there, I would have given a great deal to have such a resource available. I think some risk to take advantage of this opportunity is justified."

Now Smyslov nodded, and leaned back in his chair. After tapping on his desk a few times, he suddenly leaned forward and glared at Dmitry. "And what makes you think it so important that we have such a resource in Pakistan at this particular time? What, exactly, have you heard, Dmitry?"

Of all the reactions Dmitry had imagined, this was not one of them. Bewildered, he answered honestly, "I've heard nothing, Director. I just thought this defector was a windfall we'd be foolish to overlook."

Smyslov's glare persisted for several more seconds, and then he leaned back in his chair again. "Very well. I believe you. Does this person even want to be an agent?"

Dmitry shrugged, and replied, "We've not asked in so many words, but the handler I assigned her thinks she would be willing. Of course, she's highly intelligent, and the report on her escape from Iran appears to show her instincts are good."

Smyslov nodded absently, and asked, "When you say she's fluent in Urdu, could she pass as a native speaker?"

Dmitry frowned, and rocked his right hand back and forth. "Only by claiming to be from the region of Pakistan bordering Iran, Balochistan. She has a definite accent. However, from my own time in Pakistan I think if she said she was from Balochistan, she could pass casual scrutiny."

Smyslov nodded and then handed Neda Rhahbar's file back to Dmitry, saying simply, "Approved. Keep me advised of her progress."

As he walked out of Smyslov's office, Dmitry realized that their meeting had little to do with whether Neda Rhahbar would go through training as an agent. Instead, it was about whether Dmitry knew about something going on in Pakistan that he shouldn't.

Dmitry was glad he hadn't asked.

The Royal Palace, Riyadh, Saudi Arabia

Enes Balcan had no formal title in the Turkish government. He had something much more important - the Turkish President's complete trust. His carefully tailored suit and impeccable grooming perfectly matched his dark good looks. Never married, he had never been lonely.

Enes' intelligence and common sense were unquestioned, but not the main reason he had risen so far in Turkey's government. Instead, it was his total confidence. Enes never made a promise he could not keep. He knew the President's thinking, and never needed to bother him with details.

The stakes had never been higher. But Enes knew in his bones this would be his greatest triumph.

The Saudi Crown Prince glowered behind his vast wooden desk. There had been no traditional welcome, no pleasantries. Enes had been delivered to the seat in front of the Crown Prince like a sack of mail, and for several minutes been ignored while the Prince pretended to review documents.

Enes had said nothing, but simply waited.

Finally, the Crown Prince spoke.

"So, you must already be tired of your guests. Two royal families must be quite a handful. Well, don't worry. We're ready to take them off your hands, and give each the welcome they deserve."

Enes had no doubt that he was absolutely sincere. He also knew that the Saudis would waste no time restoring the Bahraini royal family to power. Just as he was sure that any Qatari royals foolish enough to set foot in Riyadh would be publicly executed.

"Actually, I am here to make a proposal that I hope you will agree is mutually beneficial. We have also discussed it with our mutual ally, the United States, and have their full support."

Enes saw with satisfaction that this statement had caused the Crown Prince to hesitate, and visibly rethink his approach.

The Crown Prince sat back and said, "Very well. You have my attention. Make your proposal."

Enes nodded. "First, Qatar will hand over all military assets to the Saudi government, and will have no military in the future, only a police force."

The Crown Prince shook his head. "In less than a week Qatar will be a Saudi province, and we can collect those military assets."

Enes nodded. "You can easily defeat whatever military forces remain in Qatar. But I'm sure you know that you will take casualties. And fighting them will force you to destroy their equipment, rather than adding their weapons to your own forces. Plus, we are offering you the chance to obtain all of the Qatari aircraft that flew to Turkey after the conflict. Just send pilots to fly them from Turkey."

The Crown Prince shrugged, clearly unimpressed. "Continue."

"Al-Jazeera will cease broadcasting permanently."

Now the Crown Prince actually laughed. "Al-Jazeera's studios in Doha are on the list of structures to be leveled once we annex Qatar. I think that will end their broadcasts quite effectively."

Enes shook his head. "Ending Al-Jazeera's broadcasts was one of the chief demands of your government for ending the blockade of Qatar, and we both know why. Our government has promised to provide Al-Jazeera broadcasting facilities, and nearly all of its journalists are now in Ankara. Thanks to the Internet, Al-Jazeera's programs will continue to be seen throughout the Middle East, and indeed throughout the world. Unless you agree to our proposal. May I continue?"

The Crown Prince was clearly having trouble keeping his temper, but finally managed to nod.

"Qatar will pay one hundred billion US dollars in reparations."

The Crown Prince sneered. "About a third of the money in Qatar's Sovereign Wealth Fund? Very generous! I think we'll prefer to seize Qatar's oil and gas production, and see how much that gets us. Plus whatever we find in Qatar's banks."

Enes nodded. "The Americans have already said publicly that they would impose sanctions on you if you seize and attempt to sell Qatar's oil and gas. Also, Qatar's banks are empty, with all their assets digitally transferred to Turkey days ago. Still, we can return to this topic."

The Crown Prince shrugged, but said nothing.

"The Americans plan to return to Al Udeid air base just south of Doha, and from there will both once again support your campaign in Yemen with mid-air refueling, as well as provide an on-site guarantee that Qatar will never again threaten Saudi Arabia."

Now the Crown Prince nodded. Losing American mid-air refueling support after the Qataris kicked them out of Al Udeid had been a heavy blow. It would be nice to have it back. He gestured for Enes to continue.

"I was only authorized to offer you reparations of one hundred billion dollars. I think I can persuade all concerned to increase that to one hundred fifty billion dollars. Also, as a gesture of our sincere desire for a peaceful conclusion to this conflict, my President has authorized me to offer you his personal aircraft."

The Crown Prince smiled. 'The one that the Qataris gave him in 2017, worth about half a billion dollars?"

Enes nodded. "Yes, that one."

The Crown Prince looked thoughtful. "And Bahrain?"

When Bahrain's Shi'a majority had overthrown their monarchy, their royal family had also sought sanctuary in Ankara. Refuge had been offered deliberately, for precisely this moment.

"The Americans plan to return to their naval base in Manama, and the new Bahraini government has agreed. There the Americans will ensure Bahrain never poses a threat to the Kingdom. From that base, the US Navy will also inspect any ship approaching Yemen with the capacity to carry ballistic missiles, to make sure the Iranians keep their promise not to supply them to the Houthis."

Enes paused. "The Bahraini royal family will be welcome to live out their lives in comfort in Turkey."

The Crown Prince grunted. He was sure the Bahraini royals would be paying dearly for the privilege.

Enes handed a flash drive to the Crown Prince, who looked at it curiously. Enes said, "I was given this by the Americans. They say it includes the names of all the Shi'a in your Eastern Province who have been killed by Saudi forces over the past several years, as well as supplemental documents confirming their deaths. I was told to remind you that the Americans declined to intervene in Libya until Qaddafi declared he was planning to wipe out the residents of his eastern province, Benghazi. They wish to remain your ally, but even for allies, there are limits."

The Crown Prince scowled, but for several moments said nothing.

Finally, he said, "Increase the reparation amount to two hundred billion dollars. In return we will allow all of the Qatari royal family except the Emir to return to Doha, and trust the Americans to oversee the transfer of all Qatari military assets to us. We plan to focus our military efforts on bringing peace to Yemen, and will not undertake any punitive action in the Eastern Province. We will also end construction on the Salwa Canal, both now and in the future. If you agree, I will take this proposal to my father."

Enes nodded. "Agreed. Please let me know what he says."

They both knew this was only for show. The King only had a matter of months at best to live, and had transferred nearly all power to his favorite son.

Enes hesitated, and the Crown Prince's eyebrows rose. "Something else?"

Enes shrugged, and said "It's none of my business, but I heard the address from Iran's Supreme Leader, and his offer of compensation. I had an idea I thought you might like."

The Crown Prince made a "come on" gesture with his hands. He was actually curious.

"Well," Enes said, "you could ask the Iranians to pay for a desalination plant producing fifty percent more water than the one they destroyed. As well as provide all the workers. To encourage quick completion you could also refuse to allow any Iranians to make the pilgrimage to Mecca except the workers you decide are the top ten percent performers, until the plant is completed to your satisfaction."

The Crown Prince smiled. "I like your idea. I may just use it." With a few changes, he thought, like requiring double the water production from the new desalination plant.

Enes rose. "Your Majesty, I am happy that your wisdom has found a way to peace after all this bloodshed." Moments later the Crown Prince was alone with his thoughts.

Before he had become Crown Prince he had argued strenuously against the Salwa Canal, saying it would earn the Saudis new enemies, and achieve none of its goals. He had no idea then just how right he was, but ending the project would not only save money.

No, it would also show the Saudis were capable of mercy. As would allowing the Qatari royals' return to Doha, with the obvious exception of the Emir.

Yes, he thought, my decisions will make a nice contrast with my predecessor's murder of Jamal Khashoggi. That Kashoggi's death took place at a Saudi consulate in Turkey, the country which had just helped to broker a deal to prevent the start of a wider war, helped drive the point home a little deeper.

Shahid Rajaei Research & Training Hospital, Tehran, Iran

Roya Maziar looked up from her station, and her pulse quickened as she saw Colonel Arif Shahin walking towards her. On the one hand, she was annoyed with herself. She was not a schoolgirl, to swoon when a handsome boy paid her attention.

On the other, maybe she should start listening to her instincts, unless she wanted to let her mother pick her husband.

"I am glad to see you again," Roya said, looking Arif straight in his eyes.

Arif looked at her thoughtfully, and nodded. "I as well. I wanted to be sure you had recovered from the terrible experience you had last week."

"I am fine. Have all of those responsible for killing my friend and the Supreme Leader been brought to justice?" Roya asked, her dark eyes flashing. Arif had no doubt what she meant by "justice."

"Yes," Arif replied, adding, "I placed many of those criminals in custody myself."

"Good," Roya said emphatically. "I'm certain there is a special place in hell for people who could be so cruel to those who are both innocent and defenseless."

"I'm sure you're right," Arif said gravely.

"Now that we have that cleared up, I'm glad you came by because it saves me the trouble of finding you," Roya said.

"Oh?" was all Arif could manage in response.

"Yes," Roya said, "my mother insists you come for dinner. She says it is to thank you for saving my life, and that under no circumstances am I to take no for an answer."

"I see," Arif said seriously, but with a humorous twinkle in his eye. "Of course, I was simply doing my duty. But as an officer, I recognize a valid order when I hear it."

Then he quickly wrote on a piece of paper, and handed it to Roya. "This is my personal cell phone number. Like the official number I gave you before I will answer it at any time, day or night. Unlike the other one it is not monitored by my superior officer, so you may also text me with personal messages. Like, for example, the place and time you wish me to come for dinner."

Arif and Roya smiled at each other, as Roya thought to herself that she had to remember to remind her mother that the dinner was supposed to have been her idea.

CHAPTER THIRTY TWO

FSB Headquarters, Moscow, Russia

Anatoly Grishkov was welcomed into the office of FSB Director Smyslov with one of his usual bear hugs, this time followed by a pat on the back. Then, Smyslov led Grishkov to the same red leather couch where he had learned about the mission he had finished last month.

"I am glad that at least one of you survived this last adventure, and that we were able to give you a month to spend with your family," Smyslov said as he looked Grishkov over. "From what I read in your report, either your guide in Iran, the Iranian border guard force, or an Iranian nuclear weapon could have easily cost me both of my best agents."

Grishkov shrugged. "If I were really one of your best agents, Vasilyev would be sitting here beside me."

Smyslov shook his head vigorously. "Nonsense. Vasilyev knew what needed to be done, and that it was a one-man, one-way mission. The Saudis gave us the weapon to study, which was after all the very least they could do. Our scientists say the device would have detonated if sea water had not infiltrated the casing, which happened due to water pressure. The depth for that to happen would not have been sufficient if you had both merely dropped it off the end of the pier. If you had been in the truck as well when Vasilyev drove it off to gain those extra meters of depth, all you would have accomplished is your own needless death."

Grishkov looked stubborn. "It should have been my choice."

Smyslov gave a short bark of laughter. "Would you say that if Arisha were sitting here?"

Grishkov winced at the mention of his wife. "I may have imagined it, but the last words I remember hearing from Vasilyev as I passed out had something to do with a promise he made to Arisha."

Smyslov nodded. "There you are. I'm sure she'll deny it, but I'll bet Arisha got him to give his word he'd bring you back, or die trying. And why not? You do have both her and two boys depending on you, yes?"

Grishkov reluctantly nodded. "Very well. Anyway, nothing I can do will bring him back. So, what is next for me? Will I return to Vladivostok? I have to tell you, I am not ready for any more such 'adventures,' particularly without a man I trust at my side."

Smyslov smiled. "First, let me tell you that the President is once again extremely impressed by your performance, and of course with Vasilyev's as well. As after your last mission, you will each receive one million American dollars from the President's personal fund, with Vasilyev's award going to his next of kin."

Grishkov's eyebrows flew up. "Is that a joke? Vasilyev didn't have any family."

Smyslov shrugged. "I think it's time you met your new partner." With that, he pulled out his cell phone, and sent a one word text to his assistant.

A few moments later, the door to Smyslov's office opened, and in walked a man who looked very much like Vasilyev, except about thirty years younger.

"Anatoly, meet Mikhail Vasilyev, Alexei's son," Smyslov said with a huge smile.

Grishkov remained seated, and appeared to be rooted to the sofa in shock. "But Vasilyev told me he never married."

Mikhail sat down next to Grishkov and nodded. "Yes. But you do know it's possible to father a child, without marrying the mother?"

As Grishkov turned beet red, Smyslov roared with laughter and turned to Mikhail. "I am only sorry that your father is not here to see this. I know he would have been tremendously entertained."

Wiping a tear from one eye and gasping for air, Smyslov finally said, "Mikhail's mother was also a KGB agent, who was killed during an assignment in the Middle East while Mikhail was just a baby. He was raised by his grandparents. I knew Alexei even then, and I can tell you that he asked Mikhail's mother to marry him. She refused, because under KGB rules back then she would have been forced to resign."

Smyslov paused, and said somberly, "Alexei never forgave himself for her death, even though he was on assignment in Asia at the time and could have done nothing to prevent it. He had nothing in his life except his work after that."

Grishkov shook his head. "I can't believe Alexei had a son and never told me. Did he know?"

Mikhail smiled. "Of course. He sent money to my grandparents, and I never lacked for anything. My grandparents claimed I was an orphan until I graduated from university, and had started my first job and rented my first apartment. When I came home on holiday to visit them, there he was. He said that he wanted me to make my own choices in life, and not to be pressured into following in the footsteps of his parents."

Mikhail paused. "Maybe I was being contrary. But days later, I had applied to work at the FSB."

Smyslov smiled. "It didn't hurt that he had studied foreign languages at university, and his first job was with a translation service."

Mikhail shrugged. "I'm sure that's true. Anyway, when I told him of my application, it was the only time in all the years I knew my father that I saw him angry. He told me to withdraw my application, and when I refused said he would make sure I was never accepted. I didn't see him for several years after that, but as you can see I did start work at the FSB."

Smyslov nodded. "It was obvious Mikhail had great potential. And no matter how much Alexei objected, it was not difficult to keep him busy abroad and unable to interfere. After several years, reports came to him of his son's performance in the field, and he finally changed his mind."

Mikhail smiled. "Our work only let us see each other a few times, but we made the most of each occasion. The Director has told me about your last two missions with my father. I know you are unhappy that he did not allow you to join him in concluding his last one. I can assure you that he ended his career exactly as he would have wished had he planned it. After my mother's death duty was all he cared about. He was about to be forced into retirement, and after that he would have never complained, but would have still been miserable. A hero's death instead, saving thousands of lives including his partner's? Perfection indeed."

Grishkov shook his head. "I still can't believe he never told me about you."

Mikhail shrugged, and repeated the first part of Vasilyev's favorite saying. "Tell your enemies nothing."

Grishkov gave a sad smile and repeated its end. "And tell your friends even less."

Smyslov clapped his hands and said, "Now it is time, Anatoly, to answer your question. You have had a month to spend with Arisha and the children. I wish it could have been longer, but once again there is a problem, and Mikhail needs someone he can trust to help him address it. Do you agree to your new partner?"

Grishkov held out his hand to Mikhail, who immediately shook it. "Of course I do. Where are we going this time?"

Smyslov pulled two fat manila envelopes from his desk and laid one in front of each of them. "Mikhail obtained most of the information in these files, but there have been a few additions made since he came back a few days ago. I'm sorry, Mikhail, that you have to go back to Pakistan again so soon, but I'm afraid your last report has now been confirmed."

Grishkov shrugged and said, "Well, at least it can't be as bad as three nuclear weapons."

Mikhail smiled ruefully and said, "Three? I wish it were only three."

Made in the USA
San Bernardino, CA
15 May 2019